HOPE

The World In-between Series
Book 5

IE Castellano

Laurel
Highlands
Publishing

Paperback edition published 2017

Cover by JosDCreations
http://JosDCreations.com

Laurel Highlands Publishing
Mount Pleasant, PA
USA

http://LaurelHighlandsPublishing.com

ISBN-13: 978-1-941087-36-7
ISBN-10: 1-941087-36-1

This book is a work of fiction. Names, characters, places, and incidents either are products of the author's imagination or are used fictitiously. Any resemblance to actual persons, living or dead, events, or locales is entirely coincidental.

Books by IE Castellano

The World In-between Series

The World In-between
Bow of the Moon
Secrets of the Sages
Whispers

Other Novels

Tricentennial
Where Pirates Go to Die

Short Stories

All That Lies in *Disturbance*
The Dragonlands (World In-between Series Short)
The Hunt in *Moon Shadows*
Sector Three-three in *Across the Karman Line*
Yuletide Magic (World In-between Series Short)

*To my parents
for
telling me I can be whatever I want,
encouraging me to write,
shaping me into the woman I have become,
and, occasionally, doing my schoolwork for me.*

Chapter One

The Ultimate Question

"Miss Chase? Are you with us today, Miss Chase?"

Tearing her eyes from the wooden ring resembling a flower on her pinky, Hope raised her head to look at her teacher who leaned against the metal desk left over from another decade.

"Good," the teacher said with a patronizing smile. Mrs. Kurlow always had one of those smiles at the ready. Being the last class of the day, students' minds drifted more than usual. Of course, minds drifted in her classes at any time of the day just to get rid of her drawling voice that carried a smug air. "I was hoping you would have the answer to the question I asked."

The board behind the teacher gave no indication of the question. The book sitting on the tiny writing platform that comprised her desk would have no answer. "Forty-two," Hope replied.

Snickers surrounded her. Someone had found a battered copy of *A Hitchhiker's Guide to the Galaxy* and passed it around. Just about everyone had read it.

Mrs. Kurlow's nose flared. The snickering stopped. "How does detention sound, Miss Chase?"

"Fine with me," she answered.

The bell rang. Hope quickly slipped out the classroom door.

In the hall, a girl with stringy blonde hair sidled next to her. "Did you get another letter from him?"

"Yeah," said Hope.

"Real letters. That's so romantic. Has he declared his undying love for you yet?" the girl asked in a fit of giggles.

Hope rolled her eyes. "Issy," she exasperated. "We're not like that."

"Who's not like that?" asked a tall girl with short, tight, dark curls as she strode on Hope's other side.

"Hope and her military man," said Issy.

"Mmmm hmm." The tall girl gave Hope a look of disbelief. "You haven't seen each other in forever. He obviously doesn't want you to forget him by the time he comes home."

"We're friends," protested Hope. "We've been friends for a long time. He wrote to tell me about his promotion. The youngest lieutenant promotion since his captain."

"Hey, Chandra, see what I see?" said Issy.

Chandra's tight curls bounced. "Mmm Hunter and he's got eyes for you, Hope. Wish I had guy troubles like you do," she teased.

The girls giggled. "See you in the locker room, Hope," said Issy. They left her in the hall.

"Hope." Dark hair and eyes leaned against a locker with his tie loosened.

"Mike," Hope greeted.

"Walk with me to the gym," he said.

"'Kay."

Mike matched her stride. "So, Waterson is having a party this weekend," Mike began. "Wanted to know if you would go with me."

"Can't. Going camping with my uncle this weekend."

"Please?" he begged in a low whisper. "It's Friday night. Don't make me go by myself. You need to save me from Molly—"

Hope's raucous laughter echoed in the hallway.

"I don't see anything funny."

"You've only been avoiding her since seventh grade," Hope said.

"I'll do anything to make it up to you, Hope," he pleaded.

She sighed. "Fine. But you're picking me up at my parent's house and dropping me off at my uncle's."

"Thank you," he said with a relieved smiled. He kissed her hand before disappearing into the boy's locker room.

When Hope entered the girl's locker room, she found her friends dressed for practice and retrieving their field hockey sticks from their lockers. "So?" asked Chandra.

"What did he want?" asked Issy.

"He invited me to Waterson's party this weekend," answered Hope. She opened her locker and began to change out of her uniform.

"Ooh. His parties are invitation only. Lucky girl," said Chandra.

Hope shrugged. "All seniors."

"Nuh-uh," said Issy. "You'll be there. A junior in their midst."

3

Laying her bow and quiver on the bench, Hope said in monotone, "Yay."

"What's the harm in letting Mike give military man a run for his money?" said Chandra. She winked at Hope.

"We don't want to be late for practice. See you later," said Issy.

Alone with her bow, Hope tied her leather armbands to her forearms before wandering through the gym to the far door. She watched students covered in all white padding prance back and forth. She wondered which black facemask hid Mike. A blunt tipped sword raised to salute her. She waved to Mike, then stepped out into the sunshine.

Beyond the field hockey practice fields, the archery targets formed a boundary of sorts. The others in the Archery Club already began to practice. She walked to the empty target. "You're late, Hope," a voice carried from down the row of archers.

"I'm sorry, Mister Wilde," said Hope.

The Archery Mentor approached. Even inside the school, Mr. Wilde always looked like he lived up to his name, but outside, wandering amongst the treed grounds, he could have belonged to the wild. "Is everything okay?" he asked with true concern in his voice.

"I got detention," she answered, setting an arrow.

"From?" he asked.

"Missus Kurlow." Hope released. She watched it hit the red center area.

"Hmpf. What did you do?"

Hope lowered her bow. After she told him what happened in her last class of the day, he chuckled. "I'll see what I can do," he said.

"Thanks, Mister Wilde," Hope said with a little smile.

"Do you want to tell me what's really bothering you?" he asked.

Her eyes searched the far reaches of the Whingham Academy's property. In the distance, the equestrians practiced a course. After a couple horses jumped over a fence, she focused on Mr. Wilde. His golden brown hair rustled in the breeze. Quarter inch stubble added to his rugged style. Most of the girls swooned when he passed, attempting to display a tame side while wearing a tweed blazer. She never noticed his sparkling light brown eyes or his roguishly handsome smile about which the other girls whispered. To her, he had become her advocate and friend of sorts. He fought to allow her wooden bow in competition while everyone else used composites. He encouraged her passion for the art form archery was to her. In that way, he reminded her of Declan—her first archery teacher. "I'm not really sure," she answered. She bit her bottom lip. "I kinda feel empty. Like I should be doing something else."

His eyes reflected her sadness. "I can't tell you what will fill that hole. I know that you kids get pressured in your junior year to start choosing a career path and lining up colleges," he said. "Don't let that get to you. It'll come. Let's do an exercise. Close your eyes."

She closed her eyes. Mr. Wilde's breath grazed her ear. Her back felt his thin frame mimic her body more closely than her shadow. "Can you remember the first time you fell in love with archery?" he asked.

Her feet shifted her weight away from him. "Yes."

"Picture it," he suggested.

Her mind left the school grounds. Years rewound. She sat around a campfire with Uncle Berty and Aunt Silvia, before she became her aunt. Her Fairy Godmother, Freesia, kept a watchful eye on her while Empire Guards, Otho and Tacitus, patrolled the camp under the direction of their superior, Lieutenant Edwin. The fire warmed her back as she watched Declan fire arrows at a target from the gracefully curved Bow of the Moon. Turning to face Prince Telor, Declan caught Hope's gaze. He gave her a small smile then returned to the archery lesson for the Fairy Prince. Later that evening, Declan spoke to Uncle Berty about making her a basic practice bow. After her sister learned on that bow, her father hung it in the garage. Her fingers curled around her current bow more tightly as she smiled.

"Good," said Mr. Wilde in her ear. "Now I want you to think about the time you first shot an arrow from this bow."

She pictured a cottage nestled in an old growth forest. One of the only buildings built on the forest floor, the cottage sat at the edge of Boudon—a village hidden high in the trees. She let out a small breath.

"Tell me about it," he urged in his calming voice.

"Uncle Berty promised me a bow for my seventh birthday. He took me to this little shop. I tried a plethora of bows. This one... This one sang to me when I released the string." Behind her eyelids, Hope pictured a boy with windswept blond hair, staring at her with his intense blue eyes. A tear rolled down her cheek. "I miss my best friend," she muttered.

When she opened her eyes, Mr. Wilde's kind eyes stared into hers. His hand raised to his chest, stopping there. She wiped her cheek with the back of her hand. "If you don't want to practice today, I'll understand," he said.

"Thanks, Mister Wilde, but I'd like to practice."

Giving her an understanding smile, he patted her shoulder. She raised her bow as he walked away.

After archery practice, Hope strolled back to the gym. She cared not if she missed the activity bus home. Across from the locker rooms' entrances, Mike leaned against the wall. His fencing mask dangled from his fingers. Knowing she had to pass him, she took a deep breath.

"Give you a ride home?" he asked her.

"Sure," she answered. "Be out in a minute."

"Meet you here." He pushed off the wall then disappeared into the boy's locker room.

Dressed in her uniform skirt and untucked shirt, she exited the locker room to find Mike waiting. Their arms bumped periodically while walking through the school to the parking lot.

In his car, Mike began talking. "So, my dad's gone again on another job. Taking pictures halfway around the world. Who knows when he'll be home. In the meantime, my grandfather comes home early from work." Hope nodded unsure of why he was telling her all this. "Grandpa *accidently* leaves things from work where I can see them, read them, whatever. He asks me if the colleges have good schools of journalism. I think he's trying to push me in the same direction he went."

"Is that what you want?" Hope asked.

"I don't know." Mike sighed. "Sometimes, I just feel so lost, you know?"

"Yeah," agreed Hope. She stared at the dark haired senior she had known for years. He had always acted like her annoying older brother. At that moment, she felt like he was on the verge of confessing something. She pulled at the seatbelt.

For the remainder of the car ride, he talked about expectations and pressure of going to a good university. "How are you supposed to know, right now, what you want to do for the rest of your life? What if you don't like what you've chosen?" His hands tightened around the leather steering wheel.

"Um," she said, "don't miss the turn."

He let out a breath.

"I don't know what to tell you, Mike. What is it that you like?"

"I thought it was history, but I don't know anymore, Hope. I just don't know." He pulled into her parent's driveway. "Hey, thanks for listening."

She smiled, placing her hand on his arm. "You'll figure it out. Thanks for the ride." Mike waited until she entered her house before driving away. She found her mother and sister at the kitchen table.

"How was school?" her mother asked.

"Good." Hope plopped a heavy history book on the table across from her sister. Lily scribbled on a worksheet behind her long, dark hair.

"Okay, Mom. All done," Lily said, lifting her head.

"Great," said Teresa as she peered at the worksheet. "Wash your hands and set the table for dinner."

After turning off the water, Lily spoke an incantation. Dishes and silverware floated out of cabinets and drawers. At Lily's encouragement, they pranced into the dining room.

Hope held back a scowl. She read the same sentence about World War I twice. Her eyes could not travel any further down the page before her father entered the kitchen. Dinner halted any progress on her homework.

Between bites, she told her parents, "I'm going to hang with Mike Hunter Friday night. He'll drop me off at the house."

"Why does everyone call him Mmm Hunter?" Lily asked.

Hope rolled her eyes. "His initials are M. M. Martin Michael Hunter, the third."

Lily giggled.

After dinner, Hope retired to her bedroom to finish her homework the best she could. She placed her pen on her apathetically done homework, then climbed on top of her bed. Her eyes found a wooden doll resting on her dresser. "I don't belong in this world, Ashely," she told it.

She turned her head. The wooden flower ring pressed into her cheek. Slipping her hand out from under her head, she stared at it. She tried not to remember the last time she saw him. *Her blue dress sparkled.* She was not trying hard enough. Her mind slid back to her eighth grade dance.

Obie waited in the foyer, wearing a suit. "Ready?" Hope asked from the top of the stairs. He said nothing. He only watched her descend.

"Come on, kids. We don't want to be late," said Jon. Her parents ushered them into the car. Lily waved from the doorstep while holding her Fairy Godmother's hand.

Arriving at the school, Obie took her hand to help her out of the car. He kept a hand on her back as they entered the streamer and balloon filled gym. All her friends gushed over her date. But the best was the shocked look frozen on Cassie Mennan's face. Cassie spread rumors about Hope so that no boy would ask her to the end of the year dance.

She and Obie danced, laughed, and had fun with her friends. Any rumors quickly dissipated. The night ended with Cassie stewing in the corner all alone.

Hope's parents drove them to her uncle and aunt's house where she brought Obie back through the portal. They ran to the Star Gazing Platform.

"Thanks for coming to the dance with me," Hope said.

"It was fun," said Obie.

They sat on the wood floor, staring at the stars in silence.

"Hope," Obie began. He took her hand in his. "This is my last night in the Sages' Grove."

"What?" Her eyes found his intense blue irises staring at her.

"I leave tomorrow with the Empire Guard."

"Where?"

"I don't know. One of the outposts," he said. "Even if I did know, I wouldn't be allowed to tell you."

She clutched his hand, not wanting him to go. "How long will you be gone?"

"I don't know." He scooted closer. "I had the best night with you."

"Will you be able to write to me?" she asked in a small voice.

"Whenever I can," he whispered.

She gulped as the distance between their faces lessened. His lips carefully pressed against hers. Her heart beat faster. He laced his fingers in hers. After a few moments, his face slowly inched back. He searched into her brown eyes. His eyes were full of words he did not say. "Please, see me off tomorrow," he said. "Goodnight, Hope."

Before she could say anything, he rushed off the platform. Alone under the stars, tears streamed down her cheeks.

The memory stayed close to the surface of her mind. She lifted her face off the soggy spot on her pillow. Moving to a dry part, she cried herself to sleep.

Although Mr. Wilde had gotten her out of detention like he promised, by the time Friday arrived, she needed to go to a party. She packed her weekend bag with camping essentials—bow, cloak, Fairystone pendant, Fairy Dust. Downstairs, she hugged her parents good-bye. "See you guys Sunday," she said.

"Tell everyone we say hello," Teresa said.

"I will."

The doorbell rang. Mike looked good in his jeans and careless button down shirt over a t-shirt.

"You look nice," he said. "Ready?" She nodded. "Bye, Mister and Missus Chase," he said as he grabbed her bag. After putting it in the trunk, they crossed town. "I'm glad you could come with me," he said.

"Wouldn't want Molly getting her not so little claws in you," she said. "Might mess up your hair."

Mike found a parking spot around the corner from the party. He offered his arm in which she wrapped hers as they walked. She heard Waterson's house before she saw it. Music pulsed from a large, white colonial. Mr. and Mrs. Waterson traveled overseas often, leaving their youngest son, Jason, alone with a caretaker.

Jason resembled his two older brothers so much, everyone, including his own family, would call him either Devon or Cole. He insisted people just call him Waterson instead. At least that was the story Hope heard. She only knew his first name because they were in the same French class one year.

After their long trek up the sidewalk, they reached the black double doors. Hope took a deep breath. She did not go to parties like Waterson's. Mike steered her through the house, going room to room as if they were on parade. He stopped often to say hi to people while keeping a hand on her back. In the kitchen, a keg sat in a tub of ice. Mike expertly filled two plastic glasses from the tap. Taking a sip, Hope grimaced. She hated beer.

He chuckled. "Just pretend you're drinking it," he said in her ear.

They wandered into a room where the pulsating music originated. Mike pulled her into the crowd of dancing kids. She did not recognize most of them. "Who are all these people?" she asked on her tiptoes.

He bent over, saying, "Waterson has a lot of friends from many places."

At some point, their beers disappeared. Mike's hands found their way to her waist. He guided her away from spilling beer and the careless swinging of lit cigarettes. Taking her hand, he tugged her up the steps. "Where are we going?" she asked.

"You'll see." He smiled at her. They entered an empty bedroom and closed the door.

"What do you think you're doing?" she accused.

"Hear me out," he pleaded, stepping away from her. "This is just pretend. I think we should be girlfriend and boyfriend until the end of the year. No one needs to know the truth."

"Because of Molly?"

Mike looked at his shoes. He shook his head. His brown eyes met hers. "This is for you. I'm trying to protect you."

"Protect me?"

"From the rumors." Mike stepped closer, lowering his voice. "Everyone is saying that you and Mister Wilde are... doing it."

Her insides knotted. "So to stop everyone thinking I'm a tramp with him, they'll think I'm a tramp with you," she snapped. Anger wanted to explode. "Brilliant plan, Mike."

"If you're with me, then you're not with him. The rumors will stop."

She could not believe she wasted the evening. "Take me to my uncle's *now*," she said through gritted teeth. She opened the door. It slammed into the wall. She stormed down the steps and out of the house.

Running, Mike caught up to her on the sidewalk. She stomped to the car without acknowledging him. Staring at the locked car door, she said, "How could you not tell me?"

Mike did not answer. He let her into the car, then hurried around to the driver's side. They drove in silence. On the freeway, Mike said, "Hope, I'm sorry. I didn't want anyone thinking that you are sleeping with a teacher."

"How do you know I'm not?" Her cold tone filled the car. "You never asked."

"I didn't have to. I know you," he said.

"Obviously, not well enough," she retorted.

Mike said nothing. Staring out the window, Hope watched the streetlamps pass. She did not want to add terrible rumors to her what-was-going-wrong-in-her-life list. Something had to go right. She sighed as Mike turned onto her uncle's tree-lined street.

When he pulled into the driveway, he dared to say, "I don't think anyone is home."

Hope opened the car door.

Getting out of the car, Mike opened the trunk. Hope snatched her bag from his hand. Retrieving his coat, he followed her up the sidewalk. "Hope," he begged.

The stained glass door opened at her touch. She entered the house, leaving Mike on the porch. Without saying another word to him, she closed the door.

Gaslights ignited, welcoming her into the empty house. She quickly changed into her other side clothes. After securing her maroon cloak around her shoulders, she entered the kitchen. She packed provisions in her bag, then exited through the back door.

Hope walked past her uncle's car parked in front of the detached garage. "Hope, wait," Mike called. She lengthened her stride. He ran to her side at the back of the garage.

"Leave me alone," she said without looking at him.

"Not until I explain myself." He followed her into the woods beyond the backyard.

"I don't want to hear your explanations. Go home, Mike." She stomped through the forest on a path she knew well.

"Yes, I made a mistake," Mike confessed, keeping in step with her. "Yes, I should have spoken to you first. I thought I was doing the right thing." He walked beside her in the darkness. "Where are we going?"

"*We* are not going anywhere." She stopped to glare at him.

Her cloaked billowed as she stormed away from him.

"Where is your uncle?" Mike followed closely.

She hiked up a small hill towards two oak trees.

"Hope, talk to me." He grabbed her shoulder, keeping pace with her.

They entered a pine grove.

"Hope," said Mike.

"Shhh," she said. She walked out the grove with Mike on her heels. "I can't believe you followed me here, of all places," she muttered. "I just want to be left alone. Why can't anyone understand that?"

"Here? Where are we?" he asked.

She spun to face him. "Look, you can't go back without me and I'm not going back. Not right now. Stay close, but don't get in my way. And don't ask questions."

"Fine. No questions," Mike said. He zipped his jacket as they walked. "My plan was supposed to save you from getting hurt," he explained. "You have to understand. As soon as someone mentioned a possible relationship between you and Mister Wilde, I told them that we were dating."

She stumbled slightly. "You did what?" Hope tried not to raise her voice.

"It was the first thing out of my mouth."

"I see." She paused to examine the surrounding trees. "Thanks for not letting me in on the ruse."

"I said I'm sorry. I am so, so sorry," he whined.

"Shhh. I'm trying to listen."

"To?"

She held her hand up to quiet him. Closing her eyes, she waited. The rustling of underbrush found her ears. She opened her eyes. Stepping closer to Mike, she readied her bow under her cloak. When two men with hard leather body armor emerged, the filtered moonlight shone across the embossed large tree with seven circles. She lowered her bow.

"Tonight's not a good night to hunt," said one of the men. "It's not safe out here."

"Have you come across anyone else?" asked the other.

"No," Hope answered.

"Come with us. We only have so long to get to safely inside. The night is ripe for a Griffin."

"Crap," she said quietly. With slumped shoulders, she followed with Mike by her side.

"Who are they?" he whispered.

"Empire Guard," she replied. "My whole weekend is ruined."

Chapter Two

Griffin

A massive, circular, stone Keep rose out of the clearing. Its black stone sucked in nearby torchlight while its edges disappeared into the black sky. Hope and Mike entered under a raised iron gate. An Empire Guard led them up stone stairs to a stone room. "Wait here," he said to them. A fire raged on the far wall. Off duty Empire Guards sat at long tables, eating and drinking.

Mike looked around, saying, "I feel as though I've fallen into one of your uncle's stories."

Her eyes narrowed. She did not want to explain anything.

The guard returned. "Follow me," he said. They climbed another flight of stone steps. Down a hallway, they passed a wooden door. "We have an extra bed in the guards' quarters," he said to Mike, indicating the door. "For you, Miss, we opened a section of the citizens' quarters." He led them through another wooden door.

A lantern lit part of an empty curved room. Hope spied a single bed next to the table on which the lantern sat. "Is there no one else?" she asked.

"No other citizens tonight," he replied. "You can store your things here and go down to get some food if you'd like."

She gave the guard a smile. "Thank you."

Turning to Mike, the guard said, "I'll show you to your bed."

When they left, she exhaled. Alone at last. Unfortunately, the citizens' quarters had no window. She wondered if perhaps they would allow her on the roof. After stashing her bag under the bed and hanging her cloak on the hook on the wall, she wandered to the room below.

Mike sat at a table, staring at her dark linen shirt and pants and knee high leather boots. Leather armbands covered her forearms. Her bow and quiver rested on her back. She traipsed through the room, every bit the archer.

"Excuse me," she said to one of the guards, "may I speak to whomever is in charge?" She gave him a sweet smile.

"Lieutenant's office. Two floors up, second door on your left."

"Thank you." She glanced at Mike who made a point of looking at his food.

Hope climbed the stairs of the quiet outpost. She figured that not many guards occupied a peacetime outpost, especially one out in the middle of nowhere. The second door on the left sat open. She knocked.

"Yes?" came from behind a curtain of blond. The hair hid a face buried in papers.

"Lieutenant, I have a question," Hope began.

The blond head snapped to look at her. Blue eyes studied her.

"Obie?" she said quietly.

His lips widened into a smile. "Hope," he said. He rose from behind the desk. "What are you doing here? It's so good to see you." As he approached, his smiled dampened. "How... Why are you here?"

"Do you really expect a Griffin tonight?" she asked.

His smile disappeared. "Conditions are prime," Obie said. "This outpost gets attacked regularly. After a while, you learn a lot about knowing when they're going to come."

"Is that why the people in the nearby villages aren't pounding on your doors for protection?"

Obie nodded. "They're safer where they are unless they are out in the open like you were."

"Guess there's no chance for a little rooftop time tonight," Hope said.

Within Obie's searching blue eyes swam an understanding. That understanding always gave her comfort. "I'll take you up," he said.

"I don't want to take you away from your work," she said, gesturing to the papers on his desk.

"Nothing that can't wait," he answered. Ushering her out of the room, he closed the door.

"I got your letter," she said as they walked to the staircase. "Congratulations on becoming Lieutenant."

He smiled again. "Thanks."

"Your letter said nothing about running an outpost."

They climbed. "I'm not. Lieutenant Otho returns tomorrow. I'm just filling in," he said. "You know, they say that this Keep predates the Empire. When the Empire found it abandoned, they made it an outpost. Ten years ago, they restored it with the other older ones that were still in decent shape. This is the only one that wasn't expanded. Something about the stonework that the Dwarves didn't want to touch."

"Lieutenant and Historian," she teased.

Laughing, Obie said, "This place... Most guards don't stay here long. I've done some research on the Keep. Well, as much as I could while being here."

"How long have you been here?"

"Long enough." He led her through an opened trapdoor. The few guards stationed on the roof barely glanced at them.

Rolling treed hills rippled in every direction. "Wow," Hope whispered. She leaned against the keyed stone edge. A flash of orange caught her eye. "What's that?" She pointed above the trees. Orange streamed through the distant sky.

"Dragon," Obie answered. "The border with the Dragonlands lies just over that second hill."

A second Dragon spit fire. It burned another creature in flight. "Is that?" she asked.

"Griffin!" yelled Obie. "Sound the alarm! Barricade!" He practically pushed Hope down the steps. "Weapons and positions!"

Running, she heard a bell, then slams of wood and metal against stone. "Hope?" called Mike.

"Here," she answered.

Mike ran off the staircase with a sword in his hand. "I took it from a sword rack downstairs," he said.

Banging echoed throughout the stone structure. Obie inventoried the relatively empty room in which they and the handful of rooftop guards stood. "We're here until it passes," he said.

"What passes?" asked Mike.

"Griffin," Obie said.

"A what?"

"A combo lion and eagle," answered Hope. "Don't you read?"

"This is messed up," Mike muttered.

"Maybe next time, you'll listen to me," Hope snapped.

Distant splintering carried down the staircase. "Push that furniture in front of the door," Obie ordered. "Get ready." He glanced at the sword in Mike's hand. "You know how to use that?"

"Yes," said Mike.

Claws scraped against stone. A screechy roar resounded down the staircase. The guards backed away from the barricaded door, weapons drawn. Smashes and thuds echoed from the floor above them. A tapping clicking hit each step on its way down. The half dozen of them faced the door.

The wood door shuddered with rhythmic scratching. Hope raised her bow with an arrow ready. Wood cracked. The furniture slid a little. Keeping her eyes on the bulging door, Hope dipped her finger into a velvet pouch that hung from her belt. She smeared a fingertip full of sparkling powder on her tongue.

"Did your eyes just darken?" Mike asked in a whisper. "What is that?"

"Fairy Dust."

"Sure," he mumbled.

The door broke. Pieces of wood slammed into the stone. The Griffin roared at them. Its talons thrashed the furniture while its angry, bird-like, yellow eyes glared at each of them. Sconce light reflected on its magnificent tan feathers. Its beaked snapped at the closest guard. Hope released an arrow. It bounced off the beast.

Free of the furniture, the Griffin slashed, meeting shields. Obie and Mike attacked its other side with their swords, but the blades would not penetrate its hide.

"Fight magic with magic," Hope said. She tipped an arrow with Fairy Dust.

Obie retreated, producing a blue sphere with his hand. He hurled it at the creature. The Griffin dodged. A crater pocked the rock wall.

Hope took aim. She let her arrow fly. Her eyes returned to their normal shade of brown. It struck where its feathers morphed to fur.

Screeching, the Griffin lunged. Empire Guards fell like bowling pins. They scrambled to their feet, clutching whatever weapon was within arm's reach.

Hope hit it again with a Fairy Dusted arrow.

The Griffin spread its wings, but they smacked against the low stone ceiling. Its talons reached, slashing three lines in the air. The fourth talon hit something or someone or ones. Hope only heard the contact while she aimed for its exposed belly.

Obie threw his sword to another, then brought his wrists together. "Push it up the steps!" he ordered. A golden stream of magic erupted from his focused palms.

The beast writhed under Obie's magic. Its menacing eyes searched for a way out. Hope fired arrows at its sides, attempting to steer it back to the steps.

Obie fell to his knees. His magic diminished. He struggled to keep the stream going.

Hope sprinkled a pinch of Fairy Dust into Obie's stream. The magic sparkled with a rainbow of blues and purples.

Turning, the Griffin rushed up the stone steps.

Hope followed the creature to the roof. She raised her bow while it launched off the stone. Obie placed a hand on her arm, stopping her from firing. "Let the Dragons take care of it. Clan Mithra hates Griffins," he told her. "Save your arrows. You only have a few left."

She watched it fly into the night. Bursts of Dragonfire lit the dark sky as it passed.

Obie ushered her back into the Keep. "Is everyone all right? Open the doors. Let's clean up," he said to his men.

Hope found Mike leaning against the wall, clutching his arm. "Did it get you?" she asked.

"It's just a scratch," he said.

"Let me see," said Obie, sheathing his sword. He peered at Mike's wound. "We need to dress that."

"Colin's got a nasty scratch on his shoulder, Lieutenant," said an Empire Guard.

Hope's eyes followed Obie. Colin had a deep gash in his armor that ended at his shoulder.

Obie led them into the guard's quarters. He sat them on their beds, then had them remove their shirts.

"Can I help?" Hope asked. Declan had taught her the basics of healing and she learned some from watching Obie, to whom Declan gave full healer training, and Alina, the Witch of Rowan.

Nodding, Obie mixed ingredients from his healer's bag. He smeared an ointment on Colin's shoulder. When he finished, Hope bandaged the cut.

Standing behind Obie, Hope watched him apply a thick glop over the long gash on Mike's upper arm. Mike winced with each dab of goo. Once Obie covered the glop with a dark green powder, Hope wrapped a bandage around Mike's arm.

"Thanks," Mike muttered.

"Get some rest," Obie said. "We'll check it in the morning."

Mike nodded. "This is crazy. You're crazy, Hope Chase."

Sighing, Hope answered, "You don't know the half of it."

Alone in the citizen's quarters, Hope rested her bow and quiver against the table. Only four arrows remained. She turned away from them to remove her armbands and her boots. Feeling a little dizzy, she sat on the bed. Her head plunked into her hands.

"Why did you bring him?" Obie's voice asked.

She raised her head enough to peek through the strands of brown hair hiding her face. Obie leaned against the doorframe. His leather uniform suited his muscular stature.

"I knocked," he said.

She blew a few of the strands out of her face. "I didn't," she said. "He followed me through the portal."

Obie raised an eyebrow.

"Don't look at me like that." Her hands released her head. "I planned on coming alone."

"Why?" He pushed his back off the doorframe.

Her eyes followed the mortar joints of the stone walls. "I think there's something wrong with me," she said in a whisper. Her gaze moved to the floor as she blinked back tears.

Hope bounced slightly when Obie sat next to her. "What do you mean?" he asked softly.

"I," she breathed, not bearing to look at him, "I can't hear them anymore." Tears dropped to her lap. Admitting that she could no longer listen to the trees hurt more than the silence of the forest.

"Oh, Hope." Obie wrapped an arm around her. "How long has this been going on?"

"A while."

"Why didn't you tell me?"

Forcing herself to look at him, she said, "That's not something you write in a letter."

He squeezed, pulling her closer.

"Then, there's tonight," she said, pushing herself far enough away to look into his eyes. "The Fairy Dust didn't last as long as it should have when I took it for concentration."

His thumb wiped her cheek dry. "Have you told Uncle Declan?"

She shook her head.

"Sounds like a magical issue to me," he said. "That's Uncle Declan's expertise."

"Don't tell anyone, Obie."

"I won't."

She rested her head on his shoulder. "Thanks." He rubbed her back.

After a few minutes of comfortable silence, Obie said, "I'll let you get some sleep. I'll check on your friend in the morning."

Hope gave him a weak smile before he walked out of the room.

Awaking in the windowless citizen's quarters, Hope had no inkling of the time of day. She desired an early start back to the portal. She would then go to the Empire Tree the "normal way" to speak with Declan.

While she secured her bow and quiver to her back, someone knocked on the door. "Come in," she said.

She recognized the swarthy Empire Guard who entered. "Good to see you again, Hope," he greeted. He wore a troubled expression beneath his short cropped curls.

"Is something wrong, Lieutenant Otho?" she asked.

"Your friend is not faring well," Otho said. "He needs the services of the Witch of Rowan as soon as possible. You and he will accompany Lieutenant Oberon to the Sages' Grove. Fill your quiver from our stores to replace what you lost to the Griffin."

Obie stood behind Otho. "We're ready, Lieutenant," he said.

"Speedy and safe travels," Otho said.

After restocking Hope's quiver, she, Obie, and Mike journeyed away from the outpost. Mike only carried a bedroll on his back and a water skin on his belt. Hope carried all her original provisions while Obie carried the rest plus his healer's bag.

They stopped to administer medicine to Mike. Hope watched her friend sweat during the cool spring morning. "We should reach the portal soon," she said.

"Can't use the portal," said Obie.

"I have permission for that portal. If we hold hands, we can all get through," Hope replied.

"Doesn't matter. The Empire recently expanded restrictions on the portals," explained Obie. "You can come in, but no one can go out without a high ranking Troll. With the high Griffin activity near the border, they don't want the creatures getting through."

"Great," Hope said flatly.

"Does this mean we can't go home?" Mike asked after swallowing some water.

"It means we have to take the long way to the Empire Tree and actually visit," she said. Hope watched her steps through the forest.

"And deal with Uncle Berty," said Obie. "He doesn't know, does he?"

Hope kicked some dirt. "No. I told him I was staying at Issy's." She wrung the edges of her cloak. "My parents are never going to let me out of the house again."

"My grandfather is going to think I'm crazy or on some drug when I tell him about my hallucination," said Mike.

Hope huffed. "You're not hallucinating. At least not about being in the Land of Sages," she said. She studied Mike to see how he would react. He stared at the forest floor. Ever since she met him when she was in second grade, she knew his grandfather bathed him in ignorance about portals and what lies on their other side. "I don't know what to tell you, Mike," she continued. "I don't know how he'll handle you being here."

"Whatever," Mike mumbled.

Obie had them stop two more times before making camp for the night. "At this pace, it'll take another couple of days, at least, to reach the Sages' Grove," she complained.

"Going any faster would only worsen his condition," said Obie. "Our only other option would have been to drag him on a trolley, but that requires the use of the main roads. Much longer and more dangerous."

Mike sat while Hope and Obie started a fire and cooked dinner. Even after eating, he looked pale in the firelight. Obie's light eyes held worry. And Hope only heard the crackling of the campfire.

In the morning, Hope aided Mike to his feet. He refused any assistance walking, although he stumbled over everything and used passing tree trunks for support. When they stopped for a break, Obie handed him a large stick. "What's this for?" Mike asked.

"Balance," said Obie.

Using the stick stopped Mike's constant wobble. However, his weak grip made Hope fear that they would not reach Alina in time.

As the sun crept across the sky, Mike slowed. His stick could no longer bear his weight. Obie positioned himself under Mike's arm.

Their pace quickened to their next campsite.

After eating a little, Mike curled atop his bedroll. His body shuddered. The warmth of the campfire could not reach him. Concocting a sphere, Obie stretched it to make a blanket, then wrapped it around Mike.

Hope tore her gaze away from her friend. Staring into the dancing flames, she fought her tear ducts. Mike had just been talking about what he wanted to do with his future. She peeked at him. His frail frame held the magical blanket close. Would he still have a future come morning? She closed her eyes.

A faint rustling snapped her eyes open. She raised her bow. Obie peered into the darkness with his hand on the hilt of his sword.

The firelight outlined two cloaked figures. A dark hood lowered.

"Uncle Declan," Obie exclaimed.

Hope lowered her bow. The smaller figure walked past Declan. She let out of breath when Alina knelt next to Mike, placing her bag on the ground. Hope wanted to ask Declan how they found them, but his gaze darted somewhere above them.

"What happened?" asked Alina.

Before anyone could answer, Declan breathed, "Fairy dome. Now."

She knew better than to ask. Without hesitation, Hope sprinkled Fairy Dust in a circle around them while speaking the ancient incantation.

Once the opalescent dome covered them, Obie told Alina, "Griffin."

"Who are you?" Mike asked in his weak voice.

"Don't talk. I am the Witch of Rowan. Hold as still as you can," Alina said. "Obie, remove your magic please." She dug into her bag while he reclaimed the blanket. Equipped with an herbal bundle, she peeled off his bandage. Although Obie had tended to the wound mere hours ago, a foul odor escaped from the gash. Hope pulled her cloak over her nose to keep from gagging.

Alina spoke in the runic language of witchcraft. Hope never learned much of Witch Runes beyond the few Alina could teach her. Through Alfred and other sources, she learned the ancient languages of the Land of Sages. None entranced like Witch Runes, or perhaps Alina said them that way.

The slash began to glow. Mike screamed and writhed. Alina continued her runic chant.

A gold speckled inkiness oozed out of Mike's arm. It coalesced in the air at Alina's runic urging. She covered the laceration with the herbs, then spoke to the glinting blob. Her chant ended with a sharp, "*Brota!*" The mass exploded, sending shimmering waves through the dome.

"What's that light?" asked Mike.

"Shhh," said Alina. She moved the herbs to dress his wound. After laying a blanket from her bag over him, she coaxed, "Rest."

Standing next to Declan, Hope said quietly, "I don't know how long the dome will hold."

His light eyes studied her face. He nodded. "It did its job. I'm sure that whatever was watching has left," he said.

"Not a Whisper?" said Obie.

Declan shook his head, not taking his eyes off Mike. "Your uncle sent us. He saw the three of you in the woods coming this way."

Hope hung her head. "It's all my fault." She watched Alina whisper over Mike and immediately felt grateful for her uncle's eagle eye. With a hard swallow, she sat away from the others.

Sitting next to her, Declan said, "I'm sure you have plenty to explain when we return to the Empire Tree. Get some sleep. I'll take first watch."

Her eyes did not want to meet the gaze of the man she considered her honorary uncle. "Thank you," she said in a small voice.

Walking to her bedroll, she mouthed a thank you to Alina. She glanced at Obie before laying down. He spoke with his uncle. She knew he'd never tell her secret. After wrapping herself in her cloak, sleep wanted to step aside for crying. She forced her tears to stay inside their ducts. She could not cry in front of everyone. They would see. She would have to wait until she was alone.

At some point during the night, the dome disappeared. When she stared at the tree branches she should not have been able to see, she sighed. Velvet pouch in hand, she rose from her bedroll.

"Leave it until after we eat," said Declan. He sat, prodding the fire awake. "It's still protecting us."

Nodding, she packed to go.

After eating what Alina gave him for breakfast, color returned to Mike's cheeks. He sat on his bedroll still wrapped in the blanket, watching the strangers in cloaks surrounding him. Alina retrieved her blanket, then checked his wound. "I'll need to monitor that gash for a few days," she said.

"You're too young to be a doctor," Mike said.

Hope wrapped the spare brown cloak Declan gave her around Mike. Fastening it, she said, "That's because Alina's not a doctor. She's a Witch."

"Witch of Rowan," Mike mumbled. He looked from Hope to Alina. "Alina?" He squinted at her. "I remember you. We met ages ago."

Smiling, Alina said, "Yes, we did." She turned her face away to rummage through her bag.

"Mike," said Hope, "this is Declan, Duke of Fairyland and Advisor to my aunt and uncle."

Mike gave Declan a respectful nod.

"Obie, extinguish the fire," said Declan. "Hope, break the Ring."

With the campsite cleared, they began their trek through the woods. Alina had them stop after an hour to give Mike some medicine.

"When I wake from this nightmare," said Mike, "I'm going to wonder what you put in my drink, Hope." He swallowed what Alina gave him with a grimace.

She looked away from Mike who stood in the center of them. "I wish you were dreaming, Mike," she mumbled.

Alina walked in stride with Mike. Her deep cloak changed colors in swirls every few steps. She acquired the trademark cloak during her Renaming Ceremony the previous year. Hope had been included in the small group that gathered in the woods where Alina officially became Kalina, the Witch of Rowan.

She remembered standing between two standing stones, watching her friend in the center. Her magic reinforced the protection of the Witch Stones—a circle of five standing stones, small enough to stub a toe against before noticing, that Witches used for special ceremonies. Alina opened a box passed from generation to generation of Rowan Witches. Two blades rested in the velvet lining. Large colored gemstones capped the dark hilts of each blade. Extracting the straight blade, Alina cleansed its edges in a bronze bowl of fire. After placing it on a central tree stump, she repeated the purification on the curved blade. Chanting in runes, she ritualistically stabbed the stump with both blades. The stump cracked. She reached inside. From the cracked wood, she pulled a silver pendant attached to a sliver chain. After the ceremony, Alina showed Hope the pendant. She explained that the five pointed star resting over the Rowan tree symbolized the relationship between the mundane and the magical in the healing art of Witchcraft.

The wind blew Obie's green cloak into her, bringing her back to the present. As Obie pulled it closer to his body, Hope wondered why Obie could not use his Warlock magic when he healed. Why did one have to be born a Witch or Wizard to do so? Perhaps if she understood magic better, she would not have lost hers. Taking a deep breath of cool spring air, she cleared all thoughts from her mind. She simply followed Declan's path through the woods.

When they stopped to eat, Declan said, "I don't want to spend another night out here." He hurried them through the woods until Mike stumbled.

"He's weak," said Alina. "He needs to rest."

Declan looked at the sky. "We're losing light." He draped Mike's unhurt arm over his shoulder. "Lean on me," he said to Mike.

Light still clutched on to the edges of the sky when they finally spied the treed wall surrounding the Sages' Grove. Declan half dragged Mike through the gates.

Alina led them through the village to her family's white cob house. They passed the first wooden door that led into the house. Alina unlocked the second wooden door. Inside her Witch Room, she ordered, "Lay him on the bed."

Obie helped Declan sit Mike on the bed, which was more of a low table covered with a thin cushion than a bed. Standing by the door, Hope watched Alina grab a bottle off a shelf.

The Witch held a spoon to Mike's lips. "Open," she commanded. "Swallow." She changed the bandage and reapplied ointment. "He should be able to walk mostly by himself now."

Declan helped Mike off the bed, but Mike immediately sat back down. "Hold on," Mike said. Declan gave him a nod. After a few seconds, Mike stood. The five of them walked to the Empire Tree.

Chapter Three

Silence

Ascending the steps to the Reception Room, Hope took a deep breath. She did not want to face her uncle. She closed her eyes before her head crested above the wooden floor.

On the dais, her uncle sat on his throne while her aunt sat on hers. Hope stood between Declan and Alina feet from the dais. She gulped, not knowing what punishment they had in store for her.

"Care to explain?" her uncle asked in his calm voice. He did sound angry, but she heard the disappointment in his tone. His disappointment cut into her more than his anger ever could.

She could not look at him. She stared at the rich purple drapes flanking the dais, biting her lip. "Not here," she said in almost a whisper. Daring to chance a look into his brown eyes, she said, "I'm sorry, Uncle Berty." She looked into the pair of eyes beside him, "Aunt Silvia."

Berty gave her a nod. "Alina," he said, "Theodore has set up a room for Mike to recover. Make sure it has everything he needs."

"Thank you, my Lord," Alina said.

"Mike, your grandfather has been called. He should be here shortly," Berty continued.

"Wait," said Mike. "Grandpa knows? Of course he does. This is my dream after all—nightmare actually."

Silvia smiled at him. "In the meantime, you and Alina can follow Theodore," she said. She extended her arm to where the Dwarf stood. As they left, she continued, "Obie, we'd like a full report on the Griffins."

"Yes, Empress," said Obie.

"You'll be collected from your quarters when we're ready," she said.

"My quarters? Not the barracks?" he asked.

"Your captain has reassigned you to the Empire Tree, Lieutenant," said Berty.

Obie nodded.

Standing, Berty said, "Hope, come with me."

She gave Obie a final wistful look before following her uncle up the stairs.

After she entered the Roundtable Room, Berty closed the door. "It's just you and me. Explain."

She crumpled into a chair. Staring into the reflective round tabletop, she bit her bottom lip again. Hot tears streaked down her cheeks. She wiped them with her fingers. "I didn't mean for Mike to come through. He followed me by accident," she said.

"But why use that portal at all?" he asked.

Her vision blurred. "Because I... I... I can't hear them anymore." She collapsed into a ball, sobbing.

A comforting hand touched her shoulder. With shuddered breaths, she lifted her head. Her entire face felt wet. Her eyes managed to find Berty's. They told her that he understood.

"Go to your chambers," he said. "Get cleaned up. I'll speak to your dad and to Declan."

"Thanks, Uncle Berty." She wrapped her arms around him, crying a little more. Making her way to her chambers up more stairs and across a bridge, she felt lighter.

After she showered and changed, she heard her wind chimes. She let Declan inside carrying a lump of beige material over his arm.

"Change into his." He handed her the material. "It's magic neutral. Wear only this. No other clothes, no jewelry, no weapons, and no Fairy Dust. I need to be able to see your magic flow without hindrance."

Bundle in hand, she returned to her bedroom. The blah material was actually a robe or a dress. It emitted a stale storage smell as she slipped it over her head. The coarse fibers scratched her skin. The bottom of the robe puddled on the floor while the sleeves hung past her hands. She lifted the front to walk down the steps.

Noticing her in the oversized sack with sleeves, Declan said, "Good. Come with me. Touch nothing but the robe. Your feet will obviously touch the ground, but that's okay."

Gathering the robe, she stepped out onto her platform. Obie waited by the lantern. Between Declan and Obie, she walked across the bridges to the wall. Darkness settled over the village. Her stomach rumbled. They strode outside the gates.

A cool wind made her clutch the robe closer to her body. Her bare feet tried to pull any lingering warmth from the forest floor.

After Declan seemed satisfied in a section of woods, they stopped. "Keep watch," he told Obie. "Let the hem fall to the ground and stand still until I say otherwise," he said to Hope. He looked around them a final time, then encircled Hope. While his eyes studied her, he muttered under his breath, slightly waving his wand. Finally, he stopped. "Time to go," he said.

"What did you see?" she asked.

Ignoring her questioning, he led her and Obie back to the Sages' Grove. Inside the Tree, Declan escorted her to her chambers. "Change and bring the robe to the Roundtable Room. Berty has food for you there," he said.

She ran to her bedroom, ready to shed the horrid robe. After scrubbing the dirt off her feet, she changed into comfortable jeans and a sweatshirt. She brought the robe to the Roundtable Room as instructed. Berty, Silvia, Declan, and Obie sat around the table. She handed the robe to Declan, then had a seat. "Eat," encouraged Silvia. "You, too, Obie."

Both of them grabbed food from the table.

"I apologize for not explaining what was happening beforehand, Hope," said Declan, "but I did not want to skew or influence the results. I measured the magic flowing through you. It is easier to see in the dark and the woods is the ideal location." Declan paused for her to swallow and take a drink. "Magic does flow through you. You have not lost it. It is just weak."

Closing her eyes, she exhaled.

"We need to find out why," he said. "If possible, I'd like Hope to stay here until we do."

Hope's heart lightened. She watched the conversation with new interest.

"I'll speak with Jon," said Berty.

"Martin will arrive in the morning," said Silvia. "We discussed calling this a camping accident, perhaps a wild animal attack. Bears would be looking for food this time of year. We'll hammer out a story tomorrow." She turned her attention to Hope and Obie. "We'll leave you two to eat. Get some sleep." She smiled.

"Thanks, Aunt Silvia," Hope said, returning her smile.

Hope ate as if she had only begun to be hungry. "I should have gone to Uncle Declan in the beginning," she said.

"Why didn't you?" asked Obie.

"I was scared." She stared at the few morsels still left on her plate. "Stupid, I know."

He placed his hand on her arm. "Magic can be very scary at times," he admitted.

She found herself staring into his blue eyes. "Has yours ever dwindled?" she asked in a breath.

"No," he answered. "Come on. I'll walk you to your chambers."

She gulped her remaining drink. Leaving the room, she stepped next to Obie in silence. He towered over her. His dark green cloak floated behind him. His silence carried strength. She wanted to say something, but could not find the words. Did three years of letter writing steal the words from her mouth?

Before she knew it, they arrived at her door. "It'll be okay," he said. All she could muster was a nod. She looked up at him. The intensity of his blue eyes made her look away. "Goodnight," he said, taking a step back.

"Goodnight," she said, then entered her chambers. Without lighting a lantern, she peeked out the window. Obie stared at her door. His chest fell as if he let out a breath. When he turned to cross the bridge to the trunk, she lit a lantern and climbed upstairs to her bedroom.

When she opened her eyes in the morning, Hope found herself facing her wardrobe. Her eyes traced the carved design on the door. She rubbed her head. "Mike!" Jumping out of bed, she scrambled to get ready. She threw her maroon cloak over her bow and quiver before traipsing through the tree for breakfast.

Noticing a closed door to the Roundtable Room, she wondered who sat inside. "Hope," Berty's voice called. The door opened. "Come in."

Around the table sat Berty, Silvia, Declan, and her father. "Have a seat," said Berty. Sitting, she realized that her father had only projected himself there.

"How are you doing this morning?" Jon asked her.

"Fine, Dad."

"She says she's fine," said Jon. "She looks healthy. Teresa, I can see her. She's okay." He looked at Declan. "She's okay, right?"

"There's nothing wrong with Hope," answered Declan. "The lack of magic is not affecting her in any other way."

Jon relayed what Declan said to Teresa. "Now," said Jon, "all your schoolwork will be emailed to you and whenever you send it in is fine. Your mom and I will bring your laptop."

"I can't connect to the internet here, Dad."

Jon laughed. "You can from your aunt and uncle's house."

She stopped an exasperated breath from escaping.

"We'll see you soon, Jon," said Silvia. Jon disappeared. She turned to Hope. "Mike will be confined to his quarters until Alina releases him. She and his grandfather are with him now."

"Is Mister Hunter upset?" asked Hope, afraid of the answer.

"He's more worried at the moment," said Silvia. "Go down and have breakfast."

"Thank you, Aunt Silvia."

"You can use my target to practice," said Declan. "I'll be out there shortly."

"Thanks, Uncle Declan." She hurried out of the room.

In the Reception Room, Obie did not sit at the tables, having breakfast with the majority of the Empire Tree. She grabbed something off the buffet, then scurried down the steps and out of the Tree.

The cool morning air welcomed her. Crisp sunlight filtered through the mighty branches of the Empire Tree. Taking bites of a muffin, she strolled to Declan's preferred target—at the far end of the Empire Guard practice area. He liked the seclusion. She needed it.

The guards ignored her as she took her stance in front of the target. They knew her and her talent with a bow. With each arrow she fired, she sent with it her frustration, her worries, her fears. When she emptied her quiver, her head felt oddly empty. So many trees on a beautiful day and... nothing. She collected her arrows and started again.

"Hope, hit me," said a voice.

She looked up. A Fairy Empire Guard flew around with a target. Shaking her head a little, she raised her bow, hitting the bullseye as he zipped past.

"On the ground," bellowed a stern voice.

The Fairy immediately landed. "Captain Edwin..."

"Lift up your bow," said Declan. His voice cut across the verbal lashing the Fairy received. She never heard him approach. Seeing him next to her, she did as he asked. "Higher," he said. He glanced at her bow. "Gather your arrows. Come with me."

After stuffing her arrows in her quiver, she asked, "Did I do something wrong, Uncle Declan?"

"No," he said, leading her back inside the Tree. Declan ushered her past the reception desks to the Sages' Seals on the back wall. After he pressed a circle, they entered the box beyond the door. She stood next to Declan. The doors closed. They plunged. Declan extracted his gold Watcher's Locket. He wrote a message with the rod part of the chain's clasp. She knew that message went directly to Berty.

"What is it?" she asked.

"I think I might know how your magic is fading," said Declan. "But I want to go to the Vaults to be sure."

She nodded.

When the doors opened, he led her to one of the Empire's mine carts. The cart raced through the tunnels and caverns to the Empire Vaults. Light ahead told her they would stop soon. When the cart stopped in the niche beside the Vault door, they got out. Declan opened the stone door with his touch. They entered a room with three doors that lead to the Vaults. One door slid open.

Berty and Silvia waited for them on the other side of the opening. Once Hope and Declan entered the antechamber to the Emperor and Empress' Vault, the stone doors closed behind them. Delyth and Jon stood with Silvia and Berty.

"Take out your bow," Declan said to Hope. She held her bow in her hands. "Bring the bottom end up, so we can see it," he instructed. Without question, she did as he asked. "Can you see it?" Declan asked the others.

"Yes," said Berty. "What is it?"

"Some sort of symbol," said Declan. It's familiar to me. I wish I knew why."

"I don't see anything," said Jon.

Hope examined her bow where Declan and Berty indicated. "The wood's a little different color here," she said, running her finger over it.

"Hold it up," Jon said. He released a little blue sphere of light and used it like a flashlight on the area. "Wood putty?" He looked at Berty.

"Dad would know," Berty told Jon. "Could someone have carved a symbol into Hope's bow and filled it in with wood putty so no one would see it?"

"Who would have access?" asked Delyth.

While Declan followed Silvia into the Library Vault, Hope said, "The only time it is out of my hands is before competitions when the judges examine the bows to make sure they qualify."

Declan called her into the library. While she held her bow, he copied the symbol only he and Berty could see onto paper.

"We've seen that," said Silvia, watching him draw. She opened the magical item storage vault.

Stepping inside behind everyone, Hope's jaw dropped. All kinds of items rested on pedestals or hung on the walls. Each item had a plaque underneath. The plaques told what the item was or did and to whom it belonged in either the ancient or modern tongues. She walked past the miniature Sages' Grove that used to be in the Watching Rooms. On another pedestal sat the flask Robert bought that bespelled him. She shuddered.

"Here," said Declan.

Hope followed. She passed Martin's journal resting on another pedestal. Declan indicated a pair of gloves that bore a similar symbol. She read the plaque written in the ancient tongue. "Absorbs magic from another," she translated. "Why is the rest scratched out?"

"It's not an exact match," said Delyth.

"No, but the premise should be the same," Declan said.

"The name has been removed. Whoever it was must have done terrible things," answered Silvia.

"Am I leaving my bow here?" Hope asked.

"Eventually," said Berty. "First, we need to dissolve that putty to see the carving. Then, Edwin is going to slice it."

Everything inside her dropped.

"I know," said Declan, placing a hand on her shoulder. "We'll get you a replacement. Vander makes excellent bows."

"But, Aunt Julie made this one." She loved her bow. It was so much a part of her that she could not imagine using another. She trudged out of the vault behind Delyth. Before she stepped through the door, she noticed the dummy cut in half with the Blade of the Golden Flame slumped off to the side. Her chest constricted thinking that her bow would meet the same fate.

"When are we leaving?" she heard Jon ask in the antechamber.

"As soon as we're ready," said Silvia.

"I'll speak to Edwin and Obie," Declan said.

They climbed the ladder to Berty and Silvia's chambers. "We're going on foot," said Berty. "Pack accordingly. We'll meet in the Reception Room."

No one told Hope where they were going, but Hope found that she did not care. She clutched her bow until her knuckles whitened. Entering her chambers, she slammed her bow on the table. How dare someone defile her bow. She let out a restrained scream. Then, she packed.

After changing into traveling clothes, she carried her bag downstairs. Her wind chimes rang. "Come in," she said.

Declan entered. He held up a leather bag. "Your bow goes in here. The leather will stop the drain on your magic," he said. "And since you shouldn't travel without a weapon, I brought you a borrowed bow."

With a sigh, she secured it to her bow strap on her back. "Thanks, Uncle Declan." She plunked her bow into the bag. Her eyes followed her feet as she walked with him to the Reception Room.

Teresa hugged her as soon as she reached the bottom step. "How are you feeling, honey?" she asked.

"I'm fine, Mom. Really." Teresa loosened her grip.

"We'll get this sorted," her mother said. Looking Hope in the eyes, Teresa asked, "Why didn't you tell us?"

She averted her gaze. "I don't know," she said in a small voice. "I thought I could fix it myself." When she glanced at her mother, Teresa smiled her everything will be all right smile.

"Ready?" Teresa asked.

Hope nodded. Finally noticing her sister and cousins, she asked, "Is everyone going?"

"Yes," her mother answered. "Lily and your cousins were able to be pulled out of school without a problem."

Scanning the room, she saw Mike near the wall. Martin, his grandfather, secured a gray cloak around Mike's shoulders. "Mike, too?" she asked her mother.

"He can't stay here by himself," said Teresa.

"He wouldn't be alone," Hope began, but then realized that he would know no one. "He doesn't really believe any of this is real.

And recuperating without us to help him adjust...." Whatever Mike felt or thought, Hope could not help him. She could not relate. Before ever stepping through the portal, she knew about it all. She begged Berty to bring her. Mike never asked for any of it.

"Daddy!" cried a young boy, running, arms wide, to Declan. As Declan lifted his son into his arms, Hope smiled at how much Ynyr resembled his father, except for his mop of curly brown hair and his folded wings on his back. Putting Ynyr on the floor, Declan buckled a quiver to his son's leg and checked the secureness of the bow under his wings. He then fastened a dark purple cloak around Ynyr's shoulders.

"I hear he's as good as you were at his age," said a strong voice beside her.

She glanced up at intense blue eyes. Breaking Obie's gaze, her eyes fell on his pack and cloak. "Are you coming with us?" she asked.

He gave her a nod. "Uncle Declan told me I was coming," he said. His eyes roved over the colored cloaks. "Six kids, the other sider, and you."

"And *me*?" Her eyebrows raised.

"It's been a long time since I traveled without the Guard," Obie answered.

"The Fairy Godmothers are coming," said Hope. "It shouldn't be too bad." She looked at his hard leather breastplate, then up at his face. "What do you mean and me?"

His hand plunged into a pocket. "I got you something." His eyes quickly search the room. He plunked something cold, leather, and thin in her hands.

The metal hilt of a dagger rested against a leather scabbard. "I... Thank you?"

"Back up," he said. "I'll show you how to use it on the way." He looked around the room again. "Do you have provisions?"

With provisions packed, Hope exited the Empire Tree with the large group. Out of all of them, only Teresa carried no weapon. Ever since Freesia returned to the Fairy Godmother Guild, Fairy Godmothers began to use Fairy Dust to protect their charges, if need be. Silvia made sure Mike wore a sword.

Chapter Four

Practice

Outside the wall, Mike walked beside Hope. His eyes darted from colored cloak to colored cloak. "So, let me get this straight," Mike began. "All those stories your uncle wrote—*The Adventures of Leigh and Marcus*—were true?"

Hope nodded.

"Declan, a regular person, is married to Delyth, a Fairy—"

"Princess."

"—Princess, and they have two children with wings," he continued. "Watching their children, Silvia and Berty's children, and your sister are Fairy Godmothers. Do they grant wishes?"

Hope rolled her eyes. "No. I had one as well. Freesia taught me so much about this world. And myself. I miss her sometimes."

"Where'd she go?"

"Back to the Godmother Guild in Fairyland."

"Of course there's a Fairyland," said Mike. "Why didn't Lily get the same one?"

"That's not how it works. One is chosen for you." Hope waved the air between them. "Mike, I know this must be a lot for you to digest."

Mike's brown eyes stared at her. "I...." He looked at the ground as they walked. "My cell phone doesn't work here. Grandpa said he'll tell Dad something he'll believe." He shrugged then continued walking beside her in silence.

When they stopped to camp, Delyth and Fiala, her young daughter, constructed a Fairy dome. Mike's eyes examined the pearlescent glowing dome while Declan dosed the potion Alina made for him.

Hope sat off to the side with her food. While she ate, she watched her cousins. One of them would be either Emperor or Empress. Katie, the eldest, ran around the campsite with Lily. Brenda often kept to herself. She consumed every piece of knowledge. The Whingham Academy placed her in second grade at the beginning of the school year—a year ahead of where she should be—because of her yearning for learning. Languages were her strong suit. Although not old enough to attend school yet, Walden's Fairy Godmother encouraged him to tinker. Fiala dusted her toys after Walden deconstructed them. Horrified, Delyth took away her daughter's Fairy Dust privileges. Walden never touched the half-Fairy's things again.

Every so often, Hope caught Mike shaking his head. She sometimes forgot that Katie, Brenda, and Walden were Mike's cousins as well. He sat across the fire from her. She tried to look anywhere but at him.

"Feeling guilty?" Obie asked as he sat next to her.

"A little," she admitted without looking at him.

"His choices are not your fault," Obie said. "You only have control over your own."

"I should have made sure he left before I walked out of the house," she said. Finally looking into his blue eyes, she said, "It's happening again, isn't it?"

"They're coming after you again, you mean?" said Obie.

"But both Leif and Millicent have been dead for ten years," she said. "So, who is it?"

Concern swam in his blue eyes. His hand rubbed her back below the borrowed bow. "They're working on it, Hope." When his hand reached her waist, he retracted it.

She needed the comfort Obie gave, no matter how brief, for she knew not when she would feel safe again.

After the kids and Mike retired to the tents, Obie gave Hope her first dagger lesson. "This is mainly a thrusting blade, not a slicing blade," he said. "However, if you needed to slice, it is sharp enough." Hope nodded. "Use a solid grip." His hand wrapped hers around the metal hilt. He stood behind her—her back against his chest. With his hand still on hers, he showed her how to move the dagger.

"Not exactly Edwin's methods," said Delyth.

Hope jumped. Surpassing the Fairy in height years ago, she did not see her approach. Obie immediately stepped back.

"Get some sleep," she told them. Her violet eyes met Hope's. "Absorb everything he tells you. I know what you must be going through. If you want to talk, I'm here."

"Thanks," Hope said before entering the tent she shared with her aunts and mother.

The Fairy Godmothers made packing the campsite go smoothly.

Walking through the woods, however.... She did not remember being so unruly when she traveled with her uncle, even with Obie. Fortunately, by the time they stopped to eat, the younger ones had expended a good portion of their energy.

When they continued, Hope found Mike walking beside her again. "That medicine tastes terrible," he said.

"Mike," was all Hope could say.

"So, what's up with you and the Lieutenant?" he asked.

She glanced behind her. Obie walked with a hand resting on the hilt on of his sword. "We've been best friends since I was seven," she said.

"And?"

"And we haven't seen each other in three years," she continued. "We write every few months. He's only been allowed to send one letter a month, so he alternated between me and his family. I send pictures with my letters. Recently, I sent the picture of when I won the state archery competition."

"Again," said Mike.

A smile crept across her face until she remembered the fate of her bow. She kicked a stick in her path.

"So, are you ever going to tell me what's going on with you?" Mike asked.

She looked at the trees they passed. All she heard was their footsteps. "I don't think you'd believe me."

"Try me?"

Without looking at him, she began, "I've always had the ability to communicate with the trees."

"You speak Entish?" he said.

Her eyes narrowed.

"Sorry," Mike muttered.

"It's... how I imagine telepathy working. It's like I can hear the trees' thoughts," she explained. "And when I touch one, there's a pulse of energy exchanged. A sped up Vulcan mind meld, if you will."

"That is creepy and cool all at the same time," said Mike.

She half smiled. "But, for months—I can't remember how many now, my ability has been diminishing," she said. "And now, nothing. It's so quiet." She took a few steps without saying anything. "Years ago, they came after me for my gift. Now, they're siphoning my magic without having to abduct me."

"Who is?"

"I don't know."

Mike stared at the branches under which they walked. "So, you'll always need a bodyguard?" he asked.

Hope said nothing, but wondered when she would be able to protect herself. The dagger pressed against her body.

When they stopped to camp, Obie began training. He handed her a stick, saying, "Pretend this is the dagger. Hold it in your hand. Defend yourself."

"Wait. What?" Hope tried to say, but Obie already had an arm around her neck. She stood there, doing nothing.

"Hope. Defend," he urged.

"Edwin has already taught me basic self-defense," she said.

"Humor me."

"I don't want to hurt you."

Obie laughed.

Twisting, Hope slid out of his grasp. He grabbed her forearm. She faced him, unable to move. "Now what?" he asked her. "Pretend that in my other hand, I have a sword."

Her eyes scanned his body. Muscular... broad shoulders... strong legs... about a foot taller than she.

"You have *a* free hand. No magic. What do you do?" asked Obie.

She pulled back, then charged him—right in the chest. Her stick pressed into his breastplate.

He released her. "Good," he said. His eyes glanced over her head for a moment. "Use all your force to push the hilt as deep as possible. Twist if you can."

Nodding, Hope dropped the stick.

Obie made her practice gripping the dagger and thrusting into the air until they slept.

After Delyth deconstructed the dome, Hope looked at the trees, listening. Still the forest said nothing. She had not touched her bow in over twenty-four hours. When would her magic return? She hurried to keep stride with Declan.

"Uncle Declan," she said, "do we... need to reverse it?"

His eyes examined her with a glance. "We're almost there. Just a little longer," Declan said.

She nodded, hating his cryptic answer.

Finally, they passed through the opening of a low, rock wall. Stones outlined where buildings used to stand. Goats grazed the vegetation growing inside the haphazard outlines.

"Dad got the windmill working," Jon said to Berty. Standing on the hill to the right, a stone and plaster windmill faced the winds, its canvas blades turning. A few chickens squawked beyond other former foundations.

"Your grandparents made a lot of progress since the last time I visited," said Obie as he strolled next to her.

"Grandpa is always adding something," Hope said. "Grandma lets him as long as he and the goats stay out of her garden. And Grandpa has gotten help from those passing through who pay for provisions or a night's stay with labor."

"I remember Captain Alvar, before he retired, sending some new recruits out here for discipline," said Obie. "They all came back changed." He chuckled. "I think Captain Edwin continued that tradition."

"Someone keeps building new buildings," Hope said.

"Soon, they'll rebuild this ruined hamlet," said Obie. He stared at an empty cottage. "The Pixie who adopted the Fairy boy—Aloysia and Carr, I think—do they no longer live here?"

"Years ago, all the Pixies returned to Pixisle. Carr left with them," she told him.

Flowering bushes lined the front of her grandparents' home in the center of the old hamlet. The stone and cob house always made Hope feel welcome. Down the dirt lane a little stood two bunkhouses, as her grandmother called them, to house visitors. Behind the main house, her grandfather built his workshop. Beyond that was a small barn and chicken coop. Closer to the wall was where her grandmother insisted on keeping the stables. Her grandparents did not own horses, but many travelers did.

The front door opened. Kate smiled at her visitors. "Come in, come in," she said, hugging everyone entering the house. "Obie, is that you?" she said over Hope's shoulder.

"Yes, Missus Chase," said Obie.

After hugging Obie, Kate looked at Mike then at Hope. "Grandma, do you remember Mike Hunter?" Hope asked.

"Of course," said Kate. Her eyes snapped from Mike to Obie before landing on Hope.

Hope just smiled.

"I'm sure you're exhausted and hungry," said Kate.

"Where's Dad?" Berty's voice asked.

"Check the workshop," Kate yelled to him.

"Are the bunkhouses empty?" asked Jon. "We'll get settled in there and out of your hair."

Hope followed her grandmother into the living room. Cloaks hung on pegs near the door. Bags rested next to chairs and benches. Through the next opening, the kids ran around the long table in the dining room.

"Hope," said Kate, "take off your cloak. Stay awhile. Wash your hands. You can help."

Barely registering what her grandmother said, she did as Kate instructed. George entered through the back door with Berty and Declan, deep in some conversation. After they ate, Kate handed slices of cake to whomever wanted one. Her grandmother's cakes could always make her forget her problems. She relished each bite.

Teresa and Delyth led the children and Fairy Godmothers to the bunkhouses. When the mothers returned, George said, "You promised to tell us the meaning behind your visit once the children left the house. So?"

"We need your help, Dad," said Berty. "Someone carved something into Hope's bow and filled it in with wood putty."

"And you want to remove the wood putty," said George. Berty nodded. "It'll take a little while, but we'll get it done."

"Because of this, Hope needs a new bow. We're going to go to Boudon," said Jon. "But not until we've spent some quality time with you guys."

Kate eyed Declan giving Mike a portion of potion. Her grand-mother missed nothing. After the dishes had been cleared from the table, Hope found herself alone in the kitchen with Kate. "Want to tell me what's going on?" she asked her granddaughter.

Hope squeezed Kate. Everything from her magic woes to the ru-mors about Mr. Wilde poured out of her mouth.

"Mike's heart was in the right place although his methods were questionable," Kate told her. "Now," Kate cupped Hope's face in her hands, "tackle one problem at a time. It'll all work out. You'll see." Kate wrapped her arms around Hope again. "Go claim a bed. And smile. Troubles don't melt with fret."

"'Kay, Grandma." Hope gave her a final squeeze. After grabbing her bag off the living room floor, she headed to the lit bunkhouse.

The parents slept in the rooms on the first floor. On the second floor, Katie and Lily shared a room while the rest of the kids bunked in the dorm-like attic. She noticed Mike's and Obie's packs in one of the rooms. She took the room across the hall from them. Four of the Fairy Godmothers shared the larger room next to hers.

After taking advantage of the unoccupied bathroom to wash off days of travel grime, Hope decided to practice with her borrowed bow. She had no idea how long it would be until she got a new one. She set up the cloth target Declan gave her years ago away from children and animals. Taking her stance, she fired an arrow. Alt-hough she hit center, the bow did not feel good in her hands. She shot a few more. While retrieving her arrows, she heard, "Just doesn't feel right."

Turning, she saw Declan walk towards her. "No," she said.

Declan's eyes searched the surrounding area before saying, "Be ready to leave tomorrow before the others get up."

"Okay," she said. He left her to practice.

When it got too dark to see the target, she returned to the bunk-house. In the common room, Obie sat without his armor next to Mike. They laughed together. Obie looked up as he reached for a bottle. "How's the bow?" he asked her.

She shrugged, deciding to enter. "It's a bow," she answered.

Obie poured two glasses, then handed Hope one as she sat. While she sipped, Mike scolded, "That's alcohol."

"So?" she said. "I drink mead all the time."

"You're seventeen," said Mike.

Hope laughed. "I know how old I am." Obie gave Mike a puzzled look. "You, who gave me beer at a party, are concerned about me drinking alcohol," she said with a shake of her head.

"Yeah, but your parents," argued Mike.

"They drink mead, too," she said. "Where we live on the other side, one must be twenty-one to drink alcohol legally," she told Obie.

"Why?" asked Obie. "I'd have to wait another year to drink a glass of mead even though I've been drinking it all my life?"

Hope nodded then took another sip.

"That's stupid," said Obie.

She shrugged. "There are no such rules here, Mike. My parents are cool with that. It's not like I'm binge drinking or anything."

Crossing his arms, Mike said, "Alina forbade me from drinking even a drop of alcohol until I finished the potion."

"How are you feeling?" she asked.

"I get a little weak and achy around the time for a dose," he answered. "Declan says I'm doing well."

She smiled at him.

"And I was given this sword and told not to use it," he continued. "'Emergencies only,' Aunt Silvia said. I have to let the potion do its work first." He stared out the window while their cousins scampered inside and up the steps. "I'm sorry about the party, Hope." He looked at her. "I still believe Mister Wilde is creepy and maybe a little too attentive to you."

Obie's eyebrows raised.

"It's not like that," she protested.

"Not on your end," said Mike.

"Not on his either," she said.

"Yeah. You're *just* his star archer," Mike said. "I'm the best fencer in our school and you don't see Mister Keane gush over me like that."

Rolling her eyes, she took another sip. While she finished her drink, Obie enquired about Mr. Wilde, which Mike happily answered.

"I'm going to bed," she announced. "You boys have fun." She felt their eyes on her as she walked out of the room.

In bed, she stared at the empty bunk above her. The room slept four in bunk beds. She began to feel better—like a weight was lifting. She should have told someone when she first noticed her magic dwindling. Stupid, she told herself, then pushed it all from her mind. The magic would come back. She needed to believe that. Holding that thought, she drifted off to sleep.

She woke before the sun. Quietly, she got ready. After making her bed, she shouldered her pack. Tiptoeing out of the bunkhouse, she headed for the light in her grandparent's kitchen.

Upon entering, she realized that she had not been the first to wake. Declan and Delyth sat at the table with her parents. Berty smiled at her, saying, "Sit. Have some breakfast." He clung to a mug of coffee.

Kate roamed around the kitchen in her robe. She placed a glass and plate in front of Hope. "Chocolate milk," said Kate.

As Hope devoured her pancakes and eggs, Obie entered. He sat across from her. Kate placed food in front of him as well. George, also donning a robe, poured coffee.

She noticed that, like Berty, the others only had mugs. "Why is no one else eating?" she asked.

Berty finally sat at the table. "Just you and Obie are going to Boudon right now," he explained. "Declan was supposed to go with you, but the mineral spirits are taking longer than expected to dissolve the wood putty. After a lengthy discussion, we believe that the best thing to do is to put distance between you and the symbol. In order for you to get your magic back, the hold it has on you must be broken. Physical distance should help."

Silvia entered from another room. "Are you wearing the pendant the Pixies gave us?" she asked Hope.

"Yes," Hope answered. "I thought it was supposed to protect us from old magic."

"It does." Silvia sat next to Hope. "It may also inhibit your magic from returning. The magic of the trees is old magic. Leave the pendant."

Hope removed the flat metal pendant from around her neck. She handed it to her mother.

"You should also remove your Fairy Stone," added Declan.

"But?" Hope protested.

"Take it with you—just in your bag or pocket," he said. "Fairy magic can block other magic."

It did. Whenever she used Fairy Dust, she no longer heard the trees. She untied the leather cord, then placed the pearlescent pendant that allowed her to be impervious to Fairy Dust into a pocket of her cloak. She strained to listen.

"I don't think it's going to come back right away," said Declan.

"No hurt in trying," she said.

"Now," said Berty, "Obie will not be wearing his armor. Advertising the fact that he is an Empire Guard may make you a target by telling others that you are under his protection. You two are simply going to visit his family."

"Once the symbol is exposed," said Delyth, "the children and I will fly to Boudon. Which means everyone else will follow."

Hope nodded.

After eating, Hope and Obie packed provisions. She gave her parents and grandparents a hug before heading out with Obie.

Outside the walls of the ruined hamlet, Hope touched the first tree near the path. She felt nothing but the rough bark. Obie watched her, saying nothing. They continued on the path.

About midday, Obie led her off the path, taking a more direct route to Boudon. When they stopped for a break, Obie said, "I like Mike."

Hope just looked at him.

"I can see why you're friends," he continued. "I'm not too sure about this Mister Wilde. Anyway, Mike is coming to grips with this side of the portal being real. I read enough of your books to know that it must feel like he stepped back in time."

"When the myths lived and magic abounded," Hope said with a chuckle. "You know, my grandparents really should start liking horses. They refuse. Grandpa says he's working on some sort of travel machine. It's all very hush hush. Anyway, we should have at least brought horses. Would have made the trip easier."

"Yeah, well, we have days of walking. Let's get moving."

Reluctantly, Hope pushed off a log. They kept a brisk pace until they had to make camp.

Sitting by the fire, Hope asked, "Dome or Ring?"

"What?" asked Obie.

"Dome or Ring?"

"Neither," he replied. "Either one could impair the other thing."

"But shouldn't we be safe while we sleep?" she asked.

"We'll be fine," assured Obie. "We're only days from the outpost and they patrol on horseback. But if it makes you feel better, we'll sleep next to each other and on our packs."

They slept on their bedrolls next to one another. With her head resting on her bulky pack, she dared not look at Obie. She could sense him near her.

When they awoke, Obie said, "See? Nothing to worry about." He smiled.

They ate a cold breakfast while they walked. Obie spoke little. Had the years apart eroded their friendship to a letter every other month? Before he was whisked away to the outposts, they talked about everything and anything. And now, his silence matched the trees. At least he looked at her every now and then. Still, she wondered what happened. Was this just the result of getting older and growing up? She decided to touch tree trunks at more regular intervals.

"Is it working?" Obie asked when they stopped to camp for the evening.

"Is what working?"

"Touching trees."

"Oh," she said, staring at her food. "I don't know."

"Your grandfather packed a bottle of mead for us. I was keeping it to celebrate its return." He took a couple bites of food. "I'm afraid of talking too much. I don't want you to miss hearing them."

She laughed. "It doesn't work that way."

"I know. I don't want to distract you."

She thought she saw Obie's stubbled face blush in the firelight. A weight lifted. They were still friends.

When they finished eating, they picked up their packs to get the bedrolls. Obie froze; his eyes searched somewhere behind Hope. She secured her pack to her back. Shouldering his pack, Obie grabbed Hope's hand and ran into the forest. "After them," a voice said. Their fire exploded.

They sprinted through the dark forest, trying not to trip. She fumbled with her Fairystone Pendant. Once she got it around her neck, she searched for an out of the way spot. She pulled Obie to it. "Down," she breathed. He obeyed. She quickly constructed a Fairy dome around them.

Sitting on the ground next to him, she noticed a baby tree in the cramped dome. She caressed its smooth leaves. *It's okay*, she told it. *You're safe in here with us.*

The ground vibrated as if people and horses stampeded somewhere nearby. She clutched Obie's arm. He pulled her into him. "Good thinking," he whispered into her ear. "There were too many of them." She felt his breath in her hair. "Let's get a little sleep. We can continue running in the morning."

Nodding, she stroked the little tree again. *It will be all right.* Her maroon cloak separated her from the cold ground.

Both of them awoke after a short sleep. The dome still glowed over their heads. Hope let out a breath of relief. Under the safety of the dome, they ate cookies Kate packed for them and washed them down with some water.

"I'm ready with my magic," Obie whispered. "Undo the dome when you're ready."

Hope petted the baby tree. *Bye. Maybe we'll meet again soon.* She gave Obie a nod, then removed the dome.

Nothing awaited them in the early morning darkness. They moved swiftly without running through the forest. Their feet barely made a sound. Once the sky lightened, they quickened their steps. Full daylight meant full sprinting. Hope's lightness made up for her shorter stride.

When muscles cramped, they slowed, but did not stop. They snacked on cookies and dried meat and finished their water skins. Their only stop was a bathroom break after nightfall.

Parched mouths made them open the bottle of mead. Judicious sips kept the mead in the bottle longer. Walking for hours in darkness wore on Hope. She could feel her feet hit the ground with every step.

"The forest is thinning," whispered Obie. "Almost there."

Rain pelted their hoods. Their legs moved faster.

Hope thought she saw a window like glow in the distance. She blinked. It was still there. Obie let out a breath.

Someone was home at the woodsmith's cottage and awake at whatever god forsaken hour it happened to be. They ran to the door. Obie knocked—more of a restrained pounding. "Uncle Vander," he said in a low voice. He knocked again. "Uncle Vander, open up."

Chapter Five

The Call

Metal slid. The door opened. Vander's light eyes searched the both of them. "Obie?" he said.

"Can we come in?"

"Yes. Get out of the rain," said Vander, stepping aside. "Hope?" he asked when she entered the cottage.

Hope nodded her soggy head.

After poking his head out the door, Vander asked, "Just the two of you?" He shut the door and locked it.

"The others are days behind us," said Obie.

"What happened?" asked Vander. He moved tools, clearing spaces to sit. "Hang your wet things by the fire. Place your boots there, too."

While they removed their cloaks and boots, Obie explained. "We were sent ahead to get Hope a new bow, but we came across a gang of bandits. Hope's quick thinking saved us."

Vander shook his head. "You two must be exhausted. Spare bedroom is upstairs. Sleep. Tell me all about it in the morning."

"Thanks, Uncle Vander," said Obie.

The attic bedroom held one double bed. "I'll sleep on the floor," Obie said.

"And not be able to walk tomorrow," said Hope.

"There's no guarantee of that anyway."

"Whatever. I'm sleeping here. Sleep wherever," she said, sitting on the bed. The world went dark as soon as her head touched the pillow.

When she woke, light streamed through the dormer windows. She saw a washbasin and a screen. She had no idea when Obie woke or where he slept. After stretching sore muscles, she washed and dressed. Downstairs, she found Obie and Vander sitting at the table.

"I have to report the bandits to the outpost," Obie told Vander, "but I think we should say hi first."

"You can go up through the shop," said Vander. Seeing Hope, he said, "Sit. Let me get you something to eat, then we'll get your new bow so my mother can fuss all she wants."

Hope ate and drank whatever Vander placed in front of her.

"So," Vander sat back down, "why do you need a new bow?"

After swallowing, she said, "Griffin attack."

Vander's eyes widened. "Well, if your bow is your only loss, then you are very lucky."

"Uncle Declan says it's unusable," said Hope.

"What are you using now?" he asked.

"Basic Empire bow."

"Do you like it?"

"Not really."

Vander rubbed his chin. "I have a few for you to try. I'll go set up targets. Come through to the shop when you're done."

"Have you been up long?" she asked Obie.

"Just long enough to tell him about what happened in the woods," he responded.

Noticing her empty plate, she said, "I didn't know I was that hungry."

"Don't worry, Grandma will feed us until we can't move," Obie said with a laugh.

A connecting door brought them to the back of the shop behind the counter. They continued through a side door that brought them just outside the shop. A variety of bows waited for her on a table.

Hope tabled the borrowed bow then picked up a replica of the Bow of the Moon. After shooting a few arrows, she tried the next one. When she had fired from the last bow, Vander handed her another one. Her small hand fit well around the narrow grip. The bow flared and flattened to the edges where the bowstring had been strung multiple times.

"This is an experimental design," Vander explained. "It should give more power with each draw of the string."

Hope set an arrow. She fired. The arrow buried into the straw target halfway up its shaft.

"The arrows should also fly faster and farther," said Obie.

"That's the concept," agreed Vander. "What do you think?"

"I don't know," she said. "I like that recurve bow, too."

"I know you're attached to your old bow still," he said. "Carry this one with you. Use it. Once Declan arrives, you can make up your mind. And if you want to try out a different one, that's fine, too. Just let me know."

"Thanks," said Hope.

"We can drop off the Empire bow at the outpost after we go up to the house," said Obie. "Are you coming up with us, Uncle Vander?"

"Later. I have some work to finish in the workshop first."

With all their now dry stuff, they wound up the spiral staircase to the Firth house. Obie opened the door at the top of the stairs. "Hello?" he said. "Dad? Grandma? Grandpa?"

"Obie?" Geraldine looked up from chopping vegetables at the table. Rising, she wiped her hands on a towel. She hurried to meet them. "Obie," she said, hugging him. "Hope," she greeted with a bone crushing hug. "I've missed you both. Are you? I don't see Hope's family."

"Grandma, Hope has another year of learning on the other side," said Obie. "Uncle Declan and Aunt Delyth and the kids will be here in a couple of days with others."

"Oh, good. I look so forward to seeing everyone. Your dad and granddad are out being woodsmen. They'll be home later. You look hungry. Come in and eat something while I prepare dinner," said Geraldine.

"We'd love to, Grandma, but we need to go to the outpost," said Obie. "We'll be back soon. Mind if we leave our bags here?"

"I'll put them in your rooms."

"That'll be great, Missus Firth," said Hope.

She followed Obie across the bridges of Boudon to the far lift. Once on the forest floor, they walked a half an hour to the outpost bearing the tree village's name. An Empire Guard stopped them at the gate. "Name and purpose," the guard demanded.

"First Lieutenant Oberon to see the Lieutenant in charge," said Obie.

The guard eyed Obie's cloak clasp—a symbol of his rank—then said, "Someone will take you to Lieutenant Manius, sir."

"Thank you," said Obie.

"And the woman?" asked the guard. When he saw her cloak and the bow in her hand, he said, "Never mind."

Another guard brought them through stone fortifications to a central courtyard. After crossing the courtyard, they climbed a stone staircase to an upper level. The guard knocked on a door before opening it. "Lieutenant," he said, "Lieutenant Oberon to see you, sir."

Manius looked exactly the same to Hope as when she first met him in the Sages' Grove a decade ago. Only his short, dark curls glistened with more gray and his face wore a few more lines.

"Lieutenant," said Manius, "you are out of uniform."

"Yes. I have my orders, Lieutenant."

"From whom?"

"The Emperor and the Empress," answered Obie.

"The outpost is at your command, sir," said Manius.

Hope looked from Manius to Obie, then realized that Obie introduced himself as First Lieutenant. That promotion, directly reporting to the Empire Tree, meant that Obie outranked Manius.

"No need, Lieutenant," said Obie. "I am only here to inform you about bandits running loose in the woods between Boudon and the reclaimed hamlet. We were attacked by at least a dozen well armed bandits."

"They attacked without demanding money for passage?" asked Manius.

"Several arrows were aimed and no demands were given," Obie stated. "Others also had weapons drawn."

Manius' eyes fell on Hope. "Perhaps they are not the usual bandits," he said. "I'll send a scouting party out for them and will alert Irmingard as well."

"Thank you, Lieutenant Manius," said Obie. "Before we leave, we have an Empire bow to return. It was signed out by either Advisor Declan or Captain Edwin in the Sages' Grove."

Manius gave Obie a nod, then retrieved the bow from Hope. They promptly returned to Boudon.

Alone with Obie in the lift, Hope removed her Fairystone Pendant from around her neck. She tucked it in her pocket. "Manius thinks they were not ordinary bandits. That they were there for a reason," she said. "This is proof that it's happening again, isn't it?"

He took her hand. "We'll discuss it with your aunt and uncle when they arrive," said Obie. The lift stopped. He escorted her through the village, hand in hand.

Inside the Firth home, Obie reclaimed his hand to hug his father. Hope stepped back while Cecil relished in seeing his son. "Your last letter said nothing of a visit," Cecil said, finally letting go of Obie.

"I was just recently reassigned," Obie said. "Dad, you remember Hope."

"Of course," he said, turning his gaze to Hope. "How could I—" Cecil stopped midsentence. Something in his eyes told Hope that he understood that *she* was Obie's new assignment. Obie's father hugged her. "Stay as long as you need," he said to her.

"Thanks, Mister Firth," she said.

After hugging his grandson, Leon gave Hope a welcoming hug. Geraldine ushered them all to the table, saying, "The kids haven't had a proper meal in days. They need to eat and so do you men."

Although Hope felt like family around the Firths, she still tried not to devour her meal in two gulps. While reminding herself to chew, Hope listened to the conversation about going to visit Julie and Matt for the twin's fifth birthday. Vander described how he refurbished his and Cecil's old bows for them.

"Vander says he talked you into trying that new bow of his," Leon said to Hope.

"I'm looking forward to see what it can do tomorrow," Hope replied. "I'm too exhausted to do the practice course this evening. And full. Dinner was great, Missus Firth. Thank you so much."

"So, what were you doing in wild creature country?" asked Vander.

Hope sighed. "Wrong place; wrong time. It was late. I was angry and walking. And I wasn't paying attention to where I was going." She stared at the wood grain in the plank table for a moment.

Vander made a face. "A bow can't really be fixed once it's broken," he said. "Depending on where the break is, it will always be off. They can be made into something else. I can look at it for you and see what I can do."

Her mouth opened, but unsure of what to say. Finally, she said, "Thanks, but I'm afraid it's complicated."

Cecil looked from Hope to Obie. "Well, anyway," he said, "we're glad you guys are here. There is someone I want you to meet. She'll be coming over soon."

Vander's nose wrinkled, then he quickly rubbed it. After telling everyone that he would be back later, he disappeared behind the door to the workshop. While Cecil and Leon left to check on the day's wood haul, Hope and Obie helped Geraldine clean the dishes and table.

When Leon returned, the three of them sat with him on the cushioned benches. "The lookouts have been alerted about the bandits," he said. "If they come near here, we'll know." He stopped talking when Cecil entered the house.

A tall woman with almost glowing, creamy skin and shining, bright, white blonde hair that rippled down her back floated on Cecil's arm. Her clear blue eyes caught sight of both Hope and Obie. Her dark pink lips smiled, but the rest of her face reflected nothing.

Obie watched her approach with his father. His expressionless face did not betray his thoughts.

"I'd like you both to meet Brooke," said Cecil. "My son, Obie, and his... Hope."

"It's so nice to finally meet you, Obie. Your father speaks of you all the time," Brooke said, her voice flowed like water over glass. "And you, too, Hope."

Hope gave her a polite smile and nod. Obie began asking her questions to which she laughed. Her melodic laughter made Hope's ears ring. She tuned Brooke out. Obie's words faded and all Hope heard was the rise and fall of his voice. She allowed his tones to soothe her.

"Hope?" asked Brooke.

"Hmm?" said Hope, coming out of her trance like state. "I'm sorry. What did you ask?"

"You poor thing, you look exhausted," said Brooke.

"The traveling is catching up with me, I think," Hope said with a smile. "I'll be asleep very soon."

"Of course. We can talk more tomorrow, girl to girl," said Brooke. She looked from Hope to Obie. "The kids should be finished with their chores, so I better be going. It was lovely meeting both of you." Obie watched his father walk Brooke to the door. With a wave, she left.

Hope leaned back against the cushion. Someone placed a glass of amber colored liquid in her hand. She sat up when Vander sat next to her with a glass in his own hand. She noticed Obie held one, too. "It helps make her more digestible," Vander muttered.

"You just missed Brooke," Cecil said to his brother.

Vander passed a glass to Cecil, saying, "Had some work to finish before bed."

"What do you think of her?" Cecil asked Obie.

Obie sipped his drink before answering. "She seems nice."

Not wanting to have to say anything, Hope brought the glass to her nose. A strong spiciness assaulted her. She sipped. The warm alcohol burned her throat. She finally got to drink more than a little taste of the Firth's spiced whiskey. It was exactly what she needed. She sipped some more.

The whiskey had only reached perhaps a third of the small glass. And, she only took small sips. Why did the room move slightly when she stood?

Obie led her to Julie's old room where Geraldine placed her bag. She clung to his arm for support. "Goodnight, Hope," he said. "If you need anything, I'll be in my old room. Just down the hall."

"Okay," she said. "Night nights." She detached from his arm. Once inside the room, after she managed to close the door, she fumbled for nightclothes. She settled for a t-shirt and left clothes strewn across the floor as she changed. The bed was soft. She was happy. The room would stop moving soon, she was sure.

Voices crept inside her head—indiscernible voices. They spoke gibberish nonsense. "It is time," said a clear female voice. A scream. She bolted upright, gasping for breath.

Her eyes searched the dark room. Shapeless lumps of clothing laid everywhere. The door opened. Obie took one step inside the room. His blue spheres of light roamed into every dark corner. "I heard you scream. Are you okay?"

She nodded. "Dream," she answered. "I'm fine."

"Do you want to talk about it?" he asked. She shook her head. "I'll sit in here until you fall asleep."

"Obie, I'm fine," she protested as he walked to the chair. "I'm just not used to drinking your family's spiced whiskey."

He rested his hand on the back of the chair, ready to turn it towards the bed. "Are you sure?"

She nodded.

"Okay."

Head on the pillow, she pulled the covers over her. Obie inspected the window and the room, stepping around her clothes. "You're usually not so messy," he said.

"The room moved while I was getting ready for bed," she explained.

He chuckled. "That could pose a problem," he said. "See you in a few hours." His light spheres gathered around him as he exited the room. His eyes watched her until the door latched.

Alone, in the dark, she still felt the intensity of his blue stare.

The voice haunted her while she tidied the room in the morning. It had no gender. To whom did it belong? Or was it a figment of her whiskey enhanced imagination? The smell of breakfast helped her ignore her thoughts.

A generous breakfast started the early day in the Firth house. Cecil and Leon left before first light with the woodsmen and archers of Boudon. Vander dawdled, taking another cup of Geraldine's root infusion. "I brought some extra arrows for you, Hope," Vander said with a yawn. "I want to know all your thoughts." He gulped down the contents of his cup. "I better get to the wood before the Turners and Sawyers take all the good pieces." He plunked his cup on the table then left through the woodshop door. "Wanna help sort the wood with me, Obie?" he said, poking his head back in the room.

"Be down in a minute," Obie said, smiling. "I used to love picking through the wood piles with Great-grandpa, Aunt Julie, and Uncle Vander," he told Hope. "Will you be okay?"

"Me and the practice course will be just fine," Hope answered.

"Hope won't be alone on it," said Geraldine. She turned to Hope. "Stay on the main course. The modified course that mainly the Boudonian Brotherhood use should only be done with another."

Hope gave her a sharp nod. After slinging the extra arrows over her shoulder, she walked out onto the balcony. Feet from the Firth's door, she met Brooke, who flashed her a dazzling smile.

"Hope," said Brooke, "just who I was coming to see. I'm taking Winnie and Jasper, my two children, foraging, and I wanted to see if you'd like to join us. We make pies with what we find. Usually an assortment of mushrooms, wild onions, and ramps. I can't wait for the children to meet you. You'd be such a role model to my Winnie with your archery prowess. The twins will be fifteen next year."

Hope smiled and blushed a little. "That sounds like fun," she said. "Unfortunately, I can't today. I promised Uncle Vander that I'd test his new bow design."

"Another time, perhaps?" said Brooke.

"Absolutely."

"Great," Brooke said with too much enthusiasm for the morning. "The twins and I will bring a pie over later."

As Brooke spun and walked away, a dull buzzing filled Hope's head. She placed her hand on the railing. The buzzing faded while she approached the first target.

Boudon's practice course started at the perimeter of the town, then climbed above the houses. Archers perched on platforms and bridges while hitting targets. The course also gave different views of the surrounding forest.

About halfway through the course, Hope began to like her new bow. "Interesting bow you got there," said a female voice above her. Hope looked up. A girl, maybe a couple of years older than she, peered over a small platform. Her braided white blonde hair stopped above a pin that resembled a B with an arrow piercing the middle— the pin of the Boudonian Archers. "You're good. How come I haven't seen you before?"

"Thanks," said Hope. "I haven't been here in years."

"Visiting family then?" the girl asked.

"Yeah."

"You only need to have Boudonian blood, regardless of where you live, to be in the Brotherhood of Boudonian Archers," said the girl.

"I'm related by marriage," said Hope.

"Oh. That's too bad. I'm Freddie, by the way. You are still welcome to practice with us. Come on up."

"Thanks." The buzzing in Hope's head grew. She took one step and wobbled a little. "I better not," she told Freddie. "I've had a headache all morning. Too much spiced whiskey last night." Hope laughed a little to cover her concern.

"No problem. Another time, perhaps."

She gave the girl a simple nod.

Hope walked past the next target, rubbing her temples. The buzzing inside her head remained. Aimlessly strolling through Boudon, she found herself climbing steep steps.

She reached a platform in the forest canopy. A hooded figure sat on a log stump. The hood faced her. "I'm sorry for disturbing you," said Hope.

"Nonsense, child." Wrinkled hands lowered the hood. The female Village Elder's kind eyes smiled at her. "Sit with me," she said.

Hope sat on a stump, placing the bow on her lap.

"We consider you a Boudonian for helping save our village all those years ago," the Elder said. "And all Boudonians are permitted on this platform, even without an invitation, though not many come." She looked at the swaying branches. "I love to sit and let the wind pass over me as if I were a branch of these trees. I find that just sitting here clears the head."

Hope smiled.

"You don't have to sit with me. Go wherever you feel the wind the most beneficial." The Elder gestured around the wooden platform.

Hope found a place near the railing. She watched the branches sway with the rhythm of the wind. Brown tendrils swept across her face. Her body moved with the wind. The buzzing cleared as if she were tuning into a station on the radio. *It is time. It is time. It is time.* She looked around her. A chorus of trees sang to her.

She practically skipped back to the Firth house.

Chapter Six

The Cottage in the Woods

When she entered, Brooke was placing a warm pie on the table for Geraldine, Vander, and Obie. Cecil and Leon had yet to come home. "Hope," said Brooke, "you're home just in time to have a piece of my forest pie. It should cool more, but it just smells so delicious." Steam escaped the crust when she sliced.

Inside her head, the trees screamed at her. "Don't eat the pie," said Hope, relaying the trees' message.

Finally, said a voice in her head.

Obie stepped away from the table.

"What do you mean, Hope?" asked Geraldine. "Being warm doesn't hurt it any."

"Don't eat the pie," Hope repeated. "Whatever you do, do not eat the pie."

"Why would you say that, Hope?" asked Brooke, keeping her perfect smile.

"Who are you? Where are your kids? What do you want?" accused Hope.

Brooke's smiled faltered. Both Vander and Geraldine raised bows against her. "The trees," Brooke said through her too white teeth. Red flashed behind her blue irises. Light flashed towards Hope. A yellow shield diffused it. Brooke screamed. With arrows piercing her body, she sprinted out the door.

"After her," Obie bellowed across the village. "She isn't who she claims."

Other villagers took up arms against Brooke. On the bridges, she darted through the arrows flying at her.

"She's calling for her children," said Hope.

"She's heading for the forest floor," said Obie.

Below the bridges and balconies, a teenage girl and boy waited, their white blonde hair shining against the greens and browns. The girl resembled the one who she encountered on the course. Brooke reached the lift. As it descended, the other lifts' ropes snapped, sending the boxes crashing stories to the ground.

Hope returned to the Firth house. She raced down the spiral staircase to the woodshop with Obie and Vander on her heels. Running outside, she noticed raining arrows never reaching beyond a certain point. Magic. Everywhere.

"So very nice of you to join us, Hope," said Brooke, striding away from a lift. "Makes our jobs that much easier. Sorry, your boyfriend can't join us." She swirled her hand in the air. Red flashed in her eyes. Obie pounded against an invisible wall. While he attacked it with magic, Brooke sipped from a small bottle. "Grab her," she said to the twins.

They raised their arms in unison. Magic wrapped around Hope's arms and legs, rendering her motionless. Her erratic heartbeat bounced beneath her shirt. Obie shouted silently behind the barrier. Brooke licked her lips with a lurid smile. Hope struggled against her bonds until a message flooded her mind: *Become.* The magic felt green, familiar. She relaxed. It encapsulated her.

Obie froze.

Brooke's eyes widened as she screamed, "NOOOOOOOOOO!"

The twins backed away first.

Hope could move again. She raised her bow. Her arms, bow, and clothes all shimmered green.

Brooke tripped over her skirt, trying to get away. She picked up the front to run.

Twirling the tip of her arrow in the magic, Hope set it. She watched the three flee. Her arrow flew. Brooke stumbled. Two more magic captured arrows hit the twins.

Magical barriers broke. Arrows from the village above stormed the three. Brooke and her children crumpled to the ground like stringless marionettes.

"Hope?" Obie called, running in her general direction.

"I'm here," she said. She grabbed his arm.

"There you are," he said.

Together, they approached Brooke and the twins. Her creamy skin withered to resemble crumpled paper. Her white blonde hair shrank to a couple of colorless strands on an otherwise bald head. The twins shriveled like misshapen grapes.

"What was she?" Obie asked.

"A Hag. Get no closer." Delyth landed next to them. "Ugh, and Haglings." The Fairy turned to Hope. Her eyes glanced at something on her chest. "We need Edwin. I'm going to put a dome over each of them just in case. The others are on their way. I'll be back as soon as I can. Go back to the house and wait. Both of you."

Hope and Obie gave Delyth a nod, then returned to the house through the workshop. On the balcony, Hope watched Delyth fly off in a lavender blur.

"Hope, where is Mommy going?" Ynyr asked, his hands grabbing the railing.

"Empire business. She'll be back soon," said Hope.

"Why couldn't I go, too?" he asked.

"Because your mommy has to go super duper fast," Hope answered. "Tell you what, get all settled and rested tonight and tomorrow we'll go shoot some targets."

Smiling, Ynyr hugged her. "Can't wait," he said, lifting his head from her waist. He let go and stepped back. "Why are you disappearing?"

She looked down. Green shimmer swirled in place of her body. "I don't know." Materializing, she noticed something new hanging from her neck. It looked like an acorn on a wood fiber rope. She caught Obie's eye. They smiled at each other. She became *The Wood Listener*.

When they entered the house, Jon appeared beside her. "Hope? What's going on?" he asked. "We thought we saw Delyth streak overhead."

"Everyone is fine," Hope said first. "You did see Aunt Delyth. This Hag and her Haglings attacked. Aunt Delyth placed a dome over them. I don't know if they're dead or not, but they're not going anywhere. She left to get Edwin."

Jon looked as though he listened to someone on his side of his magic. "Berty wants to know where they are," he said.

"Forest floor. Just past the bridges," said Hope.

Jon paused before saying, "We will be there in a couple of days."

"Mister Chase," said Obie, "we ran into trouble right around where you are now. Be on guard."

Jon gave Obie a nod.

"And, Daddy," said Hope, "tell them I got an acorn." Smiling, she fingered the pendent resting against her shirt. "Be careful. See you soon. Love you guys."

After Jon said good-bye, his image disappeared. Leon and Cecil froze in the doorway from the shop.

"Grandpa!" cried Fiala. "Uncle Cecil!"

Leon picked up his granddaughter, swinging her in the air while she squealed with delight.

"Was that?" asked Cecil, pointing at the space Jon's image recently occupied.

"My dad," Hope replied. "He's a Communicator. When he projects himself, he can see and hear everything while being able to talk at the same time."

Cecil nodded then hung his head. "I'm sorry, Hope," he said. "I knew nothing about Brooke other than she was a widow with twins."

"I didn't either. I just didn't like her," Vander added. "How did you know, Hope?"

A knock on the door saved her from answering. The three Village Elders entered the home. Upon seeing Hope, they bowed to her. The Firths exchanged glances. "We have come to respectfully request that the Wood Listener bestow her blessing on Boudon," said one of the male Elders.

Hope saw herself become invisible again.

"Hope?" said Cecil.

"Still here," she said. "I would be honored to bestow a blessing on Boudon, however, as you can see, the magic has yet to stabilize. I ask that we wait until the magic has settled."

"Yes, of course," said another. After bowing again, they left.

"Am I still invisible?" she asked.

"Yes," said Obie.

She sighed. The new magic puzzled her. How did one control invisibility? It just happened.

"Perhaps your magic is similar to the Elves," suggested Vander. "Except without having to touch trees. Although, finding a non-wooden surface in Boudon is impossible."

"Elves can touch trees without becoming invisible," she argued.

Vander's shoulders slumped. "I can't help with that. I've only seen... Elves go invisible. I don't know how they do it."

Obie relocated the pie Brooke brought to a shelf. "To be examined," he explained.

At some point during the bath Geraldine encouraged her to take, Hope became visible. She returned downstairs feeling refreshed. No one let her help with dinner or set the table. To get out of the way, she leaned on the balcony just outside the door. *How do I control this?* Her question to the trees remained unanswered. Instead, she knew about two Fairies flying an Elf.

Walking back inside, she announced, "I think Aunt Delyth returns with Edwin."

A couple of minutes later, Delyth entered with the Elf.

"Where's the other Fairy?" asked Hope.

"He reported to the outpost," said Delyth. She glanced at the set table. "We'll only be a minute. Hope, Obie, if you could bring us to them."

Because of the broken lifts, they had to use the rope and wood ladders to the forest floor. Delyth, however, flew. Obie released spheres of light. When Delyth opened her domes, Edwin examined the Hag and her Haglings at a safe distance. "Will they keep in there?" he asked Delyth.

"Yes."

"Then we wait for Declan," he said.

Before returning to the house, Hope and Obie gave a brief report about the bandits and the pie. Delyth encased the pie in Fairy magic as well.

While eating, Edwin started his inquiry. "Cecil, how did you meet Brooke?"

"I came across her and her kids truffle hunting near where we were collecting wood," said Cecil. "Just this past autumn. I ran into her often after that. We would talk about being an only parent—she was a widow. Her husband died a few years ago. She moved her family to a nearby cottage for a fresh start. From around Lake Vlod, if I remember correctly."

"I patrolled Lake Vlod," said Obie. "Her description of it was awfully vague."

"Do you know where this cottage is?" asked Edwin.

Nodding, Cecil said, "I've never been inside though."

"You'll take us tomorrow," said Edwin. "With Guard and Watcher escort." The Elf glanced at the acorn hanging from Hope's neck. "Do you know if your uncle had armor commissioned for you?" he asked her.

"No, I don't."

"I'll talk to Berty when he arrives," said Edwin. "In the meantime, Hope, you should not be alone. Not even when you sleep."

"I'll stay with you, Hope," offered Delyth.

"No. It should be Obie," Edwin said. "Sorry, Delyth, but Obie is trained for this. Besides, as a Warlock, he has better eye sight and better hearing than any of us."

"I get the top bunk," Hope said.

After dinner, Hope discussed the bow with Vander. "Does this mean you'll keep it?" he asked.

"Since it helped me against the Hag, how could I not?" she answered with a smile. "We haven't... How much?"

Vander waved away the notion of paying. "I won't accept any money from you," he said. Hope's mouth began to protest. "No buts," he added.

In front of the fireplace, Ynyr and Fiala played. Delyth kept an eye on her children and an ear on Edwin and Obie's conversation at the end of the table. Soon, Hope excused herself to go to bed.

After changing into her nightclothes, Hope sat in the dark, staring out the window. Droplets of rain stuck to the panes. Her eyes followed their paths down the window once they became too heavy. She wanted to know what being *The* Wood Listener entailed. No one could tell her—not the trees, nor the rain, and certainly not the window. She climbed into Obie's top bunk, feeling like a strange intruder alone in his old room.

She heard a soft knock on the door. "Hope?" Obie called quietly.

"You can come in," she said.

He opened the door, flooding the room with light from the hall.

"I wanted to give you enough time," he said. His shadow did not move. After a moment, he stepped inside, closing the door over.

Spheres of light shined from under her bunk. "If you need the light on," she began. The lights disappeared.

"I'm good," he said. The blankets rustled. "Are you?" he asked.

"Am I what?"

"Are you doing okay?"

"Well, my magic is back and then some," she answered. "Good and weird. New."

He did not say anything right away. "Aunt Delyth's giving the kids nightmares tonight with her Hags eat children stories she started telling after you left. Ynyr wanted to come with us tomorrow in the worst way. You should have seen his face when she told him about locking children in cages to fatten before roasting. 'Hags might eat Goblins, but children are a prized delicacy.'" He chuckled. "Now, I understand the term *Fairy Tale*. Ynyr will be terrified for weeks until Aunt Delyth tells him she made it up."

"I don't think she did," Hope whispered.

"What?" Something banged into the bed. "Ouch."

"I heard similar stories growing up," said Hope. "Hansel and Gretel finding the gingerbread house in the woods that was used to lure children so they could be eaten."

"By Hags?"

"Every bad female character was usually called a witch," explained Hope.

"I remember your mom telling me how the term, *witch*, was different on that side of the portal," he said. "We better get some sleep. Morning is going to come too soon and I fear we have a long walk."

Morning did come too soon. Still dark outside, Hope reluctantly dressed and headed down the stairs. Edwin, Obie, and Delyth wore armor. Cecil handed everyone day provisions.

"Where's my cloak?" asked Hope, seeing a light greenish cloak hanging in place of her maroon one.

"You're the Wood Listener now, Hope," said Delyth. "Your cloak is bound to be different. Just like you are."

Hope secured the green cloak around her shoulders. It fit her perfectly.

Cecil led them down the ladders to the forest floor where Empire Guards and a Watcher waited. "Captain," said the only woman guard. "Protection formation, sir?" she asked.

"Sergeant Sorrel, you and the Watcher will walk with Cecil. The rest in formation," ordered Edwin. The Elf kept pace walking between Cecil and Hope and Delyth. Obie stayed behind Hope as the other four guards formed the corners of an imaginary box.

The low clouds prevented the rising sun from reaching the undergrowth, keeping the forest in a dark dimness. Edwin would not permit auxiliary light.

Rain thumped their hoods. The raindrops sounded different to Hope as they hit her "new" cloak—more like the music of drops pounding on leaves. She smiled to herself despite the cold rain.

After over an hour of trudging, Cecil stopped. "I don't see it," he said. "Her cottage should be right over there." He pointed to a small clearing. "Could it have vanished?" Turning, he threw a questioning look at Edwin and Delyth.

"Something's there," said the Watcher. "Something magical anyway."

"Show me," said Delyth. Once the Watcher told her where he saw the magical disturbance, she said, "Cover your faces."

While everyone brought cloaks up, Hope clutched her Fairystone Pendant. Delyth threw a fistful of Fairy Dust. A bright light exploded in the small clearing.

When the light faded, a quaint cottage stood in front of them, right where Cecil said it should be. "There is magic protecting it," said the Watcher.

Edwin made the Watcher walk with him. When they stopped, the Elf plunged his sword into the air in front of him. He twisted the blade. A dome surrounding the cabin glowed red, then dissipated. The Watcher gave the Elf a nod.

Cautiously, they approached the door. The Watcher and a few guards walked around the cabin. "All clear," one reported.

After slipping on a pair of Empire leather gloves, Edwin tried the handle. The door did not budge. "Sergeant," he said to Sorrel, "I hear you have a special talent."

Sorrel looked at her boots.

Stepping aside, Edwin said, "Time to put it to good use."

She held her hand in front of the lock. Her spikey magic crept into the mechanism, giving it a pink glow. Her hand twisted back and forth. Hearing a click, she recalled her magic.

Edwin opened the door. "Touch nothing," he said. "Reconnaissance only."

Entering the cottage, Hope's eyesight adjusted quickly. A generous hearth spanned a side wall. Herbs and skins hung from the stone above the hearth. A table and chairs sat in the middle of the single room. Gouges pocked the tabletop. Shelves covered the other walls. Books, bottles, boxes, and other items Hope did not want to consider cluttered the shelves. Shelves decorated the area behind the steps to an upper floor up which others climbed.

"Hope, could you come up here please?" called Cecil.

Edwin followed Hope up the creaky stairs. Past the beds, in the loft like room, Cecil bent over a dressing table. He glanced at Hope as she approached. "This is similar to what Julie sends, yes?" He pointed to a rectangle tucked in the bottom right corner of the mirror.

The glossy rectangle showed a beautiful woman with cascading blonde hair and light blue eyes.

"That's a photograph. Yes," answered Hope. "She looks a lot like Brooke, but different."

"That's Fiona," said Cecil.

"In the picture?"

Cecil nodded, not taking his eyes off the photo.

"But" said Hope, "how is there a photograph of Obie's mother?"

"I don't know."

Studying the picture of Obie's mother, she noticed how much Obie resembled Fiona. As Edwin leaned in to look at the picture, Hope said, "She's not looking at the camera."

"What does that mean?" asked Edwin.

"People usually look at the camera when taking pictures. So, she probably didn't know someone took her picture." Her insides sank. Feeling wobbly, she took a step to steady herself. "Obie's mother died when he was six. Why would anyone take a picture of her?" she asked in a low voice.

Darkness pushed into the edges of her sight. Hands at her elbow and small of her back stopped her collapse. A strong grip steered her down the stairs. "She's fine. Meet us outside when you've finished," said Edwin's voice. Somewhat of their own accord, her legs released her from the cottage. The hand from her elbow raised her hood. Rain pattered on her head.

At a comfortable distance from the door, gentle pressure urged her to stop. "Are you okay?" asked Edwin, looking from eye to eye.

"Fresh air is good," she said. "What was happening to me?"

"My theory," said Edwin, "is something in there must be similar to those Fairy ruins that we stayed in that one time. I never forgot how they made me feel. This, however, is tailored to you. No one else seems to be experiencing it."

Hope remembered the ancient Fairy ruins that protected them from the Night Golems on their way to the tree line. All of them, except the Fairies, needed to recover after a night within the granite walls. Being an Elf, the Fairy ruins affected Edwin the most. She looked to him for answers. He shimmered a translucent light green.

"Why are we invisible?" he whispered.

"We are?"

"You don't know you're doing it," he stated. "Very few Elves have problems with being too invisible, but it does occur. I believe there is someone in Irmingard who can help you control your gift."

"Captain?" someone called.

"Here," he answered. "I'm going to let go now. Okay?" he said to Hope.

She nodded.

Edwin reappeared once he released his hold on her. He barked orders to the guards. The Watcher stood close to Hope. "Can you see me?" she asked him.

"If the Captain had not appeared, I would not know where to look," the Watcher said. "If I look carefully, I can see a slight disturbance in the air."

Obie approached the Watcher. "Hope?" he said.

"I'm here."

He looked in the general direction of her voice, but not directly at her. "The Captain used his gloves to close the door. The cottage will stay under watch," said Obie. "Are you okay?"

"Yeah. I just got a little light headed when I was upstairs," she answered.

"Have you eaten?" he asked her.

"Doing that now," she said. She plucked a piece of dried meat from her bag and began to chew. When Obie's gaze shifted directly at her, she figured she was visible again. They hastened with the group, minus three Empire Guards, away from the cottage.

Chapter Seven

Pictures

Hope struggled to sit upright at the Firth's table. While Edwin visited the outpost, Geraldine plunked food in front of her. "You should never have left without eating," Geraldine admonished. Across the table, Obie's intense gaze scrutinized her. She paid attention to her plate.

When Edwin entered, he glanced at her. "Better, yet?" he asked.

"I feel so drained," she said.

"Still?" said Edwin. "You must have gotten too close to some sort of magical trap in there. I'll go back with Declan. You are not stepping foot near that place again."

Obie leapt off his chair to rummage through his healer bag. "Grandma, could you heat up some milk?" he asked. Geraldine did as he asked without question. He carried a small phial to the pot. After spooning something into the milk, he tapped a dark powder out of the phial. He stirred rapidly. Finally, he poured the now dark milk into a mug.

He placed the mug in front of Hope. "Chocolate milk," he said. "Probably not as good as your grandmother's, but it should realign the magic. I always keep a little cocoa powder in my bag for magical problems."

Little brown lumps floated at the top of the warm milk. She drank it. He was right; it was not as good as her grandmother's. However, it began to give her back her strength. "Thanks, Obie. I should probably keep chocolate on me."

Ynyr sprang into a chair next to her. "Are you still going to practice with me?" he asked her.

She looked into his light eyes that stared up at her. "In a minute," she said.

His mess of dark curls bounced as he bounded across the room. "I'll get my stuff," he said.

Chuckling, she finished the bread and cheese still on her plate.

"I'll come with you," said Obie.

With arrows aplenty, the three of them climbed to the first target. Ynyr's Fairy Godmother trailed at a comfortable distance. While watching the boy take his shots, Hope said to Obie, "You know, I've never seen you even attempt to use a bow."

"Let's keep it that way. That's something no one should ever see," he said. "I understand the concept, the mechanics of it, but can't execute. However, I will happily incinerate the targets with magic if you want."

She play-shoved him in his arm. He laughed. From that moment, she allowed the Hag, the bandits, and the symboled bow to wait in a corner of her mind.

After the practice circuit, Hope and Obie spent the rest of the day with Vander, learning about carving wood. At bedtime, Obie gave her enough time to climb into the top bunk before entering the bedroom they shared. Once in the bottom bunk, Obie said, "Dad told me about the picture of Mom. Well, he showed it to me." Silence. "I've been thinking about it," he said in a quiet voice. "Someone had to have used one of those things from the other side."

"Camera," said Hope.

"Yeah. That's a lot of going back and forth through the portals with other side items."

"It's like that flask my grandfather bought," she said. "Set-up to get Uncle Berty. Brooke was all set-up to get me."

"In case that symbol backfired?" asked Obie.

"Or just to finish the job," said Hope. Her hand clapped over her mouth. She hated the way that sounded.

"Hope." Obie's voice sounded closer than the bottom bunk. Turning, she could make out his head at the edge of the bed. "I won't allow anything bad to happen to you," he said. His hand found her arm through the blankets. "Uncle Berty and Aunt Silvia should have some answers when they get here, which should be some time tomorrow."

"Aunt Silvia should have some insights about my new magic, too," Hope said. She smiled at Obie in the dark, unsure if he could see her. With renewed spirits, she fell asleep.

Rain teemed on the platforms and bridges of Boudon in the morning. The occupants of the Firth house ate breakfast while watching sheets of water blow through the forest. Delyth ate very little. Violet eyes rested on the balcony.

"The village isn't off the forest floor because of flooding," said Leon. Delyth nodded slightly without looking away.

"They'll be here soon," said Hope. Delyth's head turned. "The storm isn't affecting them. Some sort of invisible protection surrounds them."

Delyth let out a breath, then ate something. "Good," said the Fairy. She stole a glance outside. "Strong wind. Thank you, Hope."

Since the woodsmen had to stay home with the storm blowing outside, Leon joined Vander in the woodshop to wait for their new arrivals.

After an extended breakfast, Delyth began pacing. Nothing Geraldine said or did made Delyth stop for long. "Daddy will be fine," said Fiala, who kept a close eye on her mother.

"I know he will, honey," Delyth said. "Mommy has something else on her mind."

Hope caught Obie's gaze. His eyebrows raised. "They're almost at the shop," Hope announced.

Ten minutes later, the door to the shop staircase opened. Declan let everyone into the house. While Teresa hugged Hope, Edwin told them about the Hag's cottage.

Silvia glared at the storm beyond the balcony. "We need to go now," she said. "There's magic in this storm. The cottage may not be there once the storm stops."

"Do you need me to take you?" asked Cecil.

"You know these woods best," said Edwin.

Cecil led Declan, Edwin, Berty, Silvia, and Delyth back down the spiral staircase. When the door closed, Hope and Obie re-introduced her parents to his family and introduced her sister, cousins, Fairy Godmothers, and Mike.

"How's the arm?" she asked Mike.

"Stiff. The rain doesn't help much. At least I finished that awful tasting potion," Mike answered. "Speaking of awful, that storm came out of nowhere. I don't know what they did, but Aunt Silvia and Uncle Berty put up some sort of shield very quickly."

Geraldine made everyone feel comfortable and had food ready for the newcomers on the table. Hope and the Firths joined her parents and Mike at the table. "Besides the storm, how was your trip?" Vander asked.

"Not bad," said Jon. "Made good time and didn't come across anyone."

"That's good," said Leon.

Tuning out the rest of the conversation, Hope stared at the rain. She wondered about magic in the storm. What did it have to do with the Hag? Could the rain hurt her if she were out in it?

After a few hours, Berty and Silvia returned wearing concerned expressions. They beckoned everyone around the table except the children, who played in another part of the room.

"First," said Declan, "we leave tomorrow. Hope needs guidance and there is only one place she can get it. Second, we believe that the family was targeted because of your connection to Hope. We already had a long discussion with Cecil about the Hag. He can fill you in when we're gone. Third, the heads of the Hag and her Haglings have been liberated from their bodies. Any residual Hag magic will dissipate. However, I will do a thorough search for safety."

"That picture of my mother had to have been taken about fifteen years ago, at least," said Obie. "We hadn't met Hope yet."

"I know, Obie," said Berty. "The pictures are the most disturbing part of this. We believe the picture of Fiona was to aid the Hag in charming Cecil by resembling his late wife. In that cottage, we found pictures of your entire family, even Owen. There's a... possibility that Fiona's death may have been... murder."

No one said anything. Geraldine closed her eyes. "But why?" Leon said finally.

"We have more questions than answers at this point," Silvia replied. When she looked at Hope, her eyes rested on the acorn. "I think all of this was an attempt to stop you from getting that."

Fingering the acorn, Hope asked, "And now?"

"We borrow horses from the outpost," said Silvia. "Mike, I hope you remember how to ride."

Mike swallowed hard.

"Did you say pictures, my Lord?" asked Vander.

"We found pictures of all of us," said Cecil. "Obie growing up as a boy. Us in different years. Julie's wedding to Matt. All of them in Boudon. Except... except Fiona's grave." He placed stacks of photographs on the table. The pictures circulated.

"We did not find the camera," said Berty.

Mike lined up pictures on the table. "These are all taken from the same angle," he said. Looking up at Silvia and Berty, he continued, "The camera is probably hidden somewhere. Somewhere with discreet access to change the film. Unless someone sits in the same spot to take the pictures."

"What else?" asked Silvia.

He examined the pictures, feeling the paper thickness and turning them over to look on the backs. "They've all been developed on the same paper."

Vander turned the picture over in his hand. "Maybe it has something to do with this." He tapped on the paper manufacture's name on the back.

"Sort of," said Mike. "The fact that the pictures span fifteen years and all have the same paper means that some person is developing with a stockpile of old paper." He looked from Vander to Silvia. "My dad likes to buy the same brand of paper for his pictures, and he always complains when the paper changes even if slightly. This paper had to be bought at the same time in bulk. It hasn't changed. They might not even make this type anymore. I'd have to look it up to be sure though."

"We didn't find a dark room in the cottage," said Berty. "Nor did we find negatives. Of course, I highly doubt a Hag would know how to develop film."

"Dad calls it a dying art form," said Mike. "Especially with digital everything. He uses some really old cameras that he has a hard time finding film for. Anyway, my dad has a portable dark room kit for developing his photos on the road. It's about the size of a suitcase." He turned to Silvia. "Even if they used the same paper, where would they replenish the chemicals?"

Silvia made a face. "Mike, you get to find the camera."

He stared at her for a moment. "I can do that. I just need to know," he picked up a picture, "where this is."

Once the storm subsided to sprinkles, Mike left with Vander and Declan, armed with a few photographs. When they returned, Mike reported, "No camera, but I found where it was perched."

"The photographer won't be back," said Silvia.

"Are you sure, my Lady?" Leon asked.

"There's no reason to return," she said. "These pictures that we found were to help the Hag acquire her target. We also found evidence of a potion of some kind that helped her maintain her Fionaesque form out in the open. Hags rarely ever leave their underground lairs for that's where their magic is the strongest. What is odd is that she had two Haglings."

"Why?" asked Hope.

"Haglings are... They can't wander too far from the mother Hag," answered Silvia. "They are bound by the magic used to create them."

"Create?" Jon asked.

"Think Frankenstein's monster."

Both Jon and Teresa shuddered.

"What kind of monster?" asked Vander.

Jon spoke into Vander's ear.

"Parts of corpses?" Vander asked with disgust.

"Oh, no," said Silvia, checking to see if the children were out of hearing range. "That is fiction. Hags use live parts." Everyone groaned. "It is said that they collect children to use all the parts they like best to make the perfect Hagling. The magic spent trying to make one can almost kill a Hag. To have made two—twins." She shook her head.

"That's a lot of children," Delyth whispered.

"It's too much magic," said Declan.

"Could the Hag have been siphoning magic like Eirawen?" asked Edwin.

Berty almost dropped the stack of bowls that he carried to the table. All eyes snapped to him. He looked from Silvia to Declan, Edwin, Delyth, then to Hope, but said nothing. Hope wished that she could tell what her uncle thought. Why did he look at her? What did she have to do with anything? Since no one pursued the extra magic questioning further, Hope decided to not ask either.

"I don't believe there is anything for you to worry about," Silvia told the Firths. "Hope has the acorn now. Nothing can take that away."

"If all this is about Hope," said Cecil, "then how did... years before she ever walked into the workshop?"

Declan placed a hand on his brother's shoulder, then leaned in to whisper something in his ear. Cecil's light eyes scanned the room as Declan spoke.

"Madness," muttered Cecil. "But we're safe? You're sure?"

"Yes," said Declan. Hope thought something in his eyes also said, "For now."

Only light conversation joined the cacophony of chewing at dinner. Most seemed to mull over their own thoughts. After they ate, Edwin visited the outpost. While the children laughed in front of the fireplace, an uneasiness settled on the couches.

"So, Vander," Declan began, "you never did say what happened between you and Jordis."

Vander narrowed his eyes. Finally, he said, "Jordis decided to do special jobs for Vidor and the High Elf. She would visit between jobs. A couple of months before the High Elf's wedding, Jordis made a rare during-job visit. She needed to restock some provisions and get a good night's sleep. When I woke, she was gone. Haven't seen her since."

"That was three years ago," said Declan.

"One of her people, the half-Fairy, half-Elf—I forget her name—told me that Jordis took a position in Irmingard," said Vander. "The High Elf needed her or something." He swirled the contents of his glass.

Edwin's return ended talk of Vander's personal life. The Elf suggested that they retire early. Vander insisted that Edwin, Mike, and Cecil stay in his cottage. The children split themselves among their parents' rooms and sleeping in the great room with the Fairy Godmothers.

Hope sat at the window, watching a night breeze blow branches after changing for bed. When she heard Obie enter the bedroom, Hope said, "I'm sorry, Obie."

"For what?"

"Putting your family in harm's way." She could not get herself to tear her eyes from the window.

"There's nothing you could have done about any of it," he said. A warm hand slid around her waist, coaxing her away from the window. As she stood, his arms pulled her into a hug. "Don't worry. I won't let any harm come to you."

Wrapping her arms around him, she rested her head on his shoulder. After a few breaths, she disengaged. "Thanks, Obie," she said.

Obie allowed her to climb into the top bunk before he extinguished the lantern. She felt him crawl into the bed below her, then fell asleep.

By morning, the rain stopped. After eating a quick breakfast, they said good-bye to Obie's family. Vander brought them through the shop to avoid the soggy rope ladders. Sorrel waited with the horses outside.

Edwin assigned horses. Fairy Godmothers shared with their charges. Everyone else, including Sorrel, had a horse. Hope secured her pack behind the saddle. She then showed Mike how to secure his. When she mounted her horse, relief washed over her to not have to walk. Galloping away from Boudon, the parting of colored cloaks revealed members of the Roundtable wearing leather armor.

Chapter Eight

City of Elves

Her hand rested on the dagger that Obie taught her how to use in every spare moment. Her new bow rested comfortably on her back. Glancing at Declan who trotted in her peripheral vision, she wondered about her old bow and the symbol carved into it. Since no one mentioned it, she did not ask.

Silvia pushed a punishing pace. By the time they stopped to camp, they rode through plenty of forest. Under the confines of a Fairy dome, Silvia asked Hope to join her in one of the tents. She entered with Silvia to find Berty, Declan, and Edwin waiting for them.

"The bow has been left in the hamlet," said Silvia. "We have questions about the symbol, so we head to Irmingard to use their library. The Elves should also be able to help you with your magic."

"We sent word to Avery that we would be arriving, but without telling him why," said Berty. "Aunt Silvia and I will speak with him in person to explain everything."

"Don't speak about the symbol outside of the dome," cautioned Silvia. "And then only to Obie."

Hope nodded in understanding. After leaving the tent, Obie insisted they practice with her dagger until they slept.

After clearing their presence at the campsite, Silvia kept the horses at a trot—not as fast as the previous day, but fast none-the-less. Before they had a chance for a midday rest, Obie called, "Captain!" Edwin turned. "Warriors heading this way."

Mike clutched the reins tighter.

"Can you see who?" Edwin asked.

"I don't recognize him, sir, but he wears a lieutenant insignia," answered Obie.

Edwin rode his horse up to the front.

"How do you see that?" asked Sorrel. She squinted, searching the distance. "I can't make out faces, let alone insignias on their armor."

"Actually, Sergeant, it's on his cloak clasp," said Obie.

Sorrel's eyes narrowed, then she pulled her horse to the rear position.

"What's a Warrior?" Mike asked Hope quietly. He rode close enough for their knees to touch.

"The protectors of Irmingard," Hope replied.

"That doesn't help," said Mike.

"City of Elves."

"What kind of Elves? Wood Elves? Dark Elves? Light Elves?" asked Mike.

Hope rolled her eyes. "There's only one type of Elf," she said. "Like Captain Edwin."

"The Captain is an Elf?" Mike said. "But he doesn't have pointy ears!"

Suppressing a laugh, Hope said, "That's fiction."

"Fiction does have its roots in reality," said Berty who trotted beside them. "I've often wondered if some of the fiction greats ever wandered through a portal or spoke to someone who had. Don't know where the pointy ear thing originates, but if you notice people's ears, some are pointier than others. Perhaps there was a lost, pointy-eared race interbred out of existence." Berty looked around as if he examined his thoughts. "Fiction is but a guide leading to truth, which waits ready for those who see it."

As Berty steered his horse to ride alongside Jon, Mike said nothing. He put space between him and Hope—about a foot.

Not long after Obie spotted the Warriors, Hope saw their gleaming white armor riding towards them. When the two groups met, the lead Warrior said, "We have been dispatched to escort the Empire Delegation to Irmingard."

"Thank you, Lieutenant," said Edwin. "Tell me, did you have trouble finding us? We expected you yesterday."

"The forest is vast," the man answered.

Images of an ambush flashed in Hope's mind. She nudged her horse over to Silvia. "They're not Warriors," she told her aunt.

"Edwin suspects," Silvia whispered. She waved Sorrel to her other side. After breathing something to the Warlock, Sorrel glanced at Obie. She rode into the trees while Obie disappeared in the opposite direction. "Find the real Warriors," Silvia told Hope. "We will protect you."

More images flashed through her head. No, not images. A feeling of where the real Warriors were left for dead came to her. "Help is coming," she said through the trees. She felt an Elf breathe in response.

Smooth and spiky magic erupted from where the Warlocks disappeared. Weapons unsheathed. Horses knocked the false Warriors to the ground. Fairy Godmothers covered the eyes and ears of their charges.

Swiftly, the remaining pretenders surrendered. Silvia looked at Delyth who nodded. "Hope, Obie, Mike with me," said Silvia. "Jon, Teresa, follow Delyth with our children."

"Sergeant, go with Princess Delyth," ordered Edwin.

"Lead the way, Hope," said Silvia. The two groups left Declan, Berty, and Edwin to deal with the imposters.

Placing her bow and a handful of arrows on her lap, Hope followed the trail the trees provided. The trees spoke to her rapidly. She slowed her horse. "The bandits that came after us," she whispered. "Six of them guard the Warriors."

They stopped. Silvia motioned for Obie to accompany her. The two of them slipped off their horses. Drawing their swords, they disappeared.

Hope raised her bow and urged her horse forward. A bandit charged her, axe high. She released an arrow. Then another. The man dropped. Mike edged his horse next to hers.

The underbrush rustled. Mike unsheathed his sword. Hope lowered her bow. Silvia approached from the trees. She glanced at the bandit lying on the ground. "Go," she said. "Obie's tending to injuries. I'll get his horse."

Hope led Mike to where Obie hunched over his patients—the real Irmingard Warriors. "Oh, my...," escaped Mike's lips. Two dried dark stains blotched the makeshift camp. Trying not to stare at the unmoving bodies, she dismounted.

"Can I do anything?" she asked quietly.

Obie looked up. "I need a fire," he said.

Mike helped Hope gather wood and build a fire while Silvia handed Obie his healer's bag. "This wood's too wet. It'll never light," said Mike.

With a wave of her hand, Silvia lit the logs they stacked. The three of them assisted Obie tending to the surviving Warriors. They scrounged blankets to wrap around the Elves who lost their armor and cloaks and wore nothing but thin underclothes. After a couple of hours, the Elves gained some strength.

They sat up without help and all but one could feed themselves. "We never saw them until they were upon us," said an Elf between slurps of broth. "And then we were four against a dozen men."

"We sent a message about the bandits or whomever they were from the Boudonian Outpost days ago," said Obie.

"No message ever arrived in Irmingard from any outpost," said another Elf.

"That we knew about," said the first.

"Lieutenant?"

The Elf Lieutenant sipped an infusion that Obie handed him. "Two options," he said. "Either they killed the messenger, or we have a traitor within who destroyed the message."

"That was a long time ago, Garik," said a different Elf.

"Time can heal wounds or make you die from them," said Garik. "We would have suffered the latter if the good Lieutenant here hadn't also been a Healer." He looked from Obie to Silvia. "Thank you for our lives, my Lady."

She gave him a sharp nod. "We need to get to Irmingard tonight," she said. "Can they move?" she asked Obie.

"Yes, but those two need supervision," he answered, motioning to two Elves.

"We will double up on our horses," said Silvia. She placed the two least injured on Hope's horse, while the two Obie indicated rode with Silvia and Mike. Hope shared Obie's horse. Before mounting his horse, Obie removed his sword. Handing it to Garik, he said, "Someone on each horse should have a weapon." The Elf nodded, then laid the sword across his lap.

They rode at a gentle hurry. Hope believed Silvia used her magic to keep the Elves on the horses.

The white ramparts of the Elf city gleamed in the post sunset evening. Horse hooves clomped on wood as the four horses and their riders crossed the moat. Warriors waited at the gates for their rescued brethren.

Two men helped each off the horses. While Hope reclaimed her horse, Garik returned Obie's sword. "I didn't catch your name, Lieutenant," said the Elf.

"Oberon."

"I will make sure that Captain Edwin hears my commends, Lieutenant Oberon," Garik said in front of his men. He leaned on the nearest Warrior for support.

"Recover well, Lieutenant Garik," said Obie. He turned to the Healer's Aide who came to collect the men. "They all lost a lot of blood and some of the wounds were infected. Do not break the dressing until morning. They all also had a dose of willow bark infusion."

"Yes, sir," said the Aide.

A mounted Warrior escorted them through the bright streets of

Irmingard. Although her first visit to the Elf city, Hope refrained from sightseeing. She turned her head only to look at the center of Irmingard's central circle where Albrecht's Mound resided. An Elf in bright green laid an offering of pinecone buds in the center of the Mound. The Elf's head snapped up to look at Hope. She felt the Elf's dark eyes scrutinize her as if Hope spied something private. The Elf's head nodded respectfully, then turned. The Warrior steered them onto a broad road taking them away from the circle. In a few minutes, they arrived at their domed destination.

An Elf draped in dark green took their horses after they dismounted. Hope paused before climbing the white marble steps to admire the brightly colored glass dome that roofed the long building.

Inside the large double doors, Hope recognized the waiting Elf wearing the Warrior Commander's breastplate. She met Edwin's brother on the rare occasions he visited the Sages' Grove. His entire family from Irmingard stayed in the Empire Tree when Lark gave birth to her and Edwin's son. "Welcome to Irmingard, my Lady," he said. "May I enquire about my men?"

"Of course, Commander Wystan. We found four alive. First Lieutenant Oberon treated them. They are now in the hands of your Healers."

"Thank you, Empress," said Wystan. "We need to retrieve the fallen. I expect we will speak again in the morning." He bowed to Silvia. "One of the High Elf's men will escort you to the Garden." An Elf cloaked in white stood beside a marble column behind Wystan. The Commander's gaze examined Obie. "Lieutenant," he greeted with a sharp nod.

"Commander." Obie gave him a deeper nod.

Wystan glanced at Hope's acorn then her face before rushing

down a marble corridor.

"This way, please," said their guide. The High Elf's personal guard escorted them through the marble clad building. Hope learned all about the Blǫvar from Alfred who had two in the Empire Tree at Avery's insistence. The former High Elf turned Empire Scholar also taught her the ancient tongue, Elf history, and the dead pictorial Elf language. She loved spending her summers with Alfred.

Through an opening in the marble colonnade, Hope followed Silvia down a few steps. Alfred described the Garden, but his description could not fully illustrate its beauty. She paused to marvel at the expansive conservatory. Butterflies fluttered from fragrant bloom to fragrant bloom. Exotic fruit trees bore blossom laden branches. Striking flowers released a heady perfume. Breathing deeply, she greeted the Garden with, *Hello.*

The Listener has returned, murmured the Garden. Smiling, she closed her eyes while the plants greeted her.

When she opened her eyes, she found an Elf smiling at her. Braids of mostly gray encircled her head. "Welcome to the Garden, Listener. We have not officially met, but perhaps you remember me from when I visited the Empire Tree. My name is Femke."

"Yes, you're Captain Edwin's mother," said Hope. "It is nice to meet you." Her eyes scanned for her traveling companions. In a thicket of bushes, Obie stood near her parents and Mike. Her parents sat on some sort of stool, engrossed in a conversation with a few Elves. Obie caught her gaze and smiled.

"The Empress is in conference with the High Elf. Would you like a tour of the Garden? Your guard may join us," said Femke.

"That would be nice," said Hope. She waved Obie over.

Femke led them away from the others. She said nothing until they crossed a footbridge spanning a koi filled pond. "As soon as the others see you, word will spread about you," she said. "They will come to see you, talk to you, touch you, ask you for your blessing."

Hope shivered.

"Edwin told me about your magic," she continued. "I can arrange training for you. No one would bother you then."

"Yes, please," said Hope. "Would you be training me?"

"I would be honored to, however, as a member of the Raðþing, I cannot. It would be seen as a conflict of interest and I would be relieved of my post, for starters. Don't worry, I know of an excellent trainer. And, I can give advice. That is my duty, after all." Femke gestured to the surrounding plants. "The very first Raðþing of Irmingard began planting this Garden with seeds and cuttings brought from their travels or original homelands. We find serenity here all year long. In spring, the beauty and fragrance makes one want to linger until the last petal falls."

The Garden whispered about a new arrival. Hope turned. A graceful Elf strolled towards them in billowing emerald green robes. "An honor to have you in Irmingard, Listener," he said.

"An honor to be here, High Elf," she said.

"How are you finding our Garden?" Avery asked.

"Magnificent," she replied.

Avery beamed. "Allow me to introduce you to a few people before we have dinner," he said. He brought her to meet members of Irmingard's legislative body who dawdled around the Garden.

"Ah, yes, we met briefly when my grandson was born in the Empire Tree," Ryker, Edwin's father, said in earshot of the others.

Hope smiled and nodded during the introductions.

"If your schedule permits, while you are in residence in Irmingard,

Listener," said an Elf whose name slipped her mind, "our House would be honored to host you for dinner one of these evenings."

"Give her a chance to recover from her journey, Whitby," said Ryker. "The Listener rescued our Warriors today."

"Oh. Yes, of course." Whitby bowed his head to Hope. "My apologies, Listener."

"It's…" Hope was unsure of how to answer. She wondered what Berty would say. "Admiring the Garden has renewed me a bit, but food and sleep would be very welcome."

"Renewal is why we come here after Chamber sessions," said Ryker. "I hope we see you again tomorrow, Listener." Ryker bowed his silver haired head to Hope. The rest of the Elves that gathered followed. "High Elf." They bowed to him as well.

Hope and Obie walked with Avery out of the Garden. "We Elves hold the Wood Listener in very high regard," said Avery. "People here will fawn over you." He let out a small, dignified chuckle. "I'm sure Femke warned you about that already. Expect the Dominatrix to visit your suite either tonight or tomorrow. But first, dinner."

"Thank you, High Elf," said Hope.

"Please, to you, I am Avery," he said. "We keep things informal in the residence."

"Then, please, call me Hope."

The Elf gave her a smile. "Oberon," he said, "as Hope's guard, you will be mostly ignored. Though, with you around, they will think twice about coming too close. Of course, you must be prepared for people to think they can get to Hope through you. Politics in Irmingard is something of an art form. Speak with Edwin if you need help navigating that dance."

Before Obie could answer, Avery led them into a dining room

where everyone else, except the children, took seats around a long table. An elegant, willowy Elf floated from guest to guest. When her gaze found Avery, her whole face lit, making her one of the most beautiful women in the room. He held out his hand for her to take. "Listener," he said, his tone formal, "I'd like you to meet my wife, Lene."

"An honor," Hope said, unsure of what title to call the wife of the High Elf.

"The honor is mine," Lene said with a warming smile. "Do not worry; the spouse of a High Elf does not have a special title. Titles in Irmingard are earned from merit. Only High Elf is inherited. Come; share a meal at our family table."

Lene sat Hope and Obie across the table from Berty and Silvia. From the center of the table, the guests radiated in order of importance—Declan, Delyth, Edwin, Jon, Teresa, Mike, and two white cloaked Elves, introduced as Jordis, raised as Avery's sister, and Vidor, Avery's father.

Light conversation flowed around the table. The heavier words most likely spoken behind closed doors. Doors that did not open for Hope. She wondered if she wanted those doors to open for her. Could she handle the responsibility? Did she want to? What responsibility did she have as Wood Listener? She still had to finish high school.

A knock on the door brought an Elf who whispered in Avery's ear. "Who is it?" Avery asked aloud. "You may speak in front of the Empress and Emperor."

"A man calling himself the Master Woodsman is at the gate, asking to see the Wood Listener," said the messenger.

Avery stood, almost knocking over his chair, which Vidor caught.

"Make sure he has an escort to the Central Circle," he told him. "Jordis, get Katell. Hope, Oberon, come with me."

"He may not be who he says he is," cautioned Vidor.

"Then come."

Hope quickly washed down her food with a swallow from her goblet. She and Obie hurried after Avery. "Avery," she said, "Vidor may be right. I can't hear the Master Woodsman."

"You wouldn't," said Avery. "Not with all the stone."

Vidor remained a step behind Obie. Avery paused before the double doors leading to the outside to wait for a woman in form-fitting leather to join them. "Hope," said Avery, "this is Katell, the Dominatrix." He gestured to Hope. "The Wood Listener."

The doors opened of their own accord. The cool night air stung Hope's face. The four of them had to run to keep up with Avery as he galloped down the steps.

Catching his son, Vidor said in a low voice, "Decorum. We are outside." He looked around. "If not for you, then for them."

Avery stopped at the bottom of the white stone steps. "Walk quickly," he said. "We are alone out here." He led them with long, meaningful strides. As the shortest of the bunch, Hope had to take one and a half steps to sustain the pace. The broad road ended at Albrecht's Circle and his Mound.

Alfred told Hope all about the father of Irmingard—Albrecht the Collector. He used his horn to call all the Elves to area that would become the city of Irmingard. The city that protected the Elves from extinction. Albrecht placed his horn in the center of the city on a pole for all to hear the call. A series of wars, with the Fairies and themselves, ensured the removal of the horn for its protection. Only the Mound remained as tribute to Albrecht. Hope always believed that the Mound was more than the face value of Alfred's tale.

An escort of Warriors encircled an elderly man with light green robes. He looked exactly as Hope remembered. His white beard reached past the green sash around his waist. *"Hello again, Listener,"* he said inside her head. *"You heard the Mother Wood Sprite's call. Finally."*

"It has not been easy, Woodsman," Hope telecommunicated.

"I have come to make it easier," the Woodsman said aloud. In her head, he continued, *"It is after you—your power. Do not be afraid."*

"Thank you, Master Woodsman," said Hope aloud. *"I am not afraid."*

"Then, we shall begin." The Woodsman noticed the Elves beside her. "High Elf, Dominatrix, and Captain of the Blǫvar, if you would be so good as to join us." He walked to the mound then touched the offering. "There you are," he said to an Elf in the shadows. "You have waited long enough." He waved the Elf forward. When the Elf entered the light, Hope saw a woman in her mid-twenties. "And you," he said to Obie, motioning him into a position. Turning in a small circle near the mound, he said, "One of the Taproot conduits. Albrecht's Mound."

Somewhere inside, she understood what the Master Woodsman meant. Not dwelling on his words, she stood where he indicated.

Hope found herself on the pinnacle of the low mound. Obie, the Elf woman, and the Master Woodsman formed a triangle around her. Avery, the Dominatrix, and Vidor made an outer triangle with points intersecting the first. The Master Woodsman chanted in a language Hope did not know, yet understood. Although she could not translate the words, she felt the meaning resonate inside her. He called on the power of the One Tree—the tree that connects everything—the tree from which the other trees stem—the Tree of Life, the Tree of Knowledge, and the Tree of Wisdom.

A greenish brown haze engulfed her. Magic washed over her, through her. She no longer heard the Master Woodsman's words nor could she tell if his mouth moved. When the magic stilled, the Master Woodsman smiled behind his beard. *"Balance has been restored,"* he said inside her head.

After helping her off the mound, he turned to the Elf woman, saying, "Your line has kept tradition all this time." She nodded, throwing a glance at Hope. Hope recognized her as the Elf they passed who was laying the offering. "Listener," he continued, "this is your Tender. She is with you always."

"Collect your things, Tender, and come up to the Residence," said Avery.

The Tender bowed her head. As the Elf walked away, Hope noticed Obie watching her for a moment. His expression held a mixture of intrigue and disappointment.

"May we offer you some hospitality, Master Woodsman?" asked Avery.

"Thank you kindly, High Elf," said the Master Woodsman. "All I need is an escort back to the gate. Until we meet again, Listener."

Hope gave him a nod. He left in the company of Warriors. Avery smiled while he allowed Vidor to lead them back up the road.

Once inside the double doors, the Dominatrix said, "If there is nothing else, High Elf, I'm going to return to my quarters."

"No," said Avery. "Thank you."

"She's not your servant, Avery," she said.

"Excuse me?" Avery's smile faltered.

"Your mother trained her well. Permit her to do her job. Out there."

"Where is this coming from?" he demanded.

"Don't forget who you are, High Elf Avery. No one else does." The Dominatrix held a hard stare. After breaking it, she said, "Captain, Lieutenant, Listener." She politely nodded her head before striding down a marble corridor. Her boots barely made a sound.

Avery exhaled audibly. "Let's finish dinner," he said, trying to find his smile.

When they returned to the dining room, everyone smiled at her. "Lene brought us to the balcony to watch," Teresa explained.

"How do you feel?" asked Silvia.

"Fine," she said. "Should I feel different?"

"No," answered Silvia. "When you retire after dinner, explore how the magic feels within you. It will give you an idea of normal. The more aware you are to your magic, the more control over it you have."

"Okay," said Hope, nodding.

Chapter Nine

Messages

A servant showed Hope and Obie to a three-bedroom suite. After hanging her cloak and checking on her pack in the main bedroom, Hope sunk into a cushioned bench near a fireplace. "It's been a long day," said Obie, sitting in a chair across from her.

"I understand what Aunt Silvia was telling me at dinner," she said. "Know my magic so I know if something's off." A knock on the door kept her from continuing.

When Obie opened the door, Mike entered. "Looks like I'm in here with you guys," he said. "Aunt Silvia doesn't want me by myself and their suite is full." He dropped his bag next to a chair. "I think they want to talk without me." He sat. "Up on the balcony, I don't know what they were looking at, but Declan and Uncle Berty gasped at one point."

"They can see magic where the rest of us can't," said Hope.

"Must be cool to have magic," mused Mike.

"Don't you?" said Hope. "It runs in your family."

"Aunt Silvia is really my cousin once removed or something like that."

"You don't know," muttered Hope.

"What?" asked Mike.

Someone knocked on the door. "Come in," said Obie.

When the door opened, the Elf Tender took a step inside the suite. She bowed her head when she saw Hope. "An honor to serve you, Listener," she said. "Is there anything you need?"

Hope straightened in her seat. People started treating her like her uncle. Smiling at the Tender, she wondered how Berty would handle it. In the lantern light, the Elf did not seem as old as Hope first thought. "We won't be in Irmingard long," she told the Elf. "Be ready to travel."

"Tonight?" she asked.

"No. Thankfully, tonight we sleep," said Hope. "Unless we don't."

"Do you carry a weapon?" Obie asked the Elf.

She stared at Obie for a second. "I carry a small blade, Lieutenant," she said. "Did you want to examine it?"

"Not necessary," Obie dismissed. "I just want to make sure you are armed in case we're attacked while traveling."

"I've had the basic Warrior training all Elves receive," she said.

Obie nodded.

"What's your name?" asked Hope. When the Elf's gaze froze on her, she continued, "If we're going to be spending most of our time together, we should know each other's names. Mine is Hope. The Lieutenant is Obie and this is my friend, Mike, who is visiting."

The Elf's demeanor relaxed. "I am Verity of the House of Saggard," she said.

"The bedroom on the left is yours, Verity," said Hope. "Get yourself settled and ready for a big day tomorrow."

Verity bowed her head respectfully to Hope before the Elf disappeared into the bedroom.

Standing, Hope announced, "I'm going to bed."

"So early?" asked Mike.

She gave him a look that made him cower in his chair. Entering the bedroom, she closed the door behind her. Alone at last. After changing into her nightclothes, she sat on the bed and closed her eyes.

Magic coursed through her veins with every heartbeat, filled her lungs with every breath. Pouring out of every pore, the magic enveloped her. Its tendrils wrapped her in a cocoon. She pushed and prodded, checking its boundaries. As she explored her magic, her magic explored her. She found its rhythm, the melody to which it danced.

With her magic she discovered the bedroom—the bed, the wardrobe, the vanity, the stone walls, the wool rug, the lanterns, the wood door. She sensed magic through the door. A comfortable magic. Strong and refined. She reached for it, but hesitated. The other magic embraced hers.

"Hope?" said a quiet, male voice.

She opened her eyes.

"There you are." Obie's blue eyes floated inches from her face. She blinked. All of him sat on the foot of her bed. "What do you need? Are you okay?" He placed his hand on hers. "You called me," he explained.

"I did?"

"Magically," he said. "It was similar to when, uh, I was taken. When we were kids and you spoke to me through the trees."

"I didn't mean to disturb you," she said. "I just... found you."

Obie's free hand swept a rogue hair out of her face. His eyes got closer. They tilted. Lips bumped into hers. Her lids dropped over her eyes. His fingers threaded into her hair. Her hands rested against his shoulders.

They broke apart.

"Hope, I," he began.

"You should probably go," she breathed.

He softly pecked her on the lips. "Goodnight," he said. He slid off her bed. With his hand on the handle of her door, he gave her a look she did not want to read.

She emerged from her bedroom in the morning to find Obie supervising servants bringing breakfast. "Good morning," Obie said with a warm smile.

"Morning," she said. The evening's tender kisses lingered on her lips.

Before the servants closed the door to the suite, Mike strode out of a bedroom, saying, "Food." While Mike chose from the breakfast offerings, Verity joined them. "No coffee?" Mike asked. He sniffed under the lid of what resembled a silver coffee pot.

Hope loaded her plate with food. "The only place you'll find coffee beans here is at my grandparents," she said.

"But I got coffee at Obie's family's house," said Mike.

"Uncle Berty must have given it to you. He transforms all morning infusions into coffee."

He poured a little infusion into a cup. After a sip, he made a face. "This tastes like bitter mud," said Mike.

"Did you add a blossom first?" asked Verity.

Mike glanced at the bowl of yellow, red, and orange flowers next to the silver pot. "Why would I do that?"

Choosing an orange flower, Verity dropped it into a cup then poured the hot infusion over it. "Try this," she said, giving it to him.

He stared into the cup before bringing it to his lips. "Oh, that's different," he said. "A little spicy."

"Goes well with jam pastry," said Verity. She fixed a cup for herself.

Once seated, Mike asked Hope, "So, what don't I know?"

She swallowed her bite of sweet roll. "Lots of things."

"Like?"

Hope finished her roll before saying, "It's really not my place to say anything." Mike raised his eyebrows. "Fine," she conceded. "Your grandfather is a Matchmaker. He matched Uncle Berty with Silvia. He uses it also at his job on the paper."

"And that's a magical skill?" Mike asked.

Hope nodded.

"I don't understand," said Mike. "How did he know he had magic?"

"I don't know exactly, but I'm sure it was when he was young, growing up in the Empire Tree."

"What?" He set his cup down. "He grew up in the Empire Tree?"

"Your grandfather is the son of an Empress," said Hope.

Mike's jaw moved as if he ground his teeth. His brown eyes narrowed. He squished a roll in his hand. Finally, he said, "Do you know where my mom went on my third birthday?" He blinked a few times. His hands attacked a napkin. Standing, his chair banged to the floor. He stormed into the bedroom.

"Mike," Hope called.

The door slammed.

"Let him be," said Obie. "What did happen to his mother?"

"All I know is that she dropped him off at his grandparents to get things ready for his birthday. She was never seen again."

None of them said anything while they finished breakfast. A knock interrupted the silence. Obie admitted the Dominatrix.

"Listener," she said with a bow of her head, "if I could have a moment of your time before your day starts."

"Sure," said Hope. "Please, have a seat."

"I need you to accompany me," the Dominatrix said. She glanced at Hope's shadows—old and new. "Alone."

"No," said Obie. "She goes nowhere alone."

"I understand your duty, Lieutenant," said the Dominatrix. "She needs to go alone." She met his determined glare. "Where we go will wreak havoc on your Warlock magic. It is best if you do not come near."

Standing, Hope said, "It's okay, Obie. Besides, someone has to keep an eye on Mike."

Behind Obie's expressionless face, she knew he seethed. After a moment, he gave her a nod.

She followed the Dominatrix down the shining stone hall. They walked silently, even their footsteps made no noise. "I know what you're going through," the Dominatrix finally said. "And I understand the need for protection. I would have come for you last night, but after the magic, I thought it best to let you rest. Magical transference can be exhausting, even with years of preparation."

"Where are we going?" Hope asked.

"The Matrix."

Hope lost a step.

"Weapons vault," the Dominatrix clarified.

Nodding, Hope noticed the tight leather outfit the Dominatrix wore. "Is that comfortable?" she asked. "The leather."

The Dominatrix laughed. "That's not a question I usually get," she said. "The armor is almost a second skin. I have gloves for weapon work and, at one time, there was a headpiece. Its protective magic is what is special. It is old magic. Perhaps not as old as the magic of the trees, but old enough to be forgotten."

When the stone corridors dulled, the Dominatrix explained, "This is one of the oldest parts of the building." Finally stopping, she touched a stone on the wall while muttering something under her breath that sounded similar to the ancient Elf language. Blocks slid inward to reveal a doorway. After walking through, the doorway sealed itself. Crystal sconces, like those in the Scepter Room, lit the dark stone corridor down which they traveled. Other corridors branched, but the Dominatrix seemed to stay on the main one.

They stopped on a stone balcony that overlooked darkness. Air blew over the stone rail. No light escaped beyond the rail. "Everything housed here has magic or is made from or contains a unique substance," said the Dominatrix. "There are three storage levels: ordinary, special, and legendary. Off you go."

A staircase on the right disappeared into the darkness. "Where do I go?"

"Only you can retrieve," she answered. "Trust the magic. It will guide you."

Hope stood on the last step in the light. Unsure of where her feet needed to go, she tuned into her magic like she did the previous night. A path opened up before her. The magic nudged her down the last few steps.

Unlike Obie or Berty, her magic did not illuminate her surroundings. Her feet obeyed the magic's directions. Her eyes discerned nothing but darkness. She could not see her own body, let alone the hard surface on which she walked. Curiosity bumped fear from her mind. What lurked in the vault with her? Was it similar to the Magical Item Vault where her old bow was fated to rest? Perhaps the darkness kept all the magical items stable. After that thought, Hope no longer wanted to know what she passed on her path. She closed her eyes to keep them from adjusting and seeing something she should not.

When her feet stopped, she dared to open her eyes. She still saw nothing but inky blackness. Reaching, her hands found a material of some sort. She gathered every bit that called to her before leaving that spot. Returning seemed faster than the trip into the darkness.

On the lighted balcony, the Dominatrix leaned against the rail, waiting. "What is it?" she asked. Hope raised a rich brown bundle. "Let's lay it out on the table." The Dominatrix led Hope to a dark stone slab. "This stone will not disturb the magic or transfer magic from one item to another."

The brown material glowed against the dark stone. Hope unraveled slim pants and a turtleneck shirt with open-fingered gloves buttoned to the end of the sleeves. "I don't think this will fit me," she mumbled.

"It will," said the Dominatrix. "Magical armor, such as this, conforms to the body of the current wearer. This is probably woven from the bark of the Old Tree itself." Tearing her eyes off the armor, she looked at Hope. "Why don't you put it on so we see what it does."

"Here?"

"No better place to test its magic," she answered.

After stripping to her underwear, Hope pulled on the bark fiber clothing. The shirt flowed over her like a dress. With her sleeve covered hands, she held the pants up to her waist. The bottom of the legs puddled around her feet.

The Dominatrix chuckled. "I'm glad the Dominatrix can never be a male. Give it a minute," she said.

The clothing began to shrink. Hope let go of the waistband. The bark fiber fit snug as if she wore long underwear. "Am I supposed to go out like this?" Hope asked.

"Turn around."

Hope obliged.

"Hmmm. This isn't armor, per se." Hope waited for the Dominatrix to continue. "It will only provide minimal protection against weaponry. However, its magical protection should be exquisite. Wear it under your clothing." She motioned for Hope to get dressed over the bark. "You may want to invest in Dwarf made armor."

Fully dressed, Hope followed the Dominatrix out of the Matrix. When the dull corridors finally gave way to shiny ones, she noticed that they headed towards the library. She wanted to ask why the library, but soon met Obie and Verity in a table filled nook.

After the Dominatrix left, Hope asked, "How's Mike?"

"He's with your parents," said Obie.

"Can I help you?" said a voice in the main library hall.

"I hope so," a male voice answered. "I'm supposed to speak to someone about education."

"In Irmingard?" asked the first voice.

"Yes, I have a writ here signed by the Pixie Priestess that I am supposed to give to the Head Tutor," said the male.

"Ah." An elderly Elf librarian and a teenage boy stepped into view. "Wait here, please," said the librarian.

The boy entered the nook. Looking from face to face, he asked, "Are you students?"

"No," answered Hope, trying not to stare at his malformed Fairy wings on his back. "Not in Irmingard anyway." He tucked his shoulder length brown hair behind his ear. "Carr?" she asked.

"Yes."

"We used to play in the ruins before Aloysia and you left for Pix-isle," she said.

"Hope?" Carr smiled. "Aloysia tried to train me for a mixed gender Squad. Turns out, I'm not really made for brute force. So, education is my route. Of course, I know it's been centuries since Irmingard has hosted Pixie students."

"You're a Pixie? With wings?" asked Verity.

"I was born a Fairy," said Carr. "Lost my parents in the war... and my wings. They're useless. Can't even fold them properly."

"Just because your wings do not work like other Fairy wings does not make them useless," said Delyth. She descended spiral steps in the back corner of the nook.

"Princess," Carr said, bowing his head. "I didn't mean..."

"Usefulness is not determined by how something looks on the outside," continued Delyth. "Hence, why we educate." Carr averted his eyes. "The High Elf will join us momentarily."

Behind Delyth, Declan descended. His knowing eyes studied

Hope. They paused on the high neck and fingerless gloves of her bark armor that spilled beyond her clothes. "I take you had a good meeting with the Dominatrix," he said to her.

"Yes," Hope answered.

The High Elf appeared on the steps with Berty and Silvia. "If you three would come with me," he said to Hope, Obie, and Verity. He said nothing more while leading them up the staircase that reached well above a rolling ladder against the library shelves. The stairs ended at a wooden door on which Avery knocked twice. When the door opened, Avery stood aside to let them pass. "The Scrollist is expecting you," he said.

A circular, white, opaque window lit the empty room. The domed ceiling ran the entire length of the library. Off to one side stood a woman Hope did not notice at first. The woman approached wearing a long dark green robe. Braids looped around her head. "Welcome, Wood Listener," she said in a heavy accent Hope could not place. "I am the Scrollist."

That title meant nothing to her.

"I curate and protect the Library's knowledge," she explained. "Once I learned of your presence in Irmingard, I requested an audience with you. Please, have a seat." She led them to four chairs not there earlier. Once everyone sat, she continued. "I spoke with your predecessor before he escaped through a portal never to return. He knew that someday a Wood Listener would walk back through a portal. He also knew you would be a target. That is why he fled in the first place. He entrusted his journal to me so that I may pass it on to the next." The Scrollist rose.

She approached something only she could see. After pantomiming plucking a book from a shelf, a book appeared in her hands. Returning, the Scrollist handed Hope a leather bound journal secured with leather ties. "Do you read the ancient tongue?" she asked Hope.

"I do."

"Tomes rarely leave the upper area," said the Scrollist. "Magic preserves them here. I cannot guarantee that it will stay in its preserved stated for long. Read and take notes or transcribe it into the common tongue would be my advice." She returned to her seat. "I requested the three of you, because I feel it necessary that the Wood Listener's Tender and Guardian have knowledge. It is imperative that you know that there are six such Listeners, five beside yourself, but they are not all called Listeners. Today, those who are called Listeners are not actually Listeners. The other true Listeners are Crystal, Metal, Star, Stone, and Wind. The one who can bring their magic together is the Speaker."

"Like a Communicator?" Hope asked.

"No," said the Scrollist. "Sometimes, the Speaker is also referred to as the seventh Listener—the Listener of Magic.

"The different Listeners adhere to different rules. The Wood Listener has a Tender because trees have Tenders—the Wood Sprites—at least they did at one time." She paused. Nostalgia glinted in her eyes.

"The previous Wood Listener dismissed his Tender and relieved the line of its duties," the Scrollist continued, "but I see that the tradition survived despite that."

"Yes," said Verity. "We knew that one would return one day and we needed to be ready. We continued our training in secret."

The Scrollist nodded. "Good, because our Wood Listener will need help. I am aware that you have been pursued ever since your first journey through the portal," she said to Hope. "The signs... What you must know... An ancient enemy—the Elves call him the

Gatherer, loosely translated—rises. The Gatherer covets your magic. Thinks it will give power over the world. Your magic is but one part of what can destroy the Gatherer."

"I never heard of this Gatherer," said Hope.

"There are different names," said the Scrollist. "You may have heard one or two. Or not. I understand the Dragons will not name. They may reference the Imprisoned."

"You have told us two names and implied that there are more, but yet have not given a form," Obie said.

"Quite perceptive." The Scrollist focused on Obie. "There is no form, at least not of one of which I am aware. After hearing many stories over the many long years, I have deduced that it takes any form it chooses. Hence, the many names. However, they all describe a cunning and beguiling trickster in one way or another.

"We Elves believe that to truly defeat your enemy, you must understand your enemy. Go to Fairyland. Study the Histories. Particularly, *The History of the World* and *The History of Magic*. You may discover insight. In the meantime, perfect your magic."

The Scrollist stood, signaling the end of their meeting. "Thank you," said Hope, "and thank you for the journal."

"I would be honored to store yours here someday, Listener," the Scrollist said. When the door opened, they descended the spiral staircase.

Pushing off a bookcase against which he leaned, Declan asked, "Finished?"

"Yes," Hope answered.

"Good," he said. He motioned for them to follow. "Did you know this complex has a courtyard?" He brought them outside. Blue stone covered the ground between the walls of the surrounding building. Trees and benches punctuated the stone with an artful constraint. Femke waited on one of the benches with an elderly Elf.

When Femke noticed Hope, both Elves stood. The older Elf resembled Alfred a little. At second glance, only the white hair was the same. "Listener," greeted Femke, "I would like you to meet the tutor about whom we spoke."

"An honor to meet you, sir," said Hope.

"The honor is mine, Listener," he responded. "Please, call me Menny. So, what seems to be the issue?"

"My magic has recently grown and I find that I," Hope paused while she searched for the right words.

"Are not used to all that magic and have difficulty keeping it in check," he finished for her.

"Yes, especially the invisibility."

"Ahh." Menny tilted his head. "Herein lies the first problem. It is not invisibility. It is camouflage. You are not an Elf, so I can see your confusion. Of course, younger generations have trouble with that concept as well." Shaking his head, he strolled towards one of the courtyard's trees. Hope followed. "When one looks at a tree, does one see everything? No. One sees what the tree allows. It is the tree that hides us and anything with us." He touched the trunk then disappeared. When he reappeared, he said, "Your turn."

"I have a question first," Hope said.

Menny inhaled sharply through his nose. "What is it?"

"Do you not have to accept the tree's protection when you touch it?"

The aged Elf smiled. "You want to know how to convey one's acceptance? I think I grasp your predicament. As Elves, we only have one message to confer to the trees. While you, as Listener, have many. However, you answered your own question in your words."

"Accept protection," she said.

"Yes." He motioned for her to touch the tree trunk.

She felt *accept*. Menny gasped. Hope touched the tree trunk. The tree disappeared. Menny stumbled. Hope scrambled to catch him before he fell, but Obie reached him first.

"In all my years," mumbled Menny. He glanced at Obie. "Thank you, Lieutenant. This old body is not what it used to be. Help me to the bench. I need to sit a spell."

When Hope sat next to Menny, he asked, "Did you know that you did not have to touch a tree?"

"Yes. I've done it before, but it's been erratic."

He nodded. "There is much more to Wood Listener magic than I realized," he said. "I need to consult a few things. May I call on you later?"

"I'll be around the residence," Hope said. "Thank you for your assistance, Menny."

His almost clear colored eyes bounced between both of hers. "Oh, my dear." Menny placed a hand on her then left without saying another word.

After the aged Elf disappeared into a doorway, Verity sat in his spot. "That was a short lesson," she said.

Hope said nothing. Her eyes found the tree she made invisible. Finally looking at Verity, she said, "I learned what I needed to learn." Beyond her Tender, Declan shifted his weight from foot to foot. They needed to leave the courtyard.

Rising, she led Verity to where Declan and Femke stood. "Thank you, Femke. He was enlightening," Hope said. "How do we get to the Garden from here?"

Femke smiled. "Also my favorite area of the complex, even on a beautiful day like today," she said. "I know the shortest route." She guided them through marble corridors while Declan made small talk.

Inside the Garden, Declan fell in beside Hope. As Femke discussed the Garden with Verity, being her first visit, Declan said, barely above a whisper, "That was reckless." She stared into his light eyes. "You should have touched the tree *before* becoming invisible."

"But, I don't need to."

"No one should know that," he said without moving his lips.

"Everyone saw in Boudon," she argued.

"A reclusive village who are loyal to you. Besides, that could have been a one time thing. Here, you proved otherwise," Declan reasoned. "You never know who's watching or from where. Showing strengths also shows weaknesses."

Hope's lips pursed.

"You must consider not only your own safety, but of those around you," he said.

She nodded slowly. "What can I do?"

"Learn from it." His eyes scanned beyond the bushes. "Get your fill of the Garden," he said to both her and Obie. "We leave this afternoon."

Hope found a quiet place to sit. Declan's words rattled in her head. She could not undo what she did, however, she could explain it. A magical spike due to meeting the Master Woodsman caused the sudden camouflage. She did not realize it at the time and has not been able to replicate it since. Resolved to correct her mistake, she looked for Declan. She could not see him over the vegetation. Her magic searched instead.

She found him with Obie. Hers and Obie's magic touched.

Then, her magic followed Declan as he walked to where she sat. "Obie said you were looking for me," he said. His light eyes studied her. His eyebrows raised. She retracted her magic.

"Boudon is where I became The Wood Listener," she began, "so the magic was erratic and doing strange and often unheard of things. When I met with the Master Woodsman last night, he performed a magical ritual, which led to a spike in the magic, causing it to be become erratic once more. I'm thinking that by this evening, it should calm down again. I was only going over what Menny taught me in my head before I got the chance to touch the tree."

A smile crept across Declan's face. "Absolutely. It should level before we leave," he said. "The three of you should stay here and relax. Someone will collect you for lunch."

Verity wandered while Obie patrolled. Hope sat with her eyes closed until she heard, "May I sit?" Opening her eyes, she found Mike standing near a bush. She nodded.

With a sigh, he sat across from her. "I'm sorry," he said.

"You know, you've been apologizing to me a lot lately," she said.

"Yeah, well. Don't get used to it." Mike let out a half laugh. "Anyway, I didn't mean to snap at you this morning. I spoke with Aunt Silvia. She didn't know that Grandpa didn't tell me everything. I also spent a good portion of the morning with your parents." He let out a breath. "They're really cool. You're lucky to have them."

"Thanks."

His gaze roved around the Garden while his fingers pulled his pants at the knees. "Um... What do you want to do about the, uh, rumors about, uh, you and, um, Mister Wilde?" His eyes finally rested on her.

Her shoulders slumped.

130

"It's just that we're going to be back in school soon and I, well, I'm not making plans without consulting you," Mike said, "again."

"I bet you someone in the Archery Club started those rumors," said Hope, mulling over her club mates. "Gabe... He always comes in second. Or... Rosalind. She is super duper sweet to my face, but daggers behind my back, from what I understand."

"Does it matter who?"

"Yes," Hope said with a wry smile. "Because we can say that Rosalind started the rumors about me to divert attention from what was really happening between her and Mister Wilde."

Mike's jaw dropped a little. "That's brilliant and vicious," he said.

She shrugged. "I'm really sick of people coming after me, Mike."

"Excuse me, Listener," said Obie.

Hope's head snapped to look at him. A servant stood sheepishly behind him.

"Time for lunch with the High Elf," he continued.

Standing, she said, "Does Verity know?"

"She's waiting by the door," said Obie.

"Shall we then?" said Hope. She smiled at the servant, who stood straighter.

The servant brought them through the marble corridors to the High Elf's residence. The four of them were the last to arrive in the dining room. Once they found their seats, everyone began to eat.

Hope ate silently while conversation flowed around her. She ignored everything until a woman she barely recognized entered. The woman spoke to Avery in his ear. "Are you sure?" he asked quietly.

"No mistaking it," she answered.

Avery nodded. "Your husband is having lunch with your brother-in-law and, I believe, the Dominatrix," he said to her.

"High Elf," she said with a bow of her head before leaving. Vidor left the room a moment after she did.

"Is everything all right, Avery?" asked Silvia.

"Nothing that can't wait until after we finish our lunch," he said. Vidor slipped back into his seat.

"Who was that?" Mike whispered to Hope.

"Commander Wystan's wife. Gaynor, I think her name is," answered Hope.

"Wonder what she wanted. Surely not to ask the High Elf where he husband was," said Mike.

Hope shrugged.

After lunch, the Fairy Godmothers took the children back to their suites to pack. Avery addressed them, "It seems that the magic tutor, Menny, who met with Hope today has," he paused, "committed ritual suicide."

Hope inhaled sharply.

"I thought Irmingard forbade ritual suicides," said Silvia.

"Only legal for extreme cases," said Vidor. "Such as to prevent one from becoming a Vindalf. My people are investigating. It's good you were leaving today anyway."

"I'm leaving as well," said Jordis. "May I ride with you for a while?"

"Of course, Jordis," said Berty.

"Thank you, my Lord." Jordis hurried out of the room.

"We will send the Empire a copy of our findings," said Vidor.

Berty gave the Elf a nod. "We should prepare for travel," he said.

In her suite, Hope repacked her bag, adding some of the provisions provided by the Elves. Someone knocked on her opened bedroom door. She looked up. Declan stood in the doorway. "Menny's suicide was not your fault," he said. "Irmingard is politically crazy. I don't want you to think that you did something to cause him to... make his statement."

"Statement?" Hope asked.

"I spoke with the Dominatrix about it," said Declan. "Ritual suicide goes back before the unification of the Elves. A simplified version of this ritual survives today. Menny performed the old ritual. The Dominatrix says it was a message to someone. She's just not sure to whom."

"A message?" said Mike. "But the guy took his own life."

Declan glanced at Mike behind him. "Yes," he said. "Say nothing more about it. Let's just get out of Irmingard. Verity," Declan entered the suite's main room, "since you had no horse of your own, one has been acquired for you. We're meeting at the Great Doors."

All four of them had to have heard Declan's words because they finished packing in silence.

Chapter Ten

School Bound

Hope's parents waited at the doors with the children and the Fairy Godmothers. Sorrel stood between the doors and a marble pillar, watching. She greeted Obie with a nod. The rest arrived with Avery, Wystan, and Vidor.

After good-byes, the doors opened. Irmingard Warriors surrounded their horses. "For the Empire Delegation until you cross the bridge," said Wystan as he walked down the marble stairs.

Escorted by Warriors, they processed through the white city. The gleaming buildings had a beauty of their own. Hope knew she could get happily lost on any of the winding side streets that connected to the main road. Some Elves, mostly children, stood on the side of the road to watch them pass. Most of the Warriors stopped at the gates. Wystan and a select few Warriors crossed the bridge with them. After giving Edwin a salute, they turned back to Irmingard.

Once the ramparts disappeared from view, Edwin hastened the pace. Eventually, Berty led them off the road to an occupied campsite. A blue cloaked figure approached. "Empress, Emperor, thank you for meeting with us," the figure said.

"Thank you for waiting, Grier," said Silvia.

"Are these women Amazons?" Mike asked quietly as they secured their horses.

Hope recognized three of the five women in rich blue cloaks. "Pixies," she answered.

"They tower over the Fairies," said Mike.

"Fairies are small people," Hope said. "I passed Aunt Delyth when I was in sixth grade and Freesia not long after." She smiled for a moment. "Freesia left the following year."

"Your Fairy Godmother. Why did she leave?" asked Mike.

"I outgrew her," said Hope. "They only stay as long as they are needed. Then, they go back to the Godmother Guild to await reassignment."

Mike looked towards the campfire. "What's the story with the Pixies?" he asked.

"If we step away from the horses, we'll find out," said Obie.

Mike gave him a where did you come from look.

By the time they joined the others around the fire, Berty, Silvia, Declan, Delyth, and Edwin had disappeared inside a tent with the Pixies. When Hope sat next to her father to eat, the others sat like dominoes around her. "Why are we meeting with the Pixies?" she asked Jon.

"Unfinished business is all I know," Jon told her.

"Wonder what that's about," Hope said softly.

"We'll find out when we get back to the Empire Tree," said Obie. Her eyebrows raised, but she said nothing.

Eventually, everyone emerged from the tent. Around the campfire, they discussed Pixisle's progress since the liberation of the Priestess. "Captain Mabe and her crew helped spread the word that we were looking for settlers, especially men," said Zelda. "They came. Half left within the first year." She laughed. "Those who stayed or came after made good lives for themselves. The island is alive again."

"Merja has been negotiating with the Water Sprites for our passage," said Aloysia. "Progress has been slow, but we can trade. Carr can study in Irmingard. Of course, being born a Fairy helps."

Delyth said, "He is doing well."

"Yes, he is," agreed Aloysia. "Being male, he can never be a Sini like I, but with education, he can become a Terho—a leader—or an Usko." Smiling with pride, she continued, "We will see."

Tuning out the Pixie conversation, Hope found Grier staring at her. She remembered that the Pixie was something of a Watcher and probably saw her bark second skin. Obie interrupted her thoughts with self-defense practice.

At first light, the campsite broke down—without breakfast. They would eat while riding. Jordis left the group to travel with the Pixies for a bit. Hope wondered if the Elf would make her way to Boudon to see Vander.

By the time they stopped for a break, Hope's muscles screamed with every little movement. "Although I am as sore as all get out," said Mike, "I really hope I don't wake up and find that all this was a dream. You know, that I hit my head and made all this up."

Hope laughed a little. "Might as well be," she told him. "We can never talk about here in front of others."

"Yeah, but still."

Edwin corralled them back atop their mounts for another grueling ride. When night fell, they slowed. The children whined about being hungry, tired, and Walden complained that his bottom fell off.

"Not much longer," said Declan.

"You said that ages ago, Daddy," said Fiala.

"If you look hard enough, you might see the lights besides the gates," Declan countered.

Obie chuckled in silence. While the kids squinted to see lights, he whispered to Hope, "That was brilliant. I'll have to remember that one."

Hope felt her face flush.

Finally, one of the girls exclaimed, "I see them! The lights! We're almost home."

Hope squinted. Maybe she saw lights ahead. She looked to Obie. He nodded.

The treed walls of the Sages' Grove welcomed her. Climbing up the steps of the Empire Tree made her feel safe. Berty insisted that both Obie and Verity accompany her to her chambers to freshen and rest. Verity said nothing while they traveled through the Tree.

Entering her budding chambers, Hope said to them, "Put your stuff anywhere. There's a second bathroom through Freesia's old bedroom. Upstairs." She dragged her bag up the steps in the back of the room. She passed a door on her way to her bedroom. She backed up.

"There's a third bedroom," she called down the stairs.

"What?" Obie appeared at the bottom of the steps.

"It's added a third bedroom. Three!"

The wind chimes rang through her bundle of budding branches.

"Come in," said Hope, returning downstairs without her bag.

A Dwarf entered. "Hello, Miss Hope," he said. "I am here to add Lieutenant Oberon and the new addition to the door lock."

"Both of them?" Hope asked.

"The Emperor said both will be living here now."

"Of course," said Hope. "Please, meet Verity." She turned to the Elf. "Theodore is the Head Tender of the Empire Tree."

"I heard the Empire Tree had Tenders," Verity said.

"Miss Verity, Lieutenant, if you would join me outside," said Theodore.

"My room is the one with the closed door. I'm going to change," Hope said before Obie and Verity left with the Dwarf.

After her shower, she dressed in clothes that did not include bark. She combed her long, dark, wet hair then headed downstairs. Obie sat at the table without his armor. His towel dried blond hair brushed his jawline. His blue eyes followed her until she joined him. "How's the room?" she asked.

"A place for everything and almost everything in its place," he answered. "I told Theodore we were eating here tonight. I thought it best that the three of us talk without an audience." He glanced at the stairs where Verity slowly descended. "Verity," he said, "forgive my ignorance, but what exactly does the Tender do for the Wood Listener?"

"I suppose it would be difficult to do your job without knowing mine," said Verity, approaching the table. While she sat, a Tender brought their food.

They began eating before Verity explained. "My primary job is to keep the tradition of the trees," she said between bites. "I assist the Wood Listener with rituals such as blessings, dedications, and offerings. The Tender often acts as an intermediary between the Listener and others who would ask for her services. And finally, I am to be the conscious one while the Wood Listener communes with the trees."

"Will you be accompanying Hope through the portal?" Obie asked.

"The portal?" Verity looked from Obie to Hope.

"Here, I am the Wood Listener," said Hope. "There, I attend school. I'm a junior at Whingham Academy."

Verity's brows furrowed. "I do not understand."

"The world is a different place on the other side of the portal," she explained. "I am just a girl trying to get through high school with minimal detentions. No one there knows anything about portals or even a world elsewhere. Well, besides family. I come back on weekends and for the summer."

Verity scratched the side of her neck before saying, "Word will spread about you. You will get requests. People will ask for things. Some, you can grant. Others, you cannot. From what I understand, that is why many of your predecessors never spent long in one place. That and because people never quite understood the true magic of the Wood Listener. It was looked upon as just another magical title, such as Mage or Enchantress." She took a breath. "Since you are not recognized for who you are over there, then there is no need for me to accompany you through the portal. The best way I can Tend to you is to be here. I can receive your requests and organize them for you until you return."

"I would like that a lot," said Hope. "Use this room however you see fit, if that's okay with you, Obie."

"Fine with me," Obie answered. "Stay vigilant, Verity. There are people after Hope. I would hate for anything to happen to you. I must go with Hope. Perhaps you can ask to use the Receiving Room as an intermediary."

"I will consider that, Lieutenant. Thank you," said Verity.

"You can call me Obie," he said. "I'm sure we will be leaving as soon as Alina says Mike can go home. She'll check him tonight or early tomorrow."

When they finished dinner, Obie poured himself a glass of spiced whisky. He offered some to Hope and Verity; both declined. "I'm going to bed," said Hope. "I have a feeling we're going to have an early portal crossing."

"Is it difficult?" asked Verity. "Crossing the portal, I mean."

"No. Two steps and you're on the other side," she answered. "There is a time difference though, and I have tons of schoolwork to do."

Waking early, Hope packed before breakfast in the Reception Room. She introduced Verity then noticed Alina sitting at the table next to Mike. "How's your patient?" she asked her friend.

She thought she saw Alina blush. "Doing really well. Completely healed from the attack."

Smiling, Hope let out a breath. "Good. Looks like it's back to school."

Mike stared at his plate. "Do you think my grandfather would get upset if I spent the summer here before college?" he said.

"What would you tell your dad?" asked Hope.

"I haven't thought it through yet," he admitted. "Being here has given me some focus. I know what I want to do with my life." He smiled.

"Mike, are you ready?" Silvia asked.

"I just have to grab the bag Grandpa brought," he said.

"Bring it to Hope's chambers. Berty and I will take you home," she said.

Mike nodded then whispered, "Where are Hope's chambers?"

"I'll show you," said Alina.

Hope watched the somewhat exchange of smiles and looks between her friends. "Let's go," Obie said in her ear.

In their shared chambers, Hope and Obie placed their bags near their bedroom doors. When Hope's parents and sister entered, Lily said, "Why does Hope have a portal and not me?"

"One portal per family," said Jon. "Your chambers are right next to hers."

"I know, but there should be another one," Lily argued. "Be easier."

Hope silently agreed. Once Mike arrived, Alina said good-bye to everyone. "Lily, who would you like to bring through the portal? Mike or Obie?" Hope asked.

Smiling, Lily said, "Obie."

Obie extended his hand to Lily. "Shall we?" She placed her small hand in his before climbing the steps.

When her parents followed, Hope said, "My bag is upstairs." Mike ascended behind her.

"They disappeared," said Mike as Hope grabbed her bag.

"So will we," she said. "Take my hand. Only my family and I are authorized to use the portal by ourselves." His hand wrapped around hers. "No crushing my hand."

"Sorry."

She pulled him through the tapestry. They stepped into a wood paneled hallway.

"Where are we?" asked Mike.

"My uncle's house." She dropped his hand.

Mike turned to look at the tapestry behind them. "That was officially cool."

Berty chuckled. He stood in the hallway wearing modern clothes. "Time to go home," he said. He led them downstairs and into the kitchen.

While they exited through the kitchen door to the cars, Hope said to Mike, "Talk to Uncle Berty and Aunt Silvia about how you can visit this summer. It'll be fun."

"I will." Mike got into the back of Berty's sedan.

Hope put her bag in the trunk of her parent's car then sat behind her father. Lily sat between her and Obie. No one said much of anything during the forty-five minute drive home. Once Jon pulled into the garage, Teresa said, "Obie, you're in the guest bedroom upstairs. Girls, unpack then bring your schoolwork into the kitchen."

After retrieving a week's worth of assignments from the emails, Hope and Lily sprawled their books, notebooks, folders, and papers on either end of the dining table. "Okay," said Jon, "let's see what we've got."

After perusing Hope's schoolwork, Jon said, "You do your English. I'll do your physics. Mom will do your history. And either Uncle Matt or Grandpa Robert will do your trig." A weight lifted from Hope while her father delegated Lily's work.

When Matt and Julie arrived, Matt started Hope's trigonometry while Obie spent time with his aunt and young cousins. Robert and Lillian brought groceries. After stocking the fridge and pantry, they helped Lily with her work.

Hours later, most of the schoolwork was finished and Jon called for pizza. After two slices of pepperoni and mushroom, Hope returned to copying the work her family finished for her. Obie sat at the table with her, holding a plate of two more slices. "Pizza is a plus for this side of the portal," he said. "School stuff, not so great. I don't understand why your books make it so complicated. This physics," he pointed to some papers, "you calculate all this in your head and then some when you shoot an arrow or launch a spear."

"I know. But if you don't do it this way, they'll mark you down," said Hope.

Shrugging, he bit into his pizza. "Is there anything I can do to help?" he asked after swallowing.

"Give me a little time to finish this. Then you can help me load it all into my backpack," she said.

He placed a hand on her shoulder as he walked away.

Her hands ached from her wrists to her fingertips. Hope typed the last bit of her schoolwork. Lily finished before her and watched tv with their cousins. Being able to close her laptop gave her a sense of accomplishment. She slumped in the dining room chair. Obie entered. Without saying a word, he closed and stacked her books while she organized her papers into the correct folders.

"I can't believe I have to go to school tomorrow," she said, zipping her crammed backpack. "It's going to drag. I am so not ready."

"Your mom and Aunt Julie are taking me clothes shopping tomorrow," Obie said.

Hope laughed.

Matt poked his head into the room. "We gotta get going," he said.

"Thanks for everything, Uncle Matt," said Hope. "I couldn't have done it without you."

"Sure you could, just not as quickly," he said with a wink.

They walked into the foyer where Julie gave hugs. "We'll be over next weekend," she said. "I want to check out that new bow Vander made," she told Hope.

"I'm sorry about what happened—" Hope began.

"Don't be," Julie stopped her. "Things happen. Life happens. It's only a piece of wood. It would need to be replaced eventually. Only magical bows can withstand normal damage and transcend replacement. And I only know of one such bow. Okay?"

When Hope nodded, Julie hugged her.

At the front door, Hope stood with her parents, sister, and Obie while the two cars backed out of their driveway. "Do you want turkey or ham tomorrow, girls?" asked Teresa, closing the door.

"Turkey or ham?" asked Hope.

"Sandwich. For lunch," Teresa clarified. "Neither of you are buying things at school anymore. Not even from the vending machines."

"Mom, no one at school is going to poison me."

"You can't be too careful," said Teresa. "Until we find out who marked your bow, lunch is in a brown bag."

Hope knew her mother was right.

"Your grandparents brought turkey and ham. What do you want?"

"Sure," said Hope.

"Ham," said Lily.

Upstairs, Hope got ready for bed. She plucked a white button down shirt from her closet then hung its hanger on a nail in the wall. "Laying out your clothes for tomorrow?" Obie asked from the doorway.

"Yeah. I've decided to wear a white shirt rather than a blue one with my uniform skirt tomorrow," she said.

He stepped into her bedroom. "We never got a chance to talk about the Dominatrix," he said.

"Oh," said Hope. Opening a drawer, she beckoned Obie over to the dresser.

His fingers felt the bark material. "Wow," he said. "What does it do?"

"We're not sure exactly," she answered. "I'd like to try some stuff—ideally with Uncle Declan monitoring, but I need to feel my way around this new magic. I'm not... I don't know its—*my*—limitations."

"Well, if I can help in anyway, you know where to find me. Goodnight, Hope."

"Goodnight."

Jon stood in the hall behind Obie. "Do you need a reminder about how to use the lights, Obie?" he asked.

"That would be helpful. Thanks, Mister Chase." He and Jon strode to his room.

Rain slapped the window in rhythm with her alarm. After smacking the button, the buzzing stopped, but the rain continued. She groaned. Then, she remembered Obie came back with them. She got up to get ready.

As usual, Hope entered the kitchen for breakfast last. While she poured cereal into a bowl, a spoon clanged onto the table. She glanced towards the table to see Obie wiping his chin with his napkin. Before Hope sat with her sister and Obie, Jon filled his travel mug with coffee. "See you girls later. Have a good day," he said.

"Bye, Dad," said Hope and Lily.

"Lily, put yours and Obie's bowls in the dishwasher," said Teresa.

After scarfing down cereal, Hope slipped on her raincoat. Teresa handed Obie a coat from the closet. "You can borrow one of Jon's," her mother said. "It fits well enough."

During the car ride to school, Hope placed her hand on the hilt of her sheathed dagger that she concealed under her skirt. She hoped no one at school noticed it. For the first time, she wished they wore blazers like some of their rival schools. She watched the windshield wipers as if she watched a tennis match from the back row. Why she felt the need to bring the dagger to school baffled her. She stared at the back of Obie's blond head. The dagger gave her a protection beyond her bow—an added protection, one no one knew.

Teresa dropped them off under the portico with the other students who did not take the buses. They waved before walking inside the school's double wooden doors. Lily turned down the hall that led to her classroom. Hope strode to the less extravagant hallways that housed the lockers.

"So, it seems that I'm popular this morning," said Mike's voice.

Hope stacked books she did not need in her locker. "And you came to see me. I'm so honored."

"My dad didn't let me drive to school today," Mike said. "He's concerned about me fencing after school. Thinks it might be too strenuous. Grandpa convinced him to let me fence. My dad's talking to them about how I'm recovering and to keep an eye on me."

"You went through a lot. Let him worry about you," Hope said, closing her locker.

"How's Obie adjusting to being here?" he asked. They walked down the halls to morning assembly in the auditorium.

"It's not like he's never spent time here before," she said.

"But he hasn't been here in years."

"Well, he's going to have to find something to do while I'm at school," she said. "Without having to drive."

Mike said nothing for a few strides. "Would you... Do you think... I could come over sometime? Just hang out?"

She nodded. "Yeah."

"Great." He smiled. "Later." They separated to sit in their respective sections of the auditorium.

At lunch, Issy plunked her tray on the table and took the seat next to Hope. "Okay," said Issy, "you have been so busy talking with teachers about your missed assignments that none of us have gotten any answers." Hope rolled her eyes. "So, how did Mike end up on your camping trip? And a bear? Super scary? How did you get away? Are you and Mike dating? And did you hear about Rosalind and Mister Wilde?"

"I heard Mike almost lost an arm," said some girl sitting down the table from them.

"An arm? He almost lost his life," Hope said. Other tables around her quieted. She kicked herself for saying anything. However, she had to continue. "The bear came out of nowhere. It clawed Mike. I shot it a few times with my bow before good-bye bow. Luckily, we weren't alone out there and was able to get Mike emergency help. Yes, very scary. I don't really want to talk about it anymore. So, if you guys don't mind...." People resumed eating and their own conversations.

"So," Issy said in almost a whisper, "are you two a thing now?"

"Wait, what's this about Rosalind?" Hope asked.

Issy's eyes sparkled in anticipation of sharing gossip. "Oh. My. God," she began. She yammered about a rumored affair between Rosalind and Mr. Wilde until lunch ended.

Hope heard whispers of the bear story she told at lunch in her last classes of the day. As she collected her coat from her locker before archery practice, a shove in her back threw her into her opened locker. Pulling her out, Mike said, "I think Rosalind's upset the rumors about you and you know who have transferred to her."

"Great," she said in a flat voice. "Now, I have to keep a bunch of targets between us *and* watch my back."

"The price of your reputation," said Mike. He accompanied her down the hall to the locker rooms. "Go have fun out in the mud. At least the rain stopped."

Hope shook her head then entered the girl's locker room.

Near the archery targets, Rosalind scowled at her while Mr. Wilde discussed their next competition. After telling the club members to take their targets, Mr. Wilde made the rounds. "Nice shooting, Hope," he said. He walked past to spend more time with the newer members.

Hitting the target freed her. The breeze carried that after rain clean smell mingled with damp earth, tree buds, and distant blossoms. Through the parting clouds, the sun beat on her back. She removed her jacket.

"Last shot," announced Mr. Wilde. Once the last arrow thudded its target, he called, "No more shots. Collect your arrows."

Hope took time to grab her jacket off the grass and tie it around her waist. She did not move towards the targets until Rosalind did. As Hope sorted her reusable arrows from the bad, Mr. Wilde approached. "Is everything okay?" he asked. She nodded. "I see you got a new bow. I can try to change the registration to your compound bow, but the competition registration deadline has passed. You may not be able to compete."

"That's okay."

"If you had your old bow," he began.

"It's beyond repair, Mister Wilde," Hope said. "I tried, but," she shook her head.

"They took it from you," he said in a quiet, almost threatening tone.

"What?" Hope shuffled back. "It's unusable. The attack—"

He stepped forward. "You and I both know there was no bear."

"I don't know what you're talking about," she said. Mr. Wilde's kind eyes turned cold. Her feet moved her away from him, but he kept advancing.

"Don't play with me."

Instinctively, she lifted her bow. Mr. Wilde caught her hand, squeezing it until the bow dropped. "Ow!" she screamed. Her magic reached for the nearest tree. It hit a barricade.

"You don't think I'm going to let you use your regained magic," he said.

"What do you want?" she asked. Her feet could feel the tree roots through the ground as she attempted to pull out of his grasp.

Mr. Wilde licked his lips. "Why, you, my dear." He yanked her hand until inches separated them. "You're my prize," he breathed.

"No!" She wrestled to get free. His fingers dug into her hand and wrist harder and deeper. Her other hand gripped the hilt of her dagger. She tried to stomp on his feet, but they proved elusive. His knees blocked her legs from kicking or kneeing him in sensitive areas. Her back slammed against a wooden target. His body pressed into hers. She wriggled her hand between them. They tumbled to the wet ground. He landed on top of her. She pushed against his crushing weight, but he would not move. His shoulder blocked the sky and muffled her cries. Warmth spread along her abdomen. She pushed harder, screaming, praying someone would hear.

The ground vibrated with the thunder of horse hooves. "Hope?" cried Obie. Mr. Wilde rolled off of her. Fresh air found her. "Hope, are you okay?" Obie's face hovered above hers.

"Mister Wilde—"

"He's dead."

Shuddering, she raised her head off the ground.

"Don't move," said Obie. He knelt beside her. "Are you hurt? Is that your...?"

"My left hand... he crushed it," she said. Her eyes examined without moving her head too much. Wet scarlet pooled on her gray t-shirt. "The dagger. I must have—"

"Hope!" screamed Teresa. Her mother and a few others ran across the fields while Obie continued his examination of her.

"Mom," said Hope. Teresa stroked Hope's head. "He tried—"

"Did he hurt you?"

"Other than my hand..."

Obie helped her to her feet. "Can you stand?" he said.

She nodded. One of the teachers spoke quietly on her phone. Others held curious students at bay. Merely feet away, the form of Mr. Wilde laid still. No light shone in his eyes. A strange expression froze on his face. A red glint caught her eye. Her dagger stuck out of his abdomen. Blood dried on the hilt. She glimpsed at her right hand. Blood stained halfway down her forearm. His blood. Black danced in front of her eyes. Her legs gave way. Her arms flapped for balance. Distance voices swarmed around her.

"I got you. Stay with me, Hope."

"Don't. No teacher will touch my daughter. Chandra, take Obie to the locker room. Let's get her cleaned up. Mike, go to Lily. Stay with her."

"Male coming in! Anyone here?"

"Sit on the bench, Hope."

"Empty out the locker. Lock and all."

"Will do, Missus Chase. Hope, what's your combination?"

"Hope, can you answer?"

"The combination, Hope."

"Five, thirty-two, sixteen," Hope answered.

"No. That's not it, Hope."

"Twenty-seven, eight, eleven," Hope said.

"There we go."

"Let's get this blood soaked shirt off. Hope, lift your arms."

"Eeeew. She's covered. How come there's so much?"

"Hopefully, it's not hers. Just gravity."

Water ran somewhere.

"Here you go. Wet and dry."

"Going to need more wet ones." Gentleness rubbed her torso, then her hand, and, finally, her arm. "Did I get it all? Is there any elsewhere? Any more on other clothing?"

"Um, no. All good."

"Okay, Hope, time to put your shirt on. You have to work with me here. Chandra, is it? Can you do the buttons? I'll get everything in her bag."

Dark skin and hair came into focus. "Thanks, Chandra," said Hope. "Can't feel my fingers right now."

"I was talking with RJ when we saw you struggling," Chandra said while buttoning. "RJ rode his horse to the building to get help."

"Tell him thank you for me."

151

Chandra flashed a smile.

"For me, too," said Obie. "I borrowed his horse." Hope looked into his blue eyes. "Glad you could join us, Hope." He smiled at her. "I have everything. Did you want to wear your coat?"

Hope shook her head. He folded it then stuffed it into her bag. "Don't forget the lock," said Chandra. She handed it to Obie, who tucked it into one of the outside zippered pockets. Chandra quickly retrieved her bags from her nearby locker.

"Do you need help standing?" Obie asked Hope.

"Where's my bow?" she asked

"Your mom gave it to Mike," said Obie. He helped her to her feet. She tried to take either her book bag or her gym bag from Obie, but he refused.

In the hallway, Teresa and Jon spoke with a diminutive woman. "Hope," said Jon. He tried to put a protective arm around his daughter, but Hope pulled away. His face filled with concern. He turned to Obie. While they conversed, a police officer handed the woman a bag. Through the transparent plastic, Hope noticed the blood stained dagger.

Her legs wobbled. The hall swayed or maybe she swayed. Her father steadied her. "Daddy," she said. Hot tears fell. Her mother stood at her other side. "Mommy," escaped her lips. Her body convulsed as sobbing conquered her. A hand brought a tissue to her nose.

When she could see again, she and her parents sat in a comfortable room—the teacher's lounge. The woman, who Hope assumed was with the police, held a box of tissues towards her. Taking a few, Hope wiped her eyes and cheeks then blew her nose.

"I'm Detective DiValderi," the woman said. "I know it's going to be difficult, but when you're ready, I want you tell me what happened."

Hope nodded then blew her nose again. "Archery practice just ended," she said. "Mister," her mouth tried to say his name, but nothing came out. "He started talking to me about the upcoming competition because I got a new bow."

"When you say, 'he,' you mean August Wilde?" the detective asked.

"Yes," said Hope. "He... The subject changed. He... I... I was so scared. He grabbed me." She rubbed her left hand.

"On your hand there?"

"Yeah. Made me drop my bow. He wouldn't let go. I couldn't...." Her lips quivered. "He... He... He wouldn't get off." Tears welled.

"Where did the blade come from?" she asked.

"Obie gave it to me for extra protection."

"Who's Obie?"

"He's in the military. First Lieutenant and field medic," said Jon. "They're childhood friends."

DiValderi nodded.

"I've been carrying it with me ever since the attack," Hope said.

"The bear in the woods," DiValderi said.

Hope gave her a slight nod.

"What did he do when you pulled the blade?"

Hope looked at the floor for answers. "I don't know." Her hands shook as if she were trying to shake something off. "He was," her voice cracked. She tried to control her breathing. Her arms crossed her torso. "I couldn't move." She tugged at the hem of her skirt. "He held on so tight." The room blurred. Her body shook. "He wouldn't get off me." Her head fell to her knees as she cried.

"Oh, Hope," said Teresa. A gentle hand rubbed her back.

"My God," said DiValderi. "Take her home. I'll be in touch."

After a few more tissues, her parents steered her to the parking lot. Obie and Mike leaned against Teresa's car while Lily sat in the backseat with the door open. "Did you get everything?" Teresa asked them.

"Everything," answered Mike. His brown eyes found Hope's. He held her bow out to her. "Quiver is in the backseat."

She gave him a little nod.

Once Hope got in the car, Jon said, "See you at home."

Chapter Eleven

Night Mara

Silence filled the car. Hope stared out the window; the world passed as a blur. After a shower, she parked in front of the television. Someone brought her dinner. She chewed without tasting any food. Her hands barely registered the weight of the warm plate. She could not feel her fingers hold the fork. Images on the tv screen danced without her eyes knowing what they saw. Someone suggested she go to bed. In bed, she turned, trying to get comfortable. She threw off her comforter. Its weight constricted.

Screaming cut the darkness. Lights turned on. A chorus of voices called her name. Still, she screamed. Two pairs of brown eyes and a pair of blue surrounded her.

"It's okay, Hope. You're home. You're safe," the voices said.

She saw her bed on which she sat. The screaming stopped. After blinking, her mom, dad, and Obie came into view around her bed. Her room had not changed. No blood soaked anything. All she remembered from her dream was blood, blood everywhere, covering everything. "Bad dream," she mumbled. Escaping tears fell to her lap.

"Want some hot tea to help you sleep?" asked Obie.

She wiped her face. "I'm okay. My hand hurts."

"Let me see." When he touched her hand, his magic consoled hers. Her magic hugged his. Obie looked into her eyes, then breathed. "I don't see any bruising, but that doesn't mean bruises won't develop over the next day or so. Did you want something for the pain?"

She shook her head. "I'm so tired."

Teresa brushed hair out of Hope's face. "Lay back down, honey. If you need anything, you just let us know. Okay?"

Hope nodded.

"Do you want to keep a lamp on?" Jon asked.

She nodded again, sucking her lips into her mouth.

Jon turned on a lamp on her dresser then switched off the overhead light.

Hope said nothing while watching the three of them leave her in her bed. She turned on her side, falling asleep quickly. In her dreams, she felt the dagger plunge into Mr. Wilde as if it were an extension of her hand. She sliced through flesh and muscle, cut things she would rather not know, and scraped bone. Warm blood streamed over her.

She woke. Only the dresser lamp held back the darkness. Her clock said it was morning, although the sky did not agree. Birds chirped somewhere beyond her window. Sitting up, she still felt the blood bathed blade in her hand. Tears washed her cheeks.

Sounds of movement down the hall told her someone else in the house was awake. She quickly wiped her face then tiptoed to the bathroom. Cool water helped reduce the puffiness around her eyes. Returning to her room, she stared at her bed. It did not welcome her back. Slowly, she performed her morning routine.

Dressed in comfy, old sweats, she wandered downstairs. The sky lightened at the horizon. The early morning light gave the house a bluish cast. She peeked into the empty rooms as she moseyed to the family room. Plopping on the couch, she needed a reprieve from her head. She flipped through the channels on the television, watching not much of anything. Her thumb pressing the button on the remote satisfied her in some strange way.

"Hey," said Obie, striding towards the couch. "How are you doing?"

She shrugged.

Sitting next to her, he said, "It'll get better. Your mom made pancakes. Want to come and eat?"

She shrugged again.

"Come eat anyway. Eating helps," he said.

Her thumb smushed the power button on the remote. The tv screen turned black. She stared at it for a second then stood.

In the kitchen, pancakes stacked on a platter in the center of the table. Little sausages sat on a plate beside them. A plastic jug of maple syrup rested on the other side. Mugs of coffee steamed to the right of the plates. "Smells delicious. I'm so hungry," Jon said to Teresa. Hope inhaled through her nose. She smelled nothing.

While everyone around her devoured their pancakes with a knife and fork, Hope tore a soft chunk off the top pancake then dipped it into maple syrup. She barely tasted the sweet fluffiness before forcing her throat to swallow. The coffee was hot. The sausage was... sausage. After washing down three pancakes and one and a half sausages with coffee, she rose to leave.

"Sit down for a minute," said Teresa. Hope sat. "You two are not out of school today because of what happened yesterday. Neither of you will be going back to that school. In fact, your father and I discussed at length last night not sending you to any school."

"No more school, like ever?" asked Lily. A wistful smile crept on her face.

"No more going to *a* school," said Jon. "You and Hope will be homeschooled. You'll learn everything you need to know and then some. We'll go on our own fieldtrips to the museums, planetarium, forts, historical buildings, wherever. And you can spend more time on the other side of the portal developing your magic."

Lily raised her arms in the air. "Yea!"

"Hope, you haven't said anything," said Teresa.

Hope shrugged. She got up to return to channel surfing.

At some point, Obie sat on the couch with her. "How's the hand?" he asked.

She looked down. She had no idea she rubbed her hand where Mr. Wilde squeezed it. Shrugging, she held it out to show him.

"There's a little swelling," he said. "Stop rubbing it. Would you like something for the pain?"

Again, she shrugged.

"I'll be back."

When he returned, he held out a glass of water and two white pills. "For the swelling," he said.

Like an obedient robot, she swallowed the chalky pills with help from the water. She handed the empty glass back to Obie.

"Want to go for a walk outside?" he asked.

Without looking away from the tv, she vehemently shook her head.

"Didn't think you'd want to."

She looked at him.

"Talk to me, Hope," he said, sitting on the couch.

Facing the television, she finally said, "Flashes of what happened and of my dreams, which are so much worse, are right there—seeping in. I need a distraction to not think of... those things. Tv distracts me."

Hope let Obie take her hand in his. He watched whatever played on the television.

"Hope," said her mother.

She decided to look at her mother standing next to the coffee table.

"Grandma and Grandpa are here. Dad and I are going to Silverman, Silverman, and Trane's offices," Teresa said. Hope dropped Obie's hand. "Lawrence said that he didn't need to see you yet."

"They're not those types of lawyers," said Hope.

"No. Lawrence will talk with the police first. If it comes to that, he will recommend an excellent lawyer."

Hope chewed her thumbnail while saying, "I don't wanna go to jail, Mommy."

Rushing to her daughter's side, Teresa said, "You won't. You did nothing wrong." She gave Hope a hug. "Defending yourself is never wrong. Okay?" She held Hope at arm's length, looking in her eyes. Hope nodded. "Good. We'll see you in a little while."

Between tv movies, Lillian joined Hope on the couch. "It's time we played some games," she said. "Lily and Grandpa are setting one

up in the basement. A little fun will help you forget all about...
anything. What do you say?"

For the first time since breakfast, Hope turned off the television.

In the carpeted portion of the basement, the five of them played
board games. Hope laughed a little. All good feelings died when Jon
and Teresa came down the basement steps.

"Are they going to arrest me? Am I going to jail?" Hope asked
immediately.

"No," said Jon. "You will not be charged with anything. Lawrence will be getting that in writing from the District Attorney and
bring it over tomorrow."

Her hands caught her head. She laughed and cried before lifting
her head. "I was so worried. I... I killed a man." Her tear ducts
filled again. "I feel so—I can't explain it—yucky." The welled tears
flowed freely. Teresa hugged her as they rocked. Lily hugged her
other side.

Her grandparents stayed for dinner. Afterwards, she finally replied
to Mike's texts. "Sorry, I didn't get back to you sooner," she wrote.
"I've been... Anyway, I'm not being charged, so that's good. It
doesn't stop me from seeing it over and over. But thanks for the well
wishes."

Mike responded only a minute later. "That's okay. Target practice releasing anything for you?"

"Can't," Hope wrote. "My hand was crushed. Hurts too much
to hold anything. Sigh."

":(," replied Mike. "They suspended all after school activities until
further notice. Mind if I come over tomorrow?"

"Not at all."

"Great. See you tomorrow."

Hope stared at Issy's and Chandra's texts asking her how she was. She decided to ignore them for another day.

Changing into her pajamas sent pain shooting through her hand. The simple task of closing her hand around woven cotton hurt. The aspirin Obie made her take every four hours kept only the resting pain at bay. She pulled the covers over her with her right hand while positioning her left hand on the bed where it would hurt the least.

The lamp on her dresser cast weird shadows across her room. She preferred to sleep with it off, but she switched it on just in case.

Birds chirped their merry songs as she meandered through the forest. Sunlight dotted the underbrush. Bright spring green leaves danced in the cool breeze. Inhaling deeply, she could taste the nectar in the spring forest blooms. She smiled.

Run popped into her head. *Run. Run. Run. Run. Run. Run. Run.* Her bare feet shook out of their leisurely stroll as her legs moved quicker.

Her heart pounded in her ears. *Faster.* She sprinted. *He's coming.* Turning her head slightly, she glanced at Mr. Wilde chasing her.

"You can't get away from me," he taunted with a laugh. "I will get you."

Hope kept running. When she peeked behind her, she no longer saw him. Her legs began to tire, but she would not stop.

Hitting an invisible barrier, she bounced to the ground. Mr. Wilde's face blocked the sunlight. "Got you," he breathed. His body constrained hers.

"No," she said, struggling with him. The more she wrestled, the tighter he held. She wriggled. He repositioned.

They tumbled. She felt airborne for a fleeting moment. They crashed into something hard. He grasped her more firmly.

"Hope!" said a voice. Other voices repeated her name. "Hope, wake up!"

She opened her eyes. Her blanket and sheet tangled around her. She sat up. Three faces watched her. Little footsteps entered her room. Lily stood next to her kneeling mother. "Whatcha doing on the floor?" Lily asked Hope.

Hope glanced at the mattress beside her head. "I must have fallen off the bed," she answered.

"Do you need help getting up?" Obie asked.

She shook her head.

Unwrapping herself from the covers, she stood. "Do you want some help remaking your bed?" her mother asked.

Hope glared at the pile of sheet and blanket lying benign on the floor. "I think they should stay there," she said.

"How about a blanket from the closet?" Teresa asked.

"I don't want anything over me." Hope sat on her bed.

Obie looked her in the eyes before giving her a nod. He then returned to his room. Her parents and sister left as well.

Hope curled into a ball with the pillow to fall back to sleep. A few hours later, she woke, shivering. She peered over the side of her bed at the heap of blanket and sheet still on the floor. After shuddering a couple of times, she decided it was time to get up. A shower would warm her.

Her father pressed the on button on the coffee maker when she entered the kitchen. "Can't sleep?" he asked her.

"My back hurts from hitting the floor," she said. She noticed his suit. "Going to work early?"

"I won't be gone long," said Jon. "Do you want to talk about your dream?"

Hope filled a bowl with some cereal. "Not really. He was in it." Picking up the bowl with her left hand, she let it slip onto the counter with a grunt of pain. "I keep forgetting my hand hurts," she said. "Must use right hand." After pouring milk, she carried her bowl to the table.

Jon poured her a mug of coffee before he filled his travel mug. "Mom will be down soon. I'll be home before you know it." He kissed her on the head.

"Bye, Daddy."

Halfway through her cereal, Obie entered the kitchen. He smiled at her, then unsuccessfully stifled a yawn. With a mug of coffee, he sat with Hope. "How are you doing?"

"My hand really hurts."

He held out a hand for hers. Once she stretched her arm across the table, he turned it at different angles. "Looks like it's starting to bruise," he said.

"What is?" asked Teresa, coming into the kitchen.

"My hand."

"We'll get it looked at when Dad gets home," said Teresa.

Hope spent the rest of the early morning helping around the house, wincing when she used her hand too often. While she placed clean clothes in her drawers and closet, she heard the garage door open. Soon after, the doorbell rang. Lily stood in Hope's doorway. "You're needed in the living room," she said.

In their rarely used living room, Hope saw the two people she did not want to see together—the detective and her family's lawyer.

"It's okay," said the deep voice of Lawrence Trane. He stood next to the couch in a three-piece suit. "Have a seat. Detective DiValderi wants to talk about the school."

When she sat on the couch, so did he. Her mother and father sat on chairs in the corners of the room while Detective DiValderi sat directly across from Hope.

"First off," said DiValderi, "you have to sign the papers that state that no charges against you will be filed for the death of August Wilde. There is no question that it was self-defense." Her dark eyes surveyed everyone in the room. "Next, the DA wants to charge the Whingham Academy for negligence and child endangerment."

"Would I have to testify? Hope asked.

"No," answered Lawrence. "Not unless you want to. The statement you gave the police would be read in court in lieu of your appearance. It would reflect poorly on the state to force a minor to relive a horrifying experience, especially when she has been traumatized by said experience and shows signs of Post Traumatic Stress Disorder."

"We're not in a courtroom, Mister Trane," said DiValderi. "Believe it or not, I'm on Miss Chase's side."

"I believe you," he said, "but your reasons for doing so might be because you're a homicide detective who has been known to get physically ill at the sight of the dead bodies you investigate."

"That doesn't make me a poor detective, just a queasy one. I get results," she retorted.

"I know you do. You did even before you moved to homicide."

The Detective tapped her pen on her notebook. "Okay, Miss Chase, just to let you know, I've been assigned to this case because I was the first detective on the scene and I have worked in departments other than homicide. I would like to discuss any other of August Wilde's targets or of any faculty, current or previous, who may have abused their position with the students."

"Um." She tried to remember school. "There was a rumor that Missus Swain was having an affair with Ron Petrazelli who graduated two years ago," Hope said. "And, uh, there's talk that Missus Hereford, the chemistry teacher, sells an ecstasy type drug that she makes to some of the students." Her mother gasped. "Mister Davies always gives off this creepy, trying to look up your uniform skirt vibe whenever you walk by him. Um, for anything else, you'd have to talk to Issy. She knows more gossip and rumors than I do."

"Okay," said the Detective. "I have to ask these next few questions."

Hope nodded for her to continue. She rubbed her hand, then remembered that Obie told her not to rub it.

"That's a nasty bruise on your hand. August Wilde's handiwork?"

Hope looked at her hand. The dark, ugly colors splotched the back, side, and palm of her left hand. "He squeezed it when I tried to fend him off with my bow."

"She has an appointment with the doctor this afternoon," said Teresa.

"We would like a copy of the doctor's report for our case," said DiValderi, "if you don't mind."

"I'll make sure the police get a copy," said Lawrence.

The detective gave the lawyer a firm nod before continuing her interrogation. "Had August Wilde ever attempted to touch you inappropriately or had he touched you inappropriately?"

"No."

"Had he ever suggested a relationship with you beyond the confines of teacher-student?"

"No."

"Did he ever comment about your body or physical appearance?"

Hope hesitated, but never took her eyes off the detective. "Only when it involved archery. Complimenting my stance."

After jotting in her notebook, the woman asked, "Did he ever make you feel uncomfortable, like you wanted to get away from him—other than the day he attacked you?"

Hope's gaze moved to the carpet. The light green pile reminded her of grass. Grass covered the school's archery target area. She could remember times when Mr. Wilde got too close. "Yes," she said without looking up. "He would get very close, almost suffocatingly so. He never had to correct my hold or stance. There was no reason for him to be so close to me." She gave her parents a puzzled expression. When she returned her focus on Detective DiValderi, she said, "It always made me feel uncomfortable, but I didn't know what to do about it. Always after a minute or so, he would leave."

"And you would be relieved?" she asked.

Hope nodded.

"Why did you go back to Archery Club if he made you uncomfortable?"

"It's complicated," Hope answered.

"Try me."

"Ten years ago, when my parents were being held captive in Africa, someone tried to abduct me not far from my uncle's house where I was living at the time. Uncle Berty told the school that I was to keep my bow on me at all times for my protection. To justify this, they allowed me to join the Archery Club. He wasn't always the mentor. And I enjoyed winning competitions.

"He also encouraged me to do better. And told me that my only competition was myself. The times when he... were not that often. I never really worried about it beyond in that moment. I never thought that he'd," Hope did not finish the sentence.

"A witness heard August Wilde say that he wanted you. What can you tell me about that?" She gave Hope a soft look of understanding.

Hope's gaze rested in her lap to find her fingers fiddling with the hem of her shirt. "I hear it in my head," she answered in a low voice. She kept her head down. "He tells me that in my dreams—my nightmares. I don't know how to get rid of it." When she raised her head to look at Detective DiValderi, the promise of tears stung. She blinked.

No one said anything for a moment.

Detective DiValderi broke the silence. "Ask your doctor for a referral to talk to someone about those dreams, to make them stop. I know someone who does great work with veterans and cops, if you need someone," she said. "I have no more questions. Thank you for answering, Hope." She gave Hope a sad smile before standing.

Hope signed documents where Lawrence indicated. The detective took her copies then left.

"Do not worry about them prosecuting the school," said Lawrence. "We will keep you off the stand. It will take at least a month or two to build their case anyway." He said more to her parents, but she did not pay attention.

Soon after Lawrence left, the five of them drove to Hope's doctor appointment. Teresa accompanied her when a nurse called her into an examination room. After asking a series of questions, the nurse took pictures of the bruising. When the doctor came in, he sent her to the x-ray room.

She waited in the exam room for what felt like forever. The doctor returned with her x-rays. "The good news is that nothing is broken," he said. "But that is a nasty injury. It's going to take some time to heal. Don't compress it with a wrap or anything that could injure it further." He rolled over to the exam table on his stool. "You're not sleeping."

Hope shook her head. "Nightmares."

"I'll prescribe something for the pain and to reduce the inflammation," he said, scribbling on a pad. "Nightmares are common after traumatic experiences. Doctor Preston might be able to help. Her office is located on the fourth floor. I'll give her a call right now and see if she can squeeze you in for a consultation." The doctor left the room for five minutes. "She said to come right up. Her next appointment isn't for another half hour."

"Thanks, Doctor," said Teresa.

On the fourth floor, Hope entered Dr. Preston's office alone. The doctor smiled at her then asked her to sit. "Talk to me about what's going on with you, Hope," she said.

Hope gave an abbreviated version of the attack. Instead, she focused on her nightmares and her constant feeling of dread. "I can't seem to shake the feeling that he's there, peeking through the windows at me," Hope said. "I'm afraid that if I go outside, he'll grab me. I know he's dead, but he's very much alive in my dreams."

Dr. Preston leaned forward. "None of what has happened to you is your fault," she said. "You are not responsible for the actions of others. I am going to bring your parents in, and the four of us will discuss options."

Teresa and Jon flanked Hope on the leather couch.

"We can set up a weekly appointment," said the doctor. "Or if the nightmares become extremely intense, I can recommend a clinic where patients are monitored around the clock and counseling is available at any hour. There are drugs that may help her sleep without dreaming, but that won't help her get to the root of the problem or make her feel safe during her waking hours."

"I'd rather her not take any drugs," said Jon.

"No. I'll make sure you get some literature on clinics. Go home. Look them over and discuss what you want to do."

Cold drizzle fell as they left the doctor's office complex. They stopped at a pharmacy on the way home. After taking the medicine, Hope no longer felt the pain in her hand, nor did she feel much else.

Mike arrived at the end of the school day. "You look as miserable as outside," Hope said to him.

"Thanks," said Mike. He cocked his head, studying Hope. "Pain meds a bit strong? Obie, what did you give her?"

Hope led the guys to the family room. "Perskip, pre-crip, persiption," she said.

"Prescription," Mike corrected.

"Yeah. Couldn't say that." She plopped on the couch. "Whazzup, Mikey?"

"You, obviously," he muttered, sitting.

Hope sported a frown. "I'm fine," she said. She glanced at Obie who sat on the other side of her with his eyebrows raised. "Well, Obie's finer. What did you want to talk about?"

"A lawyer showed up at my house yesterday," Mike said.

Hope wanted to say that a lawyer showed up at her house today, but refrained.

"Divorce papers," Mike said. "My mother wants my dad to give her a divorce."

"What?" said Hope. "But I thought—"

"My mother was legally declared dead years ago," said Mike. "My dad told the lawyer that he had to produce proof of life first. Then, he slammed the door in his face."

"Mike," said Hope, placing her bruised hand on his arm.

Staring at her hand, he said, "Your hand looks awful."

"Don't mind it. How do you feel about this?"

"I think it's terribly convenient that after I turned eighteen, my mother seems to reappear," said Mike. "She doesn't have to bother with being a mother. My dad's furious. All those years ago, he hired a private investigator to find her. Do you know how long it took before the state could declare her dead? Anyway, I think he's been in touch with his lawyer today." He released a breath.

"Could your mom really be alive or is this some sort of scam?" Hope asked.

"I don't know. Grandma suggested a DNA test where the woman who claims to be my mother has to show up at the lab. I agree that it's the only real proof of life. But that means meeting her. Well, seeing her again if one counts being a toddler when she disappeared and not having any true memories of her. And if it is her, where has she been for the past fifteen years?"

Hope leaned across the couch to give Mike a hug. He had to catch her arm to stop her from falling. "If you need someone to talk to, you know where to find me," she said. "Unless, I had to go away to one of those clinics to deal with my nightmares and daymares."

Mike's eyebrows scrunched. He pushed her back to her seated position. His eyes darted between her and Obie. "Why though?" he asked. "Why attack you? Why then? I don't understand." He scratched the back of his head. "I better go. Need to check on my dad. I'll text you. Feel better soon, Hope."

After seeing him out, Obie said, "I don't like the way those pills affect you."

"I'll be fine," she said.

"You can't even walk straight." He took her by the arm to steady her. With a hand on her back, he steered her to a stool in the kitchen. She giggled as she tried to keep her balance.

Teresa paused from preparing dinner to watch her daughter. "That was nice of Mike to stop by," she said.

"His mom wants a divorce," Hope blurted. Hers and Obie's shoulders bumped.

Teresa stopped stirring. "What?"

Hope recounted Mike's story with help from Obie. She could not seem to remember all the details although he recently left.

"I'm calling the doctor's office in the morning. Those pills are much too strong," said Jon. He placed a stack of dinner plates on the counter.

"They work. Pain's all gone." Hope smiled.

Halfway through dinner, Hope set her fork on her plate. Churning in her stomach preceded cramps. Dinner did not want to digest. Her hand sprang over her mouth.

"Hope? What's wrong?" asked Teresa.

Not able to answer, she pushed her chair back then bolted to the bathroom. She lifted the toilet seat in time for her stomach to reverse everything she ate and then some. Once the dry heaves stopped, she noticed her mother standing beside her. Teresa washed Hope's face and made her swish water around in her mouth. Hope clutched the sides of the vanity to stop the vertigo after spitting out the water.

"Dizzy," Teresa said. She waved to someone behind them.

Strong hands grabbed her waist. "I got you," said Obie.

"I don't feel well," said Hope, collapsing against his chest.

He lifted her into his arms. "Let's sit her on the couch," said Teresa. "Jon, get some warm ginger ale."

As soon as Obie set her down, Teresa felt her forehead with the back of her hand. Jon brought her a fizzing glass, which she sipped while being watched. After giving the empty glass back to her father, she held her stomach and groaned.

"The rest of that medicine will be out of your system soon and you'll feel better," said Jon.

"My hand hurts," Hope whined. "And my tummy hurts. And I feel yucky." She rested her head against the back of the couch.

She blinked. Only Obie remained on the couch with her. He held her hand. "Where did everyone go?" she asked.

"Your dad is in the kitchen and your mom went upstairs with Lily," he said. "I told them I'd watch you while you slept."

"I slept?"

He smiled at her. "A dreamless sleep. You needed that."

Her fingers combed through her tangled waves. "Don't think I'm taking any more of those pain pills," she said. "Ow. Wrong hand." Pulling her hand out of her hair, she studied it with her tired eyes. "Is the bruising getting worse?" she asked Obie.

"It will get darker before it starts to fade," he said.

"I'm so tired." Her arm held her head off the couch.

"You haven't exactly been sleeping that much," he said. "A little weak tea before bed will do you good." He helped her off the couch.

Her parents joined them in the kitchen. They drank tea and talked about silly things. The queasiness left her. However, the lethargy remained. Barely able to keep her eyes open, she finished her tea then went to bed. She pulled the covers over her one handed seconds before drifting to sleep.

"Hope, you need protection," said her doll, Ashley, from her place on the dresser.

Sitting up in bed, Hope asked, "Protection from what?"

"It's coming," said the doll. Ashley's painted wooden lips moved as well as her painted wooden eyes.

"What is?"

Ashley stood. Pushing against the mirror, she ran to the edge of the dresser, then leapt. The doll landed on the bed. "The one who sent Wilde. The one who wants your magic," said the doll. "Get ready."

A wave of panic hit Hope. "No one can have my magic," she said.

Soft laughter filled her bedroom.

"A Mara," Ashley said softly. "Don't let it on your chest."

"I'm sitting up," said Hope.

A murky mist swirled past the lamp.

"No, Hope. You're sleeping," said Ashley. "This is a dream."

"But—"

"I'll protect your sleeping body the best I can."

The mist twisted into a solid form. When elongated, sharply pointed ears took shape, Hope gasped. She did not want to see the rest.

Gathering her magic, she said, "Get out."

A hunched back with a protruding spiked spine solidified.

Her magic wrapped around her, but she did not have her arrows to propel at the creature. And the police still had her dagger.

The Mara flexed long, claw-like fingers.

Hope wished Obie was with her. "Get out!" she yelled.

It flashed a grotesque smile.

Why could she not push magic like Obie? She shoved her right palm forward. The magic moved. She aimed for the Mara. "I said, GET OUT!" Screaming, she projected her magic.

Its yellow eyes widened with surprise. The smile dropped. The Mara evaporated.

She heard her name being called through a gauze.

"Good job, Hope," said Ashley. "Wake up now."

Hope sat up in bed, knocking something hard to the side. Her parents, sister, and Obie ran into her room. She looked at her blanket. Ashley lay on her bed. Not just a dream. Pulling her knees to her chest, she began to rock.

"Hope, what's wrong?" her mother asked in a frantic voice. She asked a couple of times before Hope looked at her.

"He knew," was all Hope managed to say over and over and over.

Chapter Twelve

Marked

"Who? Knew what?" Teresa asked.

"Mister Wilde knew about Hope's magic," said Lily.

Hope froze. Her eyes found her sister. She nodded.

Jon backed up to the door. "Berty. Berty, wake up," he said while walking into the hall.

"Put on your bark armor," said Obie.

"What? Why?" asked Hope.

"Trust me. Just wear it."

"What bark armor?" asked Teresa.

"From the Dominatrix," said Obie. "I'll leave the room." Lily walked out with Obie before he closed the door.

Her mother helped her change out of her pajamas. Once the shirt and pants connected, she felt as if she breathed for the first time in a long time. She wrapped a robe around the clinging clothing before opening the door.

"How'd you know?" she asked Obie who stood right outside. After failing to pull the gloves over her injured hand, she left them in the drawer.

"Hunch," he answered. "You said he knew." He leaned against her dresser. "He had to be the one who carved the symbol into your bow. Not all at once, but over time. You don't know what kind of magic he used against you before," he did not finish his thought.

Teresa gave Hope a squeeze.

Entering her room, Jon said, "They're coming over. I'll put some coffee on."

The kitchen clock said almost four in the morning. She downed a glass of water before the doorbell rang. The dream dried out her mouth. Actually, screaming her magic towards the Mara made her mouth and throat dry.

When Jon led Berty, Silvia, Declan, and Edwin into the kitchen, Hope asked, "Where's Mom?"

"Upstairs with Gerta," Jon answered. "Sorry about the bedroom, Obie, but Lily needs her Fairy Godmother here."

Obie nodded then helped Jon hand out coffee to everyone.

When Teresa joined them, she led them with their coffee to the dining room. Once they settled around the table, Silvia said, "Tell us everything."

For the first time, Hope recounted the attack in detail, what he said, what he did. "He blocked your magic?" Silvia asked.

"From reaching the trees. It was more of a barrier. I was able to reach the roots though. I tried to send Obie a message."

"I received it," said Obie. "We were on our way when I got it."

"And I raced to that school," said Teresa.

"This Wilde fellow had to be the one who carved your bow," said Declan.

"I concluded that as well, Uncle Declan," Obie said.

When pairs of eyes rested on her again, Hope continued, "I was so afraid to use too much magic. I didn't want anyone to see. How would you explain it?"

"Understandable," said Berty. "These dreams. Describe them for us."

"The first night, I was walking. Then, blood out of nowhere filled everywhere—no, more like flooding. It slowed my walking. Soon, it was waist high and I could barely move. It just kept rushing at me. I thought I was going to drown in it. The next night, he chased me through the woods. He put up his barrier again. When he caught me, we struggled. Tonight, a Mara visited. I somehow pushed magic at it. It vanished."

Berty gave her a look she did not recognize. Titling his head, he asked, "When did you start wearing the magical armor?"

"Just before you arrived. Obie strongly suggested I put it on. It made me feel better. Tonight's dream was way too real. Ashley warned me and…." She covered her face with her hands. Through her fingers, she saw Berty and Silvia exchange a glance.

"Why?" Berty asked Obie.

"It seemed right," Obie answered.

"But you could have made her a draught for a dreamless sleep," said Declan.

"Yes. However, Hope has been complaining about how her hand hurts. Every time I examine it… I know what Hope's magic feels like. Her hand area is off and it's been progressively getting worse as the bruise darkens. I've been thinking about it and I think Mister Wilde marked her."

"Explain," said Silvia.

"This mark is the bruise while usual marks on people are tattooed, branded, or otherwise drawn," he said. "I'm thinking that the mark will only last as long as the bruise does."

"When did you learn about marks?" asked Declan.

"While stationed at the outpost—the ancient Keep by the Dragon-lands. There's a room with old books. I'd read them from time to time. Well, the ones I could read. They're not all written in the common tongue."

"No library type room was ever reported being found at that outpost," said Edwin.

"It's there. I've been in it," said Obie. "Come to think of it, I've never seen anyone else there."

"You found it because you're a Warlock," said Silvia. "That's why the Griffins attack. Obie, you are taking us to the outpost. Hope, you must come as well."

Teresa agreed. "I think it's best for you to be on the other side," she said to her daughter. "You need to exercise your magic without the restraints of the modern world. Your father and I will take care of things on this side with school and the investigation."

"We need to be able to freely explore the Keep for as long as it takes," said Silvia.

"If we say it's a building inspection, no one will be the wiser, especially if we arrive with a Dwarf," suggested Edwin.

"What if we transferred everyone except essential personnel for a survey and repairs and reinforcement?" Obie said.

Edwin studied Obie for a moment. "Make a list of those staying, Lieutenant. Only Guards we can trust implicitly stay, regardless of rank." He turned to Berty. "Can we send that list now?"

"As soon as it's in my hand," said Berty.

"I'll write Otho a letter," said Edwin.

Jon gave both Edwin and Obie pens and paper. They sat on opposite ends of the kitchen table, writing.

"We'll take the portal in the woods. Have Hatcher open it for us," said Berty.

"While we're there, Delyth should construct a Fairy Ring around the Keep to protect against Griffins or other things," said Silvia. "We could use Colvin's expertise to find any other hidden rooms."

"What about Verity?" asked Hope.

Silvia sipped her coffee. Finally, she said, "She should join us. You should not separate while on that side of the portal." She asked Teresa, "Can you have them at the house no later than four this afternoon?"

"Absolutely."

"Retrieve anything from your chambers that you may need," Silvia told Hope.

When Obie and Edwin finished, Edwin gave the papers to Berty. Holding the papers, Berty's brown eyes unfocused as if he saw into nowhere. With a slight movement of his hand, the papers disappeared.

Hope returned to her bedroom after the others left. Standing at the foot of her bed, she stared at a lifeless Ashley partly covered with blanket. "What's on your mind?" asked Obie. She felt him standing behind her.

"In the dream, Ashley moved on her own. She jumped onto my

bed," she said. "When I woke, she was there, right next to me on the bed. Obie, I'm scared. I'm scared to sleep."

His hand rested on the small of her back.

"I don't think Edwin had a Mara in mind when he told me that I couldn't be alone even to sleep," she said.

"No," agreed Obie.

"Don't worry, Hope," said Jon.

She turned to see her father enter her room. "I'm scared, Daddy."

"I know. Start packing. We're heading to Berty and Silvia's as soon as we're ready," he said. "This house is not safe enough. You can wash and nap there."

Hope hugged Jon tightly. "Be ready soon," she said.

When she let go, Jon said to Obie, "Stay here while she packs and she'll go into the guest room with you while you pack. You are not to leave her side."

"Yes, Mister Chase."

The sun peeked over the horizon by the time both cars were packed. Obie and Hope rode with Jon while Teresa took Lily and Gerta. Once they drove into her uncle's driveway—crossing the property's protective boundary—Hope relaxed. Inside the house, Hope and Obie decided to gather their things from their chambers first.

Emerging from the tapestry caused Verity to jump. "Sorry," said Hope. "Didn't mean to scare you."

The Elf stood on the steps looking from them to the tapestry. "I wasn't expecting," she said. "I thought we were leaving later. I am not ready yet. The Empress just informed me."

"Don't worry," said Hope. "We're just picking up a few things. I want to be packed before I take a nap." She covered a yawn. "We'll be on the other side. I assume you'll be coming across with the others."

Verity nodded.

Hope gave her a smile while Obie entered his bedroom. She turned to enter hers.

"Wait."

Hope spun back into the hall.

"Does it hurt? Going through the portal?"

"Not at all. It's like parting a sheer curtain."

Verity released a breath. "One more question. Will we be returning here?"

"Absolutely," said Hope. "I don't know how long we'll be gone. Pack everything you think you'll need that'll fit into one bag. No horses on this trip. If you can't carry it, leave it here."

"Thank you," said Verity. "I'll be ready soon."

Hope collected traveling clothes from her wardrobe before she and Obie stepped back through the tapestry.

Her parents insisted they sleep in the bedroom with the twin beds—just in case. Hope finally slept without dreaming. A ding on her phone woke her later in the morning. Obie laid on the other bed with his eyes open. He watched her. "I'm fine," she said.

She checked her phone. Mike sent her a text: "Police crawling all over the school. They're sending us home now. Come over?"

"At Uncle Berty's," she sent back.

"Be there soon."

Placing her phone on the nightstand, she said, "Mike's coming over."

"Again?" he asked, rising from his bed.

Hope ignored the somewhat suspicious tone in his voice. "I'm going to take a shower so my hair dries before we leave," she said.

In the house's back sitting room, Obie glared at Mike who conversed with Teresa about the happenings at school. Hope tapped Obie on the shoulder. He gave her an innocent look. Teresa excused herself when Hope sat.

"No longer under the influence?" asked Mike.

"I, uh, had an adverse reaction to the medication last night," she said.

"I got swabbed very early this morning," Mike said. "Dad waited at the lab for the woman who says she is my mother. With his lawyer. I couldn't...." He looked around the room. "I've never been in this room before. So, they let us out early. Told the seniors today was our last day. Still won't graduate until June, but whatever."

"Mike, what's wrong?" asked Hope.

"What if my mother has been alive this entire time? What if she left because of me? Stayed away because of me?" Mike's jaw moved, but nothing else came out of his mouth. He sighed. "I can't go home. Not right now."

Pity washed over Obie's face. He stood. "Mike," he said, jerking his head to follow.

She trailed the two through the kitchen to the back porch. Obie disappeared into the garage for a moment. He returned with two practice swords. After throwing one to Mike, they began sparring. She sat on the porch to watch.

Mike showed good skills, although clearly not comfortable with the heavier sword. Obie seemed to hold back as if to keep the match even. The clanging of metal had a soothing rhythm.

The screen door opened. Silvia exited the kitchen with Mike's father. "Hello, Aunt Silvia, Mister Hunter," said Hope.

Mike's father gave her a polite hello as though he could not recognize her. "How's your hand?" asked Silvia.

"It hurts, but I won't take any more of that medicine the doctor prescribed," said Hope.

Silvia watched her nephew watch his son before calling both Mike and Obie to the porch.

"Is there a problem, Em——," Obie's eyes flashed to the man standing beside Silvia, "Missus Chase?"

"Dad," said Mike as he reached the porch with the sword in his hand. He glanced around. "This is Lieutenant Obie Firth. The good friend of Hope's I told you about."

Mike's father blinked then gave Obie a nod. "Mike, your grandparents are waiting for us in the living room," he said.

Color drained from Mike's face. "What is it?"

"We have to talk," his father said. "Decisions to make."

After handing Obie the practice sword, Mike allowed his father to usher him inside the house.

Obie left the swords on the porch as he and Hope followed Silvia into the kitchen. A teapot and cups rested on the table. Silvia motioned for them to sit. "I know about Mike's mother," she said without preamble. She poured cups of tea for both of them before sitting across from them. "The DNA was a match. She is alive. As for where she's been, well, my brother and I have our suspicions."

Realizing what she meant, Hope's jaw dropped, dribbling tea down her chin.

"Yes," affirmed Silvia.

"Why come back now?" Hope asked.

"You." Silvia sipped some tea. "Things were put into motion well before I ever became Empress," she told them. "Berty is discussing our suspicions with Tong right now." She swallowed another sip. "We are afraid that Mike will be used to get to you. To save both of you, his grandparents are trying to convince his father to let us protect him."

Hope slumped back into her chair.

"May I ask what that includes, my Lady?" asked Obie.

"Silvia," said Mike's grandmother from the swinging kitchen door, "we're ready for you."

"I'll be right there, Martha." When the door swung closed, Silvia answered, "He'll be assigned his own guard. You will not be responsible for his protection."

Once Silvia left, Obie took Hope's hand. "I don't understand all this, Obie," Hope said. "I feel like a plague—hurting everyone I touch."

"Don't think like that," Berty said. She never noticed her uncle enter the kitchen. "Your magic was being sought before I ever brought you through the portal, before you were ever born."

"But why, Uncle Berty? Why me?"

Berty sat in Silvia's vacated chair. "Because there is more to your magic than your ability to communicate with trees," he answered. "You need to speak with the Mother Wood Sprite. She holds answers." Rising, he said, "Obie, help Hope pick out a weapon that she can use with one hand in the garage. The police won't be giving back the dagger anytime soon."

As Hope and Obie crossed the driveway to the garage, she asked, "How long until I can hold my bow, do you think?"

"It may take a while to fully heal." They climbed the stairs to the second floor.

The large room at the top of the stairs held an array of weapons, armor, and targets and dummies for both defense and practice. "What do you mean a while?" she asked.

Obie dug into a chest. "A month, maybe two."

"Maybe two?" She groaned.

"Try this," he said, handing her a blade. "Longer than a dagger, shorter than a sword, relatively light. And, take this." He gave her another blade, more dagger like.

"I have Fairy Dust," she countered, staring at both blades.

"And I'm a Warlock. I still use a sword. Plus, I carry my bone dagger and another blade at all times."

"Point made."

The longer blade had a scabbard that hung from her belt. The dagger snuggled into a simple leather sheath, which slid perfectly into her boot.

Carrying voices made them pause at the screen door to the kitchen. "I want to know how you will protect my son."

"Dad—"

"No."

Hope closed the screen door softly. The two of them crept closer to the swinging door between the kitchen and the hall.

"We will assign him a bodyguard," said Silvia's voice.

"To be his shadow everywhere he goes?"

"Marty, we've been over this," said Silvia.

"I want specifics."

"The best way you can protect your son is to be ignorant," said Berty.

"He's my son. I have a right to know."

"If anyone can keep your son safe, it's my brother and his wife. They've done the same with my daughter," said Jon.

Hope glanced at Obie then pushed open the door to the hall. Mike and his father faced each other in the foyer. Berty bridged the hall and the sitting room. Stepping forward, she saw Jon on the staircase landing. As she approached Berty, she peeked inside the sitting room. Martha sat on a settee, shaking her head. Both Martin and Silvia stood in the foyer. Martin crossed his arms. Silvia eyes caught Hope's advance.

"Mister Hunter," said Hope. "I don't know exactly what you've been told, but how do you propose to protect Mike against forces you've never seen? If he's in danger from his own mother.... With us, he has a fighting chance."

"Forces? Us?" said Marty. "I know a terrible tragedy has befallen you, Hope, but don't think for a moment that surviving your attack makes you invincible."

"Invincible?" Her tone raised. "You have no idea what I have been through, what I have seen since before I ever met your son. Terrible tragedy? I *killed* someone. Someone I thought was on my side, a teacher, a mentor. And I killed him." Tears brimmed. "His death haunts me night and day. I may never be free of his ghost. Terrible tragedy indeed. Don't, I beg you, put Mike into the position where he might have a 'terrible tragedy' of his own, especially not his own mother." She swallowed back an urge to cry. "No, Mister Hunter, nothing has made me invincible. I am angry. I am angry that someone somewhere has put me in the position where I constantly look over my shoulder and may have to fight for my life again and again." Her eyes narrowed, glaring at him. "Mike is suffering. You want to be there for your son and protect him the best you can? Trust your family." She paused for a breath. "If I have learned anything from these 'terrible tragedies,' it's that we have two choices:

be the victim or be in control of your destiny. I made my choice. Make yours." Breaking her glare, she climbed the steps.

Jon placed an assuring hand on her shoulder as she passed. At the top of the steps, Lily stood when she saw Hope coming. "What I can I do?" Lily asked her.

"Protect Mommy and Daddy and the rest of our family. Use your magic well, Lily," Hope said with a hug. Over her sister's head, she saw her mother smile.

In the bedroom, Hope checked her backpack. "Who is this enemy?" said Obie. He sat on the bed in which he slept earlier. Hope cocked her head to the side. "Mike's mother was essentially a spy, then abandons her post," he continued. "Unless she was reassigned."

"I don't think it was originally about me," said Hope. "I think it's about Aunt Silvia. She is a powerful sorceress in her own right, and then being Empress on top of it. I think I'm being used as a means to an end. Extremely powerful magic resides in the Empire Tree and I am the Wood Listener. Having my magic would mean getting to Aunt Silvia and the Scepter easier. The Empire Tree is a branch of the Great Tree of the Universe of which my magic is a part." She sat on the opposite bed. "I understand this now. And I won't allow myself to be used. The question is: how do we stop this enemy we know relatively nothing about?"

"We'll find a way," said Obie.

They sat in silence.

"Looks like I'm coming with you," said Mike. He stood in the doorway, holding an old canvas bag. "My grandfather had it packed for me. Can I put it here before we go?"

Hope nodded.

As Mike set his bag next to the chair of the desk, an older male voice called, "Mike." His grandfather stopped in the hallway, looking into the rooms. "There you are." Seeing Hope on the bed, he said, "Those were strong words, Hope. Living your life on both sides is not easy." He turned to Mike. "I chose a side and stayed. To make life easier, I decided never to tell anyone about the world in-between the portals. Not even my own family. Your dad will accept this in time. I didn't get a chance to give you these." He handed him a sheathed sword. "This sword is a Hunter family heirloom, passed from male to male. I think you found it once." He smiled. "And this," he gave Mike a folded light blue bundle, "is the Hunter family cloak. You'll notice Silvia wearing the same color. Both of these hold the magic of the Empire Tree—the magic of the Scepter. Because of your bloodline, the magic will work for you."

"But, Grandpa, how will you protect Dad and Grandma?" asked Mike, holding one heirloom in each hand.

Martin smiled. "Don't worry. There is more than one set for there is always more than one Hunter male protecting this side of the portal."

"Thanks, Grandpa." Mike hugged him.

When they broke apart, Martin said, "Stay safe and take care of each other. Hope, Lieutenant."

After his grandfather left, Mike stood by the door, taking deliberate breaths. He kept to himself throughout lunch. While Obie gave Hope blade instruction, Mike sat on the porch, not watching them.

Berty called them inside. They followed him into the dining room where their entourage gathered around the table. Through magic, the dining table had enough seats. Hope sat between Verity and Obie. Mike found a seat next to Hatcher.

"Mike," Silvia started.

"I don't want to be called Mike anymore," Mike said. "I want to go by my first name from now on."

"Okay, Martin," she said with a slight smile, "Sergeant Sorrel is assigned to you as your guard."

Mike nodded, looking across the table at Sorrel.

"Hatcher, what have you decided to do once we cross the portal?" asked Berty.

"I think it would be best if I accompanied you to the outpost," he answered.

"How will you explain the presence of a Troll at an outpost?" asked Colvin.

"I'm the Gatekeeper," said Hatcher. "The outpost is an ancient Keep with gates. I can survey the gates while you survey structural stuff."

Colvin rolled his eyes.

"What?" snapped Hatcher.

The Dwarf chuckled. "You're getting feisty in your old age, my friend," he said.

"Watch who you're calling old."

"You've got as much gray in your little curls as I have in my red beard," said Colvin, patting his wiry, long beard.

Laughing, Hatcher said, "You're so sensitive." Colvin laughed with the Troll.

"I have a question," said Hope. The laughter subsided.

"Go ahead," said Silvia.

"How did Mike's mother, sorry, Martin's mother come through a portal if they've all been closed?" asked Hope.

The smile melted from Hatcher's face. "Well," he began, "she may have crossed a portal prior to their closing. There could be portals that we don't know about. Or," he swallowed, "she could have used another form of Porter magic. The portal tapestries are a good example of alternative Porter magic."

"Can she... track me?" Mike asked.

"While you are in this house, no," answered Silvia. Her hands reached behind her neck. She removed the warding pendant that the Pixies gave her. "Wear this. It will protect you from old magic. Since we're related, it will work for you as it does me."

"Thank you," he said, taking the pendant.

"I wanted to leave when it was darker," said Berty. He glanced out the bright window. "But, I'd rather leave as soon as we can. Does anyone have anything else to say?"

Those familiar with how Berty and Silvia ran their Roundtable shook their heads. The few others sat in silence.

In the foyer, everyone secured their packs and cloaks. Hope said good-bye to her parents and sister. "Lily," said Berty, "before we go, I want you to wear this." He fastened his warding pendant around her neck.

"Won't you need it, Uncle Berty?" she asked.

"As Emperor, I'm protected by the Empire Tree and the Scepter," he told her. "You have your magic, Lily, but you won't be a full Enchantress until you're fifteen. Let this aid you."

"Thanks, Uncle Berty," said Lily.

After hugging his niece, he addressed the cloaked gathering. "When you step through this door, you will look different. Don't be alarmed. The magic will last until we reach the portal."

Berty opened the stained glass front door. Silvia led them out of the house. Cloaks and traveling clothes morphed into modern jackets and jeans. Only Declan and Delyth wore modern clothes on a regular basis when they visited Declan's sister, Julie. While Edwin shifted uncomfortably without his Empire Guard armor, Hatcher and Colvin stared at each other's clothes. Crowding beside Hope, Verity smiled at the changes. Sorrel, on the other hand, seemed unphased.

As Berty closed the door behind Mike, Silvia ushered them off the front porch. Sorrel lost her cool demeanor when a car drove past. "Don't stare," whispered Obie. They walked along the sidewalk. Another car passed, then an SUV drove the other direction.

"What are those and why do they make so much noise?" asked Sorrel in a low voice.

"Horseless carriages," answered Mike. "And the noise comes from the engine that runs them."

"Are they magic?" breathed Verity.

"Do you have one of those?" Sorrel asked Mike.

"I don't personally own a car," he answered, "but I usually drive my Dad's when he's away."

"Only if you consider a combustion engine magic," said Hope.

"George lent me a book about those once," Colvin said. "Fascinating stuff."

"Is that the book I caught you reading upside down?" asked Hatcher.

"No. And for the last time, it fell and I was picking it up, not reading it," huffed Colvin.

Turning to watch a neighbor unload filled plastic bags from the trunk, Hope giggled to herself.

Reaching the end of the road, Silvia stepped into the woods with the others on her heels. When the sounds of the modern world faded, everyone relaxed. Reaching the portal, they stopped. Berty lifted his magic as Hatcher approached the space between the two oak trees.

The Troll muttered in Trollian while performing an elaborate gesture holding a blue crystal. Silent, he inserted the crystal like a key. The portal pulsed blue. Hope marveled at the blue disc before it disappeared from her view. Hatcher waved them through as he held the portal open.

Once across, the group waited outside the pine grove for Hatcher to lock the portal. He emerged, tucking the crystal into a pouch.

Edwin took the lead through the forest. The sun began to set before they reached the Keep. Hope did not remember it taking her so long, but other issues preoccupied her mind.

The two guards at the gate saluted their Captain. The group filed into the empty room just inside the gate.

"Lower the gate behind us," Edwin ordered.

"Captain Edwin," Otho greeted as he descended the stone staircase.

"Is everything ready, Lieutenant?" Edwin asked.

"Yes, sir."

Edwin nodded. "Princess?"

Delyth stood under the gate. "Are there men on the roof, Lieutenant?" she asked.

"Yes, Your Highness."

"They will be fine as they are," she said. "Because of the speed that I will draw the Fairy Ring, secure the wooden door after lowering the gate. I would hate for anyone to be affected. I'll enter from the roof." She stepped outside the gate.

As the guards locked the gate, Otho brought them upstairs. "Is this a different type of inspection?" he asked.

"Colvin will be inspecting the structure while Hatcher inspects the doors, preferably the one that leads to the roof," said Berty. "This is the most frequently attacked outpost. We would like to know why."

"Most of the guards were all too happy to get a transfer," said Otho. "There have been two more attacks since Lieutenant Oberon left. Luckily, we had help from the Dragons. Tong came to our aid on both occasions. Mithra does what they can before it reaches our border." He opened a door. "We did not get a chance to completely ready the citizen's quarters."

"Not a problem," said Silvia. When she walked through the door, a lantern ignited. Standing outside, Hope heard wood scrape against the stone floor. "This will do fine, Otho. Thank you."

Delyth approached from the staircase. She gave Berty a nod.

"We also have plenty of beds open in the guard's quarters," said Otho.

"Our presence here is distracting enough," said Silvia. "We'll let them sleep in peace."

"We're going to freshen up from out travels and meet you in the dining hall," Berty told the Lieutenant.

"Very good." Otho bowed to both of them before leaving.

Chapter Thirteen

Keeping

Silvia set up the curved, windowless room so everyone had a bed and a table or nightstand. Lanterns graced every other table. She placed Edwin closest to the door, and Hope and Mike would sleep the furthest from it. Hope found comfort in that and that Obie had the bed next to her.

While Hope stored her bag under the bed, Silvia stood at the foot of the bed. "Keep your bow with you," Silvia said. "No one needs to know that your hand hurts too much to hold it."

Hope agreed. They were at war. Berty and Silvia trusted no one unless personally vetted. Everyone in that room had been, everyone except Verity. Thrust upon them, no one knew much about the Elf except her status as Hope's Tender. Did that status make her trustworthy? Unsure, Hope realized what better place to get to know someone than in a Keep where no one could leave.

The half dozen Empire Guards in the dining hall stopped all conversation when they entered. Otho stood first.

"Please sit," said Berty. "Bring your chairs around." All of them sat around one of the long tables. "Princess Delyth has constructed a Fairy Ring around the outpost that will remain for the duration of our stay. Those of you who are not familiar with a Fairy Ring should know that no one other than a Fairy can cross one whether it be via land, sky, or underground. Advisors Colvin and Hatcher will need someone to show them the damage sustained from the Griffin attacks. Our other objective is to discover the reason behind these attacks. We will entertain all theories. They can originate from you or from other guards stationed here at any time. We would like to hear rumors and superstitions. Nothing is too silly or too far-fetched."

"You may have noticed First Lieutenant Oberon and the two civilians who were present during the attack when the Griffin breached the Keep accompany us," Silvia said. "We would like anyone who was there to be with us as well when we examine the area in a moment."

"Only two remain; the others were transferred," said Otho. "Stefan is on roof duty and Sergeant Francis is sleeping. He should wake soon for his shift."

"We'll collect the Sergeant on our way up," Edwin said. "Lead the way, Lieutenant Otho."

Only Sorrel and Verity stayed behind while they followed Otho through the Keep. Edwin stopped everyone while Obie fetched Francis. Stifling a yawn, the guard hastily bowed to Berty and Silvia. "Let's go, Sergeant," said Edwin.

The staircase ended at the floor of the attack. Another staircase continued upwards on the other side of the Keep. The splintered wood had been cleared, but the door to the upper staircase had not been replaced. Otho sent Francis to retrieve Stefan.

Declan strolled around the room, looking at things Hope could not see. He stopped at the remnants of a magical blast. "Your work?" he asked Obie.

"Yes," Obie answered.

When the two guards returned, Edwin asked for a retelling from both guards' points of view. Hope tuned out their words until one said, "The archeress spotted the Griffin. Her. Over there. We sounded the alarm and followed procedure." She turned, not wanting to relive it.

"Hope," Edwin called, "where were you when the beast broke through the door?"

"Uh," she looked around the room. Walking towards the center, she said, "Around here, I think."

"And you shot it with arrows?" he asked.

"Yes, but they bounced off until I tipped them with Fairy Dust," she said.

The Elf gave her a nod then turned to the men, asking more questions.

"According to the Dragons, the Griffin was considerably weakened and they easily destroyed it," said Edwin. "Thank you both," he said to the guards. "You may return to your duties."

Edwin continued upwards with Berty, Silvia, Declan, Colvin, Hatcher, and Otho. When they returned, Colvin said, "We'd like to revisit here in daylight, Lieutenant."

"Of course."

After they ate, a handful of off duty guards spoke with Berty, Silvia, Delyth, and Edwin. Declan suggested that Obie familiarize the rest of them with the Keep. Obie happily walked them through the outpost he knew well. His tour ended at their sleeping quarters.

Exhaustion caught up to Hope as she changed. Climbing into bed, she ignored nighttime preparations and conversations. Somewhere, Delyth's voice relayed a story from one of the guards. The cadence of incoherent words lulled her to sleep.

The forest called to her. She sped through darkness into a green tinged light. Standing among trees and lush underbrush, she glanced around. Something felt wrong. "No," she said. "I will not be part of this. I will not play your games." Bird songs filled her ears. A family of deer pranced along a hidden path. "No!" Hope said again. Her hands covered her ears. "No!" she yelled. She closed her eyes. "No! No! No! No! No!"

She shook. Her hand was being pulled away from her ear. "Hope. Hope. Wake up."

Obie's magic touched her. When she opened her eyes, Obie stared at her. She sat up. Lighted lanterns illuminated worried looks on faces. "Sorry," she said in a small voice.

Berty sat on the foot of her bed. "What happened in this dream?" he asked.

"It was trying to pull me into a false sense of security. I refused." She looked around the room. "I didn't mean to wake all of you."

"It's okay," said Silvia. With a wave of her hand, she moved a wooden screen between Hope's and Verity's beds. All lanterns except the one on her nightstand extinguished. Another wooden screen blocked the view of Mike and Sorrel.

Declan joined them in the screened area. Wordlessly, he asked to see Hope's hand. His brow furrowed as he examined the bruise.

Something in the space around her drew his attention. "Touch her," he said in a whisper to Obie. When Obie's hand touched her shoulder, Declan turned to Berty. "Did you see that?"

Berty nodded. "Very interesting."

"Obie's magic disrupts," Declan breathed. He pointed at her hand. "The Master Woodsman knew what he was doing. To stop the nightmares until," he tapped his own hand, "you have to touch—"

"While sleeping? In the same bed?" whispered Obie. Hope's face grew hot.

"I know it's awkward, but it's the only way," Declan whispered. "You can't keep a shield over her while you're sleeping. And you're not staying awake while she sleeps. Holding hands is enough."

Hope averted her gaze from everyone, especially Obie.

"Hope, stay where you are. You two, by me," said Silvia. Hope's bed vibrated as it widened. "There," Silvia continued, "it shouldn't be as uncomfortable."

As soon as Hope felt Obie sit on the enlarged bed, the screens moved and the lantern extinguished. Obie moved on the other side of the bed. She looked over, but could not see him in the dark. When her head hit the pillow, Obie adjusted the blanket to cover her. He inched closer. His warmth radiated towards her.

"It will be okay," he breathed in her ear. His arm slipped under hers. Taking her hand, he threaded his fingers between hers.

She squeezed his hand, then tried to sleep.

When she opened her eyes, they still held hands. Lantern light in the curved room meant that others woke as well. She tried to pull her hand out of his, but his grip tightened. "Obie, I'm going to get up now," she said.

His hand released hers. "Okay," he answered without opening his eyes.

"Are you all right?" Verity asked while they changed in the women's dressing room.

"I've been better," Hope admitted. "Nightmares every night since the attack. This is the first night I fully fell back to sleep. So, I guess that's progress or something."

"Is there anything I can do?" the Elf asked.

Hope gave her a small smile. "No, but thank you. It means a lot."

Before leaving the curved citizens' quarters, all of them took turns asking how Hope was. Delyth offered to talk if she needed it. Sitting at the long table during breakfast, Hope realized how large her extended family became.

After breakfast, Hatcher and Colvin left to examine the damage in the sunlight. Obie brought the rest of them to the room where he found the books on marks. The doorway melted into the surrounding stone. If Obie had not pointed it out, Hope would not have known it was there. Inside, the shelf filled room occupied the space between other rooms. A short, book lined hall connected two bulbous rooms, each with a couple of tables in the center.

Declan skimmed the books Obie gave him, then stacked them on a table. "I'm going to read these later," he said. "Mike, Sergeant, come with me." As the three of them exited, Hope followed her aunt and uncle's lead by reading the titles on the shelves.

Most of the books had leather bindings with metallic lettering. Browsing, Hope noticed the majority of titles in the ancient tongue, a smattering of ancient Fairy, and fewer in ancient Elf. "There are books in ancient Dwarf and Trollian in here," exclaimed Delyth.

"I found a few written in Pictell," said Silvia.

"This one's in Runic," Hope said, recognizing the symbols on the spine.

"Can you read it?" asked Berty.

Hope pulled the book off the shelf. She placed it on a table while Berty lit a candle. The gold runes had worn off the blue leather. After examining both the front cover and the spine, she could not make out all the runes to discern a book title. Seeing if the ancient book's pages could still be read, she tried to lift the cover. "It won't open," she said.

Berty studied the book. "That's because it's locked—magically." He looked at Silvia. "Declan should be here for this."

"Then, we'll wait for him," she answered.

They continued perusing book titles until Declan entered. "I found something that might be interesting."

"Might be?" asked Delyth.

"Well, there's a teeny problem," he said. "Come."

Declan led them into the bowels of the Keep. "I've never been down here," said Obie. A door opened into a circular room with symbols carved into the stones on the walls. Holding lanterns, Mike and Sorrel flanked an entrance in the wall that led to a dark somewhere.

"Where does that go?" Silvia asked.

"That's the problem. Beyond the Fairy Ring," said Declan.

Delyth peered into the doorway then glanced at Hope and Silvia. "I don't want to explore this unprepared. Let's come back," she said.

Agreeing, Silvia suggested they take a break.

Hope's break consisted of lunch then spending time of the roof with Obie, Mike, Sorrel, and Verity.

"I think I'd go mad being stationed here," said Sorrel.

"It's not so bad," said Obie. The other guards turned an ear to listen. "I was here for almost two years. The villagers are nice and the Dragons can be amusing."

"Two years? That's a long time for anyone to be at one outpost," Sorrel said. "I like change—outposts, camping patrols."

"Is that a Dragon?" asked Verity.

Obie and two of the roof guards searched the sky where Verity pointed. "Yes," said Obie. A sleek, blue shape tucked its wings then dove into the forest canopy. Distant roars kept them company while they scanned the skies for non-Dragons. After a couple of minutes, Obie let out a breath.

"Do Dragons come close often?" asked Mike.

"Dragons can't cross the border," said Hope. "Except one."

Mike threw Hope a startled look.

"Hope," called Delyth. Her head popped over the makeshift roof door. "Declan would like to see you. The rest of you can stay up here."

After pushing off the keyed stone wall, Hope descended with Delyth through the Keep.

"How are you doing?" asked Delyth.

"Fine."

"Mentally, I mean. When someone is after you, it takes a toll and not just physically. It can play with your mind, eat at your soul. Don't be afraid or ashamed to let it out. Even if you have to wait until the bruises heal. It's a process, and you don't have to go through it alone."

Hope knew about Delyth's poisoning and the previous Historian's vendetta against the Fairy royal family. If anyone understood, Delyth would. "Thanks, Aunt Delyth."

Inside the hidden library, Declan inspected Hope's bruise. "See?" he said to Hatcher. "It's a transportation mark."

Hatcher peered at Hope's hand through glasses perched on his nose. "Then this deviation must be the location, the originator," said the Troll.

"What does that mean?" asked Hope.

Removing his glasses, Hatcher said, "Porter magic. This magic is used on vessels for transportation to a certain location. The mark would be put on, say, a box. Then whatever is in the box would be transported to the location indicated in the mark. On you, it was used to take your magic. However, you have a multiple anchor, so it did not work. Instead, the connection is being used the opposite way."

"The nightmares," she said.

"Yes."

"What do you mean by multiple anchor?" she asked.

"Your magic has a three-point anchor," Hatcher explained. "You, your Tender, and your Protector. According to Porter magic, the more anchors something has, the harder it is to move."

"Actually, Hope and her magic have a seven-point anchor," said Declan.

"Seven?" Hatcher cleaned his glasses with a cloth before placing them back on his nose.

While looking at Declan, Hope titled her head.

"I saw it from the balcony," Declan explained. He set his locket symbol side up on the table. "Look at the six pointed star as two triangles." His finger outlined the star in the symbol. "The Master Woodsman arranged the High Elf, the Dominatrix, and the Commander Wystan in the apexes of one triangle and Obie, Verity, and himself in another. You, Hope, were in the center." He tapped the eye in the center of the star.

"According to this," Hatcher said, nose over a page, "the Porter magic will stay as long as the mark stays intact."

"So once the bruise starts to fade, so will the nightmares," said Hope. "Obie was right."

"Yes," said Declan. "However, the magic may prolong the duration of the bruise. The good news is that Obie's magic breaks this magic. It is the nature of Warlock magic."

"Then, Sorrel's would as well?" asked Hope.

"Not as completely. If she had been one of the anchors, then yes," Declan answered.

Hope nodded as she pulled the sleeve of her bark armor over her wrist. She buttoned the glove to the sleeve while Berty and Silvia entered the room with Colvin.

"The only thing I know for certain is that it's not a Dwarf access tunnel," Colvin said. "In fact, the Keep pre-dates Dwarf construction in the Land of Sages. From what I've ascertained, the Keep pre-dates the ruins under Fairyland, which, to my knowledge, were the oldest stone structures in the Land of Sages."

"Did you get a look at that book?" Berty asked Declan.

"Yes," said Declan, "but I can't read Runes and there aren't any pictures. This is something the Guild Master should study. However, I don't feel that the book should be removed from the Keep."

"It'll take some time, but I could copy it onto paper and send it to him," said Berty.

Declan slowly nodded.

"The tunnel needs to be explored," said Silvia. "Though, I don't think that Delyth, Hope, and I should go alone. Breaking the Fairy

Ring leaves the outpost vulnerable."

"What if we protected it another way," said Hope. All heads turned to listen. "If Aunt Delyth lifts the Fairy Ring, I can use my magic to protect the Keep."

"But we already know that Fairy Dust can be used against Griffins," said Delyth.

"I know my magic is untested," said Hope.

"It could work," said Declan. "We can't draw a new Ring; we don't know where the tunnel leads. Griffins tend to attack at night. We can do the change of magic at first light."

"Edwin and I will show Otho the tunnel tonight in case it needs to be guarded," said Berty. He turned to Hope. "I want you and Obie to come down with us tomorrow."

Hope nodded. "What about... Verity? Do you guys not trust her?"

"Verity is part of *your* inner circle," said Berty. "The Master Woodsman trusts her."

"But then why did my predecessor dismiss his Tender?"

"We don't know," said Silvia. "Add it to the list of things you should ask the Mother Wood Sprite."

Before disappearing with Berty, Edwin set up blade training for Hope, Mike, and Verity. He had Obie and Sorrel practice their magic. The guards not sparring with them watched.

When Edwin returned, he observed each of them fight a guard. "You have good technique and natural instincts," he said to Mike, "but you're obviously not used to your weapon. Even if you just practice swinging your sword on your own, it'll help." To Verity, he commented, "I recognize your basic Warrior training. You need to practice on your fluidity and, eventually, raise your skills." After studying Hope's spar, he said, "I commend you for picking up a secondary weapon. You fight like an archer using a blade. Understanding principles and technique only help in a pinch. It is better to differentiate." He took a training sword off a rack. "Let me show you. Everyone watch, you can learn something."

Her insides dropped. She gaped at the Elf who trained her uncle, her father, and even Obie. Her grip moistened the hilt of her blade. She gulped. Then, she remembered that he taught Delyth as well. Why did everyone have to watch?

He swung. Their blades met. The vibration of metal striking metal ran up her arm into her back. "Hope," he said, "like the bow, the sword is a part of you. However, the bow is an internal weapon whereas the sword is external. You draw energy when you pull the bowstring, releasing the energy in an arrow. Here, the energy draws through your feet, releasing through your arm."

"Oh." She adjusted her grip.

Edwin smiled. "Again."

The Elf swung from a different angle. She blocked. Zinging ran nowhere. She moved how Obie taught her, how she had seen others move.

When training stopped, Edwin said, "Good. I think that's enough practice for one evening. Let those muscles heal."

After washing, Hope sat on the bed, combing her hair.

Edwin entered the curved room. "Hey, Declan," he said. "Just so you know, Hope's getting really good at using her back up blade."

"I know how to use my back up blade," said Declan. He pulled back the blanket of his bed.

"Skinning game doesn't count," Edwin said.

Declan shook his head. "Use is a general term."

The men laughed.

"High praise from the Captain when he talks about you," said Obie, gingerly sitting on his side of the bed.

"I think he was chiding Uncle Declan," said Hope. She tossed her hair between her and Obie then continued combing.

Silvia addressed them once everyone settled. "We're heading down the tunnel tomorrow. Sorrel and Mike will be on guard in the room with Otho and a guard of his choosing. Verity will be there as well. Her job will be to ring the warning bell. One ring is for help. Two bells: Griffin spotted. Three means Griffin breech. Constant ringing: evacuate. I'll go over this again in the morning with the guards."

Obie took Hope's hand again as they laid down to sleep. "Get some sleep tonight," she said to him.

"I will if you do," he answered.

Hope woke in darkness. She squeezed Obie's hand to know if he was still there. "Morning," he whispered. "Delyth's getting up now."

"You can see in the dark?"

"Her wings are starting to glow."

She squinted, searching the dark. "I see nothing."

"Huh. Did you sleep well?"

"No nightmares. It would be nice if this room had a window," she said.

A lantern lit then another. Hope sat up, remembering that she promised to protect the outpost with *her* magic.

Hope and Delyth left the dining hall with Silvia after she explained that with the new magic, people could leave but not return. Silvia magically unbarred the door and lifted the gate. In a lavender blur,

Delyth removed the Fairy Dust. Once the Fairy crossed the threshold, Hope called on the magic of the trees. She accepted their protection from everyone who wished the outpost and all contained therein harm. When the magic changed her, she touched the stone. A shimmer of green pulsated through the stone. Hope waved her other hand, closing the door.

"It is done," she told them.

When the three of them rejoined the others, Otho asked, "Can guards still go on the roof?"

"As long as you stay within the stone. It walls in the roof, so yes," she said.

Berty ushered the group down through the Keep. Saying nothing, Declan studied the stone. Reaching the last room at the bottom, the Watcher stopped in the middle of the circular stone room. His eyes moved from symbol to symbol. "It's like they're awake," said Berty.

Looking around, Verity shook her head. "They see magic," Hope said to her.

The symbols seemed different to Hope as well. "Wait," she said. She gazed from symbol to symbol. "Uncle Declan, I think you need your wand and your locket. There's a message in these symbols."

Holding his locket by the chain in one hand and his wand in the other, Declan crossed the room several times. "Watcher symbol. Crystal. Blowing cloud. Star. Anvil. Keystone. Tree. And a key with an X over it," he said. "Blowing cloud... wind. Anvil probably means metal."

Verity gasped. "The Scrollist. The Six Listeners."

"What are the Six Listeners?" Declan asked, spinning to face her.

"Wood, obviously," said Hope, "but also Crystal," she walked to each symbol, "Wind, Star, Metal, and Stone. The Watcher Symbol—

six anchors and the seventh in the center." She stared at Declan.

"But the key is crossed out," he argued.

"Recite the riddle, Declan," said Berty.

Declan nodded. "When the wand, the sword, and the bow unite with the past, the present, and the future, will the key unlock the Cavern. A worthy Keeper will solve this riddle."

"And you are of the Order of the Keepers," said Hope.

Again, Declan nodded.

"If the Keepers predate the Watchers, then so should the symbol. It's on the lockets only given to Keepers," said Berty.

"What if," Mike interjected, "the Keeper who solves the riddle is one of the Six, but not the Key?"

Declan stared at Mike for a moment then glanced at the symbols. "Sorry, Berty," he said.

"I was never meant to solve this riddle," said Berty.

"Anvil, metal, sword?" said Declan, wandering around the room. "Star. Estelle reads the stars, sees the future. Stone, a keystone, an integral part of a foundation," he glanced at Delyth, "foundation—the past. The present, the present." He paced. Stopping in front of Hope, he said, "What is more present than a tree? Crystal and Wind..." He paced again, muttering incoherently. "Crystal. The Scepter." He glimpsed at Silvia. "Magic. Of course, the wand detects magic. Wind—" He stopped. "Oh. Huh." A small laugh escaped. "This is the Keeper's Keep. The information here should lead us to the Cavern... somehow."

Hanging his locket around his neck, Declan held his wand in front of him. He lit the tip of his wand like a flashlight, then led them into the opening in the wall. Only Hatcher and Colvin carried lanterns. Their light died on the black stone. The blue light from Berty's and

Obie's magical spheres illuminated enough to see one another. The tunnel began a wide spiral downwards as if they traversed around the outside of the Keep. The lanterns extinguished. "I didn't do it," said Colvin.

"Magical breeze," said Berty. His spheres divided into more, albeit smaller sources of light. The bluish cast gave the black stone an ominous aura. Claustrophobic, Hope wanted to run back up the tunnel. Caught in the middle of the group, she dared not.

A bell echoed down the tunnel. They froze. A second bell stopped mid-ding. Why? Images popped into Hope's head from the outer walls' point of view. A tawny creature flew over the Keep. "The Griffin can't see us," she said. "Just flying in our direction."

"Otho realized that as well," said Berty. "That's why he stopped the bell. He didn't want it to hear us."

"Brazen for a daytime attack," muttered Hatcher.

No one answered him.

Declan urged them forward, sending no one back. They trusted her magic. Warmth spread from her stomach. She smiled slightly in the semi-darkness—she finally belonged. While they traveled deeper, she decided that the magical side of the portal would be her home. She would start in Fairyland. Learning more languages would be her first goal.

"Interesting," said Declan, pausing the descent. "A magicfall. I guess we must go through it."

Hope saw nothing but darkness where the Watcher looked.

"What does it do?" asked Delyth.

"I don't know."

"I'll go first," said Colvin.

"But you have neither magic nor a magical object," said Edwin.

"After I show it's safe for non-magic, Hatcher will follow," Colvin said.

Narrowing his eyes, Hatcher shook his head at the Dwarf.

"I'll go," said Silvia. Before anyone argued, she stepped past Declan. She bounced a magical sphere in her hand. "I think it's a test, not a magic wash."

"A detector," said Declan.

Hatcher and Colvin joined Silvia. "Does that mean something is tallying inventory?" asked Edwin. No one answered. He and Delyth walked under the invisible magicfall.

Obie grabbed Hope's hand before she stepped forward. Declan gave his nephew an approving nod. A slight shiver crept down her body as the detection washed over her. Finally, Berty and Declan walked through. All the blue spheres disappeared. Declan reignited his wand tip before continuing. While Berty released his light spheres, Obie did not. He kept his hand connected with Hope's.

Declan stopped again. The light from his wand illuminated a dark door. "Extinguish the light," said Berty. Darkness pressed against them. Feet shuffled on the stone. Metal locked into metal. A door swung on creaky hinges. Golden light bathed Berty and Declan.

After a moment, they stepped into the light. The rest followed.

Gold covered every surface of the round room beneath the Keep. Hope surveyed the walls, floor, and ceiling. Nothing but gold. Not even a light source. "Is the light coming from the gold?" asked Delyth.

"It glows like Grunnan," Colvin said softly.

"What is this? An altar?" asked Edwin. He examined a golden slab balanced on a golden pedestal in the center of the room.

Joining him, Berty ran his fingers on the top of the slab in a star pattern. When his finger returned to the apex where he started, the center eye opened. He reached inside, then extracted a hand filling golden object.

"A sethbravin," exclaimed Delyth.

Berty magically rotated it in the air. On one side, a Watcher's symbol—a six pointed star with an eye in the center—was carved into the gold. Six pointed gold rods pierced the inner corners of the star. The center of the eye, where an iris would be, held a clear crystal.

"How does that direct us to the Cavern?" asked Colvin.

"It doesn't," answered Berty. "It opens it, or rather the magic that sealed it." The object came to rest on his palm. "We'll have to see what the rest of this stuff in here has to offer."

"What stuff?" asked Hatcher. Beyond the gold slab, the room contained nothing.

"Well, that makes things more difficult," said Declan.

"Maybe there's a way to turn off the magic. A switch, perhaps?" said Hope.

Berty's finger tapped air. "Maybe, Hope, maybe. This is the same gold as the lockets. Give me a minute," he said.

Berty turned in a circle. His magic work always intrigued Hope. Unless he hurled Dragonfire, his magic had a subtle quality to it— more like hers. It worked in the background. Seeing. Changing. Moving. At times, he could barricade, but it never held for long. Strong, old magic coursed through his veins. Hope admired his subdued strength and the way he intellectualized magic while also feeling it.

After a minute, tables, shelves, and other objects appeared around the room. Nothing was made of gold.

Silvia approached the shelves. "All these books have translated copies. The original language, ancient, and modern," she said.

"There are books here in Trollian and Goblish," said Hatcher. "I never knew Goblins wrote books."

"What an opportunity to learn these ancient languages," said Hope.

"Alfred should be here," said Delyth.

"So should the Watcher's Guild," said Declan.

Colvin's hand reached to touch what looked like a wind-up toy on a table, then stopped. "If this Keep has been abandoned for thousands of years, who translated everything into the modern tongue?" he asked.

"The magic did," said Declan. "I can't read the ancient tongue. And neither can Berty." He looked at her uncle. "You can't. Not without wearing that ring."

Not being able to see her uncle's face, Hope asked, "Should we start reading and taking notes or…?"

"That's exactly what *we* should do," Silvia answered. "However, until your bruise fades, you should not."

Hope's jaw dropped a little. "Oh. Do you think that whatever I learn could be accessed?"

"We can't take that chance, Hope. I'm sorry."

"Hope, I think it's time you saw the Mother Wood Sprite," said Berty. "I have a feeling that your magic will still protect us."

Nodding, Hope understood the danger of leaking whatever secrets the golden room hid. "Obie, Verity, and I will leave as soon as we can," she said.

"Take Mike and Sorrel," Silvia suggested. "He is safest with you. Will Edwin be able to get back into the Keep without you?"

She looked at the Elf. "Yes."

"Then Edwin will retrieve Alfred and the Guild Master," said Silvia. "Take enough provisions to not stop in the Sages' Grove."

"Someone would be either expecting us to return or leave from there," Hope surmised.

"Exactly," said Silvia. "Travel safely."

Chapter Fourteen

Tren

Hope and Obie climbed back to the symbol room. While Obie relayed a message from Berty and Silvia to Otho, Hope said to her inner circle, "There is nothing more for us to do here. We should get ready to leave."

In the windowless quarters, Hope repacked her bag to make room for provisions. When Berty entered the room, Hope asked, "Is everything okay?"

"I want to make sure you have enough money to pay for passage, lodging, or meals," he said, digging into his bag. He handed her a heavy sack.

"This is too much," she said without opening it.

"Take it. You never know when you'll need extra money," said Berty.

She dropped the leather pouch into her bag. "Thanks, Uncle Berty."

With provisions packed, they ate while waiting for Edwin. He and Colvin finally joined them at the table. The Elf checked and double checked their supplies before they left the outpost.

Yards away, Hope turned to look at the Keep. The black stone structure had disappeared. In its place, a thicket of trees blended seamlessly with the surrounding forest. "Are you sure you can get back?" she asked Edwin.

They all turned. "Impressive," said Edwin. "I'll be fine."

"I wouldn't," said Colvin.

"Good thing you have me," Edwin said, clapping the Dwarf on the shoulder.

A distant screech cut off Colvin's grumbles. They hurried into the cover of the trees. Obie constantly checked the skies as they trekked. To Hope's relief, nothing found nor followed them. She still could not grip her bow.

With the trees' guidance, Hope suggested a sheltered campsite. Edwin agreed, then prepared food from his provisions for all of them. After eating, he made Hope, Verity, and Mike practice with their blades, showing them different techniques.

Hope drew a small Fairy Ring around their campsite for protection during the night. Edwin would not stay in a dome without Declan or Berty who could see through the opalescent glow. He released Obie from night watch duty so that Obie could block Hope's nightmares. Sleeping while holding hands with Obie proved awkward on bedrolls. Obie's bedroll almost touched Hope's to make sure neither hand slipped out of the other's.

On the second morning since leaving the outpost, Edwin said over breakfast, "Colvin and I will reach the Sages' Grove tomorrow. You cannot come too close to the village. Take a path more west. We'll go the direct route. Don't stop in the hamlet either."

Hope nodded as she chewed.

After breaking the Fairy Ring, Hope thanked Edwin for everything. They said good-bye and walked separate paths. Soon, the Elf and Dwarf strode out of sight. When she could no longer hear their rustlings in the underbrush, Hope felt strangely alone. Edwin's presence brought her a bubble of safety. Although she improved with a blade, not being able to use her bow made her feel defenseless. Her hand had not been healing as quickly as she would like—as warned. Not wanting to imagine how rusty her archery might be, she released a frustrated breath.

"Anything wrong?" asked Mike.

"Just the usual," she answered. The trees sent her a message. Her head turned to look at a spot behind Mike. Both Obie and Sorrel unsheathed their swords. "A dog being pursued by a man," she said.

"What are you talking about?" said Mike barely above a whisper.

A soft clomping, then a rustling of vegetation reached their ears. A large pawed, brown bundle burst out of a bush.

"Hugh," a man's voice called. "Hugh, where are you?"

Wagging its tail, the puppy barked twice as though an answer. It sat at Mike's feet, looking up at him with its big brown eyes. It turned to look behind as if to ask what was keeping its owner. The puppy barked again.

A man in a lavender gray cloak bumbled their way, pushing bushes aside with his walking staff. "Hugh, there you are. Why did you wander off like that?" He patted his thigh. "Come here, Hugh. No bothering these nice people." His gray eyes noticed Obie and Sorrel, then rested on Mike. "Lord Hunter," he said with a bow of his head, "I apologize if my dog disturbed you. He's only a puppy. I still have much to teach him."

"He's not bothering anyone," said Mike. He looked from the dog, who sniffed the ground with enthusiasm, to its owner. "I don't believe we've met."

"No, my Lord. I recognize the Empress' color and you're traveling with Empire Guards. You must be close family because you're too old to be her son." Sunlight glinted off an exposed portion of a silver crystal hanging around the man's neck. "May I offer my assistance in whatever brings you away from the Empire Tree, Lord Hunter?"

"Who are you again?" Mike asked.

"This is Sean," said Hope. "Warrior Mage and bearer of the Staff of Lightning. He accompanied my uncle often and fought in the Battle of Fairyland."

Sean's gaze snapped to Hope. He stood up straighter. Studying her green cloak, he gasped. "I didn't recognize you without your maroon cloak, Miss Chase. Unless you're Missus..." He looked up at Obie. "You must be Declan's nephew." Obie gave him a sharp nod. "You sure got tall and broader than your uncle."

Shaking her head, Hope rolled her eyes. "We need to get moving. Sean, are you coming or not?" She figured another magic user would be useful.

"Sure," Sean said. They started walking. "Come, Hugh," he said, slapping his thigh. The puppy bounded to his side. "Where are we going?"

"This way," answered Hope.

Sean frowned, but nodded.

After making camp and collecting firewood, Hope constructed a Fairy dome. Sean stared at the swirling opalescence, frowning. "These still glow all night, don't they?" he said.

"I don't want to be overheard," said Hope.

"I thought Whispers no longer posed a problem," he said.

"The problem is we don't know what's out there," she answered. "And I don't want to see what happens when your dog tries to cross a Fairy Ring. Anyway, if you're coming with us, it's only fair to disclose what we're doing. First, we are heading to the northern coast. Second, our lives may be in danger. Third, upon knowing this, if you no longer wish to come, we understand."

Sean looked form Hope to Mike. "Who's in charge here?"

"She is," said Mike.

"I'm with you," said Sean. He laughed a little. "What's an adventure without your lives being in danger? A Chase, a Hunter, a Firth, an Empire Guard, and a maiden." He laughed again.

"Hope, Martin, Lieutenant Oberon, Sergeant Sorrel, and Verity," said Hope.

Smiling and apparently lost in his own thoughts, Sean gave his puppy scraps of food.

Obie ignored Sean. He sat beside Hope to examine her hand. "Squeeze," he instructed. Her fist lasted only a moment while she grimaced in pain.

"That's a nasty looking bruise," said Sean.

"I was attacked," she said.

"By whom?"

"Doesn't matter. He's dead." Her voice came out flat and lifeless.

Sean shivered. "I mean, who are we up against?"

Replacing her fingerless glove, Hope said, "That's what we're trying to find out."

Sean stroked between his puppy's ears. "I assume you can't use your bow," he said. "Are you using another weapon or do you have magic like the Emperor?"

"My magic is different than my uncle's. I have a blade."

"You all seem to have blades," said Sean. He turned in Verity's direction. "Aren't you an Elf?" She nodded. "You should be able to use a bow well."

Her face flushed. "I—I—I—I... I'm not that type of Elf."

"You're not from Irmingard?"

"Lived there my entire life."

His brow furrowed. "I don't understand."

Verity fidgeted with her cloak. "At thirteen or fourteen, we all get basic Warrior training. Some join the Warriors. Some join the Empire Guard. Others take up a trade or continue their education. It mostly depends on your family—your House. I hail from the House of Saggard. We are an erudite House. Most Elves carry blades for protection."

"But Elves are such naturally talented archers," Sean countered.

Chuckling, Verity dropped the edges of her cloak. "You have never been to Irmingard. Most areas, such as where I lived, are not conducive to archery. A blade is more practical a weapon."

Sean looked at his sleeping puppy while rubbing the back of his neck. "There are some things I'll never understand," he mumbled. "Anyway," he glanced at them, "I'm going to try to sleep under the glow." The dog woke when Sean moved. It sat, watching Sean. Once he laid on his bedroll, the puppy curled up next to him.

The cute scene made Hope smile.

"How do you want to handle watch, Lieutenant?" asked Sorrel.

"Can you see out?" Obie asked in return.

"No."

"Fairy domes render us invisible to the outside. No one can see us or hear us. No one, not even a Fairy, can enter or leave. It will protect us until Hope removes it."

Sorrel said nothing for a moment. "Why did we not use a dome when the Captain was with us?"

"Because none of us are Watchers," said Hope. "Only Watchers can see out."

A frown flashed on Sorrel's face.

Obie's gaze landed on a small tree within the dome. "We're not completely blind in here, Sergeant. Get your sleep."

Lying on her bedroll, Hope's gaze followed the swirls of opal-like fire swimming across the dome. Obie held her hand. She thought he lay an inch or so closer to her than the night before. Her mind wandered to the times she "camped" in her backyard under a Fairy dome, wishing Obie was by her side. Her hand tightened around his for a moment before closing her eyes.

"How does it stay lighted all night long?" Mike asked over breakfast.

"Magic," said Hope.

"So," said Mike, "how long will it take us to get there?"

"Last time, it took a week on horseback during winter," said Obie. "I figure a week and a half if we walk quickly and later."

Mike said nothing more.

Before breaking the dome, Hope consulted with the small tree she deliberately included. Through its roots, it could tell her what lay beyond the dome. "All clear," she said. After thanking the tree, she murmured the ancient Fairy incantation that released the magic.

Obie led them northward, keeping to the forest trails and off the roads. Sean's puppy, Hugh, trotted beside them, sometimes playing with twigs or other findings. Keeping a hand on the hilt of her sword, Sorrel's eyes swept the forest.

Mike walked with Verity, chuckling at Hugh when he scooted between their legs. After spitting a stick that he carried between his teeth onto the ground, Hugh started barking. He darted beyond Obie, barking at nothing or something no one could see.

"Hugh, get back here," Sean ordered.

The puppy ignored him.

The magic between the trees changed. "Dragon," Hope said to herself.

A black boxy head appeared in front of them. Hugh backed up until he hit Obie's legs, still barking. A black body snaked through the trees. "Greetings, Listener." The Dragon bowed his head in respect.

"Hello, Tong," she said. Hope stepped forward, shushing the puppy. "To what do we owe the honor of your appearance?"

"I have been looking for you. You are not easy to find. The trees hide you well," said Tong. "It is a good thing that you are my Match's kin. I had to track you by the smell of your blood." His golden mustache twitched.

Hope gulped. "Why were you looking for me? What's wrong?"

"There are more than just Griffins escaping God Mountain," he said. "Our ancient enemy pursues you. I've alerted the clans. You search for answers. I wish to help. The Emperor told me where you're headed. I cannot take you all the way there, but I can get you as far as Gnome Knoll."

Hope smiled at the Dragon. "That would be very appreciated."

"Get on my back," Tong said.

Sean scooped Hugh off the ground. He hurried to climb the Dragon's back with his puppy and staff. Shaking his head, Mike mounted the Dragon next. Verity approached cautiously. While Obie made sure everyone was secure on Tong's back, Hope sat in the space behind Tong's head where Berty normally sat. Once Obie straddled the Dragon's back behind Hope, he tapped her shoulder, saying, "Okay."

"We're ready," Hope said to Tong.

Her hands pressed against the tiny, cool, black feathers that resembled scales as Tong's squat legs pushed off the ground. Green and brown blurred around them. She focused on the back of Tong's head, but it did not stem the rising dizziness. When she closed her eyes, a weightless free-falling sensation overtook her senses. They had dematerialized. Usually, she loved riding on the back of the Dragon. To her, it felt like being on a rollercoaster, only better. However, this time, dizziness mingled with queasiness. She attributed the nausea to her bruise, somehow. Once her stomach returned to normal, she counted to ten, then opened her eyes. Pine assaulted her nostrils.

Tong landed in a small clearing surrounded by towering pines. After taking a settling breath, she slid off his back. The pines cast long shadows across the grassy knoll. The sun was sinking. "Thank you, Tong," she said, rubbing his head. Tong closed his eyes, a look of enjoyment swept across his boxy face.

"I'll be following and watching as closely as possible," said Tong. "People tend to fear me. Which is understandable; I *am* fearsome." He smiled for a moment. "For some reason, I cannot cross the water, invisible or visible."

"It's okay. You've done so much already," said Hope. She took another look at the shadows, then asked the trees which way to Tren. "Let's get going," she said to her companions. Verity and Mike wobbled slightly. "We need to be inside the gates before sundown." She led them into the pine forest.

"Why? What happens at sundown?" Sean asked, catching up to her.

"They close the gates," said Hope.

"And the probability for a Gnome attack increases," Obie added.

"Gnomes?" said Mike.

"Trust us. You'd rather not know," said Obie in a dark tone.

After a few steps, Mike said, "I want to know."

Hope sighed. She checked to see if they all followed closely, including the dog. "Do you know why people place brightly colored statues of Gnomes in their yards?" she asked.

"I'm guessing it has nothing to do with lawn ornaments," Mike said.

"Gnomes traditionally attack at night in groups of three or four. They destroy gardens and crops, disturb livestock, sometimes killing them, and attempt to get inside homes where they ravish food stores. When caught, their bodies were put on display as a warning to other Gnomes—think Vlad the Impaler, but without the impaling. Oftentimes, the bodies would be painted in bright colors so that they could be easily seen at a distance. Gnomes would then avoid those homes and find other prey," Hope said.

"Who's Vlad?" asked Sean.

"People who weren't quick enough to catch Gnomes used likenesses," continued Hope. "Eventually, making statues."

"That's really gruesome," said Mike.

"Who's Vlad," Sean asked again.

Ignoring him, Hope said, "Now, they attack in large swarms. There had to be hundreds of them last time. They were endless and nothing seemed to stop them."

"Gnomes?" Sean asked.

"Yes, Gnomes," answered Hope. "That's why we need to get inside the gates before sundown."

Sean was silent for a moment. Hope relished in the sounds of the forest. Then, he said, "Who is this Vlad?"

"A brutal, brutal nobleman who lived hundreds of years ago on the other side of the portal," she explained.

No one said anything until they emerged from the woods. A spike wall barricaded the landscape from view. "So, those spikes keep the Gnomes out?" asked Mike. They hastened their pace to reach the gate.

The guards flanking the gate stood straighter when they noticed Empire Guards entering. Hope wondered if Obie and Sorrel should have removed their armor. *Oh well, too late now.*

Workers toiled in the fields alongside the road that connected the outer and inner gates. A few raindrops plunked Hope's head, causing her to raise her hood. Cool, steady rain fell by the time they reached the inner gate. Both Sorrel and Obie pulled their cloaks closed over their armor. Only the tree insignia on their cloak clasps gave away their Empire Guard status. The guards at the gate treated them like everyone else—without notice.

The busy, paved streets of Tren teemed with people hurrying one way or another. Water rushed along the gutters in the center of the streets. They weaved through the city, making their way to the harbor. Light rain turned into pouring rain by the time they reached the docks. Hope asked a dock attendant for directions.

He pointed without saying a word.

"You frightened him," Mike whispered in her ear.

"It's the ship's captain who frightens him."

Finally reading *Nerida* painted on the stern of a ship, Hope stopped. She surveyed the all-woman crew. The rain did not slow them from rolling barrels or craning crates onto or below deck. She approached a woman overseeing the loading from the dockside. "Excuse me," said Hope. "Where are you headed?"

The woman whipped around. "What does it matter ta ye?"

"I wanted to enquire about room for passengers," said Hope, trying not to stare at her gold teeth and only look into her good eye.

"Run along and play, girlie."

"Kara!" reprimanded a voice from the gangplank. "What have I told you, over and over again? Civility in port or you go back to the depths."

Kara's lip twitched into a sneer.

"Back to work." A woman, a head shorter than Hope, stepped onto the dock. Her rich red and gold sailing uniform stood out against the gray surroundings. A wide brimmed hat covered her cascading dark hair woven with gray. Hope recognized the gold and gemstone hilt of her cutlass that hung from her belt.

"Captain Mabe," greeted Hope.

The woman flashed a smile, then bit on the mouthpiece of an unlit pipe. "What can I do for the Empire?" she asked, pipe still between her teeth.

"We seek passage to Pixisle. Are you heading there?" asked Hope.

"How's Declan?" Mabe asked in return.

"Married," Obie quickly answered.

Mabe chewed on her pipe. "Aye, but we don't leave until tomorrow." She removed the pipe from her mouth. "No mangy mutts and no Elves."

"He's not mangy," argued Sean.

"I don't make the rules, except about the dog. No dogs on my ship." She glanced at Verity. "Elves are forbidden to cross."

"Perhaps if we spoke with—" Hope began.

"I'm not risking my ship and crew because the Empire has a problem with the rules put forth by others," said Mabe. Her lips pursed. "Tell you what. See Tan in the Hen and Wren. Get a room and food. The Elf will be safe there with the dog until you return. I want no trouble with the Empress... or Declan. We leave with the tide tomorrow. Be here or find another way."

"How much?" Hope asked.

"A ver each. I trust you have it." Mabe returned to her ship.

With drenched cloaks, they stepped inside the Hen and Wren. A fire roared next to the desk that blocked stairs to the upper levels. Another, albeit more generous, fire warmed an open common room on the left. Beyond the round tables, a wall of windows overlooked a gloomy harbor.

"Whatcha be needin', loves?" asked a sturdy woman who emerged from behind a pair of swinging doors under the stairs.

"We're looking for Tan," said Hope.

The woman laughed. "Mabe sent you. I'm Ya-ya," she said. "Leaving with her tomorrow? You'll need some rooms." She grabbed keys from under the desk. "I have two left."

"One of our party is staying with the dog," said Obie.

"Not a problem," said Ya-ya. "What a cute puppy. Follow me." She led them up the stairs. Unlocking the first room, she said, "The puppy and its keeper can stay in here." A few doors down, on the other side of the hall, she unlocked the second room. "This'll sleep four." Ya-ya opened the murphy beds above the two twin beds. "The rooms come with full meals."

"Thanks, Ya-ya," said Obie.

"It'll be eleven rons four cops for them both."

Hope dug into her pack for the money Berty gave her. "How about I give you a ver and that'll pay for tonight and secure the room for while the rest of us are away. Balance to be paid upon our return."

"Sounds good to me," said Ya-ya. She tucked the silver coin into a pocket. "Supper starts soon. Come down when you want." After handing Hope the keys, Ya-ya walked back down the hall.

"Hope and Obie need the room with the bed," said Verity. "I would like to bathe before we eat."

Hope nodded. After figuring out which key opened which room, she handed Mike the second room's key. "We'll be down the hall."

In the first room, Hope set her pack on the floor next to the table and chair. Obie peeked behind a door. "Bathroom," he said. After hanging her wet cloak on the cloak rack, she extracted the coin purse from her bag, then dumped its contents onto the double bed. Obie helped her group and count the coins.

"I don't want to keep all this money on me," she said. "Besides, Verity will need it most." She separated five vers from the bunch. "That covers the boat."

"Will you give any to Sean?" Obie asked.

"No." She made five piles of coins. She, Mike, and Verity would get the majority of the coins. Obie and Sorrel would hold emergency back-up money. No one would expect a guard to pay for anything when with a charge. Hope split her money into different pockets.

While Obie took his, Hope scooped Verity's into the coin purse Berty gave her.

Obie left to retrieve Mike first.

"Hope," called Jon's voice.

"Dad?" said Hope. Her father appeared in the room.

"Good. You're alone. I didn't want to startle the others," he said. "Just checking on you. See how you are and what you're doing."

"We picked up Sean. Tong brought us to Tren. We leave tomorrow with Captain Mabe," reported Hope.

The door opened. Mike entered with Obie. Noticing Jon, Mike stopped. "Mister Chase, when did you get here?" Mike asked.

"Ah," said Jon. "I'm not. Hope will explain."

"Dad, I'd like to know why we weren't told that Verity couldn't go," Hope continued.

"I'll have to ask," said Jon.

"Well, rules from the Water Sprites would have been good to know from the onset," Hope said, annoyance pouring from her voice. She took a breath. "How's everything on your side?"

"Everything's great. Mom and Lily say hi." Jon turned to Mike. "Your grandfather says not to worry about missing your graduation. Your mother has left. No one can find her—not even her lawyer. We think she may be looking for you. And, she could be employing magic in her search. Keep your eyes peeled." He faced his daughter. "Well, that's it. Stay safe and I'll check in on you soon."

"'Kay, Dad. Love you guys."

"Love you too, honey," he said, smiling. After giving them a little wave, he disappeared.

"Your dad has magic?" Mike asked.

"And my sister."

Mike said nothing. Obie steered him towards the coin filled bed. While Mike examined each of the different coins, Obie and Hope explained the money to him. "If you forget or need advice on a price, ask Sorrel," said Obie. Mike left, sending Sorrel to collect her share of the money.

When Hope and Obie gathered the others for dinner, she handed Verity the coin purse. Downstairs, laughter and conversation filled the common room. They passed customers too busy eating and drinking to glance at them. Sean found a table near the windows overlooking the gloomy harbor. Soon after they sat, a waitress brought food and ale. Sean requested some scraps for Hugh, who ate his dinner while positioned between Sean's feet.

Lightening flashed, silhouetting ships against the clouds. Rain lashed the windows. The fire and never-ending tankards of ale kept the other patrons happy. Only those at her table glanced outside when the wind smashed raindrops against the glass. "Can't imagine being out on a boat, even tethered to a pier, in this weather," said Mike who gaped out the window.

"Aye, nasty storm," answered an old man from the next table. His weathered hand clutched a battered tin tankard. He brought it up to a mouth hidden behind a full, wiry, gray beard. His cloak told stories of blustery storms and wave-washed travel to distant shores. The ancient mariner sat alone, the ale his only company. "What brings agents of the Empire this far north?"

Hope stopped chewing her food. Neither Obie nor Sorrel revealed their armor. How would he know? Unless… he saw them on the docks, speaking to Mabe. "Our business is our own, old man. What's it to you?" said Sean. Hope swallowed her food, thinking that she would have used a bit more tact.

The man laughed. His cloudy sea eyes rested on Verity. "We don't see your kind up here," he said to her.

"It's personal," interjected Hope. "Our business, that is."

"I thought the Empire was here sorting out our Gnome problem."

"If we were, we wouldn't be sitting in this place," said Sean.

"The Empire is well aware of the Gnomes, sir," said Obie.

The old man snorted into his tankard. "Those little, evil things brutally murdered me wife an'a me daughter," he said. Revulsion dripped off his words. "What has the Empire done? Nothing! Nothing at all to protect us!" He spat on the floor.

Obie's nostrils flared. "It is not the Empire's job to protect one from every single thing," he said, his voice flat but direct. "Protection is an individual's job—to protect oneself, one's family, and one's property. If one is so inclined, even one's neighbor. Laws of this land dictate what the Empire can and cannot do. It is up to each community to request the Empire's help, if so needed. Citizens can also petition directly to the Empire, especially if they feel their community is not doing its job. The Empire is but a resource, a tool, for its citizens, not a nanny nor a scapegoat for their problems." He paused for a breath. "Please accept our sincerest condolences for your family, sir. Know that the Empire has firsthand knowledge of the Gnome problem. They are working on that along with other problems that plague the Empire."

Grunting, the old man slammed his tankard on the table then clomped to the door.

After throwing glances around the table and shrugging, they finished their meal, listening to and watching the room around them. Thunder shook the inn. Sean bought another round of ale. Successive lightning strikes showed boats crashing against the piers.

Pipe in hand, Mabe strolled past their table. "That storm's a nasty piece of work," she said. She sat at a small corner table. Leaning back on a chair, she lit her pipe.

"What? Does she not care?" Mike asked in a low whisper.

"Very much so," said Obie. "My uncle says she's an excellent Captain. No one better on the water and very protective of her ship."

She puffed on her pipe as a waitress set a glass down in front of her. Obie's eyes followed Ya-ya to Mabe's table.

"On land, different story," Obie continued, his voice so low the others had to lean in to hear.

"How does he know?" asked Mike.

"He spent some time in the region."

"Why doesn't he know more about Gnomes?" asked Hope.

He shrugged. "We should get some sleep."

Sean chugged the rest of his ale before they climbed the stairs to their rooms. Hope watched the others leave her at her door. A part of her wanted to go with them. Drunken singing carried up the steps, mingling with the grumbles of thunder. Obie held the door open for her. Stepping inside the room, she searched its emptiness. She jumped when the door closed behind her.

"Are you okay?" he asked.

Being alone, especially alone with Obie, scared her. They were friends, best friends. And what more? She bit her lip. A lip Obie's had touched, kissed. She held onto the table for stability. "I don't like leaving Verity here alone," she said.

"I know," said Obie. He unlaced his boots. "Can't you protect her like the Keep?"

She sat in the chair beside her pack. "Might do more harm than good," she said, tugging off her socks. "She'd be invisible."

Grunting in agreement, he removed his armor.

She turned her head although he wore a shirt underneath the leather and padded tunic. "I'm going to use the bathroom to change," she announced. Not waiting for his response, she retreated to the tiny room with her hastily unpacked nightclothes.

When she emerged, he had already changed. He entered the bathroom while she put her clothes away. She sat in the bed, covers drawn. Her heart pounded. She could not get herself to lie down.

Walking out of the bathroom, Obie did not look at her until he found the bed. He glanced at her before climbing on the empty side. "Didn't mean to keep you waiting," he mumbled. "You ready?"

She nodded. He extinguished the candle on the nightstand. Lying down, they held hands.

"Why does it only come when I sleep?" she asked him in the dark.

"I've been wondering the same." He squeezed her hand. "I think it's because you—anyone—don't have control over your magic when you sleep. Or at least not as much. Maybe whoever is doing this needs that vulnerability." He paused. "I wish I had a better answer for you."

"It's a good theory, but that doesn't explain how the symbol on the bow worked."

"I know. That bothers me." The bed bounced while he shifted. "We'll figure it out. That's why we're here." A flash of lightning showed Obie on his side, facing her, his free hand crossing the barrier between them. She closed her eyes, waiting for the contact. It never came. The bed bounced again. She fell asleep.

In the morning, Hope dressed in what felt like soggy clothes. The storm subsided, but a city strangling mist settled, reaching every door and window. Verity brought her things into the room, Sean on her heels. "Sean, I know how to take care of a dog. Don't worry," she said.

Hope laughed to herself. She handed Verity the key.

"I'll walk with you to the ship," said the Elf.

They trudged through the cool mist to the harbor. Hugh stayed under Sean's cloak. When they arrived at the Nerida, they said good-bye.

"Be careful," Hope said to Verity.

"You, too," the Elf answered.

Sean spoke to his dog. "Be good, Hugh. Listen to Verity and protect her. I'll be back before you know it." Hugh licked Sean's face. Sean kissed the puppy on the head. Hugh stood next to Verity, as if he understood, to watch his master board.

A crew member showed them to the room the five of them would share. Hammocks hung bunkbed style. Built-in trunks lined the walls for secure storage. They stored their packs, then climbed back to the deck. Verity stood on the gray pier, returning their waves while the Nerida sailed out of dock.

Chapter Fifteen

Pixisle Passage

The misty fog dangled over the sea. Waves reached to kiss the cloud as if welcoming the airborne water back home. Not far from the docks, the harbor and its city faded into the gray mass. The low hanging cloud saturated everything—the deck, the railings, the ropes, the sails, the cloaks, their clothes underneath all the way to their skin. Uncomfortably soggy, they returned below deck.

They found a room with a fire lit in a furnace-esque grate. Sitting, they huddled around it to find a little warmth and perhaps dry their damp clothing. Mabe soon joined them. She puffed on her pipe a few times, squinting at them through the smoke. "I know you," she said. "You were the girl on my boat with the Empress." She stared at Hope before turning her attention to Obie. "And you're the boy." She laughed. "The Pixies come and go now, a handful at a time. Is there anything I need to know? I'm not risking my neck, my crew, or my ship."

Hope laughed a little to lighten the mood in the room. "We're just visiting," she said.

Chewing on her pipe, Mabe examined her. "With two Empire Guards who couldn't stay with the Elf girl?"

"It's complicated, Captain," said Hope.

"It always is."

"For either one to have stayed would have been a dereliction of duty," said Hope, not knowing from where her words came.

Mabe leaned back in the chair. Staring straight at Sean, she said, "And where do you fit in?"

"Adventure," Sean answered. "And if I find a wife in the process, I'll make my mother happy."

Laughter burst from Mabe. She held onto her chair as to not fall off in laughing fits. Composing herself, she said, "Most of the Pixies married years ago."

"She doesn't have to be a Pixie," muttered Sean.

Wiping her eyes while still chuckling, Mabe left them.

Sean stared at the floor. "Love is elusive," he said in a quiet voice. His staff rolled between his fingers. "Berty loved Silvia so much he was willing to give his life for her. How do you find that? How do you know?" After a couple of breaths, he walked out of the room, leaving the four of them alone.

"Do you really trust him?" Sorrel asked Hope.

Hope stared at the doorway through which he left. "He's... weird. Always been weird. But, trustworthy and a good fighter."

"Shouldn't he have stayed to protect Verity? It's his dog, after all," Sorrel said.

Her eyes found Sorrel. Her mouth opened, then she closed it. "It's better that he's with us," she finally said.

"Why?"

Hope shook her head at her.

"I deserve to know something," Sorrel snapped. "We all can't have high ranking Empire Official relatives."

"You're out of line, Sergeant," Obie reprimanded.

"Oh, yes! Please, remind me of my rank," said Sorrel, sparks of pink crackled in her hair. "That I didn't get promoted like *you* did."

Obie's hand clutched the arms of the chair in which he sat. "Control your temper and maybe your rank will improve," he said.

"Ha! Practicing for your next job?"

"What next job?"

"Captain of the Empire Guard!"

Standing, Obie took a half step away from the chair. "Perhaps, I should also remind you that your assignment is only until the end of the summer. Mine is for life." Her magic retreated. "Plus, remind you that at the Battle of Fairyland, the Empress herself gave you a new life. And you've been squandering it being jealous and angry. Shape up, Sergeant. The world owes you nothing you haven't earned." Turning on his heel, Obie pounded out of the room.

Sorrel's chest rose and fell with each breath, staring at Obie's vacated seat. She, too, stormed away.

Mike looked at Hope. "Guess it's just you and me."

A bell rang from somewhere above them. Crew raced past the doorway. Hope and Mike rushed after. The crew gathered on deck, facing their Captain. Fog chomped over the railings, devouring all from view. Mike grabbed Hope's hand before they, too, disappeared into the gray.

"This is no ordinary fog, ladies," said Mabe's voice, clear and distinct. "All non-essential crew must remain below deck. Keep all portholes closed. The bell will ring until we can see again. Our navigational instruments fail against it. This fog has magic." Mike squashed her hand.

"If I may, Captain," said Sean's voice from somewhere on the fog engulfed deck.

"Go ahead," said Mabe. Hope wondered if anyone else detected the strain in her voice.

Wood tapped against wood. A glow lightened the fog around the top of Sean's staff. He spoke in the ancient tongue. Lightning sparked through the fog. The fog dispersed. Women ducked away from the traveling sparks. The lightning from his staff pushed the fog off the ship.

The Staff of Lightning transformed from a simple walking staff to its full glory. A clear crystal topped the ancient wood. A few inches from the crystal, hung a lone feather whose purpose Hope never knew.

"Good thing Sean didn't stay with Verity," Mike said in her ear. She agreed while she watched Sean work.

Sean moved to the bow of the ship, staff striking the deck with each step. Facing the fog, he lifted the Staff of Lightning. The language of the ancients rolled off his tongue.

"What's he saying?" whispered Mike.

"He's calling to the latent electricity in the fog to meet with his," said Hope. "Could also translate as spark or current."

Lightning forked from his staff into the fog. When the lightning crackled to another part of the cloud, the fog dissipated. Breaths escaped the crew as gray water became visible once again.

"May we move forward without harm, Mage?" Mabe called to Sean.

"Yes, I will continue to divert this... fog," Sean answered.

"No staring. Let the Mage do his work," Mabe barked. "Onward, ladies!" The women scattered.

Dropping Hope's hand, Mike said, "Why don't we explore the ship?"

Not seeing either Obie or Sorrel, she agreed.

Ten years ago, she and Obie explored the Nerida. Not much changed—only herself. Their tour finished in the galley where they found Obie. Grabbing some food, they sat with him.

"Are you okay?" Hope asked him.

Obie grunted.

"So, how long will it take us to reach.... Where are we going again?" asked Mike.

"Pixisle," answered Hope. "Days."

"And you can only reach this Pixisle by boat?"

"That would be a very long bridge," said Hope.

"What about magical ways?" Mike asked.

"I don't know. Even Tong couldn't cross," she replied. "It might not be possible."

Mike's shoulders dropped into a more relaxed position.

Before evening fell, Sean managed to part the fog enough for them to escape to clearing skies. He shot lightning at it from the stern to stop it from following. "No other ships will be penetrating that fog without help," Mabe told Sean. Hope believed that to be somewhat of a compliment.

She slipped away to their cabin while crew recalled stories of their adventures. Alone, she sat on a hammock. To whom did the fog belong? The magic in that fog was meant to ensnare. Who? Them? Her? Someone else? If that magic could be on the water, then why could Tong not traverse the water? Was there a certain point where magic could not cross?

When the door opened, her mind ceased questioning. Sorrel entered, softly closing the door behind her. The female Warlock stood in front of Hope. "I came to apologize," said Sorrel. "I spoke out of line and allowed the demons inside to take over."

"You need to be saying this to Obie," said Hope.

"I've already spoken to the Lieutenant."

Not knowing what to say, Hope nodded. When Sorrel still stood there, Hope said, "Inner demons?"

"I... lived in fear most of my life," Sorrel began to explain, clutching the trim of her dark green cloak. "My parents died when I was young and my uncle raised me. He," she looked away from a moment. "Let's just say he was a cruel man. Joining the Empire Guard... saved me. Somewhere, my fear turned to anger and I became envious of those who had families to return to during leave and holidays—places they called home. I never returned to my uncle's house. Staying with the Empire Guard... It's a strange place for a woman. There aren't many of us. Those who are, usually are Elves. It's... They're different."

Hope nodded again.

"I know I lash out too much and too often. Protecting Martin is an opportunity that I don't want to mess up. I am making the effort to be better." Her hands released the edges of her cloak as she turned to leave.

"Wait," said Hope. The woman spun to face her. "We are on open water. An insignificant little dot among the waves. Take off your armor while you're out here. Free yourself from your anger and let those demons drown."

Sorrel cracked a smile. "Thank you."

Leaving Sorrel in the room, Hope wandered about deck. The cargo ship was smaller than she recalled, or perhaps she was bigger. She remembered the pitching with the waves as more fun. Cracks in the cloud cover revealed stars. She leaned against the railing. Shining tales broke the surface of the water every once in a while. They entered the domain of the Water Sprites. No magic would dare follow them. Hope smiled.

When she returned to the cabin, Obie rose off a hammock, free of his armor. "How... How do you want to work this?" he asked.

"I want to test a theory," she said.

Sean paused searching his pack while Mike raised his eyebrows at her. Obie patiently waited for her to explain.

"I believe we've crossed into Water Sprite territory," said Hope. "And I think their magic blocks other magic. So, I want to see if the nightmares will also stay away."

"I don't think you should, Hope," said Obie. "That *thing* was in your bedroom. There's no wooden doll to save you."

"What thing?" asked both Mike and Sean simultaneously. Sorrel raised her head off her hammock.

She waved away their question. "But you'll be in the hammock right below me," she said.

"What if it's not enough? I won't know you're in trouble until you're screaming. By then, it could be too late," said Obie.

"I want to try."

"Hope," he took both her hands, "you've been inaccessible for nights, now. This... wacko could be waiting for you with who knows what."

She yanked her hands out of his. "You have always assumed the role of my protector, assignment or not. Why can't you trust me?"

Obie flinched as if she slapped him.

She strode out of the cabin, slamming the door behind her. The salt air stung her moist eyes. She slunk onto a coil of rope. In the dark, hot tears streamed down her face.

Obie sat on the deck next to her. Their knees touched. "Hope," he said in a soft voice.

"Go away."

He inhaled audibly. "No," he said. "I do trust you, Hope. I've always protected you because I—I've always cared. Even if this wasn't my official duty, I'd still be here. Hope, I'm afraid that I wouldn't be able to reach you in time. What if I can't save you?"

His light eyes shined like the stars. They pleaded with her. She wiped her cheeks with the back of her hand. "You're right," she said. "I haven't had a chance to read that journal before it disintegrates. Nor, do we know enough about this wacko, as you call him."

Obie's fingers dried her damp cheeks with his soft touch. Reaching her hair, they paused before curling her dark hair around them. Then, he withdrew. "Being on this boat affords you time. Take advantage of it."

Hope nodded.

Obie pulled her to her feet. Together, they returned to the cabin.

"I noticed that these hammocks are secured by notches in these vertical rails," said Mike as soon as they entered. "If you take the top one off the notches, you could slide it down to the bottom notches. Your hammocks can be side by side."

Obie inspected the top hammock. In a couple of minutes, the top hammock slung next to the bottom hammock.

"Guess I'm in the back one," said Hope.

"Need help?" asked Obie.

She shook her head. "Thanks, Mi—Martin." She climbed into her hammock, getting her foot caught in the front one. As soon as she settled, Obie climbed into his. Their cloth cradled bodies banged into one another. They linked hands before falling asleep.

During the night, the clouds cleared, revealing soft blue morning skies. Afraid the sea spray would destroy the old paper, Hope sat in an inner room, reading her predecessor's journal. Pages loosened from the binding as she turned. She took notes about rituals, blessings, and meetings in the modern tongue.

"You've been at this for hours," said Mike, entering the room. "Come out and get a little sun. It's beautiful."

Dropping the pen on her notes, she stretched her hand. She groaned as she leaned back in the chair. "I would, but it's important I get through this." Mike sat on a chair he pulled next to the table at which she worked. "So far, I've been learning about what it means to be me. What others expect of me. Not that I have to do everything his way." She pushed her hair out of her eyes. "I need to know why he left before we reach our destination."

Mike peeked at the open page of the journal. "That must be the ancient language."

"Yeah. I'm translating the important bits to English."

Smiling, Mike said, "You're amazing, Hope Chase."

She looked away from him, laughing a little.

"Can I fetch you something to eat or drink?" asked Mike.

"Already done," said Obie. He placed a plate and goblet on the table for her.

Mike made a face.

"Can I ask you about Sorrel, Hope?" Obie asked, standing on the other side of the table from Mike.

After thanking him for the food, she said, "And why I recommended she not wear armor?"

"Yes."

Hope nibbled on a piece of hard bread. "I won't tell you our personal conversation, but she needs to do so in order to deal with her anger issues."

"I hope it works for her," muttered Obie. "I'll leave you to get back to your work." He glanced at Mike. "Don't forget to get some fresh air."

"You have worry issues, Obie," Hope said with a smile. "Just a few more hours."

"'Kay," said Obie. He glanced again at Mike before leaving.

"Do you need anything else?" Mike asked her.

"Nah, I'm good. Thanks though."

Once Mike left, she returned to the journal while absentmindedly eating and drinking only when she remembered that she had food. Eventually, her eyes could no longer decipher the words on the page. She stopped reading. The food that Obie brought had long gone. She needed something more to eat and a little sunlight would not go amiss before it plunged beyond the horizon.

Hope spent the next day in the same room hunched over the journal. Interesting, but nothing jumped out as pertinent. "I should have had Uncle Berty copy this for me," she muttered, flexing her cramped hand.

Pages of notes later, Obie checked on her, bringing lunch. "How goes it?" he asked.

She shrugged, then took a long drink. "Thanks." She stared at the opened journal. "He wrote down *everything*. Well, he left out his more private habits. So far, it tells me absolutely nothing about what we're facing. Maybe tomorrow. Maybe I should read the back first." She rubbed her eyes. "But, I'm afraid I'll miss a sign of trouble or something."

Obie nodded. "You're not taking as many notes?"

"Only if there's a change in a ritual or blessing or something."

He nodded again. "See you later," he said with a smile. "This ship's not the same without you." He stood. "And I think it's shrunk."

Hope laughed. She watched him leave, then returned to reading.

She found herself in that room again right after breakfast the next day. The journal grew tiresome. Then, the "journaling" abruptly stopped. He wrote, "*I have decided to leave through the portal and never return.*" She transcribed, word for word in the ancient tongue, all he wrote after. When she finished, she closed the journal. Obie found her staring at her pen. Her head snapped up to look at him.

"What's the matter?" He froze midstride, plate and goblet in hand. "Did you find out?"

Hope gave him a slow nod. He approached the table. When he sat, she tore off a chunk of bread, saying, "I don't want to talk about it right now."

"That bad?" he whispered.

Chewing, she did not answer.

Obie sat with her until she finished eating.

"He dismissed his Tender, so that he—his Tender—would be safe," Hope said finally. "The Empire knew of the problem. They sent guards who all died protecting him." Her eyes looked anywhere but at him.

She felt his hand on her arm. His magic reached for hers. The magics embraced. "I won't let you replace me," he said.

Finally, her eyes found his. "It's not that," she said. "*They* knew. The Empire *knew*."

"Come on. Let's get some fresh air," said Obie.

Hope squinted when they emerged on the deck of the ship. She inhaled the salty air as she followed Obie. "Yeah. Not feeling better," she said.

He made them stop near the railing. "That knowledge could have been lost," he said to her. "So much of it was."

"I know. Still," she said, watching waves swell.

He placed a hand on the small of her back as they leaned against the railing. Neither uttered a word until the usual nothings at dinner.

"There's nothing to do on this boat," Mike complained when they returned to the cabin for their cloaks.

"I'm sure our esteemed Captain could find you something," said Obie.

"There's always cards," said Sorrel. "I play with the crew all the time."

"I don't know how to play," Mike said.

"I'll teach you," said Sorrel.

"You've been awfully quiet, Sean," said Hope, fastening her bright green cloak around her shoulders.

"Just thinking," he answered.

Hope nodded, not wanting to know what churned in Sean's mind.

Above deck, she gazed at the stars glowing against the night sky. She noticed how the sea seemed to sparkle at night.

"With me," Mabe said at her shoulder.

Her insides froze. Mabe climbed the stairs to the bridge. Hope followed.

When she joined Mabe at the railing of the bridge, Hope asked, "Is there a problem, Captain?"

Mabe stared out at the sparkling dark sea. "What kind of personal business brings my ship under the watchful eye of the Water Sprites?"

"The glows... Those are Water Sprites?"

"They are relatively close to the surface."

Hope swallowed. "My business, while sanctioned by the Empire, is personal in the fact that I am being hunted by an entity known as the Gatherer. I come to Pixisle for answers. I need to defeat this Gatherer. I need my life back, Captain."

"Then it is you they sense," said Mabe. "Expect contact before you return to the mainland. I suspect your enemy is their enemy." Mabe nodded. "No harm will come to my ship. That's all I needed to know."

Escaping the bridge, Hope found Obie on the main deck. She told him what Mabe had said.

"You're probably right about being protected while in their territory," Obie conceded.

Hope shrugged. "Probably best to err on the side of caution."

Around midday the following day, the woman in the crow's nest spotted Pixisle. Ship activity increased in anticipation of docking. They retreated to their cabin to get ready to disembark.

With Sorrel donning her armor, they returned to the deck wearing their packs and cloaks. The ship eased into its dock along the single, long pier that disappeared into a hole in the cliff. Hope remembered walking through that hole to the town beyond with Silvia and Obie.

Harbor Pixies boarded the ship. A couple inspected the cargo, while another approached them, holding a clipboard. "Names and reason for visit," she said.

"Lord Hunter and his party on Empire business," said Sean.

"Oh," said the Pixie. She scanned her papers. "I do not have anything about expecting anyone from the Empire."

"You don't know how the Empire works, do you?" said Sean.

The woman breathed sharply through her nose. "I don't know who Lord Hunter is," she said.

Sean stepped closer to the Pixie. "Oh, for crying out loud," Hope muttered under her breath. She told the Pixie, "Lord Hunter is the ambassador for the Empress who, regrettably, could not attend in person. He has been newly appointed, so you would not have heard of him." Hope smiled. "He is here with his guard." She made a broad gesture towards Sorrel that could have been interpreted to mean Sean and Obie as well.

The Pixie looked Hope up and down. "And *who* are *you*?"

"I am the Wood Listener."

Fumbling with her pen, she said, "Of course, forgive me."

"We are here to see the Pixie Priestess," said Hope. "And you are going to write down Lord Hunter and not me on your sheet there." She gave the woman another smile.

"Yes," said the Pixie. "A Sini will escort your party to the Grand Temple. You may head into town."

Hope caught a glimpse of Mabe packing her pipe while shaking her head and wearing a wry smile. The Captain stayed aboard while they and some of the crew crossed the gangplank. Strolling along the pier, they passed one other ship docked there. The few men on and around that ship only gave a faint acknowledgement of them or any of Mabe's crew. The women sailors had an intimidating reputation.

A dark tunnel carved through the towering cliff that disappeared into the sea, granting them access to the town. Steep, winding streets wove around buildings dug into the mountainside. They passed the pier level warehouses, unsure of which street to take.

A woman draped in what resembled a blue sheet approached them. She eyed Mike. "You must be Lord Hunter," she said.

"You are Asini?" he asked.

The woman smiled. "My name is Lumi. Welcome to Pixisle, Lord Hunter. Merja awaits. Come."

Mike looked at Hope with question in his eyes. She gave him a small nod. "Thank you," said Mike. Lumi led them along the low street and away from the town.

Soft green branches swayed in greeting to Hope. Warmth grew inside her. "Every year since the Breaking, the island has become more beautiful," Lumi said. "Even winter is beautiful. I believe that was when you were here last." She gave Hope a pointed look.

Hope wondered how much this woman knew. "Yes, it was winter," she answered.

"It is an honor to have two of the Breakers with us," said Lumi.

Hope stopped, causing Obie to stumble into her. "How do you know who we are?" she asked the Pixie.

"We celebrate the Breaking every year. The magical signatures of the Breakers are well known to the Sini," the Pixie explained. "And I have never seen the trees happier to have their Listener in their midst. The portal to the Grand Temple is ahead."

The trees did not contradict. Hope continued walking.

They arrived at a small crossroads. The multiple branching pathways ended at what Hope believed to be portals. "Take only the path I use or you'll end up somewhere else on the island," cautioned Lumi.

Hope stepped through the portal with Obie close enough to touch. Lumi waited for them in the center of another, much larger, portal crossways. A trickle of women moved from portal to portal; to where, Hope did not know.

From the portals, they walked along a path flanked by white stone colonnades. If she looked at the columns a certain way, Hope thought the white had a bluish hue. Blue blossoms blanketed woody stems of a vine that roofed the pathway. Further down the path, speckled stone paving replaced the dirt. The vines disappeared above a real roof.

The portico brought them into an austere blue stone room. "We have restored the Temple," said Lumi. "Not the altar, of course." The small room opened into a massive octagonal rotunda with an oculus in the center of its domed ceiling. Sunlight streamed through, illuminating the clear crystal altar broken in half.

"I think it is now more beautiful," said a woman's voice. Hope recognized Merja as she approached. Her brown hair floated past her blue draped shoulders. Silver shoes clicked on the stone. The Pixie Priestess had not aged since her rescue—the Breaking. "Welcome to the Grand Temple, Lord Hunter, Listener, High Sage, Warlocks," said Merja. "We have prepared a feast in your honor."

"You've been expecting us?" Hope asked.

"We have been expecting you for the past couple of years," said Merja. "We eat. Then, we talk."

A blue corridor took them to a softer room. Draped blue material framed frescos and windows. A gentle breeze caressed the room, fluttering their cloaks. Women in blue carried platters piled with food and carafes filled with drink to a long table in the center of the room. Merja indicated an alcove in the wall where they could hang their cloaks, drop their packs, and wash their hands.

They sat on high backed upholstered chairs around a brightly colored cloth covered table. Women in rich blue joined them. Many sported blue markings on their exposed arms and décolletage. One also had markings on her face.

Merja stood to address them, stopping Hope from trying to discern different patterns in the women's markings. "Sisters, today we welcome back the Breakers, the Wood Listener and Warlock. We also welcome their companions, Lord Hunter, High Sage, and Warlockess. The Sini Sisterhood are honored to have you dine with us in our Grand Temple." She sat.

Food and conversation flowed around the table. "Those symbols on your skin," Mike asked, "are they permanent?"

"Some are," answered the woman with the markings on her face. "Those indicate rank within the Sini. Others are painted for different celebrations, time of year, rituals, and things like that." As she pointed to her markings, Hope ignored the rest of the conversation.

"I can't stay here any longer, Merja," said a woman down the other end of the table. Her declaration ceased all other conversations.

"Verena, I know you and Kirsi grow restless," said Merja.

"We need more than one squad searching the mainland," Verena said.

"I agree with you," Merja said.

Verena shut her mouth, obviously expecting more of an argument.

"You are to leave with the Listener, Verena," Merja continued. "You will take Ilta, Pinja, Matilda, and Soile. Kirsi will have her own squad with Lumi, Ine, Ritva, and Blejan.

"Two squads?" asked Kirsi.

"There will be five," Merja said. "When Grier returns, Aloysia and Zelda will lead their own. I'm afraid the threat grows stronger." Her eyes found Hope. "Hence, why the Listener was late in hearing the call."

Hope nodded to herself.

"So, it's true," said the woman with the marked face.

"It is as we feared, Ine," said Merja.

"How do we stop it?" asked another woman.

"You don't know?" said Obie.

"We spent three hundred years in suspension," the woman argued.

"But you're a Sini," said Obie. "You were warded."

"Yes," said Ine. "However, most of us were just trying to survive the madness of this island. We could *do* nothing and consult with no one. We spent a good portion of our time trying to get Merja free. We believed that in doing so, the spell over us would break and we could finally seek our revenge."

"Three hundred years is a long time to stew," said Sean.

Ine smiled. "Yes, it is."

"To answer your question, Matilda, we will convene after dinner with our guests to discuss our options," said Merja. "But first, the Wood Listener has somewhere to be."

The Pixies served a mouthful of an anise tasting drink at the end of the meal. Merja said to her guests, "Someone will show you to your rooms, then we'll meet. Listener, you may refresh your provisions before you leave."

"I'm leaving now," Hope said, mostly to herself. "Yes, that will be a good idea."

A woman waited for them to retrieve their things from the alcove. While the others joined the woman, Obie stayed with Hope. "You cannot go with her, Lieutenant," said Merja. "She must do this on her own."

"But she—"

Merja held up a hand to quiet him. "Worry not. She will be protected here."

"Do you have everything?" he asked Hope. His muscles tensed as if he willed himself to stay in place.

After packing extra provisions, Hope gave Obie a nod. While she secured her cloak clasp, she realized that she traveled to the Mother Wood Sprite alone. The last time she was alone.... She did not want to think about that. Her hand smarted while she adjusted the straps of her pack.

Obie's blue eyes pierced her before he forced himself to turn. She watched him trail after the others down another hallway. Merja then led her to a different covered opening to the outside than the way they entered.

"She has been reclusive of late," said Merja. "I believe she will not speak to anyone until she speaks to you."

"Where do I go to find her?" Hope asked.

"You will find out," Merja answered with a small smile. She motioned to the lawn that met the temple.

The grass beyond the stone both beckoned and taunted her. She wanted to get as close to the Mother Wood Sprite as possible before the sun set, which she knew would be soon, especially that far north. Her magic did not make light. Or fire. She had to do both the old fashioned way.

Chapter Sixteen

Sprites

Her feet stepped into the grass. One after another, they propelled her forward—away from the Grand Temple. She expected the trees on the island, after the Breaking, to be talkative like those on the mainland. Silence enveloped her. *"Hello. How are you?"* she asked them. Nothing. Perhaps she headed in the wrong direction.

She turned around. Trees surrounded her. No path. No Grand Temple. No one. Not even the grassy lawn. Her heart skipped a beat. Shallow breaths surfaced. Her good hand wrapped around the hilt of her blade. Her eyes searched for signs of movement. Nothing. Not even a breeze. Did she step into one of her nightmares made real?

"What do I do?" she breathed.

Her magic answered, turning her invisible. Magic filled her, encapsulated her, and spilled from her.

The trees welcomed her in her more magical state. She moved towards the presence of the Mother Wood Sprite. Trees seemed to part for her. She walked through concentric circles of young trees, progressively getting younger. The circles ended with a ring of saplings. Hope felt the energy of an empty ring—sprouts ready to push through the dirt.

In the center stood a gnarled tree. Its many branches reached for the sky. Long, weeping willow like leaves glittered in the dying sunlight. The mother tree shook. Branches became arms. Roots popped from the ground, turning into legs. The trunk smoothed into skin. A many limbed woman stretched her naked torso. Her light green hair shone against her pewter skin. Maple eyes studied Hope.

"At last, Wood Listener," resounded in Hope's head. The Mother Wood Sprite spoke. "My babies are almost ready." She spread her arms wide, indicating the circles of young trees. "They await your awakening."

Hope understood what she had to do, but first, she was supposed to ask the Mother Wood Sprite questions. If only she could remember. Her hands grabbed the sides of her cloak. Her left hand hurt. The bruise showed as a dark area in her otherwise green magic. "Mother Wood Sprite," she said, "I will happily awaken them after you answer my questions."

Some of her arms crossed. Others rested hands on her hips. "Fine," she conceded.

Hope uncovered her bark armor to show the bruising. "Someone the Elves call the Gatherer is after my magic. This mark gives it a direct link to me via my dreams."

"Still," said the Mother Wood Sprite. "Your magic can cure that blemish and sever the magical link. The Elves... ever since their city of stone, haven't fully understood anything. This Gatherer, as you call him, likes to play tricks on his victims and uses various tools. He excels at dream magic. There are other names for him. Sandman. Dreamwalker. Dreamweaver. Et cetera. We call him Hobbamok. If you are not careful, you can get stuck in an alternate reality and never know the difference. Such as with the Pixies. Hence, why I hibernated when the sand came."

"How did the sand get here?"

"Ask the Water Sprites," she said with a tone of disgust.

"How can he be defeated?"

"He needs to be beaten at his own game."

"Then why want my magic?"

"If you understood what your magic could do, then you would know why he covets it so. You are the only one he cannot trap in his usual way. Therefore, the mark. You must remember, he has had hundreds of years to find a way to obtain the Wood Listener's magic. And you are only the latest Listener. Life is in the balance, Wood Listener, in all its forms." She paused as if allowing Hope time to absorb her words. "Now, cure yourself and awaken the new Wood Sprites."

Hope closed her eyes. Magic traveled up her arm to her wrist and hand. The pressure of Mr. Wilde's hold released. She peeked at her hand. The bruising disappeared. No more ugly darkness. Not even a little yellow spot. She made a fist without pain shooting through her hand and wrist. Joy overwhelmed her. Then, she turned her attention to the rings of trees.

Her magic tornadoed around her. The vortex burst, showering

the trees with magic. Seedlings erupted from the soil. Like watching a fast forward time lapse, each ring of trees reached maturity in a matter of minutes. They swayed, shaking off their bark. Wood Sprites, as different as the trees they once were, frolicked under the raining magic. Giggles resounded. Hope thought of Miradelle, the addled Wood Sprite she cured with her touch years ago.

"Well done, Listener," said the Mother Wood Sprite. "You shall meet them again once they choose their names and leave here."

Hope smiled.

"You will find the path to return you to the Grand Temple from whence you came. Good luck, Listener."

As Hope strode away from the Wood Sprites, a normal forest emerged and with it, a path. Night settled across the sky hours ago. Hope followed the path by starlight. In the distance, lights from the Grand Temple shone brightly. A door stood open for her. When she entered, a blue clad woman set a book she was reading on a table, then stood.

"Welcome back, Listener. Your room is this way." The woman brought her through unadorned hallways. Not even a sconce sat against the walls. Clusters of crystals hugged the ceiling every so often, lighting quads of doorways, a pair on each side of the hall. She opened a door in one of the quad groupings. "Your room. Sleep well, Listener," she said.

"Thank you," said Hope, entering the room. She turned. "Wait." The woman paused her attempt to leave. "I lost track of time. Is it very late?"

"Everyone went to sleep a couple of hours ago."

"Ah. Thank you again." Hope closed the door. A crystal cluster lamp—the sole light source—rested on a small circular pedestal table.

The twin bed looked… hard. A series of hooks on a rack completed the room's furnishings. Oh, and a freestanding washbasin.

After changing, she studied the crystal lamp from all angles. A soft tapping on the door interrupted her examination. Opening the door, she admitted Obie.

"How do you turn the lamp off," she asked him quietly.

"Automatic when you get into bed," he answered. "Did you find her?"

"Yes. Look!" She showed him her unbruised hand and wrist.

"She healed you."

"No, Obie. I did! I didn't know I could," she said.

He let out a breath. "No more nightmares."

"No more nightmares," she repeated.

"And?"

"And, I'll tell you the rest later." She placed her hands on his arms, willing him to understand that she did not feel private. "Two things I want to do first—sleep and try my bow."

"Okay," he said. "I wouldn't be doing my job if I didn't check on you."

"I know. Thank you, Obie. Are you sure about the lamp?"

He chuckled. "Trust me. It's annoying." He looked at her like he was trying to read her thoughts as he walked to the door. "Goodnight. Sleep well," he said before leaving.

As soon as Hope got into bed, the lamp shut off. She turned on the stiff, board-like bed, trying to find a comfortable position. Finally laying on her side, she wrapped the blanket around her right hand. She got used to Obie's hand in hers while she slept.

She woke when her lamp out shone the sun. "No nightmares." She smiled in relief, then dressed.

A Sini waited outside their cluster of rooms. She instructed them to leave nothing in the rooms. They would leave after breakfast.

Breakfast consisted of a pile of slop on a plate. Hope wanted to leave right then, but Merja insisted on conducting a conversation. "Everything went well?" she asked Hope.

Deciding it would be better to be cordial, Hope said, "Very well. Thank you for everything."

"You are quite welcome, Listener. It is the least we can do after all you have done for us. I take it the island will be inundated with Sprites soon."

Hope let out a little laugh, remembering them dancing and playing. "I believe so."

"The island will come fully alive at last," said Merja. "It has been so long since we have had Sprites." The woman smiled with reminiscence.

Taking advantage of the lull, Hope stood. "Merja, I must insist we leave now. It's not just the Empire that's in danger, but lives. Mine and Lord Hunter's in particular."

"The delicacy of diplomacy is lost on you," Merja said. "You cannot go back without a portal guide."

"Actually," said Sean who also stood, "we can. We'd prefer not to, but you may leave us no choice."

"Nor can you leave without eating a fulfilling breakfast," said Merja. "You have barely touched your food."

"Why are you delaying us?" asked Sorrel.

"Of what do you accuse me?" asked Merja.

"Last night, you seemed against this Hobbamok and today, you seem… to have made a change in your outlook," Sorrel answered.

With a hand over her chest, Merja gasped. "I have not and I will never!"

"We told you about the moves being made against us," Sorrel continued. "And yet, you delay. Why? Time is of the utmost."

Merja closed her eyes. "Selfish reasons. I would not expect you to understand." When she opened them, she would not look at any of them. "Forgive me, Listener. I had hoped for a visit from her. I do not think she will visit me anymore, but with you here, I thought maybe. Silly, I know. But when one spends three centuries in monitored isolation... I thought maybe you could spare the time while the Empire counter moves, but I see now...." Her eyes followed the vignettes of the fresco on the opposite wall. "Sometimes, I think that time...." She looked at Hope. "Go with my sincerest apologies." Tossing her head back, she rose in one fluid motion, then left them at the table.

"Okay, then," said Hope. "Back to the ship." She grabbed her pack from behind her chair.

"How do we get out of here?" Sean said.

"I memorized the way back to the portals," said Sorrel, securing her pack and cloak.

"But we only walked it once," said Mike.

"Just something I've always been able to do," she countered.

Sorrel navigated the blue corridors back to the vine covered colonnade that brought them to the portal crossing. "We came out of that one," she said, pointing.

"Doesn't meant that one will take us back," said Sean. "Stand back." He stepped in the center of the crossroads. When his staff raised over his head, lightning from the crystal struck every portal simultaneously. All the portal discs flashed blue. "The same one will take us back and now, it's open, but so are all the rest. I don't know for how long."

Sorrel led them through the correct portal. Sean ran through last. They hurried along the path away from the portals. "You don't think Mabe would leave without us?" said Obie.

"She won't get paid in full if she does," said Hope.

"Let's run. Just in case," said Mike.

Silently agreeing, they ran until the path became the street of the port town. In town, running turned into speed walking. They maneuvered past people, wagons, trolleys, and rolling barrels. Once they emerged from the hole in the cliff, Hope noticed the Nerida still loading crates. "Good," she said. "Let's hurry anyway."

When they boarded, Mabe said, "Finally. I don't have to miss the outgoing tide by going after you."

Hope and Obie exchanged a look before they all headed down to their cabin to store their packs. When they returned above deck, one of the two squads stood watching Pixisle grow smaller. Hope, too, stared until the beige cliff diminished. "Remind me, Obie," she said, "not to come back."

"Gladly," said Obie.

"Captain!" one of the crewwomen called as she dragged another woman by the hair. Two other crew members followed, one carried a bag.

"Well, well, well, what do we have here?" said Mabe, stepping down from the bridge.

"Stowaway." Leading with the fistful of hair, the crewwoman threw the woman at Mabe's feet. Her bag slid into her legs.

Mabe's finger lifted the woman's face. "Passage is not free," Mabe said with hard authority.

"No!" one of the Pixies screamed. She restrained another brandishing a knife.

"You know the law," said the knife wielder.

"No!" the Pixie screamed again.

"She must die. Let go of me or face the consequences of your dereliction."

The stowaway remained on her knees, facing Mabe.

"Pixie laws do not apply on my ship, especially on the open water," said Mabe as the one Pixie released the other. "I will not tolerate bloodshed unless *I* am spilling the blood. Do we understand?"

The one Pixie sheathed her knife while the other collapsed in tears. "Fine, Captain. We can wait until we go ashore. No free Pixie may go to foreign shores and live without permission."

Sean stepped towards Mabe. "I will pay her passage," he said. He pressed coins into Mabe's hand. Turning to the kneeling woman, he said, "You are now indebted to me and no longer free."

The woman bowed to him from her kneeing position.

"Gather your things and follow me," Sean ordered.

The woman scrambled to pick up her bag, checking to make sure none of the seams split.

After Sean led the woman below, Sorrel muttered, "Can't wait to be on the mainland."

Hope agreed. She had enough of the deck, the ship, and everyone aboard.

The Pixie woman shared their cabin. She and Sean stopped talking when the rest of them entered. "This is Vanamo," Sean introduced. "She is Beljan's sister—the squad woman who didn't want her to die." Her eyes looked at each of them from her place on one of the empty hammocks. Sean, however, stared at Vanamo. When she said nothing, he prodded, "Well? Tell them what you told me."

Vanamo swallowed, then said, "Although I am grateful that the High Sage—"

"Sean," he said.

"—Sean interceded, they may still try to kill me."

"Why?" asked Mike.

Her eyes closed. "Such is our life."

When Mike opened his mouth to say more, Hope shook her head at him.

"You're welcome to travel with us, Vanamo," said Hope.

"Thank you," Vanamo said with a bow of her head. "I go where High Sage Sean goes until my debt to him is paid."

None of the Pixie squad spoke to them, which suited Hope. She no longer wanted to deal with Pixies.

During breakfast the following morning, Mabe sat next to Hope. "A word," Mabe said. Rising, she and Obie followed Mabe into a richly decorated room that displayed treasures won in battles at the stern of the ship. A door opposite the one they entered probably led to Mabe's living quarters.

"My officers inform me that we've made good time overnight. Too good, in fact." Mabe stared at the two of them with her pipe clenched in her teeth. "Any magic?"

"None of our magic works like that," said Hope. "You should ask the Pixies."

"Already have. They told me to ask you."

"I don't know what to tell you," said Hope.

A banging on the door made Hope jump.

"What is it?" Mabe called.

"Maelstrom, Captain," said the woman at the door.

Swearing, Mabe pushed past them. They hurried after her.

On the bridge, Mabe stopped swearing long enough to bark orders. She peered through her telescope. Obie, with his Warlock enhanced eyesight, gasped. His jaw opened and shut a few times. His finger moved around and around in a swirling motion.

"Captain! We can't get out of its tug!"

Mabe swore again. She covered her eye with the telescope. "Curse them Water Sprites," she muttered, then swore under her breath. "Batten down everything, including yourselves, if you want to live," she bellowed.

Sails folded. Doors and potholes slammed. Coils of rope unraveled as it tied down everything. Women tied themselves together as extra rope became scarce.

"Trust me," Hope said to Obie. He followed her without question to one of the railings. Facing the rail, she stood with Obie beside her. Mike and Sean lined up on her other side while Sorrel stood next to Obie.

Taking note of each's position, Hope closed her eyes. She ignored the chaos of the ship and set her magic free. The deck vibrated beneath her feet. Someone screamed. Vines grew out of the planks on which they stood, wrapping around their legs and waists. When the five of them were secure, she opened her eyes.

The dark sea spun into a whirlpool. The ship gained sickening speed. A wall of water replaced the sky. Faster and faster they circled the vortex until they abruptly stopped.

The form of a massive sea creature approached the edge of the water wall. At first, Hope thought it to be a whale, but the more Hope could see, the more it reminded her of images of Neptune except with blue-gray skin and seaweed-esque beard and hair. It wielded a gleaming trident, just like in the myths. *"Kveðjan, Holtaka,"* Neptune said. Her mind immediately translated the rest from the ancient tongue he spoke. "Apologies for the dramatics, but I cannot break the surface without recompense and bringing you to me any other way would cause you to drown. Here, we cannot be heard by any who try to listen.

"A long time ago, the Dragons came together to fight Hobbamok in what is now known as the Great Dragon War. There are few remaining who remember why they fought this war. I am one.

"Hobbamok has the capacity for both good and evil, like most, however, unlike most, does not know the difference. It craves power. Always quested for it, thirsted for it. Over time, it found an effective way to take the power of others. After choosing its victim, it traps him or her in a perpetual sleep. While the victim sleeps, it siphons power through events in a dream. This power transfer is not permanent, merely borrowed. There are two known ways to stop the transfer. The first and easiest, in a sense, kill the victim. That is if you can get close enough to the victim's sleeping body without falling prey yourself. The second, the victim wakes.

"The Dragons, many who fell to it, knew it needed to be stopped. They could not kill it, so they imprisoned it. Then, they killed all the victims they found. They believed that they neutralized its threat. When they formed their clans and their districts, they collectively forgot about it. Of course, refusing to name or discuss it can bring about that type of forgetfulness.

"Eons later, when the Empress transferred it to its current home, she added a magical barrier protection. This layer stopped the transfer of power from any remaining victims. However, this barrier relied on the strength of the Scepter. Wise, at the time. Eventually, the barrier faltered. Hobbamok slowly gained strength while biding its time.

"It claimed more victims while being imprisoned. However, not enough to be noticed. Enough to build its plan. It desires revenge on the Empress, the Dragons, and any who stand in its way. Those poor Wood Sprites. Nothing could stop their petrification. The Mother Wood Sprite's behavior baffles me. She should be angrier at the petrification of her Sprites. This new batch cannot replace the ones she lost." He shook the words away from his mouth. "*You* need to stop Hobbamok."

Hope swallowed. "Why me?" she replied in the ancient tongue.

"Your magic is one of the oldest and one of the strongest in the world. If you can bring together the other Listeners, you can stop it permanently."

She shivered.

"Beware your Pixie companions for they know right from wrong, but many do not care. Individual basis only."

She nodded.

"One final thing. There is a trunk—" His head turned. Water Sprites approached. They spoke a language Hope could not understand. Facing her again, he said, "Time to go." He said no more. His massive form swam away as the ship rose to the surface.

The sea closed in on itself, spinning the Nerida like a top. Once the ship stopped, the vines retreated into the wood. Sean rushed to the rail. As he leaned over, Hope turned away. Retching echoed throughout the deck. Splashes disturbed the still water. The sails raised.

Mabe cursed as she untangled herself from the wheel. "Stupid, waterlogged Sprites! Leave us in a dead spot." Her fist banged the rail. The sails caught no wind. No currents ran in the glass smooth water. They would be stuck for a while.

"If any of you can stir the wind," Mabe bellowed, then cursed.

The ship's wood hummed beneath Hope's feet. "Captain," she said, "I can do nothing to coerce the wind, but I can give the ship oars."

Smiling, Mabe said, "By all means."

Hope stood on the deck with her eyes closed. She willed the wood to make what it needed to propel itself through the water, trusting the ship to know. The Nerida sprouted three rows of oars on either side. Flippers pushed out of the stern. The wood told Hope when it was ready. "Okay," Hope said to Mabe. "Take hold of the wheel and steer."

Mabe cackled like a madwoman as her ship sliced through the calm sea at her touch.

Sneaking below deck, Hope grabbed her journal. She wanted to write down what the Neptune-like Water Sprite said in the ancient tongue. Her pen hesitated over the blank page. Neptune had concerns about others listening. What if someone could read what she wrote as she wrote it, no matter what language she used? Capping her pen, she placed it on the journal's empty page.

"Was the Mother Wood Sprite as intimidating?" Obie asked from the doorway.

Hope shrugged.

"Sean's not feeling too well. The spinning got to him. He's laying down. We're to give him quiet," said Obie. He entered the room, then took a seat next to Hope.

"This is awesome," said Mike, strolling into the room with them. "Hope, your magic is the coolest ever."

She laughed. Leaning back in her chair, she asked him, "So,

you're sure you want to be called Martin? Not Mart or Marty? Maybe just Mar? Or Tin?"

"You're also annoying."

Her laughter filled the room. "It's just that I want to call you by the name I've always called you. But, I'm afraid to say it. It feels as though there's magic attached to your name."

He slid into a chair. "You think so?" Mike's palms rubbed his knees. "I don't know. Everyone here seems to have magic except me. Well, except for the crew. They don't have magic. And the Empire Guards I met have no magic. I'm gonna eat something." He left without giving her a chance to respond.

"I couldn't imagine feeling so lost," said Obie. "Word is we might reach Tren tomorrow. I don't want to be on a boat for at least another ten years. Let's avoid water travel."

Agreeing, she let out a little laugh. "I just want to get Verity and go home."

Obie's smile waned as he fidgeted with his fingers. "Have you thought about where home is going to be? Now that you don't have to go back and forth so much anymore."

"Haven't had a chance," she said. "I did read that when not traveling, home should not be easily accessible to those who seek me." She watched him tug on the hem of his cloak. "I'm thinking we'll just find it—home."

"We?"

"You, me, Verity."

He nodded without looking at her.

"Whatcha thinking?"

Shaking his head, he mumbled, "Nothing." He ran a hand through his blond hair. "It's been a long couple of days."

She closed her journal, looping her pen inside the leather tie.

Tren's harbor appeared early the next day. They agreed to leave Tren immediately since they would have plenty of daylight to get out of the region. Before entering the harbor, Mabe called for Hope to join her on the bridge. "The oars," Mabe said, "is it possible to keep them?"

"I," Hope hesitated, "don't know. I can leave them when I get off the ship. They may or may not disappear at some point."

"That is fine. I'll take them for as long as I can get them." Chewing on her pipe, Mabe reached into her pocket. She plunked a small parcel in Hope's hand. "For the magic. Open without prying eyes."

Alone in their cabin, Hope opened the cloth parcel. She gasped. A pair of gold and emerald drop earrings rested in her hand. They were worth much more than the payment of their passage. Wrapping the earrings carefully, she packed them in her bag.

As soon as the gangplank reached the pier, Hope and the others disembarked, including their new Pixie companion. The Pixie squad, having to wait for their horses, could not follow.

Sorrel led them away from the Nerida, into the city. They hurried through the streets full of merchants hawking wares straight from the docks. Reaching the Hen and Wren, Obie and Sorrel searched with their superior eyesight for the Pixies before ducking inside. When Ya-ya pushed through the door under the stairs, Hugh bounded towards Sean. "Good. There might still be time to save your friend," she said.

Hope's jaw opened. She could not find words.

"She was abducted yesterday in the market. The dog came back to alert us. Smart dog, that one. Search parties were sent, but found nothing, not even a trace of her. The city guard suspects magic at play. I left her things in her room in case she came back."

"I'll get them," said Sorrel. When Hope nodded, Sorrel took the key from Ya-ya, then disappeared up the steps. Hope paid the balance for the room. Ya-ya insisted they take provisions free of charge.

Outside the inn, Hope looked to Sean. He crouched in front of his dog. "Hugh, find Verity. Lead us to her."

The dog barked.

Hugh sniffed the air, then darted up the street. They chased him to a stall cluttered square. He circled a few of the stalls, then barked twice to get Sean's attention. Nose in the air, he trotted to the gates. They ran after him, out of the inner and outer gates. Hugh paused by the outer wall, then followed it to the edge of the woods. Back and forth he paced, sniffing the ground and growling. Then, he led them into the forest.

The trees told Hope that Verity had been carried past them. Hugh eventually stopped in front of a large tree at the edge of a tiny clearing. He encircled the tree twice. Hope placed her hand on its trunk. The tree told her all she needed to know, flooding her with images of things she did not want to see.

"Verity was here," she said. "Tied to this tree. Tall men wearing dark cloaks. Two of them. Gray tinged skin. Elves. No. Vindalf."

"Who's Vindalf?" asked Mike.

Ignoring him, Hope removed her hand. "They," she did not want to tell them what she saw. "They tortured her. Weakened her. I don't quite understand what they did to her. They left her here. A woman found her. Untied her and took her. Just before nightfall. They—they vanished."

"Where is she?" Sean asked Hugh.

Hugh ran around in a few circles before taking off in a direction.

His puppy running slowed as he sniffed the air, then quickened when he found a scent. He led them to a hovel partially covered with earth and vegetation. After sniffing the door, he sat facing it.

"Good boy, Hugh," said Sean in a whisper, rubbing the puppy's head. He released his staff. It hovered beside him as he unsheathed his sword. Slowly, he opened the door. Hope winced when it creaked. Hugh entered the hovel by Sean's side. The rest of them tiptoed behind him.

A lone light flickered in the back of the dark hovel. Candles rested on a shelf and side table. A shape bent over another. Candlelight showed a long dark braid down the back of a woman. In one deft swipe, Sean's sword point rested at the woman's neck. "Put it down and back away from her," he said.

The woman set a bowl on the table. With her hands up, she peeked at Sean. "I'm giving her broth. She needs help. She's very weak," she said. Standing, she took a few steps back until her back found the wall.

Verity laid on a heap of blankets, her eyes closed. Hope knelt beside her. Taking her wrist, she felt for a pulse. Her paler than normal skin felt like ice. A weak pulse thumped through her veins. "Verity? Verity? Can you hear me? We've come to take you home."

No response.

Hope wondered if she could heal the Elf like she healed herself. She hesitated, knowing that the Vindalf performed some sort of magic on her. Magic that originated beyond the tree line—twisted magic, like the former Elves themselves. Her tree magic could harm her Tender. Verity needed the Witch of Rowan.

"She shouldn't be moved," the woman said with an eye on Sean's blade. "Not until she gathers some strength."

"She won't," muttered Hope.

"No time," Obie said. "Something's coming."

"Vindalf?" asked Hope.

He held a hand up for silence. "Sounds lower to the ground and many," he said. He sprinted to the door. "Gnomes!" he yelled into the hovel.

"In daylight?" said the woman. "Impossible. Close the door. We'll be safe here until they pass."

Hope stood. "They won't pass. They'd surround us. There'd be no escape." She turned to the others. "Mmmm Martin and Pixie, grab Verity. Sean, have your dog lead them to Tong," she ordered.

The woman's eyes watched her intruders. "Mike?" she said.

"My name's Martin," Mike said without looking. He lifted Verity into a sitting position while Vanamo swung her legs.

"Mike," she said in a soft voice. "My little Mikey. You're all grown up."

Mike glanced at the woman. "I think you have me confused with someone else, lady." His voice carried a hard edge. He and the Pixie hoisted Verity off the blankets.

"No. You're Martin Michael Hunter, the third. I'm your mother, Mary Hunter."

He froze, almost dropping Verity. "No, you're not. My mother died years ago." Ice clung to every word. He lifted Verity under her arms. "You got her?" he asked Vanamo. The Pixie clutched her legs.

Hope grabbed her bow while Mike and Vanamo carried Verity out of the hovel.

"Mike!" yelled Mary, running after him. "I'm sorry. I'm so, so sorry for leaving you. I had to. I had no other choice. It was the only way to save you and your father."

Tipping arrows with Fairy Dust, she scurried outside. She shot the arrows in a line. "That should slow them and give us time to reach Tong," she said to the others while securing her bow. "When they break that, use magic. Don't let them touch you." They sprinted after Mike and Verity.

Running with them, Mary kept yelling things to Mike. Hope only heard half of them. "I never stopped loving you or your father. Believe that." Hope tuned out Mary, listening to the trees instead.

"Mary, if you want to live, get back inside while there's still time," Obie said to her.

Tears streamed down Mary's cheeks. She stopped. "I hope someday you'll forgive me, Mike." Mike's head turned in time to see Mary vanish. In the distance, a door slammed shut.

"A wave of black things are coming," warned Sorrel.

"Keep running! Faster!" yelled Hope. "Where's Tong?"

Ahead, the Pixie stumbled, dropping Verity. Mike yanked both women off the ground. Obie threw magic behind them. The trees urged her to run faster. Sorrel copied Obie. Lightning shot from Sean's staff. The pops of exploding Gnomes carried through the forest.

"TONG!" screamed Hope.

Barking reached her ears. Hugh found the Dragon. She willed her legs to keep moving. They raced towards the barking. Sorrel flopped flat on her face. Obie pulled her to her feet as Sean sent sparks at the Gnome horde.

"Go! I got this," said Sorrel. Facing the oncoming wave of dark, little beasts, a spiked pink barricade erupted from her hands. The Gnomes munched her pink wall, exploding with every bite. More spilled over. There was no reprieve. They kept running.

Hope finally spotted Tong's sleek, black form beyond the trees. Mike and the Pixie struggled with Verity. Sean rushed to help. "Get on the Dragon. I'm right behind you," said Sorrel. She turned to the horde.

Obie jumped onto Tong's back. He grabbed Verity from Mike, Vanamo, and Sean. "Hope!" Obie yelled, leaning Verity against his chest. While Mike helped the Pixie onto the Dragon, Sean snatched Hugh off the ground.

The Gnomes devoured Sorrel's second pink wall. "Sorrel!" Hope called, running to the place behind Tong's head.

Pink magic spilled out of Sorrel. She alone held the Gnomes at bay.

Hope's eyes scanned the black Dragon's back. She counted five heads and the dog before she climbed atop Tong. "Sorrel, let's go!" she yelled.

A thunder-like clap boomed. Pink light blinded. All stilled and silenced.

Sorrel was gone.

The Gnomes froze as a heaping line of black. Hope lost her breath. "Sorrel!" cried Mike.

Hope's mouth hung open. "Empire Tree, Tong," she said without moving her mouth.

He pushed off the ground. They dematerialized.

Chapter Seventeen

Answers

Once the blurred free fall ceased, the air dried Hope's cheeks. Tong circled the Empire tree, then curled around the Star Gazing Platform. Mike and Sean took Verity from Obie. Free of the Dragon, Obie lifted Verity into his arms. "I'll take her to her room. Get Alina," he told Mike.

Mike rushed into the Tree.

After sliding off Tong's back, Hope placed a hand on his snout. "Thank you, Tong," she said.

"I will incinerate every last Gnome," he said to her.

She nodded, watching him let go of the platform.

Sean and the Pixie followed her down the wooden steps into the trunk of the Empire Tree. Obie took deliberate steps onto the bridge leading to their chambers from the Scepter Room platform. Draped in her cloak, Verity hung limp in Obie's arms. Hope looked away, then continued down the stairs. Echoing footsteps reminded her that she did not walk alone.

Reaching the Reception Room, she found her father sitting at a table. "Daddy," she said. Tears obscured her sight as they carved new paths down her cheeks.

"Hope," Jon said. Wood scraped wood. "What happened?" He held his daughter close.

"We lost Sorrel," she said into his shoulder.

"What do you mean, you lost her?"

She pushed her head away. "She—she exploded."

"Exploded?" asked Alfred. Hope noticed the aged Elf sitting at the table with another—the former Empire Guard Captain.

"In a flash of magic," she said.

When Mike returned with Alina, Hope said, "My chambers." Alina nodded, then the two of them rushed up the stairs.

Alfred stood. He wore traveling clothes. "Come, child, you better tell us what happened in the Roundtable Room. Sean, you and the lady can have a seat," he said.

Hope started up the steps with the Elf.

"Who said that?" Jon asked. He looked around the room. "Wait, slow down. Sergeant Sorrel?"

Stopping, Hope gasped.

"I can't see you, but I can hear you, Sorrel," said Jon. He glanced at Alfred. "We'll get to the bottom of this."

"Alvar," Alfred said the to the former Captain, "please come up with us."

Jon and Alvar joined Hope and Alfred on the steps. They walked up the flight to the Roundtable Room. Alfred shut the door while the others sat around the roundtable.

"Where is Uncle Berty?" Hope asked.

"They are all still at the outpost," said Alfred. "Hatcher and I just returned from there today." He sat in his usual chair. "Your magic is most impressive. No one can get inside without having already been there or led in by someone who has."

"I'll contact Berty," said Jon. He sat in silence for a moment. "I can't get through. It's like I hit a force field."

"Oh," said Hope, shocked that her magic blocked her own father. "Maybe...." Obie's magic transferred while holding hands. She took her father's hand. "Try again."

Jon's eyes saw without seeing. "Berty," he said.

Hope could see the room under the Keep. Berty, Declan, Silvia, and Delyth poured over what resembled a map on one of the tables. Looking up, Berty said, "Jon. And Hope."

"You can see me?" she said.

"And hear you," said Berty. The others looked at her. "What's wrong?"

She breathed in deeply. "Went to Pixisle. It was a mess. Yes, I spoke with the Mother Wood Sprite. There's two more Pixie squads roaming. I chatted with the leader of the Water Sprites. Verity, who we had to leave behind, was abducted and tortured by Vindalf. She's... Alina's with her now. There is a woman calling herself Mary Hunter. Says she's Mi—Martin's mother. Then Gnomes attacked in the middle of the day. Sorrel defended. She—she," Hope looked around the room for the best way to put it. "Sorrel... boom in a flash of magic. Tong brought us home."

Berty's eyebrows scrunched. "Sorrel boom?"

"Daytime Gnome attacks," said Delyth.

"She was doing her Warlock thing against the Gnomes. There was this magical explosion. She disappeared. Dad can hear her."

"I suppose you or Declan could see her," Jon said.

"Oh, and Sean joined us," Hope added. She noticed Declan's grimace.

"Ede," said Silvia, stepping forward. "Take Sorrel to see Ede. He might be able to help her. Jon, you'll have to go because only you can communicate with her. Bring my nephew and someone to be a guard."

"Jon, you need the key to Ede's Palace," Berty said. "Magical item storage in the Vaults. You will be able to get in going the regular way. Hope, you've seen the key, so you can help. It's on its own pedestal. Once you have the key, go to Grunnan and ask Goscislaw for a Guide. Make sure you have at least a week's worth of provisions. You don't know how long you'll be down there."

"We are leaving here tomorrow," Berty continued. "We found the location of the Cavern. Hope, we need you and Obie to bring Estelle. Have Obie assign someone to protect Estelle while traveling that he trusts. If you leave tomorrow as well, you'll know how to find us."

"Anything else?" Jon asked.

"Ede's a bit crazy," said Declan.

"Great," muttered Jon.

"Good luck," said Berty.

"We'll be seeing you soon, Hope," said Silvia.

Jon brought them both fully back to the Roundtable Room. "You heard our side," he said to the Elves. They nodded. "They suggested Ede. We need someone to be our guard."

"I'll go," said Alvar. "I've been there. That may help deal with

Ede. He's... eccentric."

"Yes," Alfred agreed.

"We also need a key from the Vaults," said Jon.

"I can take you to the Vaults," said Alfred. "I assume you will be needing a Guide."

Jon nodded.

"Then, best to leave for Grunnan from down there," said Alfred. "While you get ready, Hope and I will check on Verity. We'll meet you in the Reception Room."

She brought Alfred to her chambers where Obie and Mike sat at the table. "Alina is with her now," said Obie.

"Please, have a seat, Alfred," said Hope. "Martin, Dad can talk to Sorrel." Mike's eyebrows raised. "There might be a way to save her. You're going to see a Mage named Ede. Get ready to go."

"You're not coming?" he asked.

"Uncle Berty needs me elsewhere," she said.

He placed a hand on her shoulder before leaving.

"We leave tomorrow," she told Obie.

Alina walked down the stairs. "I'm not sure what the Vindalf did to her," she said. "I might have to take her to Irmingard."

"May I see her?" asked Alfred.

"Yes, third door," said Alina. She sat with Hope and Obie while the Elf walked up the steps. "I'll do everything I can for her," she said to Hope.

"I know you will, Alina," said Hope.

When Alfred returned, he said, "I'm going with you, Witch. I remember seeing something about this in the High Elf's private archives, I think. We'll take the carriage and leave at once."

"Shall I carry her down now?" Obie asked.

"That won't be necessary. I'm putting her on the stretcher," said Alina. "You can bring her bag to the carriage."

At the door, Alfred stopped. "Obie, I'm bringing my Blǫvar, but I think Verity should have her own guard, given what happened. It might be a good idea for you to assign an Elf, if possible."

"Me?" asked Obie.

"You're the highest ranking Empire Guard in the Sages' Grove, First Lieutenant. He should ride in the carriage." Alfred left.

Obie picked up Verity's bag, then escorted Alina out of their chambers.

Alone, Hope brought her pack upstairs. After dropping it just inside her door, she entered Verity's room. Her cheerful room with is colors and fabrics contrasted with the Elf solemnly laying on her bed. She pulled a bench next to the bed to sit. "I'm sorry I couldn't protect you better," she said. "I'm sorry I had to leave you. I'm sorry that being associated with me led to you being hurt. There is so much that I am coming to understand. There is so much I have to learn. Alina, the Witch of Rowan, will heal you. And, you'll be safe in Irmingard." The door opened downstairs. "Time to go. Get better soon, Verity." Hope placed her hand on hers.

She got up to let Alina next to the bed. Alina snapped open a cloth and wood stretcher that hovered beside the bed. Her hands coaxed the stretcher under the Elf. When Verity was secure on the cloth, Alina guided it out of the room. Hope followed.

Everyone waited in the Reception Room. All eyes fell on the Elf on the stretcher. Alfred approached Hope. "Estelle will bring you and your father to the Vaults," he said. "Sean informed me about Vanamo's predicament. She is coming with us as an attendant."

Hope nodded.

The Elf lowered his voice. "Have faith, child. Don't blame your-self for this."

Hope nodded again. "Thank you, Alfred."

Theodore emerged on the staircase from the Receiving Room. "The carriage is packed and ready to go," the Dwarf told Alfred.

Alfred thanked him, then ushered Alina forward with Verity.

As the Elves and Witch descended, Hope turned to the Dwarf. "Theodore, we will need additional provisions for tomorrow morn-ing," she said.

"The Lieutenant already informed me," he said. "Since I am ac-companying your father to Grunnan, Anthony will provide everything you will need."

"Very good," she said.

"Are we ready?" said Jon. "Sorrel?" He listened. "Good. Make sure you follow and let me know you are still with us periodically."

"I'll wait here," Obie told Hope.

She nodded.

"Estelle?" asked Jon.

"Ready, Lord Chase."

"Call me Jon."

Estelle smiled. When she noticed Sean, her smiled faded.

In the back of the Receiving Room, the five of them and, she pre-sumed, Sorrel crowded into the box behind the Sages' Seal covered doors. The doors closed. They plunged into the depths below the Empire Tree.

"We'll wait in the mine cart," Alvar told Jon. Mike's head tilted as Hope and Jon entered a cart with Estelle. She waved until her cart began to roll into a tunnel.

The familiar route to the Vaults did not ease her mind. The

rhythm of the metal wheels gliding on the rails brought wave after wave of guilt. Two, who may or may not return from their current states, suffered because of her. Vibrations stirred the empty pit in her stomach. Guilt churned into anger.

The cart stopped. Stone doors opened. She entered the Magical Item Storage Vault with Jon and Estelle. "Ede," she said to herself. She remembered a seven sided key with a mother of pearl handle. Berty showed it to her once on a dark cloth. Her magic stretched to search for the key. Her feet brought her to a pillar that held a plaque which read, "Key to the Palace of Ede."

"Here," she announced.

Jon found his way to her side. "Well, that's not like any key I've ever seen," he said. He scooped it up with the cloth on which it laid. Wrapping it, he tucked it into a pocket. He caught Hope's eye. "They wouldn't be sending us to Ede if they didn't think he could bring Sorrel back."

"I know."

"Oh, Ede's quite mad," said Estelle, joining them. "He could do wonders. Specializes in old, forgotten magic. Works since he is old and forgotten. Shall we?" She motioned to the door.

On the way back, Hope's anger subsided. Alfred told her to have faith. She needed to hold on to that. When they arrived in the small cavern with all the carts, Jon pulled her aside. "Let your mom dote. She worries," he said. "Be careful on your way to Berty and Silvia. See you soon." He gave her a hug. "Don't worry. Everything will turn out."

She nodded.

Hope and Estelle watched Jon pile into the cart with the others. Once the cart rolled from view, they walked back to the magical elevator.

"Starjen are on the move," Estelle said while the box ascended.

Hope wondered why Estelle told her this.

"It is as if they battle each other for position."

"What does that mean?" Hope asked.

"One star cannot light up the night sky as well as many," Estelle said.

The doors opened. They walked up to the Reception Room in silence. "Where's Sean?" asked Estelle.

"He took the dog for a walk," said Obie.

"Mommy, can we get a dog?" asked Lily.

"We'll discuss it when your father comes home," said Teresa. "Hope." She gave her daughter a big, swaying hug. "How are you sleeping?"

Hope showed her mother her arm.

"Wonderful. You must be starving," said Teresa.

Sean returned in time for the Tenders to bring dinner. He sat at the opposite end of the table from Estelle. Throughout dinner, Hope caught him staring at the Astrologer. Did he have a question that only the stars could answer?

After dinner, Teresa suggested they spend time in the family's chambers. "I wish I could, Mom," said Hope. "I have to repack and I'm exhausted and drained."

Teresa gazed into Hope's eyes then kissed her forehead. "Goodnight, sweetie."

Hope trudged up the stairs with Obie lagging a few steps behind. Inside their chambers, she plopped on one of her old poufs. Obie went upstairs. When he returned, he no longer wore armor. He pulled a pouf next to her, then sat.

"Obie," she said, "what if we fail?"

"Wanna tell me about it?" he said.

Words poured out of her. She told him about the journal, the Mother Wood Sprite, and her conversation with the Lead Water Sprite.

He took her hand in his.

"It's too much. I don't know what to do," she confided. "I'm still trying to figure out me and," she sighed.

"You are not alone," said Obie. "We'll meet up with everyone soon and we'll make a plan. I think they already have one that you're definitely a part of."

She gave his hand a squeeze. "Thanks, Obie." She stared at the ceiling for a moment. "I'm so glad you're here with me."

"Always," he said.

She pulled his hand to her heart. The rest of him slid off the pouf. He knelt beside her. "Estelle told me about how it takes more than one star to light the sky," she said. "She must have known I was thinking about going after Hobbamok on my own. That's the third time being told about bringing together the others."

"That's what's going to happen," he said.

Her eyes found him. "It's been awful not being able to tell you things." When she sat up, his arm slid around her waist.

"Anything else?" he asked.

She shook her head. "You know what I know."

He smiled as his blue eyes danced. Leaning closer, his lips reached for hers. He showered them with sweet, tender kisses. When their lips parted, their foreheads rested against each other's. "I miss holding your hand at night," he said.

She giggled. "Me too. Just not why."

"No." He kissed her again. His lips moved to her cheek. He leaned back, holding both of her hands in both of his.

"What?" she said.

"I want more of this," he said.

"This?"

"Us."

She smiled as his eyes studied her face.

"Is that a yes to us?" His lips moved wordlessly, waiting for her answer.

Her smiled opened into a laugh. Her cheeks flushed with warmth. She nodded. "Yes to us," she breathed.

He closed the gap between them in an instant. His arms wrapping around her felt so natural. "Good," he said in her ear. After a moment of just being close to one another, he sighed. "We need to pack." Holding her closer, his head nuzzled next to hers. He breathed into her hair, then pulled back. "Going to let me see those earrings Mabe used as payment?"

"Ooh. I'm definitely leaving those here," she said. After showing Obie the emerald earrings, they repacked their bags.

Obie kissed her goodnight beside her bedroom door. They entered their respective bedrooms to sleep.

A handful of people sat in the Reception Room when Hope and Obie went down to breakfast. "Where's Lily?" Hope asked her mother.

"I let her sleep," answered Teresa.

Hatcher entered from the room below with the Firths and Jordis. "Dad," said Obie, "is it their birthday already?"

Teresa rose from the table to greet Obie's family. "You're two days early," she said to Leon and Geraldine. "Please, join us for breakfast."

Jordis stayed standing while the four Firths sat. She surveyed the others at the table. "Where are the Empress and Emperor?" she asked.

"Not here," said Obie.

"Who has authority here?" Jordis asked. She looked from Obie to Teresa. "With whom do I speak?"

Estelle stood. "And you are?" she asked the Elf.

"Specialist Major Jordis of the Blovar."

Estelle nodded as if she understood something. "Hatcher and I are Advisors to the Empire. You may speak with us and First Lieutenant Oberon in the Roundtable Room."

Hope watched the four of them disappear up the staircase.

"She must be why you're early," said Teresa to Obie's family. "How was your journey?"

"Long and uneventful," said Leon.

"How are you, Hope?" asked Vander. "How is the bow working for you?"

"Fine." She did not have the heart to tell him that she only regained the use of her bow a few days ago.

After a few minutes, they returned. Jordis sat next to Vander, then whispered in his ear. "I understand," Vander said to the Elf.

"She is coming with us," Obie said to Hope as he sat down.

When they finished their quick breakfast, Estelle secured her midnight blue cloak. "Will you need anything before we leave, Jordis?" she asked.

"No, thank you," Jordis responded. "It has been a pleasure seeing you all again," she said to the Firths. "Have a good time visiting your family."

While Obie said good-bye to his newly arrived family, Teresa gave

Hope a hug. "Be safe," she told her daughter. After a quick hug with Obie, Teresa walked them to the staircase.

Hope led the other four out of the Sages' Grove. Once in the privacy of the trees, she slowed to ask where Berty and the rest were. The trees gave her glimpses of Berty, Silvia, Declan, Delyth, and Edwin trekking through the forest. A path from them to her formed. "This way," she said, leading them in the direction the trees indicated.

With her focus on reaching Berty and Silvia, Hope plowed through the forest at a punishing rate. No one said anything. The day grew warmer and the breathing heavier. At one point, Sean carried his puppy. "Can we slow down?" he asked her.

"Not if we want to meet them," she said. "They're not coming towards us, like, at all. They travel away from us."

"How about a short break?" he suggested.

"They're days ahead of us."

"I have to… go," said Sean.

She stopped. "Fine. But we walk later and earlier." She hated losing time. Moving gave her a purpose. Moving kept thoughts elsewhere. She sat on a log. Perhaps she resembled a bump.

"I don't know if Estelle has the stamina for this pace," Obie whispered.

Hope shifted her gaze to her group. Estelle wiped her blonde hair out of her face. Her breaths seemed deliberate. She shook her shoulders and bounced slightly on the balls of her feet in a subtle attempt to stretch sore muscles.

Groaning with frustration, Hope closed her eyes. She saw the others walking through the forest. A sigh escaped her mouth. She nodded.

"Ready?" he asked.

When she opened her eyes, Obie's outstretched hand hovered in front of her to help her off the log. She took it. He lifted her to her feet. They held hands while she surveyed the others. Jordis closed her water skin while Estelle refused Sean's help but patted Hugh on the head. Once Estelle took a couple of steps, Hope continued their trek.

Although they traveled slower than Hope would have liked, she postponed making camp until the last possible light. After constructing a Fairy dome, Hope tried to relax within its protection. She did not taste dinner, but ate anyway. Jordis eyed the opalescence. "This is Fairy magic?" the Elf finally asked.

"Yes," said Hope. "Perfectly safe. Just don't touch it."

"Even for Elves?"

"It's never affected Captain Edwin," Hope responded.

Jordis nodded.

"Are you going to tell her?" Obie asked. His gaze held the Elf frozen for a second.

She recovered with a cold, "Excuse me?"

"Tell the Listener about the magic tutor in Irmingard."

"I don't take orders from you, Lieutenant," Jordis said.

Obie ignored the Elf. "Menny worked for Hobbamok," he said to Hope.

Closing her eyes, Hope's shoulders drooped. Of course, he did.

"Lieutenant!" screeched Jordis.

"I don't take orders from you, either," countered Obie. "The entire House of Erland is being investigated. Captain Edwin's family."

Hope shook her head. When she opened her eyes, she addressed Jordis. "Menny's suicide was a message—a message to Hobbamok. Menny resigned as his agent."

"How do *you* know?" Jordis asked.

"Because Hobbamok has been after me for the past decade," said Hope. "Hobbamok needs others to do its bidding since it's been imprisoned for so long. The family is innocent. Irmingard might as well investigate itself. It all makes sense." She looked at the four of them. "The Scrollist told us to know history. The Water Sprites gave me that history. Sean is that history—or part of it."

Sean's gray eyes widened with fear as he shifted on the ground where he sat.

"If I have this right," she continued, "Hobbamok is imprisoned by Scepter magic. Leif, the former Scholar, tricked Sean in an attempt to get the Staff of Lightning. Which, Leif wanted in order to get the Scepter. When that didn't work, he invaded Fairyland to try to obtain their magical stone. Again, to use to get the Scepter. Leif, who had been working for Hobbamok, killed himself after losing the Battle of Fairyland.

"Griffins were then used to bombard the Keeper's Keep, because the Keep houses vital information about finding the Cavern. The magic from the Cavern can maybe override the Scepter or help grab the Scepter.

"I am only being chased because the Scepter is protected by the Empire Tree. Control that Tree and control the Scepter. Menny understood tree magic better than most. That's also why Hobbamok petrified the Wood Sprites or ordered their petrification. Hobbamok has been trying to get inside the Empire Tree. Only the Scepter can truly free its prison."

"None of that will matter to some in Irmingard," said Jordis. "There are those who wish to oust the House of Erland. They are too close to the High Elf. The Warriors might not even work with the Empire Guard as long as Edwin of Erland is Captain."

Hope pressed the budding headache out of her eyebrows. "Declan was right. Irmingard politics are crazy."

"The Empress and Emperor will not be bullied into changing the Captain of their Guard," said Estelle.

"I should think not," agreed Jordis. "The House of Erland will be evacuated if necessary."

"Wystan is Commander. I highly doubt he'd leave," said Obie.

"Normally, I'd agree, but his wife's with child. They haven't announced it yet," said Jordis.

Hope raised an eyebrow. "How do you know?"

Smiling, Jordis answered, "It's a talent."

Hope urged them to get to sleep early to get an early morning start. On her bedroll, Estelle held her star pendant over her eye. "I can't see the stars through this," she said. She tucked the pendant inside her shirt.

"Sorry, Estelle," said Hope. "Fairy magic can block other magic."

"I will need a minute in the morning to consult starjen before we leave here," she said.

"Okay," said Hope. Her eyes found Obie who slept near. He smiled then blew her a kiss.

When they woke, they removed all traces of the campsite before Hope broke the dome. In the dark morning, Estelle consulted the stars through her pendant. "Okay," said Estelle as she allowed the starburst to lay against her skin. The pendant peeked above the collar of her shirt.

Hope led them in the direction where she last saw the others. Once Delyth's Fairy dome disappeared, the trees let her know where Berty headed. She adjusted her track to meet theirs.

Around midmorning, Estelle spat, "Stop it!" Hope did not know if she reprimanded Sean or his dog. When they stopped for a break, Estelle asked, "What are you doing?" Her words could have slapped someone.

Sean took a step away from her. "Being a friend," he responded.

Not acknowledging he said anything, Estelle tied her hair back. "*We* are *not* friends," she said in a tone that chilled the warm morning.

They continued through the forest in silence until Sean whined, "Why not?"

"Friends write to each other."

"You could have written to me," he said, sounding exasperated.

Hope glanced behind her to see Sean shrink under Estelle's glare. Silence overtook once more.

When the trees alerted Hope about the others stopping for the evening, she pressed on for another hour before they camped for the night under another dome. Building the fire and making dinner felt strained. Hope had no intention of wading through the thickening air between Estelle and Sean. However, she could not say anything to either one. Whatever happened or not happened between them was none of her business. She only wished that they resolved it sooner rather than later.

Around the campfire, Sean banged his spoon in his bowl like a petulant child. Finally looking into the fire, he said, "I know I said I'd write." He bit his lip while Estelle said nothing. He chanced a glance at her. "I started countless letters. Most got as far as, 'Estelle.' Some asked how you were. I never got any further. I didn't know what else to say." He set his bowl down beside him. "My life outside of this," he motioned around the camp, "is inconsequential. Nothing worth writing about. Certainly not worth hearing about my dull day to day. Especially, when *you* do great, important things every day. Why would you want to know about me? Or even bother conversing?" His eyes found his shoes.

"You're a stupid, stupid, man, Sean," Estelle said in a quiet voice. She moved to another part of the domed campsite. Hugh settled next to her legs.

Sean buried his head in his hands.

Hope looked over at Obie. He shrugged.

With an odd look of pity, Jordis sat next to Sean. She did not wait for his head to leave his hands to begin speaking to him. Hope could not hear what she said, nor did she want to eavesdrop. She regretted not making her dome large enough to practice her archery. Leaving the others to themselves, she and Obie talked until they fell asleep.

The following day, Estelle ignored Sean while he chanced glances at her. Estelle pushed their pace, which made Hope happy. However, unsaid words congealed around them.

"We're making good time," Hope announced after they set up camp.

"Good," said Estelle. Her normal wistful voice hardened.

"Estelle," Sean said softly, "I'm sorry. How can I earn your forgiveness?"

Finally looking at him, Estelle blinked a few times. "Let me think about it."

A brief smile flashed on Sean's face.

Obie slipped his hand in Hope's. The small contact warmed her inside. She held that warmth throughout the night.

In the morning, Estelle permitted Sean to hand her her pack. He grinned like an idiot. Hope ignored both of them for the remainder of the day. She focused on getting them closer to Berty and the others.

That evening, after slurping the end of his stew, Sean said, "Don't you think it's strange that we haven't come across anyone?"

"We're not taking any road or even a game path," said Obie.

"But not even a hunter or a trapper," Sean said.

"That's because we've entered wild creature country," said Hope. When all eyes landed on her, she found her fingernails interesting. "I don't mean wolves, bears, and large cats either. Magical creatures."

"Like Griffins," said Obie.

"Among other things."

"Great. All I have is a dog. Where's the Dragon when you need him?" said Sean.

"Hugh's no ordinary dog, Sean," said Obie.

Sean petted Hugh's head. "But, he's still a puppy. He can't do anything against a Griffin or...." His gaze found Estelle.

"If we walk a little faster tomorrow, we should catch them," said Hope. "We're really close."

Estelle forwent her morning star consulting so they could start earlier. They trekked faster without any prodding from Hope. Sean carried Hugh who did not squirm to walk on his own. Without stopping, they pushed through the forest. Hope's muscles burned, but she kept moving without complaint. Every rustle turned heads. Hands stayed close to weapons.

Midafternoon, Hope announced, "They're just ahead." After five minutes of quick walking, they caught sight of colored cloaks. Declan's dark purple tinted cloak billowed when he spun to face them.

"Made good time," he said to them. The others turned. None looked surprised to see them, even with Jordis tagging along. Hope surmised that Berty spied on them as she did him.

"Emperor, Empress, I have—" Jordis began.

Silvia held up a hand to stop her. "Not now," she said.

Jordis nodded.

"Good to see you again, Sean," Silvia continued. She eyes the dog under his arm. "You've made a friend."

"His name is Hugh," said Sean.

Silvia raised an eyebrow, but said nothing. As one large group, they continued through the forest. Edwin kept a slower pace than Hope did. Her muscles thanked him. When they finally stopped for the night, Delyth constructed a large dome around their campsite. Silvia magically erected tents. "I believe you need to speak with us, Jordis," said Silvia as they sat around the fire.

"Yes, Empress." The Elf surveyed those around the fire, then continued. "First, news concerning Irmingard. There are those who cast doubt on Menny's suicide. They say that he was murdered and it was staged to look like ritual suicide. Blame is being thrown on the House of Erland."

"Of course," muttered Edwin.

"A formal jury has been launched to investigate," Jordis said. "What is conclusive is that Menny had dealings with the one known as the Gatherer. Unfortunately, many believe the Gatherer to be mere myth."

"They said that about Vindalf as well," said Edwin.

"If I may, Captain," said Jordis.

Edwin gestured for her to continue.

"When I arrived at the Empire Tree, First Lieutenant Oberon in-formed me about Hobbamok being an older name for the Gatherer. The Wood Listener told me that she believes Menny's suicide was a message to this Hobbamok. If this is true, then there are other agents of Hobbamok in Irmingard. Our peace is... Rane's death only delayed our civil war."

"Verity, Alina, and Alfred are in Irmingard," Hope told the Elf. "Verity, my Tender, was attacked by Vindalf working for Hobbamok. It also sent Gnomes after us during the day." She addressed Berty. "Tong is eradicating Gnomes as we speak."

"They should be fine. War won't erupt overnight," Jordis assured. She discussed how Edwin's parents were suspended from their duties during the investigation and Gaynor's pregnancy. "Wystan is keeping it together, somehow."

"Lark, my wife, has family in Calledin. Violet's Inn," said Edwin. He gave her a piercing stare. "Those families are so.... Well, you understand the consequences better than most. Avery still has no heir." He shook his head.

"That's not entirely true," said Jordis. "Before he married Lene, Avery loved another. She was not from the right family to be his wife. Anyway, she bore him a son. Died in childbirth. Vidor's raising him as part of the Blǫvar just as Rane raised me." The fire mesmerized her. "Avery loved her so much, he'd give up everything for another day with her." She wiped her cheek. "He called me back to help him with the rumors and the like. Lene is nice enough, but it's for *her*, he shuns formality."

"How old is his son?" Delyth asked.

"Three."

"He has to be the boy Fiala befriended," Delyth said to Declan.

"Would the mantle pass to him, regardless of whether or not Avery and Lene have children?" asked Declan.

"I don't know," Jordis answered. "I searched for Hobbamok's

agents outside of Irmingard. I found none, yet. Only the remains of those who got in their way. One of which is a Fiona Firth."

Declan closed his eyes and brought a fist to his mouth. Obie's whole body froze. He stared at the Elf. His mouth moved. "It's true. Someone murdered my mother," he said. "Does my father know?"

"Your mother stumbled upon an agent and was going to expose everything. I found a partial log of those killed for 'the cause.'"

"Partial?" asked Berty.

"It was burnt."

"Excuse me," said Obie. He rose. Hope watched him disappear behind the tents. When she caught Silvia's eye, her aunt gave a slight nod. Hope politely removed herself from the report.

She located Obie sitting in the grass close to a tent wall. His head was buried in his knees while his entire body shook. She never saw him cry all those times he spoke of his mother. Kneeling beside him, she placed an arm around his shoulders. As he leaned into her, her other arm wrapped around his knees. She held him while he cried.

Finally, the sobbing subsided. He breathed deeply as if trying to catch his breath. Raising his head, he said, "It was like losing her all over again."

She kissed his head then swept his hair out of his face. Her fingers wiped the wetness from his cheeks. "It's okay, Obie. I'm here." Those blue eyes searched into hers with such an intensity.

"Obie?" said Declan. Obie broke his gaze. They both looked up at Declan standing a few feet away. "Are you okay?"

"I will be," Obie answered. He held on Hope.

"Can we talk?"

Obie expelled a forceful breath. "Okay."

Declan gave Hope an "alone" look.

"I'll be by the fire. Make you something warm to drink," she told Obie.

Reluctantly, Obie let Hope slide out of his grasp. She gave him a small smile before returning to the others.

When Hope joined them, Jordis had finished her report. Silvia said to Hope, "Tell us all that happened once you left the Keep."

Hope started at the part where they met Sean. She talked about Tong, the inn, and having to leave Verity.

"I wasn't sure if the Water Sprites lifted that ban or not," said Silvia. "They should have made an exception for the Tender."

Continuing, Hope replayed their foggy journey across the sea, then meeting with the Pixie Priestess. When she mentioned the Mother Wood Sprite, Berty asked, "Did she give you the answers you sought?"

She groaned. "She was annoying and completely self-centered. All she cared about was awakening the new Wood Sprites. As if I wouldn't." Obie and Declan emerged from between the tents. "The only real good she did was teach me how to heal myself. Of course, I probably had to get rid of the bruises in order to wake the Sprites. She grudgingly answered my questions and still managed to tell me nothing. I don't know. The whole thing was annoying. Pixisle itself was annoying."

"Can I see your hand?" asked Declan.

Hope removed the fingerless glove then rolled back her sleeve. As he examined her hand, she continued her story.

Silvia stopped her to ask, "Merja tried to keep you there?"

"You healed this yourself?" Declan sneaked his question after Silvia's.

She nodded to them both.

"Excellent," said Declan. He let go of her arm.

Replacing her glove, Hope told them of returning to the ship and the Pixie stowaway.

"Where's the Pixie now?" asked Berty.

"Alfred took her to Irmingard. I don't know where she is now," answered Hope. "Sean protected her the entire trip except when we met the Water Sprites." She told them about the whirlpool and her conversation with the head Water Sprite.

"He left just like that?" said Delyth.

"I wonder what trunk he spoke about," said Berty.

"I would've liked to have seen Mabe's face when her ship sprouted oars," said Declan.

"She paid me to keep those oars," said Hope.

Declan's eyes widened. "She parted with something. Mabe's getting soft in her old age."

"Back in Tren you discovered Verity missing," said Silvia, steering the conversation.

"Hugh led us to Verity," said Hope. "She…. The trees told me what they did to her—the Vindalf." Hope paused to stare into the flames, wishing they would burn the details from her mind. She then described finding Verity with Mary Hunter. Both Obie and Sean added details about the Gnome attack and Sorrel's explosion. When Hope's tale ended, only the campfire talked.

Chapter Eighteen

Endings and Beginnings

Of the four tents, Hope shared hers with Estelle and Jordis. Both women seemed preoccupied in their own minds. Hope had no thoughts for the moment. She told her story. Her mind felt empty. No longer in charge of anything, she relaxed. She drifted off to sleep as another tossed in her cot.

Hope woke to find Jordis' cot empty. "You don't understand. I need to leave," Jordis' voice pleaded.

"We understand more than you think. Stop harassing my wife," said Declan's voice.

Hope and Estelle exchanged a glance before getting ready. When all packs and cloaks were secure, Silvia magically cleared the campsite. Once Delyth deconstructed the dome, Jordis hiked in the opposite direction.

A small bird chirped. Edwin held out his hand on which the bird landed. He removed the paper tied to its leg. After quickly reading, he called, "Jordis." The elf ran back to them. Edwin held the paper towards her. She read. Wordlessly, she gave the paper back to Edwin. "My wife will meet you there," he said. She nodded. As Jordis left again, Edwin whispered to the bird. With a chirp, the bird flew away. He tucked the paper into his cloak, then led them through the forest.

When they stopped, Edwin and Berty huddled. Hope believed her uncle looked at the paper. Curious as she was, she knew she could not ask about it in the open. She glided next to Obie. "How are you doing?" she asked.

"I'm okay now," he said.

"I'm glad." She wrapped her arm around his. "I'm here if you need me." Their fingers entwined. She relished in their closeness. Looking at the others—her extended family, Hope finally felt like she belonged. The forest of the Land of Sages—her home—her place in the world. She smiled as she let go of Obie's hand when their break ended.

After making camp, Edwin unfolded the piece of paper he received that morning. "The Witch of Rowan somehow discovered that the High Elf's wife is barren. Anselm, Avery's son, left Irmingard with Alfred. They stopped in the hamlet where the Emperor's parents live. My wife and son will be going there as well as Jordis," said Edwin.

"I peeked at them throughout the day," said Berty. "Hedda rides with Lark."

"Good," muttered Edwin.

"Verity is still recovering, but she is doing well," Berty continued.

"From what I gathered, after receiving the magical treatment she needed, they said that she needed proximity to trees to complete her healing. No one questioned. They left in the carriage taking Anselm with them at Vidor's behest. The boy calls Alfred, Grandfather, and is having the time of his life following my dad around."

"How could that little bird have flown back to the Sages' Grove this quickly?" asked Sean.

"She doesn't have to make it back," explained Edwin. "The lark only has to be in range to relay a message. It has to do with the bond between the bird and my wife."

Berty looked at Declan. "I've been studying the maps," said Declan. "We're still a day or two from the Field of Gold which we need to cross to eventually access the Ladder of whatever it's called. Now, Sean and Obie, since neither of you are one of the seven, you might not be able to enter the Field." Both men nodded.

After eating, everyone dispersed. While Edwin checked the map again and Sean spoke with Estelle, Hope stood by the flap to the tent Obie shared. "May I come in?" she asked.

After a second, Obie said, "Yes." Entering, she noticed him placing his armor on the cot.

"In case, um, we need to leave you," she fidgeted with the cloth around the bundle in her hands, "I, uh, I'm letting you borrow this." She held out the bundle for him.

Taking it, he unwrapped the cloth. "Hope," he said, looking at her. "Your Fairystone."

"And my bag of Fairy Dust." She took a step towards him. "You won't be able to construct a dome, but you can make a Fairy Ring or add Dust to your magic or edge your sword with it."

"My magic? I thought Fairy Dust blocked other magic."

"Most magic. You're a Warlock. You're unique. I've sprinkled Fairy Dust in your magic before. If you don't need to use it, great, but I just want you to be safe." She turned. As she walked to the tent's entrance, his grasp stopped her.

He swept her into his arms. "Thank you," he breathed. Sean entered. They broke apart.

"Goodnight," Hope said before leaving. She fell asleep still feeling Obie's arms around her.

Hope found the early morning particularly beautiful. Gray clouds rolled over the treetops. Birds chirped. The smell of rain threatened to burst into pouring moisture. She loved it all. Verity would fully recover. Going to the Cavern would stop Hobbamok. Only Sorrel was left. She had to get her body back. Raindrops kissed her face and hair. She raised her hood.

They walked for hours before the rain blew past. The trees sent her a message. "People," she relayed. "Dad. Martin. Alvar. And Sorrel. Coming our way."

When the four of them came into view, Mike looked elated. "I found them," he said more to himself than anyone else.

"Good to see you back with us, Sergeant," said Edwin.

"Good to be back, Captain," said Sorrel.

"You can tell us all about it when we make camp," said Berty.

Catching Hope's eye, Mike smiled. He walked with a new confidence. The trip to the Palace of Ede changed him somehow.

Around the campfire that evening, Berty asked, "How was Ede?"

"Of questionable sanity," said Jon. "Sorrel's predicament fascinated him enough to focus. I don't quite understand it and, for the life of me, couldn't tell how he did it or what he even did, but it's done." Jon adjusted his glasses. "Half the time, he kept referring to me as you," he said to Berty. "He knew exactly who Martin was though."

"I'm a Hunter," Mike said with his eyes alight.

Hope tilted her head. She wondered why his surname excited him.

"That's my magic. I'm a Hunter," said Mike. "I can find things and people and stuff. Do you know how useful that will be when I become an anthro-archeologist? This is too cool."

Laughing, Hope said, "That explains a lot, actually."

"Why didn't you return to the Empire Tree?" Silvia asked in an accusatorial tone.

All Mike's happiness evaporated. "But, I thought—" he said in a small voice.

"I'm trying to keep you safe!" Silvia raised her voice. "Your mother is out there!" She gave Mike a penetrating stare. "Why is Sorrel blinking?"

Hope's eyes found the guard. Sorrel resembled an old, broken, neon sign with a random pattern of blinking before it died. Declan rushed to her side. "Bring her into the tent," Silvia ordered. She and Berty stood while Declan ushered Sorrel to the tent. "Jon," said Silvia as they walked behind Declan. Jon followed.

"Was going to Ede a test?" Hope asked.

"What do you mean?" asked Delyth.

"To see if he worked for Hobbamok," she answered.

Delyth's jaw dropped a little.

"I don't think it's that simple," said Alvar. "While Ede doesn't come across as exactly loyal to the Empire, his allegiance does not lie elsewhere. He is his own. What he did for her might not have been enough."

"Sorrel fascinated Ede," said Mike. "He said that female Warlocks rarely lived past the age of ten. Wouldn't say why."

"Nature. Brutal, brutal nature," Sorrel said as she emerged from the tent.

"Is everything okay?" Mike asked.

"I'll be fine."

"Martin," Silvia called. She waved him into the tent.

Mike walked to the tent as if he had been called to the principal's office. The crackling fire illuminated conversations between Edwin and Alvar, Obie and Sorrel, Estelle and Hugh—one sided, but Sean tried, and Delyth and Jon. Hope stared at the dancing flames. Her mind danced with each fiery tongue. Why was there not a Fire Listener? Would not the elements be elemental? There was no Water Listener either, but Water Sprites existed. Were there Fire Sprites? "Dragons," she breathed. "Dragons are Fire Sprites. *And* Air Sprites?"

"What are you mumbling about?" Mike asked as he sat next to her.

She shrugged. "Nothing really. What did Aunt Silvia want?"

"Talk about my mother. She thinks I should find her. And I will. Once you guys get where you're going." His brown eyes reflected the flames. Mike no longer sat next to her. This boy she knew—her friend—became Martin somewhere in the world below the surface.

"Is Grunnan as cool as I've imagined?" she asked him.

His eyes sparkled. "Cooler." He described the city's golden glow and mountain-esque pyramids reaching towards the top of the cavern. "And their tunnel system is crazy complex. Without our Guide, we would've gotten so lost. And riding around in mine carts, I felt like I was living a videogame. So awesome." He chuckled. They both stared into the fire.

Obie glanced in her direction. His chest rose and fell. After ending his conversation with Sorrel, he approached. "Martin, can I talk to Hope alone, please?"

Martin got up and walked away without saying a word.

She wanted to ask if something was wrong, but she waited for him to talk.

After getting comfortable, he asked, "What are your thoughts about me leaving the Empire Guard?"

"Is that what you were talking about with Sorrel?" she asked.

"No. She wanted to talk Warlock magic. I haven't discussed this with anyone. It's been on my mind for days." His blue eyes searched into hers. "Would you still have me if I weren't an Empire Guard?"

"To protect me?"

His fingers brushed hair that was not in her face. Moistening his lips, he glanced at hers. "In your life. Would you still want us?"

"A girl does like a guy in uniform," she teased.

His face dropped.

"Obie." She grabbed his arm. "I don't care if you're in the Empire Guard or not. You're my best friend. Nothing will change that."

"What about... beyond?"

"Beyond?"

"Beyond best friends."

Her hand still rested on his arm. What would be beyond best friends? Except.... Oh. Her stomach somersaulted.

"Hope?"

She smiled at him. "Obie," was all she could say. Her other hand slid into his. He gave it a squeeze, then returned her smile.

"When we get back to the Sages' Grove, I'll hand in my resignation," he said.

"And then?"

"Then, I'll just be a Healer. I can do that when we travel. I'll still have my sword. And I can commission armor from the pay I've saved."

"I was going to use those earrings to commission armor in Grunnan," she said. They laughed.

"Lieutenant, Sergeant, Sean," Edwin called. He and Alvar led them into one of the tents.

Hope noticed Jon staring at her with a strange look on his face. Before she could figure what his look meant, Berty distracted him.

"Giving Obie your Fairystone was a good idea," Silvia said as she took a seat next to Hope. "I feel better about leaving them if we need to. I'm sorry I put you in the crosshairs, Hope. I realize its after me and the Scepter."

"It's not your fault, Aunt Silvia."

"The Empire has a habit of forgetting its history. It rewrites, conveniently leaving out some of its more sensitive items," Silvia said. "Buried secrets can destroy, no matter how deep. Hobbamok has a long memory. There are not many who can match it. And of those who remain—memories are fickle, selective. No one can remember all of it."

"But this isn't just about memories and secrets," said Hope.

"No," Silvia conceded. "Vengeance. Revenge on a world that desired and fought to be free of what Hobbamok was prior to Dragon imprisonment."

"What was it?"

Silvia looked into the flames. "No one knows," she said. "The Dragons might. In mythologies all around the world, there is a time before. If we search deeply enough, it might be there."

Hope stared into the flames as well. Neither said anything.

Sorrel shared the small tent with Hope and Estelle. The Warlock moved differently than before the explosion—Hope could not explain it. She watched the guard check the cot and get into bed. When Sorrel noticed Hope watching her, Hope said, "How are you feeling?"

Shaking her dark blonde hair loose, Sorrel answered, "Odd. Like I have too much magic for my body. The Mage said it will take some getting used to. I worked some pretty complex magic blocking those Gnomes."

Hope nodded. She understood that feeling of overflowing magic all too well.

No one said much the next morning. Estelle checked the stars before they left the empty campsite. After tucking her amulet behind her shirt, she gave Silvia a meaningful look. Saying nothing, Silvia nodded to Edwin to lead.

With four added to their group, hiking through the forest felt slower to Hope. Berty, however, kept breaks short. The dense forest canopy filtered sunlight so well, Berty had both Obie and Jon release spheres of light along with his own.

"Something shining up ahead," warned Obie. Hope saw nothing but trees and undergrowth.

They stopped. Declan turned to Hope. "What is it?" he asked her.

She touched the nearest tree trunk. Images flashed. "Gold, a clearing of it. Like dense grass," she said.

Declan smiled. "It exists." He pushed them faster through the woods.

Chapter Nineteen

Field of Gold

The forest ended in an unnatural line. They stood at the edge, Edwin and Alvar feet behind them, gazing at a field of golden grass. The grass waved and rippled in the breeze. Sunlight sparkled on the crests of each ripple. Edwin stared at the dense, waist high grass. "Is this…? Does the magic of the trees end here?" the Elf asked.

Hope knew he meant like the tree line to the north where the Frost Giants stalked the frozen land. "No," she said, relaying the answer of the trees. "You're safe if you cross."

Edwin nodded. "Now what?"

"We set up camp," said Silvia. She had Obie and Alvar choose a campsite with a view of the golden field. Hours before the sun set, a fire roared, roasting small game. Martin wanted to leave after a quick rest. However, Silvia forced him to hunt and forage with Declan, Obie, and Alvar. "There's not always a village or farm," Silvia said to him. "You need to know how to get food for yourself." When the men returned, Declan taught him how to prepare the game they caught.

After a filling meal, Martin shook hands with all the men. He spent a little longer with Obie, saying words Hope could not hear. Silvia gave him a hug, wishing him luck. Finally, he stood in front of Hope. "This has been," he said without finishing. "Even with everything, I'm glad I followed you through the portal." He paused for a breath. "I expect to be gone a while. See you in August before I go off to college." Beaming, he gave her a strong hug.

"Stay safe..., Martin," she said.

Martin and Sorrel gave them all a wave before the dense forest gobbled them.

Hope watched everyone else be busy with one thing or another. Declan and Berty called Obie to the edge of the forest. Estelle studied the stars with the aid of her amulet. Delyth and Silvia escaped to the privacy of one tent while her father ducked into another. Since Delyth would not construct a Fairy dome around the campsite, Edwin, Alvar, and Sean paced the campsite perimeter with Hugh on their heels. Turning on the spot, Hope found a place to hang her target. She fired arrows for something to do.

"Mom and Lily say hi," said Jon's voice behind her.

She lowered her bow to look at her father. "How are they?" she asked.

"Well," he said. "Mom persuaded the school to say you finished eleventh grade. They're mailing your transcripts." He adjusted his cloak. "Not much left for you to do to get your GED. With some hard work, you'll have it by Christmas. We'd like you to get that out of the way first, before you... do other things."

"Before I get too heavy into Wood Listener duties," Hope said.

"Yes. As well as anything else." Jon glanced at his brother, Declan, and Obie returning to the camp.

"I thought about going to Fairyland to learn," she said.

Her father's eyes followed the men to the tents. "Good," he said. He smiled at her. "You finish practicing. I want a word with Uncle Berty."

When it became too difficult to see the target in the darkening forest, she collected her arrows and target. She joined the others around the fire. "Wearing the locket is a good idea," said Berty.

"What's after the Field of Gold again?" asked Edwin.

"The Pride Fall Path," said Declan.

"Prideful?" said Sean.

"Pride Fall," Declan said, emphasizing fall.

"Is there a particular way to cross the field?" asked Estelle.

Leaning forward, Declan placed his elbows on his knees. "Instructions are vague." He rested his head on his hands.

"There's an odd whispering over the field," said Berty. "No one else can hear it. Might be more clear when I wear the locket."

"Doesn't Captain Edwin represent metal?" said Obie. "Is the field not gold?"

"It's magic," said Declan.

"*You* see magic. I see through it," said Obie. "Doesn't gold conduct magic?"

Declan opened his mouth then closed it.

"That's why I'm going first tomorrow," said Berty.

Hope's body stiffened. Creaking reached her ears. Her eyes

roved, trying to peer into the dark forest beyond the firelight.

"Those would be more of the wooden protectors setting up around our camp," said Silvia.

The trees showed Hope the bark beings settling into watchful stumps.

As they readied for bed, Estelle dropped her bag on the ground. Her night clothes and cloak followed. After hastily throwing them on her cot, she excused herself from the tent. Hope fell asleep before Estelle returned.

Anxiety spread through Hope during her morning routine. Although she hated leaving Obie and her father behind, she wanted to reach the Cavern already. They, Berty and Declan, concluded that only the seven of them should venture into the field. Declan kept telling them that he had no idea how long it would take them. While eating breakfast, his feet tapped. His restless bouncing knee annoyed Hope. She could not look at Declan. The strumming and drumming of his fingers on everything increased her anxious mood.

Finally, Berty secured the locket around his neck. "We'll see you soon," he said to the men they were leaving.

Hope saw no one else's farewells as she hugged her father. "Stay safe," said Jon.

"You, too, Dad."

Obie accompanied her to the edge of the campsite. "Hope, I," he said, staring into her eyes. "I... I will watch over your father."

"I know you will," she said, taking his hands in hers. "We'll be back before you know it. Please, wear the pendant, Obie."

One hand slid out of hers. It reached inside the neck of his shirt. He pulled out the pearlescent carved Fairy wings. "Been wearing it since you gave it me. Had to see if it blocked my magic. So far, so good," he said. After pushing the pendant out of sight, he grabbed her hand again. He kissed her forehead. "You better go."

Words caught in her throat. She did not want to leave him. He had been with her through everything. Almost everything.

"You'll be fine," he said as if he read her mind. "You won't be alone."

Smiling, she squeezed his hands. Without a word, she slipped her hands out of his. Turning away from him, she walked next to Delyth and Estelle.

Berty led them to the edge of the golden field. After a moment, he stepped into the golden grass. One by one, they followed. They dared not walk anywhere but in the path he carved though the gold. Delyth waited for Hope to enter behind Edwin.

The grass glittered at Hope's waist. Each blade of grass was a leaf of gold. The blades swayed with the breeze, twinkling in the sunlight. Garbled whispers fluttered across the tops of the grass. "Do you hear that whispering?" she asked Delyth in a low voice. Delyth shook her head. The whispering increased the further they walked. She remembered that Berty could hear something as well. However, she could not see him over Edwin. Hope clapped her hands over her ears to block the incessant whispering.

Declan shrieked behind her. She turned. He stopped. His arms flew wildly around him. "Can't see anything," he said. Panic edged his voice.

"It's all right, Dec," said Delyth. "I'm right here." She placed his hands on her shoulders. "Walk with me, darling." Delyth nodded for them to keep moving.

Spinning around, Hope followed Edwin again with her hands clamped to her head. The pounding in her ears fought for release.

She settled for cupping her hands over her ears.

Edwin flickered. She caught glimpses of Estelle through him. "Is it the field?" he asked. Finally, he disappeared. Hope thought her eyes caught a slight disturbance where she knew the Elf to be.

"I think the gold magnifies our magic," said Silvia.

He returned with his hand on the hilt of his sword. "I could cut through the grass," he suggested.

"No," said Berty. "We must keep it intact. I believe us to already be on the Pride Fall Path."

A steep, snowcapped, gray mountain loomed beyond the Field of Gold. Rising out of the grass, a faint gray path wove into its folded feet. Hope's eyes rested on Edwin's dark green cloak. Her hands flattened her ears. She preferred the rumbling of her eardrums over the grumbling of whisperings.

Eventually, the gold gave way to gray. Hope lowered her hands. The whispering ceased. Declan released Delyth with a mumble of thanks. Berty turned to look at them. He caught Hope's eye. His look told her that he heard the whisperings as well. Their magic was entirely different, yet the gold found a link. Perhaps in their blood? Neither spoke of it. After making sure they all exited the field, Berty led them up the path.

The mountain and its excessive folds towered. Looking up at its imposing form, Hope figured it would take days just to reach the middle. Maybe the Ladder of Whatever would show up sooner rather than later. She doubted it. They walked along the winding path as it climbed ever higher and steeper. Their pace slowed as breathing labored. It felt like hours passed. The sun, however, seemed to be in the same position in the sky since their arrival on the mountain.

Reaching a small grove of pines near a bend in the path, Silvia had them stop for a break. Hope leaned against a rock. She washed down a piece of jerky with water. The increase in altitude affected all of them as they caught their breath. "I don't think it's a good idea to go any further today," Silvia told them. Estelle closed her eyes in thanks.

No one moved or spoke for a while. The climb exhausted them. Hope wondered if the magical field drained their energy more than hiking the steep path. She stirred her magic, greeting the trees that sheltered them from the sun.

A deep bellow echoed within the folds of the mountain. Seven pairs of eyes searched for its source. Declan and Edwin readied their weapons, moving to the edge of the trees. Delyth's wings unfolded as she ducked out from the grove. Hope kept her bow ready under her cloak. A second bellow reverberated off the rock.

The trees sent Hope a message: *It knows.*

Flapping of enormous wings reached her ears. They scrambled out from under the trees, searching the skies. A car sized bird soared, darkening the cloudless sky. The mountain trembled beneath her feet when the bird bellowed a third time.

The massive black bird circled once before landing on the path in front of them. Its white markings resembled an overgrown penguin. It waddled as if shaking the wind out of its feathers. The dark bird shrank into a dark form of a man. Declan aimed his arrow.

The man's black clothing made him look like a marauder from a lost era. A black hood shrouded his face. Hope shivered. She knew exactly who stood before them. And, she knew why.

"So good of you to come," he said, his voice hoarse. "I have been following you for, well, quite some time." His laugh tumbled down the path.

No one said anything.

"Surely, you did not think that I would allow you to reach it," he said. His words were clear, his tone cold. He threw off his hood, revealing a face that could encompass everyman. His dark hair hid other colors as if he could not decide which. His mottled skin reflected the indecision of his hair. "Though, I was not completely convinced that you would make it to that forsaken Keep. I was growing tired of Griffins. And you, my dear," his nondescript eyes fell on Hope, "I am thrilled you are here as well. We meet at last." His smile sent chills spiking through her body. "However, it would have been easier if you... well."

"What do you want?" Silvia asked.

He laughed as if enjoying himself. "What we all want, deep down." His gaze washed over them. "Don't pretend you are going to shoot me, bowman. Your worthless little arrows can do nothing to me. I will admit I coveted the Bow of the Moon, but only to shoot at what was left of my magical cell. It cannot kill me." He smirked.

Hope wished she had her Fairy Dust.

A Dragon roared somewhere beyond the mountain. He laughed again. "Those insipid Dragons. So enamored with themselves." He sounded bored, but Hope knew that he despised them. "Eirawen did a great service. Oh, yes, she was mine. Many have served me well. Many still do." He cackled. "Foolish little ones seek me, though they know not why. They search for power, for greatness. I give them what they want, for a price." His stared fixated on Silvia. "All those I have ever known... in one way or another, speak of you with such reverence. I see you now. You are only a woman. Perhaps a reverie. An ideal." Tittering, he continued, "Yes, yes. However," seriousness settled over his face, "you *will* release me. You will *restore* me." His arms opened wide as if to embrace the mountain itself.

Silvia took a step forward. "*You* are mistaken."

His arms dropped.

An odd feeling ruminated in Hope's stomach. While hooking her bow to the strap across her back, she reached out to the trees via the roots. The trees showed her images of Obie. He put his arm out to stop Alvar. "Stay in the camp," Obie warned. "Sean, grab Hugh. Hope just sent me a message."

"What happened?" asked Jon.

"Something's wrong," answered Obie. He addressed the trees, saying, "I understand." He looked at the other men. "We're being put under Hope's protection. Hobbamok joined them."

"Hope!" said Jon, scrambling to the trees.

Obie struggled with Jon. "No, Mister Chase. Her instructions are clear. We must leave it. And no spying on them. We cannot attract attention to ourselves."

Vegetation grew around them, closing them inside. Hope pushed the images from her mind, knowing they would be safe. Her eyes stayed on Hobbamok.

The shapeshifter—assuming the form of a man—looked down on them like a bull ready to charge. "Fine. You leave me no choice, *Empress*," he said with contempt. He waved a dismissive hand at her.

"No!" screamed Berty. He leapt in front of Silvia. After a second, Berty crumpled to the hard earth.

Chapter Twenty

A Chance to Dream

All breath exited Hope's lungs as if someone punched her in the gut.

Silvia's hand twitched. "Where do you think you're going?" she said to Hobbamok. Her icy tone alone seemed to freeze the man mid-shapeshift. Without taking her eyes off Hobbamok, she jerked her head at Declan. Obeying, Declan examined Berty.

"Alive," said Declan, "but—"

"Sleeping," finished Hobbamok. He released a hollow, mirthless laugh. "You cannot hold me forever, Empress. And, if you so happen to kill me, he will *never* wake. Do not worry, I will give him lovely dreams." His laughter shook the mountain and Hope to the core.

Anger quenched the shaking. She knew what kind of dreams he

gave. Branches sprang through the dirt around Hobbamok. His laughter died. A tree like cage enveloped the shapeshifter. Silvia's hold on him broke. He shook the bar-like branches, then immediately stepped away.

A cold laugh emitted from Hope's chest. "The more you fight, the more confined you'll be," she told him. She approached. "In there, you cannot change shape. You cannot communicate with others. You cannot absorb anyone's magic." Stopping, she admired her cell. "You are correct, of course. We cannot kill you... yet. But life can always become less... comfortable." She smiled at him. Walking away from him, the cage shot fifty feet into the air, balancing on a thin trunk.

Silvia collapsed beside her husband. "Berty, oh, Berty," she sobbed. "You saw the magic. Please, wake up. Please. I need you. Your children need you."

Branches grew out of the ground where they huddled. A floor wove beneath them. Railings secured the sides. Hope grabbed a rail, indicating to the others to do the same. Silvia stayed kneeling next to Berty's sleeping body. The platform lifted them off the ground. Root like legs raced the seven of them down the mountain path.

Hope stood at the edge of the platform as it sliced through the Field of Gold. Enclosing vines parted, baring the elevated campsite. The four men moved away from the opening. The platforms merged.

"What happened?" asked Alvar. His gaze rested on Silvia and Berty.

"Berty!" cried Jon. "Is he?"

"Magical sleep," Declan answered.

"How do we wake him?" Jon asked.

"I don't know," said Declan.

Hope's high hide expanded around them, building shelters, sleeping quarters, chairs, tables, and a cooking pit. The part cradling Berty extended over the golden grass. Exhausted, Hope dropped into one of her chairs.

Declan clutched his opened Watcher's Locket. "Silvia," he said.

She tore her eyes away from Berty. Tears streaked her face. He lowered the locket towards her. When her hand passed over it, a scene popped out of the oval, landing in the center of the tree camp.

"Are we? Is that?" said Edwin.

"Berty's view," said Declan. "We're seeing his dream through his eyes." He set the locket on one of Hope's tables.

They gazed at the insides of a beige bedroom that Hope did not recognize. The plain furniture looked decades old. "That's Berty's old apartment, I think," said Jon. "The one he lived in right before moving into the house."

Berty strode into his living room. He dug into a messenger bag that sat on an armless computer chair. After zipping it closed, he pressed a round button on his computer. He watched a screen load, then checked his email.

"Could his dream have brought him back in time?" Hope asked.

"Anything's possible," said Silvia.

Berty picked up the piece of paper next to his keyboard. He had waited in his editor-in-chief's office while Mr. Hunter scribbled the address of his next interview. After handing him the note, Mr.

Hunter chuckled about how the interview would be a 'magical experience.'

"Seven two seven Oak Street," muttered Berty. Placing the handwritten note under his cell phone, his hand swept through his dark hair. Bits of a dream surfaced—bows and swords and dancing feathers. Magical experience indeed. "This interview has to go well," he said. He entered the address into his navigational device then set it beside his phone.

He rubbed his stubble ladened chin. The shower called to him. He could not be late for his first interview given to him personally by the editor-in-chief of the newspaper. Stretching, he groaned. Mornings were never his thing. He shook the sleep from his head. "I better go meet this Silvia," he said, walking to the bathroom. "Hopefully, it'll— Maybe I shouldn't eat spicy food so late."

In the bathroom, he leaned over the sink. Tired brown eyes stared back at him. Thoughts of an enormous tree swam in his mind. He pulled his shirt off over his head. "What a weird dream."

The World In-between Series

Chosen to enter a portal, a modern man discovers the realm of magic where myths, lore, and fairy tales reside.

Book 1: The World In-between

Berty Chase gets caught in the battle for magic, invoking ancient magic that changes his life and the lives of those around him forever.

Book 2: Bow of the Moon

Trying to restore order in the Empire causes Berty to join the race for the legendary Bow of the Moon and its bearer.

Book 3: Secrets of the Sages

Revealing ancient magical secrets begins to unravel the world as Berty knows it, possibly losing everything and everyone he loves.

Book 4: Whispers

The anti-imperialists have been using Whispers to stay ahead of the Empire. To win the war, Berty must stop the one controlling the Whispers—the Whisperer.

Book 5: Hope

A decade after the war ended, the Empire realizes their peace was a farce.

Book 6: Dreamweaver

What the Dragons will not name has escaped its prison and seeks revenge on the descendants of those who imprisoned it. Coming 2017

Book 7: Currently Untitled

Coming 2018

Companion Story: Yuletide Magic

Before hearts entwined and battles fought, a little girl invoked the ancient magic of Yule.

Companion Story: The Dragonlands

Towards the end of the age of Dragons, the Dragon Clans fought to keep their kind alive.

About the Author

IE Castellano is an American author and poet living in the Eastern United States. Falling in love with the mechanics of the English language at an early age, she started writing poetry before venturing into fiction. She loves history (especially ancient), mythology, archeology, and anthropology. Anything IE reads, sees, or does could wind up in one of her books in some manner. With her propensity to ask, what if, she writes speculative fiction—authoring the dystopian sci-fi novel, *Tricentennial*, and the contemporary epic fantasy series, *The World In-between*.

For news and a current list of her writings, visit her blog: IECastellano.blogspot.com. Contact IE at IECastellano@zoho.com. Connect with her on Google+ and Twitter.

www.ingramcontent.com/pod-product-compliance
Lightning Source LLC
Chambersburg PA
CBHW050552260626
47157CB00002B/538